EDEN'S GARDEN

For my mother,
who gave me the joy of reading

EDEN'S GARDEN

by
Juliet Greenwood

HONNO MODERN FICTION

First published by Honno
'Ailsa Craig', Heol y Cawl, Dinas Powys,
Wales, CF64 4AH

1 2 3 4 5 6 7 8 9 10

ISBN 978-1-906784-35-5

Published with the financial support of the Welsh Books Council.
Cover design by Simon Hicks
Printed in Wales by Gomer

Prologue

1996

He was late. Carys stopped by the stone archway, her breathless, headlong rush abruptly halted.

Maybe he'd forgotten. She took a deep breath. Her fingers closed around the precious scrap of paper in her pocket, clutching it tight. She was being silly. There must be something happening up at Plas Eden. His aunt could have sent him on an errand. Or his grandmother asked him to walk the dogs for her. Something he couldn't help.

He probably thought it would take her ages to escape. It hadn't been just Mam and Dad and her sisters, but well-meaning cousins and neighbours crowded into Willow Cottage that morning. And the eager questions through the winding streets of the little village where everyone knew her name and, today of all days, wanted to know her business.

A white delivery van passed by on the road behind her, slowing as it reached the main entrance, then speeding up as it set off up the driveway to the crunch of tyres over gravel.

Well, she wasn't staying here alone, just a few steps from the main road, for all to see and laugh at. Carys lifted the rusty latch of the wrought-iron gate and pushed the protesting metal open just enough to wriggle inside the archway, pulling it to with a sharp squeal.

Entering the curve of the high stone walls was like stepping into another world. The road and the village, with its glimpse of the sea on the horizon, vanished. Trees surrounded her, their branches swaying slightly in the breeze. As the leaves parted, she could make out a blue expanse of lake. Steep green lawns led down to the water's edge, topped by the imposing, ivy-clad facade of Plas Eden.

It was strange, seeing the house from this unfamiliar angle. Close to, Plas Eden was slightly shabby, in a homely, comforting sort of way. Between the ivy, white paint peeled

3

away from the masonry. Moss collected where roof slates had slipped or broken, and the skinny beginnings of a tree sprouted from a broken edge of guttering on one side.

From here, reflected back at itself in the waters of the lake, it looked more like a National Trust place. The kind you went round in hushed voices with a guide, careful not to touch the gilded furniture behind swathes of protective rope, or go anywhere near the ancestral portraits by Reynolds and Gainsborough, each priceless and alarmed up to the hilt.

If only David were here next to her, filling her world with his presence and telling her it was all going to be okay. Carys shut her eyes, holding on to the soapy, real-wool smell of his jumpers, the smile that lit up the seriousness of his face. The warmth of his arms around her and the rapid beat of his heart when she leant against him.

Maybe she'd got it wrong. Maybe he hadn't said the first archway, but the second, further down the path, deep inside the Plas Eden grounds. At the entrance to the secret hollow where the statues lay.

Carys peered uneasily through the trees. 'Eden's ghosts', the village called them. She'd heard Mam and some of the older people talking about the statues sometimes, their voices taking on that sad, wistful tone they used when they remembered something lost forever. David had always promised to take her there, but somehow he never had. It was as if they were too precious, and the memories they held too painful for him to share, even with her. Until now, perhaps.

Well, action was better than just waiting, Carys told herself. And David *might* be there, wondering where on earth she'd got to. In any case, it wasn't as if Eden's ghosts were real ghosts; just weathered statues, carved out of stone.

She set off down the path, between ancient oaks and birch

4

saplings, towards a circular pond. As she reached the bank, she could make out the greening figure of a woman marooned within the blackly glinting remains of water, holding out a vessel of some kind, as if in forlorn offering to passers-by.

Carys shivered. All those stories Dad had told them about the Plas Eden gardens came flooding back. Stories of fountains shooting great sprays high into the air. Of cleverly constructed waterfalls and secret hideaways. Of flowers set in swathes of colour around benches and rose-covered arbours. Of grapes and melons and a kitchen garden that had once grown everything a great house could possibly need.

At the time, the stories had seemed like a fairytale. Something that belonged to a castle far away, with princesses in towers and knights in armour, not to a tiny village tucked away in the Welsh hillsides. A village that, even to her loving child's eyes, had been unmistakeably shabby, and was now, with her newly adult gaze, about as run down and back of beyond as you could get.

Carys swallowed. That gap between house and village hadn't mattered at all when they'd been kids. She'd been welcomed at Plas Eden to keep the Meredith boys company, especially after other friends began to make their excuses, as if merely being there would bring enough ill luck to last a lifetime.

It hadn't seemed to matter this past year, despite that crease of worry between Mam's brows, and the wariness of David's Aunt Rhiannon. They were old people who didn't understand, she'd told herself. And it wasn't as if she was going to mess up her exams or get herself pregnant. No way. She was eighteen now. An adult. She wasn't stupid. Nor was David.

'Cari!'

She breathed deep in relief as David came hurtling down towards her, mop of fair hair catching the sunlight, stones flying this way and that into the ferns along the edges of the path in his haste.

'Hi,' he said, coming to a halt, apology written all over his face.

'Hi.' Cary smiled, feeling oddly shy. Her stomach was making its usual abrupt plunge off a cliff edge, while all her limbs tingled as if they belonged to somebody else. Usually, she would rush straight into his arms, where the tingling would soon merge into the take-your-breath-away sensations that left her barely able to stand.

But today was not a normal day.

'I'm sorry.' His smile was rueful. 'I was on my way out, but then that idiot phoned again. Aunt Rhiannon was still teaching her art class, and I didn't get to the phone in time. So Nainie took it.'

'Oh.' Carys bit her lip. Nainie was David's grandmother, the owner of Plas Eden and seriously old. 'Was she okay?'

'She was a bit upset, so I waited until Rhiannon got back.' He scowled. 'I know he's a Meredith and some kind of cousin, but he's still a total arse. Nainie's had enough to deal with, without cousin Edmund going on and on about how we're ruining Plas Eden and he could have done it better, and he should have inherited it anyhow. He was back on about that again, and how he was coming over, or sending some private investigator to "sort us out".'

'What a horrible thing to say! Poor Nainie.' Carys had always had a soft spot for old Mrs Meredith, who was gentle and kind, and never seemed to notice whether Carys was a girl from the village or the daughter of landed gentry.

'Oh, she'll be fine.' David was wry. 'Edmund was still ranting away like anything when Rhiannon got back. He won't listen to me because he says I'm too young and I've been brought up on their "lies", and all that garbage. So I put Rhiannon on. She'll tell him where to get off, no problems.'

Carys grinned. She'd overheard enough gossip in the village to know that Rhiannon was still regarded as an outsider with outlandish London ways. The 'London' bit was mostly Rhiannon's flowing dresses of bold, multicoloured patterns, worn with Doc Martin boots and a silk scarf in her fair hair. Along with a habit of speaking her mind.

Carys hadn't personally been at the receiving end of the speaking-her-mind bit, but there was something slightly exotic and uncontrollable about Rhiannon – like a brightly feathered bird of unknown temper, whose beak looked uncomfortably sharp. She didn't envy anyone in the path of Rhiannon's temper, once she got going.

'Well?' David had brushed today's drama at Plas Eden to one side and was watching her expectantly.

Carys took a deep breath, the butterflies back in her belly. 'I got one 'B'. That was for Biology.'

'And?' He was still watching her, confidence in his eyes. He'd meant it, all those months he'd said he believed in her. Which had been slightly unnerving, because it wasn't how it was meant to be. That was not the Golden Rule of Finding a Boyfriend, at least according to Mam and every magazine Carys could lay her hands on. Listen to a boy. Show how interested you are in his concerns. Don't talk too much, especially not about yourself. Above all, never, ever show signs of being cleverer than him.

David Meredith, being heir to Plas Eden, was of the unmistakeably Lord-of-the-Manor kind, and so – as far as Mam and the magazines were concerned – the 'B' alone should have done for her, good and proper. He should have been at least halfway to Australia by now.

'As', she confessed.

'I told you so!' She was caught up and swung around and around, until she was dizzy. 'Three As and a B. Hey, you could get into Oxford with that.'

'I don't want to get into Oxford.' Her family weren't like the Merediths: she would be the first *ever* to get to university. That was quite scary enough, without any thought of posh people looking down their noses at a Welsh village girl with just her grant to live on and no sense of style.

'But you *could.*' He was beaming at her in unmistakable pride. 'And that's what counts.' He grinned. 'Huw'll be pissed, when I tell him. He only got a B and two Cs. He'll have to go to his second choice, or try through clearing.'

Carys tactfully hid a smile. She couldn't help it. David and his brother had been to Rushdown, the only private school in the area. Rushdown was a magnificent Victorian mansion perched on a cliff just outside the nearest town, with views over the sea and Talarn's famous ruined castle. Carys and her sisters had had to make do with Talarn Secondary, with views of the local housing estate and a slightly dubious reputation. But Carys had still managed to get better A levels than both Huw and David. In fact, the best results in all of Talarn, according to the reporter from the local paper. Who had still concentrated on getting lots of shots of the pretty girls, slightly to Carys' relief.

'Come on.' David grabbed her hand and led her through the second arch to a series of stone steps where the trees thickened, allowing only the faintest touch of sunlight to trickle through into the undergrowth.

'Where are we going?'

'To the statues, of course. I want this to be really special.'

Carys allowed herself to be guided along, down the steps

and into the deepest, most hidden part of the garden. The bottom step opened up into a flat expanse of ground filled by young oak and slender, silver-trunked birch. Leaves flickered, sending a sighing into the branches above them.

'Come on,' said David, feeling her hesitate. 'It's okay, there's nothing scary. It's just a bit overgrown, that's all.'

As they made their way between the thick ferns and moss, Carys found her eyes adjusting to the gloom. Faint streams of light fell into green pools on the ground, like the aisles of St Asaph Cathedral where Dad had once taken them to hear the singing: not because he was particularly religious, but because it was beautiful. High above, the branches opened up into a clear circle, revealing a distant glimpse of sky.

'It's a glade,' she said, her voice hollow and echoing.

David turned, his eyes glinting in the reflected light. 'You're not superstitious, are you?'

'No, of course not.'

He pulled her close to him. 'This was Mum and Dad's favourite place. We all used to spend so much time here when me and Huw were little. It felt like our own little world, where we could always be safe. Except Mum would never let us stay once it got to dusk: all that stuff about glades being special places for the Druids and the Celts.' His voice had become thoughtful. 'They thought woodland glades were places between worlds, where the living and the dead could meet.' She felt him shudder. 'When I was a kid, I sometimes used to think, used to hope, even...' His voice trailed into silence.

Carys held him tight. David's parents had both been killed in a terrible train accident on their way to London, when David was nine. Carys had only been seven, but she remembered vividly the pictures of the twisted wreck that had filled the papers and the TV news for weeks afterwards. She

9

knew there was nothing she could say to him. There was nothing anyone could do or say. Just be there with him, until it passed.

'We can go,' she suggested.

David shook himself. 'It's all rubbish, of course. That stuff about glades. And there's no point, really, trying to hang on to the past. Now's what matters. You and me. Anyhow, I'm supposed to be showing you the statues.' Pride entered his voice. 'So? What d'you think? Pretty cool, eh?'

She'd forgotten about the statues. Carys peered around her, not quite sure what she was looking for. Slowly, as her eyes adjusted, stone figures began to emerge from the darkness between the trees. They were taller than she had imagined: life-size, each resting on a large slate base. Stone eyes gazed out at the intruders, solemn and watchful, like pieces on a chessboard, waiting for the next move.

And their faces – as the carved features sharpened all around her, Carys felt a sliver of cold sneak down her spine. They weren't like any faces of statues she had seen before. They wouldn't quite leave you alone. As if, Carys thought, they were real people, caught inside a stone shell.

'Who are they?'

'They're supposed to show famous Celtic myths.' David brushed the nearest statue with affection. 'See, this one is King Arthur pulling Excalibur out of the stone. Those two over there, the ones kissing, they're Tristan and Isolde, who fell in love when they shouldn't have done. And the dog is Gelert, who saved Prince Llewellyn's baby from a wolf.'

'Who's this?' asked Carys, her eyes caught by the figure of an old woman bent over a large pot, her face high-boned and fierce with determination.

'That's Ceridwen. She was a witch. Only Aunt Rhiannon

10

always says we should call her a "wisewoman" instead, because that makes her sound less wicked. That's her stirring her cauldron for a year and a day to create her magic potion.' David pulled away encroaching nettles to reveal a small boy with a round, mischievous face; one finger to his lips at the foot of the pot. 'And that's her servant, little Gwion Bach, who drank the three magic drops by mistake and was turned into the poet Taliesin.'

There was something familiar about the little boy's face. Carys frowned, her mind searching. Something about the eyes and the turn of the nose, and the wide-eyed expression of astonishment mixed with delight. Something so familiar it eluded her completely and left the tips of her fingers prickling.

They were all clean, it struck her. Unlike the woman in the fountain, all the statues were clean of moss and ivy. Even of lichen and birds' droppings. As if, among all this neglect and wilderness, someone was still caring for them. Someone who might be watching them at this moment, now. This time the prickling went through all of her and lingered on her scalp.

'They're beautiful,' she murmured.

'Aren't they just. Mum got some people from the BBC interested in making a film about them once. They were really excited about it. The statues could have been famous.' The pain was back in his voice.

'Who's this?' asked Carys hastily, pointing towards the figure of a young woman sheltering beneath a metal arch, its rusting swirls almost completely overgrown with honeysuckle. Unlike the other statues, the girl appeared to have no feet, but rose up like a mermaid, smiling and eager from a sheaf of stone flowers.

Luckily, it seemed to be the right thing to say. David was instantly distracted. 'That one? Isn't she pretty? I think she's my favourite. That's Blodeuwedd. The woman made out of flowers.'

'Oh.' Maybe not the right question, after all. Carys found the unease creeping back inside her belly. Mam used to tell them that story, when she and her sisters were little. About a woman made out of flowers to be the perfect wife for a hero. Except she wasn't perfect, but turned out bad in the end. She ended up horribly punished, turned into an owl, an ugly creature to spend her life despised and alone.

Carys frowned at the laughing figure in front of her, her feet still willow, her skirts etched in buttercups, one hand stretched skywards trailing a garland of irises and dog roses: as if she wanted to grasp the sun, moon and stars and pull them down like a cloak around her, and set off across the universe, a traveller in search of strange lands.

She didn't know, the woman made out of flowers; she didn't know, as she sprang into eager life, how it would all end. No one knew, at the beginning of things, how anything would end.

'So now we can tell them.'

Carys turned back to where David was watching her, love and pride glowing in his eyes. 'Tell them?'

'About us. Officially, I mean. About us getting married.'

'But I thought we were going to wait?' A rush of fear went through her. 'After all, I'm going to be away for three years.'

'But that doesn't stop us getting married now. You can still go to Manchester. It's only a few hours' drive away. I can come and visit you at weekends, and you can come back for holidays. I could teach you to drive. I could get you a car as a wedding present. Then you could come up and down as much as you wanted.'

It was supposed to be the happiest day of her life – wedding

12

day itself excepted, of course. It *was* the happiest day. It was all she had dreamed of: passing her exams and then spending the rest of her life with David.

So where had the unease come from? The panic that was now shooting up and down inside her? Carys discovered her fingers closing once more around the paper in her pocket. Until she had seen it written there, officially, in black and white, impossible to deny or to be taken away from her, she had never imagined how powerful the effect of seeing those three As on her A level results would be.

It had been like a world opening up. A new world. One she had never quite believed existed, or at least that could never, ever exist for her.

'Maybe we should wait.'

'Wait?' He was frowning at her. 'What on earth for?'

'There's no hurry.'

'No, but there's no reason to wait, either.' He grasped her hands. 'Don't you see, Cari? It's exactly the time. Aunt Rhiannon's right: the estate is getting too much for Nainie to manage, especially with this stupid Edmund business. I'm twenty-one next year and, fingers crossed, I'll be finishing my degree at Aberystwyth. So it's time I took over properly. It's going to be really good, you know. There's so much we can do. I've been talking with the outward-bound people in Talarn about setting up courses. Canoeing and rock-climbing. That sort of thing. The west wing isn't bad, it wouldn't take much to get that up and running for guests, and that would leave the rest of the house for you and me and Nainie. And Rhiannon, of course. Plas Eden is Rhiannon's home, too. But she'll be teaching her art classes and she says she wants to start doing exhibitions of her paintings again, so she won't be around much.'

'So I'll just be there to look after the house and Nainie?' She hadn't meant to say it, not baldly, like that. She was sorry the moment the words spilled out, but it was too late.

'Of course not.' Bewilderment spread across his face. 'Cari, I'd never think of you like that.'

No, he wouldn't. Not intentionally. Just as he would never mean to hurt her. She had to try to make him understand. Once inside the confines of Plas Eden, absorbed into being a Meredith, it might be too late.

'I don't know what I want to do,' she said, slowly. 'As a career, I mean. What I want to *be*. I suppose Dad's right; I should take the business and accountancy degree so that that way I can always earn money, and then decide what I really want to do.'

'I'd never stop you, Cari. And I'll always support you, you know that.'

'Yes, I know. But supposing I want to travel for a bit? Like you did, in your gap year? You've seen loads of places and I've never even owned a passport.'

'That's simple: we can go together.'

'I suppose so.'

He must have heard the lack of enthusiasm in her voice. 'That's an excuse,' he said, frowning.

'No, of course not! That's not what I meant.' If only she could marshal her thoughts and put them into words, so that he could understand. Only the thoughts were so new and this sense of yearning to be on her own, and for once in her life to rely solely her own wits and test herself, so unexpected, she didn't even know where to start.

'If you don't want to marry me, you should just say.'

'That's not it!' She was close to tears, happiness slipping like sand between her fingers. All she had to do was stop. To smile

14

at David and say 'yes', and it would all be all right again. Yet somehow, she couldn't.

'It has to be something.' She couldn't bear the hurt on his face. 'What you mean is, you're not sure. Not sure that you love me.'

'Of course I love you! More than anything.'

'But you can't be certain.' He was watching her, a deep frown between his brows. 'It's that singer guy, isn't it? The one who's just got that big record deal.'

'Merlin?' Carys stared in disbelief. 'Don't be ridiculous.'

'He's on his way to New York. That's what the papers are saying. You said you wanted to travel. And I saw the way he was looking at you in the Taliesin that time.'

'I didn't ask him to,' she snapped, furious at the injustice.

'But you didn't tell him where to go.'

'Only because I didn't want to cause trouble. That's what people like me do. It's okay for you. People listen to you. Everyone knows your family owns Plas Eden. Mine were just servants. Your servants, in fact. That's what the village was made for in the first place, wasn't it? For us all to be servants at Plas Eden.'

'Don't be silly, Cari. No one thinks about that any more. What does it matter? I'm right; it's just an excuse. Either you want to marry me, or you don't. It's up to you.'

Before she could say another word, he was striding off up the path, wounded pride in every step, until he vanished from view.

It wasn't too late. She could run after him. Apologise. Do something, say something. Anything to keep him.

Instead, she stood there with the leaves rustling about her like whispers, stunned at having anything like that burst out of her. This was a new Carys. One she hadn't known before.

15

A Carys who couldn't go back inside her box. A Carys who couldn't unsee the look in Rhiannon's eyes that declared Carys would marry David because catching yourself the local lord of the manor was all village girls like her aspired to. That David could have done so much, much better for himself.

Carys fought back the tears. Her mind was a whirl, but still she did not move. A new world had opened up in front of her. A world without David. A world that was vast and empty, and where she didn't know how to start to make her way.

And now there was no way back.

Part One

1898

Where did it begin? Really begin?

The moment, I suppose, when I decided I would not end there, in the dark, foul waters of the Thames. Until that moment, I had never known the will to live could be so strong.

My purse had gone, as soon as I stepped out of the railway station, stunned by the rattle of trams, the call of hawkers and newspaper sellers and the rush of the city around me. I'd seen them since, as I wandered the streets, hour after hour: small boys, their hands diving like quicksilver into pockets and baskets. The smart-looking woman with feathers in her hat and a lace collar, her muff brushing against the girl just in front of me, bracelet vanishing into nowhere as the thief walked on casually, hands deep within the fur.

I had a few coins that had been thrust thoughtfully into my pockets, along with a slip of paper beneath the notice of any pickpocket but, for me, a new life. A life I did not care to preserve, a life I did not want.

'Thinking about it?' a woman said, as I paused on Westminster Bridge, the black flow of the river far beneath. Around us, midnight bells began to toll.

I did not reply. I pulled my scarf tight around my face, shutting out the throat-catching mist creeping up along the waters, and the woman with her attempt at kindness beside me.

'I've thought of it myself,' she added, 'after my eldest died.'

That had me turning, despite myself. 'Your eldest?' I could just make her out in the flickering lights. She was bare-headed, hair whipping around her in the river wind, its fish-laden hint of the sea almost drowned by the stench of city filth.

'My Maud,' she said. 'Ten, she was. Such a pretty little thing, and never a cross word. You wait for it, don't you, with the babies. But not when they grow. Not when you begin to see the woman in the childish face.'

'I'm sorry.'

My companion shrugged. 'But then what good would it have done? My man, he's not a bad man, when he can keep the drink out of him. And I could not leave my boys to the care of another woman.'

'No,' I murmured. I could see the move of shadows as she pulled her coat more closely around her.

'Do you have a place to go?'

'Yes,' I replied, a little too hastily.

I felt her hesitate. But then she stepped away. 'It's safest to keep moving,' she called over her shoulder.

She was right. All through the darkness I walked. In every shadow, every doorway, men and women slept. Children crouched close together as the air chilled towards the October dawn. I could feel their eyes watching me, as I passed. Once a shout came after me. Once footsteps. But, for the most part, I was left alone, with my quick, purposeful stride, the scarf close around me, so that I could be any woman, any age, or maybe even no woman at all.

As the dawn came, I knew I was weaker. That I could not face another night like that one. That I no longer had the strength to turn this way and that to escape a man's voice or footsteps behind me.

I thought I was lost in the tangle of alleyways. I had been to London, of course. But that was a lifetime ago, for the Season. That was a London of brightly lit streets, of laughter and music. Only the barefoot children shooed back into the shadows by the coachman or the footman waiting at the door gave a hint of another world. A hint I did not care to take. As my Uncle Jolyon said, we gave money for the poor at church each Sunday, and was it our fault if they chose to drink it away? Now I was in a world I should never have known.

But then I turned a corner, and there it was: Kennal Place, Lambeth. Immediately in front of me the great iron gates that were my passage to life.

I could have walked away. Followed the streets back towards the river, this time without a friendly voice to dissuade me. This time with a sense of purpose carried through.

What made me hesitate for that moment?

'Have you been waiting long? I'm afraid the gates don't open for an hour or so yet.' He was tall, well-dressed in a top hat and dark coat, one hand resting on a silver-topped walking cane.

'Oh.' I became aware that my hands were filthy, the hem of my dress heavy with dirt, and that I smelt of the city streets.

At his voice, a bent little man limped his way out of a building at one side of the gate. 'Morning, sir,' he said, pulling the bolts and turning the key so that the gates swung slowly open. 'Not a bad morning, all things considering.'

'No indeed.'

The gateman spotted me at once, with a sharp and obviously well-practised eye. 'Shoo!' he said. 'Off you go, young woman. No admissions until nine o'clock. No pestering Mr Meredith. And no loitering, neither.'

The man with the silver-topped cane turned back towards me. He had a narrow, purposeful face, and restless blue eyes. His movements were rapid and decisive. A man of action, I would have guessed. Not the action of a soldier, but one who thrived in the fast-moving world of trade and commerce. I knew such men: my Uncle Jolyon had paraded me in front of them often enough. I was not parading now.

21

But they were sharp, those eyes of his. He was watching me as if he knew that in an hour or two – a minute – I would not be there. And he was not going to give me up – unpromising material that I clearly was – without a fight.

Something inside me stirred. 'I have a letter,' I said.

Mr Meredith's eyebrows raised. 'A letter?'

I was scrabbling in my pockets, as if my life depended on it. 'A letter of recommendation.' I found it, and held it out towards him. Grubby and crumpled, but still intact.

He took it without comment, his eyes resting on the handwriting of the envelope. 'You had better come this way, Miss…?'

'Mrs,' I said. 'Mrs Smith.'

He glanced up, eyes resting briefly on my ringless hands. 'You had better come this way, Mrs Smith.'

I followed his rapid strides across a paved courtyard, towards the red brick of the building, stained and grubby with soot, even to my eyes. We did not go through the front door, but to a smaller entrance around one side. He let himself in with a key, and I followed.

'Come in,' said Mr Meredith, as I hesitated, my eyes adjusting to the darkness. He opened an inner door, pulling back shutters to allow light into a room with a large mahogany table at its centre, shelves of books and papers lined along each wall.

I took the seat he motioned to absently with one hand, and sat while he took the letter to the light of the window.

'So you are seeking a position as a domestic,' he said at last, turning his back towards me, and placing the letter in his pocket. His hands were already shuffling through the papers on his desk as if he could not wait a moment for the business of the day to begin.

'Yes.'

22

'Hm.' His eyes were indeed sharp. He had seen more than the lack of any semblance of a ring on my hands. I shoved their smoothness out of sight beneath the folds of my skirt.

'I'm a good worker.' Which was, for all I knew – or anyone else, for that matter – true. 'And honest.' Which was possibly not quite so true, but seemed the right thing to say.

I could feel the fight getting back into me. 'Stubborn', my uncle used to call me. 'Wilful, foolish, unwomanly' was what he meant. At the time it mattered; I thought it would be my undoing. I never guessed then that one day it would be what kept me alive.

'I don't doubt it.' Mr Meredith glanced up at me once more. 'This is a charity hospital, Mrs Smith. The work is hard, you need a strong stomach, and the pay is more than usually poor.'

'Oh.' I'd lost my sense of hunger a lifetime ago – and for the rest –

'Do you have lodgings?'

'Lodgings?' I stared at him.

'No matter.' His tone was without comment, thank Heaven. 'Many of our women live in. I'm sure a place can be found for you. Matron will be down shortly. She'll see to it.' He bent over his desk again, rapidly slitting open letters with a small knife the handle of which gleamed with mother of pearl.

'Thank you,' I murmured. There was a fire in the grate. A small one, but enough to send warmth through me. What with that and resting on the chair, my head was beginning to spin.

He had already forgotten me. He drew a fresh sheet of paper towards him, dipped his pen in the inkstand next to him and began to write with a swift, confident hand.

I blinked hard, trying to focus. Just behind the desk hung a small watercolour in a wooden frame. There was no great skill in the brushstrokes. A woman practising her accomplishment, no doubt. I wondered if it had been painted for him by his wife. Except the frame was lacking in suitable gilt and the odd cherubim or so to glorify its clumsiness of execution. And there was no wedding ring on his hands, any more than on mine.

I kept my eyes on the picture more to keep myself awake than from any curiosity. But all the same it caught me, drawing me in. The skill might not be there, but after a while I could see there was love in every brush stroke, in every leaf, stone and window of the pale building rising up between trees.

A name was carved into a small wooden plaque on the bottom of the frame.

'Eden.' I had not realised I had spoken aloud.

'Eden?' Those blue eyes were on me once more. He followed my gaze. 'Ah, the house.' He smiled. A gentle, tender smile. A smile he would give to a lover or a child. I pushed the thought away, as fast as it came. 'Appropriate, don't you think, having your childhood home named after the first paradise?'

'Mm.'

'Paradise lost,' he added, a little wryly. He had forgotten I was there. 'Or it will be when my brother Caradoc has finished with it. At least my mother still has strength to battle against the ruin of her precious gardens.' He caught my eye, and remembered me again. 'Plas Eden was once a beautiful place. I thought I was glad I was not the eldest son. I thought that left me free to do as I wished. But that last time I went back there…' He shook his head.

'I'm sorry,' I murmured, unsure what to say. Personally, I'd scream if I was dragged back through the door of a grand house again. Scream the place down, kicking and spitting and scratching and tearing eyes out first. Not that I was going to

24

mention this. Not now the will to survive was beating within me once more.

'But you don't want to hear about Plas Eden,' he said. 'Odd: I'm not known as a man who gives confidences.' He smiled. 'You have an understanding face, Mrs Smith.'

Understanding. Well, I'd been called other things, many other things, but not 'understanding'.

I liked the sound.

Even though I knew that if the letter in his pocket had told him half the truth about me, the word would never have passed his lips.

Chapter One

2011

It had been a cold spring that year. Snow still lurked in gullies high up on Snowdon's flanks, even though the tourist season was making its long, slow stir out of winter torpor.

Cyclists had appeared on the roads and forest tracks in the last few weeks, followed by walkers with new boots and smart new rucksacks, sending the tinny jingles of mobile phones echoing round the hillsides. This was much to the scorn of the serious climbers who had remained all winter armed with pick axes and crampons and enough serious fleeces, breathable jackets, snow goggles and leg guards to equip a small expedition to Everest.

On the promenade below Talarn Castle, where Cardigan Bay curves its way between Harlech and Aberystwyth, taking in the glories of Trawsfynydd nuclear power station along the way, the Mabinogion café was still half-deserted.

'By the window, don't you think,' remarked Gwenan Evans, leading the way inside. 'It always was a good view over the sea.' The few diners turned instinctively at the decisive tones. The sight of the tall, well-built woman with strongly defined features, whose expensive suit and short, firmly styled hair had defied all attempts of the sea winds to ruffle them, sent them scurrying straight back to their plates.

'That looks fine,' replied Carys, hastily. The desire to run and not have to face this – at least not now, this minute – was stronger than ever.

'Just so long as there's not a draft,' put in her younger sister Nia, pulling her faux fur collar more closely around her.

'We can always move,' retorted Gwenan. Her eyes rested on a small round table, conveniently set for three and far enough away from the majority of the diners to ensure some measure of privacy. She pulled out the nearest chair with brisk efficiency. 'I take it this is okay?'

'Fine,' said Nia, tucking her neat figure gracefully into the chair nearest the window and crossing her slender legs.

'Yes,' murmured Carys.

'Good, good.' Gwenan removed the laminated strip of menu propped between the glass salt cellar and a small vase of silk freesias and frowned at its unpromising contents.

With the arrival of the waitress, whose first language appeared to be Polish rather than Welsh or English, tea and coffee were ordered. The sisters sat awkwardly, with nothing to occupy their hands while they waited, the urgent business of the day hanging like a steaming cauldron between them.

At last, the tray arrived: tea in a little metal teapot, with a matching pot of hot water and a miniscule jug of milk. The coffee, rather surprisingly, came in the sophistication of its own miniature cafetiere; the effect was rather spoilt by the garish mugs with an assortment of kittens on their sides, and the sugar in the kind of small sachets that invariably find their way into pockets to lurk back home 'just in case', until so stiff with moisture that their only possible last resting-place is the bin.

'Well?' demanded Gwenan, in her undisputed position as eldest, dispensing tea, coffee and milk in the correct order.

'I thought she looked remarkably well,' said Nia.

'Of course she's well. They wouldn't be considering releasing her,' returned Gwenan.

'I was only saying.' Nia sounded hurt.

'She did look *much* better,' put in Carys, gently.

Nia smiled, her ever-sensitive feelings soothed. 'Mam seems happy in the nursing home. And the staff are very nice, and she has all that physiotherapy,' she added, brightly. 'I suppose, really, the sensible thing would be for her to stay there. After all, she has made the break; it wouldn't be like her going into a home from her house, would it?'

'Have you any idea how much a home like that costs?' Gwenan was frowning. 'Even if we sold Willow Cottage, we couldn't keep her there for many years. Not even with the way houses have gone up: she isn't that well off, you know.'

'There must be cheaper ones.'

'Have you seen them?'

The silence came steaming up between them once more.

'Mam did say she wanted to stay at home for as long as she could,' said Carys, at last. 'And she'll be able to get help. They are very keen on keeping people in their own homes, nowadays.'

'But she'll need constant assistance for the first few weeks. Months, even.' Gwenan stirred sugar into her second cup of tea. 'Mam's recovering from a broken hip, for heaven's sake. That's a serious business. She can't just be left to cope on her own. It wouldn't be right.'

'No,' agreed Carys, slowly. She gazed out through the window onto Talarn beach, where she had once spent the hot summer days of her childhood. Endless days, when Mam and

Dad were always there in the background and always would be: solid, unchanging, the firm and perfect centre of her world.

Her eyes followed the children straying as far as they dared from the secure circle of their parents, running back every now and again for a quarrel to be adjudicated or a grazed knee kissed, before setting out again into the vast expanse of beach.

This was one of the real moments of growing up, she thought. One they didn't tell you about: not like having sex for the first time; landing your first job; signing the mortgage on a house; having kids of your own, even: all the things that are supposed to be the rites of passage to the adult world.

There were things that weren't supposed to happen in life. For Mam, it would be to outlive any of her daughters. For them, it was to find Mam after her fall as suddenly no longer Mam, but a small, shrunken creature with frightened eyes, who had no control over her own future, and who had, in an instant, so it seemed, become the child while they had stepped into the parents' shoes.

Of course, she could walk away. Run. Carry on with her life and pretend this had never happened. She was an independent adult: no one could force her to do anything. And yet –

This was Mam's life: her one and only life. Just because she was becoming frail – and the very fact of tripping over in the street had frightened her, let alone the surgery to replace the hip broken beyond all saving – didn't mean they could just abandon her. As if she didn't matter.

And it was only for a few weeks. Maybe a month or two.

'Obviously, for me it is out of the question.' Gwenan was still stirring her tea, slowly, and with care. 'Not with these new stores we've just taken over. It's a critical time: I really cannot leave the business at this moment, and I have little enough time to spend with Charles and the boys as it is, and with Tim starting his A levels. I can still take Mam out for days, and for holidays when she's well enough. Of course, later on, when things quieten down with the business, I'll be more than happy to do my bit.'

Nia put down her spoon. 'Well, I can't leave William and Alexandra, not with Alexandra's GCSEs this year, and William making the move to secondary school this September. And Sam is under terrible strain, you know. It's not easy being a Head Teacher these days: he needs all the support we can give him. I've got to think of my family. This is their entire future we're talking about. I'm sure Mam wouldn't want me to abandon them.'

'We could share it,' said Carys. She looked up to find herself the centre of attention, with two pairs of brown eyes fixed firmly on her and no signs of looking away again.

'It could be a good opportunity for you,' said Gwenan.

Carys blinked. 'Opportunity?'

'I thought you'd been talking about moving into something different. Smallholding, or something? That was the point of that gardening course of yours, wasn't it?'

'Horticultural,' muttered Carys, between her teeth. 'Horticultural Course.' 'Gardening' made it sound like a hobby, rather than the soul-searching, life-changing decision it had been.

What was it about a woman who didn't have children? Mam had treated Gwenan and Nia as equals ever since their babies had appeared, but she still seemed to see Carys as a child. Which, Carys always considered in irritation, was hardly fair at all, given that she held down a successful career for years, paid her bills, and was now the proud half-owner of a stylish flat in one of the better parts of Chester, and had definitely grown-up sex with Joe, thank you very much.

31

So what if she and Joe had decided from the outset they didn't want children? They weren't the only couple to make that choice. She had friends with children, and friends without, and both were equally happy and fulfilled in their choice. It wasn't some kind of failure or laziness. Many people envied their freedom, their ability to pack their bags and simply go with the latest last-minute bargain for a fortnight in Venice, or the carefully planned motor home trips around New Zealand and America. It was her choice and Joe's, and nobody else's business.

'I always swore I would never have a child unless I passionately wanted one,' she had tried to explain to Mam, when her mother was in one of her why-don't-you-and-Joe-get-married phases. 'And where I had the kind of life I could build around them, not simply dump them in day-care and pretend they hadn't happened. What's the point of that?'

'Your dad and I, we had nothing, not even a house, when we had Gwenan,' Mam had said. 'You're not getting any younger, you know. One day, you'll regret it.'

'Plenty of women have babies in their thirties,' Carys had replied. 'Their forties, even, nowadays. Once they've got their career off the ground.' But Mam had turned away, without saying anything, the slight tightening of her lips a sure sign that she saw this as Carys avoiding the issue in a very Carys kind of way.

Carys hadn't brought up the subject again and made sure she quickly turned the conversation the moment she found it straying towards dangerous waters. Not even in the long months last year when the dream of a more self-sufficient lifestyle, with home-grown veg, chickens, and maybe even the odd goat or so, had begun infiltrating itself into her mind, bringing with it possibilities of another kind.

But it was a bit too late to mention that particular vision now. Carys looked up to find Gwenan watching her closely.

'What I mean is that if you're serious about a smallholding, Carys, this would be your chance to take the time to look around.'

'Round here?' Carys stared at her in dismay. 'I was thinking more Devon or Cornwall, or somewhere like that. This is hardly growing country. Unless you're a sheep. And in any case, when I said I wanted to change direction, I did not mean into full-time carer. And what about Joe?'

'Oh, but it's not forever, and we've said we'll help,' said Nia.

'When we can,' put in Gwenan.

Carys eyed them in exasperation. 'I didn't say I *wouldn't* be the one to look after Mam. I just don't want it to end up a permanent thing. I do have a life, you know.'

'A couple of months,' said Gwenan. 'That's all. By that time we'll know if she can cope or not. Meantime I'll have a good look at nursing homes, see if we can find one that's more reasonable, so that if she can't cope she will have somewhere to go.'

'We've got to at least give her the chance,' said Nia, plaintively.

Carys winced. In one way, her sisters were quite right: you couldn't just abandon children, whatever call came on your time. She *didn't* have their responsibilities.

It was only a few months. And, let's face it: what was there in her own life at this moment that couldn't be put aside for a month or so when – unlike Mam – she still had a lifetime ahead of her? But what if Mam never got better? What if she couldn't cope? Mam had always been so independent. Irritatingly, exasperatingly independent, refusing even help in her beloved little garden.

Carys felt her stomach knot. The walls of the café suddenly seemed to crowd in around her, making it hard to breathe.

What would happen if one day she was faced with the choice of continuing, or Mam being carted off to some gloomy place of vacant starers propped up in armchairs until they were wheeled off to be fed, or to the indignity of the toilet or being cleaned, as if they had never been anything more than babies? How, then, could she be heartless enough to abandon Mam and put her own life first?

She'd never had much sympathy for Victorian spinsters, expected to attend on their aging parents. And not just Victorian, either. Several of Mam's friends had never married, looking instead after invalid mothers, or widowed fathers, until marriage and career seemed out of the question at all.

'I wouldn't do that,' she'd always told herself, like the child who knows the monster isn't going to get her. 'You can always find ways. There are always ways out.'

Of course there are, came the thought stealing into her grown-up mind: but somebody, somewhere, always pays the price.

Carys quickly shoved such thoughts away. Mam's long-term future was a bridge they would have to cross later; there was nothing she could do about it now. Instinct told her that the longer Mam was in the nursing home with everything done for her and not even the washing-up and tomorrow's meal to focus her thoughts and keep her body moving, the harder it would be to get her back to her former independence. The problem Mam faced was now, this moment. The rest would have to wait.

'I'll think about it,' she conceded. 'I need to talk it over with Joe, and see if I can arrange things with work and college.'

The moment the words were out of her mouth, she felt her sisters relax.

'Good for you,' said Gwenan.

'You're such a star,' murmured Nia.

'There's only so much I can do over the Internet,' said Carys, sharply. 'I'd still need to go back to Chester for meetings. Plus I can't just completely abandon Joe, you know.'

'We'll make a rota,' said Gwenan. 'Nia and I will come and take over for a couple of days when you need it. That's fair.'

Nia nodded vigorously. 'Oh, yes of course. We'll do all we can to help, Cari.'

Spots of rain had begun hurling themselves against the window, sending the last remaining families on the beach scurrying for shelter. Within minutes, an entire throng, complete with sandy feet and buckets and spades, made their way in through the café door with the exasperated nagging of parents and the loud shrieks of a small child deprived of the sea.

Gwenan finished her tea and began stacking the mugs neatly on the tray. 'We'll go back and tell Mam, then.'

'She'll be so pleased,' smiled Nia.

'Mmm,' said Carys, wondering if it was still not too late to run away. Of course, Mam *would* be pleased. No, not just that: relieved. The fear would fade from the back of her eyes. She would protest that there was no need for any of her girls to do such a thing, she could manage very well and Carys was young and had a life to lead.

But the fear would have gone, all the same.

Bill split and duly paid, Carys followed her sisters outside into the car park. Salt brushed her lips. The air was cool, edged with the damp scents of grass and the sharpness of seafood. And in truth, thought Carys, suddenly, she was doing this for Mam, but maybe she was also doing it for herself.

'The past is always with you, until you turn round and face it, and then move on again,' her best friend Poppy, who had a

35

philosophical streak, was fond of saying. In recent months, Carys had come to agree with her.

Poppy's past was a troubled one, that had ended up in a children's home and then foster care. Carys' past was here, amongst the mountains rising up behind the shabby little seaside town. And in the smaller – and even shabbier – time-passed-by village in the hills, where every road and path led towards the rambling grounds of Plas Eden.

'Ready?' called Gwenan, pressing her key fob, sending her Volvo into a paroxysm of flashing lights and clicking locks.

Carys nodded, and hurried through the sun-streaked rain to join her sisters.

Chapter Two

✿ 'But I really don't see why it has to be down to you,' said Joe, just slightly plaintively, stacking the dishwasher in his usual methodical fashion.

Carys took a deep breath. 'I can't just abandon her. She's my Mam.'

'I thought you didn't get on with her. You were always telling me how you couldn't wait to get out of there, once your dad died.'

'But she's still my mother. Family, you know? Messy things. Don't always go to plan. They're very nice at the Home, and it's lovely. But you can tell she hates it. She hates being dependent, and she hates having no control over her life. You should have seen her, Joe. She looked so scared. Not like Mam at all. At least if we can get her back home, she has a chance of being able to fight for her independence. Even if that means having carers coming in every day for the rest of her life, and us spending more time visiting her. Me and Gwenan and Nia, I mean,' she added, as he looked up, his dark eyes wide with alarm.

'Well, I still don't see why you've ended up with it all.' He straightened, pushing the dishwasher door shut and setting the cycle churning. 'I don't see why you let Gwenan and Nia get away with things like that. You really ought to stand up to them more.'

'That's all very well in theory. But the reality is that they both live miles away and they have children settled with school and friends, and exams coming up. So what am I supposed to do? Punish Mam?'

'Surely there has to be somebody else. Some aunt, or something.'

Carys finished sorting the baskets of laundry and began feeding the washing machine with last week's whites. 'It's not like that anymore,' she replied, doing her best to keep the irritation out of her voice. 'There aren't just loads of old aunts stashed away looking for something to do. Not even in Pont-ar-Eden. Everybody works. Even pensioners, nowadays. Haven't you been into B&Q lately?'

'Then maybe she would be better off in a Home.'

She was tired. Her shoulders ached from days of tension and the strange bed of the B&B, followed by the drive back to Chester. She had a hundred and one things to do before work tomorrow morning, and her emotions were a rollercoaster, rendering her patience more than usually thin.

'Is that what you'd do, if it was *your* mother?' she snapped. He frowned at her, as if affronted by the suggestion. 'Elaine isn't that much younger than Mam,' she added for good measure, feeling her temper dangerously close to getting out of hand. 'And it could well be, one day.'

Except, of course, it wouldn't. She saw his eyes slide from hers, as he turned to fill the kettle. Joe was a man. The one with the career. The one rising rapidly through the ranks of Morley and Westcott, on track to be partner before he was forty. Morley, Westcott and Young, Chartered Accountants. That was the future, written in stone.

It would be Joe's sisters, Anna and Phyllis, mothers and career women both, who would step in, should anything happen to his parents. The assumption was there, unspoken.

So much for equality. She wasn't sure whether to laugh, cry, stamp her feet, or burn any bra she could lay her hands on. You go through life thinking it's all sorted. Equal opportunities. Equal status. Nothing to stand in your way. And, okay, you hear about the pay gap and the twenty hours or so the average full-time working woman spends on domestic chores, but that isn't you. That's not the way you live your life.

'I thought we agreed…' she began. His back was rigid as he turned the tap, shutting her out. Carys bit her lip. She could hear herself turning into some old nag going on endlessly about compromise and commitment. As if they hadn't been through this before. As if they hadn't worked this all out, once and for all, two years ago. Or so she'd believed.

Compromise and commitment. She would never have stayed with Joe if she hadn't believed he'd seen her point of view. Joe always did what Joe wanted to do. She'd only understood this during the last few years, when – for her at least – spending every holiday rushing off to some activity-packed tour of India or Greece had finally began to pall. It wasn't that she didn't want to travel, just not all the time. She'd seen too many lost souls wandering from one exotic beach location to the next, in a rootless searching for some magical Nirvana that might be out there, somewhere.

She no longer wanted to work in a job that bored her senseless, desperately making up for the time lost inside the office with expensive meals and holidays. She needed a centre to her life. Something to build on for the future. She'd thought Joe had understood. A cold shiver snuck in through her tiredness. Had that, after all, been Joe agreeing with her simply to avoid a fight? Had he assumed, all this time, that it was just a phase, and that one day he could make her change her mind?

She pulled herself together. She was tired and stressed and not thinking straight. Hadn't Joe proved enthusiastic about the idea of investing their money and their energies into escaping the rat race to a country cottage in Devon with a smallholding attached? He'd agreed that they would have a far better quality of life with a business of their own that they could run together.

It wasn't as if she was asking him to give up his brilliant career. As long as she'd known him, Joe had been talking about setting up his own Accountancy Practice and – as he had agreed – where better than a small town within easy reach of the Devon countryside? Somewhere with lower costs than a big city and less competition. Plus sun, sea and surf, and a less frenetic pace of living. A kind of life where they might, after all, consider raising a family.

Far from driving them apart, the plan had pulled them back together again. She had financially supported them as Joe went through his final exams. Then he had taken over in his turn, enabling her to work part-time so that she could fulfil that dream of a horticultural course. Surely he wouldn't have done that if he hadn't meant it?

'Coffee?' said Joe, his back still turned.

'Thanks,' she returned, mechanically.

'Or there's some wine left in the fridge?'

She didn't want to fight. And, above all, she didn't want to fight with Joe. 'Yes please,' she whispered, finding herself struggling with tears.

'Ah, come here.' He turned round, gathering her into his arms. Cari snuffled ignominiously into his shoulder. 'There's no need to make a decision now. We can talk about it tomorrow.'

'Joe…'

His lips brushed her hair gently. 'Bath,' he said. 'With all those girly smelly things. And candles.'

'I don't want …'

He kissed her firmly on the mouth, silencing her protest. 'There's nothing we can't discuss later.' His eyes were soft on hers, his smile the boyish charm she could never quite resist, however cross he might make her. 'Go on, off you go. Your waiter here will bring you a glass of the finest and then order the takeaway. What do you fancy: Indian or pizza?'

'Pizza,' said Carys, feeling herself relax and giving him a watery smile.

'Excellent choice, Ms Evans. Good comfort food. Just what the doctor ordered. And I'm sure I can unearth a tub of Ben and Jerry's in the freezer for afters…'

ᏬᎧ

'It's a quite lot to ask of him,' said Poppy, mildly, eying her friend with a thoughtful air.

Carys sighed. 'Yes, I know. I'm sure the women at Tylers think I'm mad, even thinking of going off for a couple months like that without him, and they wouldn't blame Joe if he just upped sticks and left me.'

They were sitting in the tiny conservatory that opened up into the neat rectangle of Poppy's garden, and which was about the only baby-free space in the house. Unless you counted the eternal whirr of the washing machine stealing in from the kitchen, that is.

'So,' said Poppy, who never beat about the bush, not even in the throes of very new motherhood. 'Just why do you want to do it?'

'I don't.' Carys met the raised eyebrows of Poppy on bullshit

41

alert. That's what she loved about her friend. No getting away with anything with Poppy. 'Oh, I don't know. It'll sound silly.'

'Try me.'

'When I left Pont-ar-Eden village, all I could think about was getting away. You're only thinking about the future, aren't you, when you're eighteen. I suppose now I'm older – and starting to think about maybe having children after all – I suppose I want to kind of lay it to rest. If that makes sense? I'm about to change my life. Maybe it's time to put the past properly behind me, once and for all.'

'Sounds reasonable to me,' smiled Poppy. She sipped her tea for a minute. 'There are no twins in Stuart's family, you know. At least, not as far as we can make out.'

'You mean, so it must come from your side?'

Poppy nodded. 'Yeah. Weird, eh? I never thought about it, until they told us there were two in there, and that it tends to run in families.' She frowned. 'They were nice and tactful, and everything. But it just came up naturally while we were all chatting, and it felt horrible, the fact that I didn't know. That I'll probably never know. I might even have a twin out there, somewhere. So yes, I know exactly where you're coming from.'

There was a moment's silence.

'And I suppose it's a kind of test,' said Carys, at last.

'Ah,' said Poppy, as if she had been waiting for this. 'Joe.'

'Yes.' Carys sighed. 'We've been together so long, and I still really love him. But he's always had this idea he can sweet-talk me into doing what he wants to do. I thought after that time we nearly split up he'd changed. He seemed so shocked that I might actually leave, and so hurt. I thought he'd understood that I can't always be the one that compromises, that I have my dreams, too. He's been so understanding since then about me giving up a respectable career and going back to college, and the stuff about moving to Devon and setting up a business and starting a family. He's been fine with the practical things. It's just …' She let the sentence trail away. She had always been able to say things to Poppy she could never say to anyone else. Not even Joe. But she couldn't say this. Not even in front of Poppy, who'd seen more of the nastier side of life before she was five than most people would see in a lifetime.

Poppy cleared her throat. 'Mmm,' she said, with un-Poppy-like vagueness. 'That's the thing about having kids.' She raised her head as the baby monitor on the sideboard crackled into life in agreement. Carys found herself holding her breath, too. There was a whimper, followed by the beginnings of a cry, which faded almost immediately away. Poppy began demolishing her piece of carrot cake with the urgency of an explorer who might be called upon to restart the trek at any moment. 'They change things, however much you think they won't. And once you've got them, there's no going back. Stuart adores the girls, and he's amazing. But I do have friends who feel abandoned, because their husbands still have their careers and their friends, and their lives have scarcely changed at all.'

'I've thought about that,' said Carys, the wobble back in her stomach. 'I can't help feeling that Joe still thinks that if he's nice to me and cooks me meals he can get me to give up this idea of looking after Mam. That I'm not really serious and he can talk me round. And if he's like this about a couple of months looking after my mother…' She met Poppy's eyes. 'I really thought he wanted a different kind of life, too. You can't force someone to change. Not without fighting them all the time. And that's not the way –'

The whimper was back. More insistent, this time. 'They'll be awake soon,' said Poppy. 'Once one wakes up, they soon wake up the other. Two screaming babies for the price of one. Yummy.'

Carys laughed. Her friend might talk tough, but you only had to see Poppy with the twins to see that she adored them, and would fight to the death before anyone could harm them.

'It's fine, I'll go,' came a masculine voice, as the proud father himself – bleary-eyed and slightly dishevelled around the edges – returned from hanging out the morning's washing on the line in the garden, just in time to hear the whimper swell to a cough, followed by a splutter, which merged into a definite wail. 'Nice cake, Cari,' he added, with a grin, cutting himself a slice with a practiced action, followed by a quick slurp from his wife's tea. 'See you in a minute, ladies.'

'Perhaps I'd better go,' said Carys, slightly regretfully.

'And not see the babies?' Poppy waggled a finger at her. 'Don't think you can escape that quickly. Stuart will never forgive you. You've never seen a man so proud of his achievements. You'd think he'd given birth to them himself. I'd finish your tea, though. Once they arrive, chaos reigns.'

Above them came the soothing sounds of Stuart relapsing into baby-speak as a second wail erupted to echo the first.

Carys giggled. She had known Stuart through work for years, almost as long as she had been friends with Poppy. The transformation of Mr Sex-on-Legs, smart-suited alpha male into doting dad from the moment Poppy's bump appeared, never ceased to amaze her.

'I know,' said Poppy. 'Architects don't change nappies.'

'Suits him,' said Carys. 'To be honest, I thought you were mad when you two got together. I'd never have put him down as the fatherly type.'

'Oh, he's an old softie really, underneath all that strut,' said Poppy fondly. 'Bit of an old-fashioned family, that's all. Got to keep the front up, don't you know? His dad would throw a fit if he knew anything about our real lives.' Her grin was mischievous. 'I'm always careful to appear ever so dutiful whenever we visit, and I haven't sworn once.'

'Never.'

'Hey, it keeps the family peace, so no skin off my nose for a couple of days every now and again. The least I can do for Stuart loving the real crotchety, loud-mouthed with serious issues, no-holds-barred, me. It's a manhood thing.'

Above their heads, the wails had softened more towards burbling, to much creaking of floorboards and running of water, along with encouraging mutterings from Stuart, who was clearly taking on single-handed the heroics of a double nappy-change to give them a few more minutes in peace.

Carys sighed. She and Poppy were almost exactly the same age, only a few days between them. It was strange to think now that at their joint thirtieth birthday party, just three years ago, neither of them had even considered the whole settling down and having children thing. They'd eyed without envy the friends nursing fractious babies, or chasing toddlers with minds of their own and an ability to get into all kinds of trouble. They'd pitied the ones who left before the dancing really got going to relieve the babysitter and get as much sleep as they could before the next day began. What kind of life was that? they'd whispered to each other over their champagne. Especially when compared to the three weeks backpacking round Thailand that stretched in front of them to mark this momentous milestone in their lives.

It seemed that the crossover from their twenties to thirties had changed them both in more ways than simply the appearance of the first fine lines and a B&B unaccountably gaining in appeal over a sleeping bag in a tent.

'Joe said it was just hormones, when I first started thinking about children,' she said. Women were like that, he'd informed her sagely, she remembered with a wince. It was the approaching thirty-five and the biological clock ticking that did it, according to Joe. 'Maybe he thinks he can get me to change my mind about that, too.'

'I thought you said he's become quite misty-eyed these days whenever you've visited friends with kids?'

'That's true.' Carys gave a wry smile. 'But that's when we've been able to hand them back after a few minutes. He likes the idea of taking them to football matches and teaching them how to surf. I'm not entirely sure he's got his head around the rest of what having a family means.'

Above their heads, nappy changing appeared to have been successfully completed, and was being followed by a tuneless, but enthusiastic rendition of 'Hickory dickory doc', accompanied by fresh-nappy squeals and chortles.

'At least Tylers have been good about me working away from the office for a couple of months,' Carys remarked, attempting to regain her optimism. 'I have to admit, I didn't think they'd be that reasonable.'

'And risk losing you?' Poppy, she discovered, was watching her closely. 'You underestimate your skills, Cari. Where else are they going to find someone as efficient and experienced in dealing with accounts? And I know from Stuart that you've a really good reputation for building relationships with clients. I'd have thought letting you do accounts over the internet, rather than you using up your holiday and taking the rest as unpaid leave, was a price worth paying, as far as Tylers are concerned. Pity about your course, though.'

'I know.' Carys swirled the remains of her tea, gloom threatening to descend once more. 'Brilliant timing, eh? It would be just when they're going to be doing so much of the practical stuff. I haven't said anything to Joe yet, but I can see me having to redo the entire year. We were planning to start looking at smallholdings this summer, but now it looks as if we're going to have to put it off for another year, at least.'

'Gardening,' announced Poppy.

Carys blinked. 'Gardening?'

'Set yourself up as a gardener while you're at your mum's. I know it's not the same as working on a farm or in the grounds of some grand mansion, but at least you'll be doing practical stuff, and you'll be learning.'

'I'm not sure…' began Carys.

'It can't take much to set up, surely? We've got loads of tools in the shed Stuart and I aren't going to use for years. Better they get used than rot. That was one of the first things we decided on, when we knew we were having twins: hire a gardener to mow the lawn and cut things back for the duration. It wasn't easy to find one. A really good one, that is. You can choose your own hours, fit them around Tylers stuff and your mum. At least you'll know you're making a start along the way you want to go. Sorted.'

'Oh, it's not the practical side,' said Carys. 'It's just I'm just not sure they have gardeners in Pont-ar-Eden. It's not that kind of place.'

'Rubbish. We're not talking major landscaping here. There's bound to be someone who wants a lawn mowed or a hedge trimmed. I bet lots would prefer a woman, especially an older woman living on her own. There have to be some posh houses. And didn't you say there was some big house next to the village. Garden of Eden, or something?'

'Plas Eden,' said Carys, slowly.

'There you are.' Poppy was triumphant. 'Didn't it have a famous garden? One with a funny name?'

'Blodeuwedd's Garden,' provided Carys.

'That's it. I knew there was a garden there, somewhere. Blod-' Poppy struggled. 'Blod- what was it?'

'Blodeuwedd. *Blod-ay-weth.* The woman made of flowers.'

'Even better.'

Cary smiled. 'She's not a real woman. And there aren't even many flowers in the garden. At least there weren't the last time I was there. It's the story from the Mabinogion.'

'The what?' said Poppy, who made no bones about the gaps in her education, largely due to a youthful habit of truanting in favour of various unsavoury pastimes. She had more than made up for this lack since, but clearly not as far as Celtic culture was concerned.

'The Mabinogion. It's a series of really old Welsh myths? They're supposed to go right back to ancient Celtic gods and goddesses. Blodeuwedd was a woman created out of flowers by a magician, for a man who'd been cursed by his mother never to have a human wife.'

Poppy snorted, loudly. 'Yeah, right. Old man makes woman for some geek who's never been kissed. You can just see what they'd come up with: porno starlet with a permanent Brazilian and no brains. Stepford wives, here we come.'

'Not quite no brains. He was supposed to be un-killable, but she fell in love with somebody else and worked it out anyhow.'

'Yeah, well,' said Poppy, scornfully. 'Live by the robot, die by the robot.'

'Except he didn't die. Not really. But she got punished, all the same.'

'Typical.'

Carys swirled her tea again. 'I always felt sorry for Blodeuwedd, being made to be only what someone else

48

wanted, with no choice and no chance of living her own life at all.'

'Not exactly a happy story to call a garden after, if you ask me.' Poppy gave a wicked grin. 'I'll bet you it was some lord of the manor telling his womenfolk what to expect if they didn't toe the line.'

'Probably,' replied Carys, gloomily. Out of the corner of her eye, she became aware of an exceedingly sharp-eyed gaze from Poppy, who was sitting bolt upright and quite clearly gearing herself up for the interrogation of the century.

'Oooh, aren't they gorgeous,' cooed Carys hastily, as a creak of the stairs heralded the arrival of Stuart balancing one fluffy-haired, slightly damp-faced and wobbly-smiling twin on each arm, each clutching a very dog-eared cloth animal of the vaguely bunny variety.

'This is Miranda, and this is Miriam,' announced Stuart, bending each appropriate arm towards her with irrepressible pride. 'Say hello to your Auntie Carys. Tea-time, I think.' He handed his lavender-smelling parcels over to Poppy. 'I'll just put the kettle on.'

Carys watched as tiny, perfect little fingers, with tiny, perfect little pink nails, clutched at her outstretched hands, with the general intention of directing them towards one mouth or the other. Somewhere near her heart, a terrible ache had begun. The ache of the full realisation of what this illness of Mam's could mean, and of a future maybe lost forever.

'There's a story there, somewhere.' She looked up to find Poppy still watching her. Maternal adoration hadn't quite banished the sharpness of her gaze.

'I'll take the cups through, shall I?'

'Don't think you'll always escape that easily,' called Poppy after her, as Carys fled.

They put me in with one of the maids, in a room at the very top of the charity hospital. It was small, with just space enough for two beds tucked either side under the eaves, with a small chest of drawers dividing them.

Lily her name was. I took her to be no more than eighteen. At first, she appeared a little afraid of me, but as she grew accustomed to my presence she began to chatter in the brief moments we spent there between our work and sleep.

I had never thought myself as old before, but Lily made me feel ancient with her constant talk of the pair of winter boots she was saving for and sighing after a fashion plate she had purloined from a discarded newspaper. And when it was not her hair or her clothing she was fussing over, it was the young man she was stepping out with each Wednesday afternoon, her half-day off.

The questions she asked! As if, in my supposed state as a widow, I knew everything there was possibly to know about the male sex. I could hardly say I felt I knew nothing at all, and even less, if possible, than I had known before. But at least, for the most part, she didn't stop to listen, any more than in other of her ramblings, leaving me to murmur something every now and again but mostly left free to pursue my own thoughts.

And I had been, as ever, too quick to dismiss her. A few days taught me that, when it came to essentials, Lily's head was screwed on. Her Tom might bewilder her at times, but she knew enough to keep herself out of serious trouble. Helped, maybe, by the sight of so many wretched women and their tiny, sickly babies too weak to cry, and who died, more often than not, in the few steps between the gateposts and the infirmary. Perhaps it was the girls, some no older than twelve, who came in disfigured with the disease already eating away at them. Enough, it had to be said, to kill even the most reckless of youthful ardour.

And she had a kind heart. In so intimate a space, it was impossible to hide my lack of even a nightdress. My story of my bag being stolen as I reached Paddington – which was true enough, the money in my stolen purse having been intended to buy an appearance of luggage – touched her immediately. Within hours she had begged and borrowed a few bare necessities – although I didn't dare question the source of the threadbare, but spotlessly clean, nightdress – with a promise to take me to the best places to stretch my wages, as soon as they arrived.

At the time, I have to confess, I had my doubts I would last long enough in my new post to see such a thing as wages. Had it not been for the shortness of my cropped hair, I doubt whether I could have escaped for more than a day without being seriously questioned about my former occupation.

'Fever,' I explained to Lily, when she couldn't quite contain her horror at my non-existent locks. I considered adding that it was the same fever that had killed my husband. It seemed a nice touch. But maybe one too far. So I let it rest.

Lily, however, accepted the fact without question, as did Matron and the rest of the staff at the hospital. After all, it was a charity hospital, and more than one of the nurses and the domestic staff had arrived as patients.

And meanwhile, I learnt to use muscles I had never used before. I had never thought there could be so much fetching and carrying, scrubbing and cleaning in the entire world. And the steps! Wherever I went, there seemed to be steps for buckets of clean water to be carried up, and dirty to be carried down. Every part of me ached so I could scarcely move.

By the third day, my little reserve of strength had all but

given out. I carried on as best I could, with fear clenching itself hard in my belly that if I could not sustain myself in this place, then what would I do? The river, by then, had lost its appeal.

By late afternoon, my arms ached, and my head was swimming. I was on the bottom step of a staircase, polishing the dark wood of the banisters, when the world began to spin around me. I shut my eyes to steady myself, leaning for a moment against the cool wood in front of me.

'I have to say, that looks less than comfortable.'

I jumped to my feet, cloths and polish scattering around me. Had I been asleep? At the very least, it would have looked like it. And of all the people…

'I'm sorry, Mr Meredith,' I muttered. There's nothing like fear to make pride go into hiding. 'It won't happen again. I promise.' I'd kiss his boots, if he asked me.

'Mmm,' he said. Those blue eyes of his were watching me. 'I've an idea I may know what you need.'

I felt my fists clench. Maybe not all my pride was gone, after all. I don't know whether he saw the action, but if he did, he ignored it. 'Well, come along, Mrs Smith,' he said, walking towards a door at the far end of the corridor. 'And don't worry, I'll speak to Matron.'

Wonderful. I could just see Matron – a small wire of a woman, rumoured to have been trained by Miss Nightingale herself – and her reaction to such information.

So, either way, I was a lost cause. Which meant I wasn't getting myself into this one without a fight. I hobbled after him as best I could, the dark-painted walls of the corridor weaving in and out, and the tiles of the floor undulating alarmingly, in flying carpet manner, as I made my way through.

'Take a seat, Mrs Smith.'

I stopped in my tracks as I reached the doorway, my head

steadying in the influx of fresh – or the nearest the city could offer as fresh – air. I was in a small garden at the heart of the hospital. The broad leaves of plane trees reached above me, yellow and scarlet in their autumn colours. Dried leaves detached themselves and spiralled slowly downwards every now and again, although their cover still almost hid the brick walls rising all around the little space.

For the first time since I had arrived in London, I was aware of birds chirruping away, their little voices echoing against the bricks, along with the sound of running water. Sparrows, seemingly quite unafraid, alighted by my feet and settled to drink by a small pool surrounded by greenery.

From nowhere, a memory stirred. I was back on that long stretch of sand, beneath the rocky cliffs of Treverick Bay, on a day so still the sea lay turquoise and motionless, apart from the splashing of small feet amidst the shallows. The sun was gentle on my face, and the sound of childish laughter filled the salt-tinged air.

In an instant, the old ache was back, deep in my heart, strong as it had ever been.

'Please, do take a seat,' he repeated gently, bringing me back to him, with a start. I could think of worse acts of obedience. I sat down on a wrought iron bench in the warmth of the sun. Within minutes, he had returned.

'Coffee!' I couldn't remember when I had last tasted coffee. Wine, I could have turned down with ease. But the mere smell of freshly-brewed coffee was my undoing. He watched me with an unexpectedly youthful grin as I took a sip and leant back, savouring the moment. 'Thank you,' I murmured, and to hell with all consequences.

'No matter.' He placed something else by my side: a fat square slab of fruitcake.

I swallowed. 'I can't…'

'Yes you can. Cook's best *bara brith*, all the way from Plas Eden. Best thing for those recovering their strength from a fever.'

His voice was firm, without being highhanded about it. Despite myself, it made me smile. Hunger came out of nowhere, as it had not done in a long time, setting my senses alight. My stomach informed me I wasn't about to pass up on this bounty, no chance at all.

'Thank you,' I said.

'Good,' he replied. He would sit down beside me. Engage me in conversation. I braced myself, keeping my gaze on my cup, aware that he had utterly disarmed me with his thoughtfulness. 'Take all the time you need,' he was saying. I looked up, but already he was striding away, sunshine streaking through his fair hair and turning to gold the quietly falling leaves.

I swore to myself I wouldn't; but I knew, deep in my heart, that was a memory that would stay with me for the rest of my days.

And, for his kindness, and his asking nothing in return, I hoped – I couldn't quite, even then, bring myself to go so far as to pray – that he, on the other hand, would forget it entirely.

Chapter Three

'An industrial estate?' Rhiannon Lloyd looked up abruptly, splodges of watercolour dripping from her brush like terracotta rain onto the sketch on her knees. 'You are planning to turn Plas Eden into an *industrial* estate?'

'Not exactly industrial.' Huw Meredith frowned at his aunt, smile fading rapidly. 'More like a conference centre with purpose-built units for local business.' He brightened. 'Maybe craft shops, and studios for local artists. You're always saying there's not enough light in Eden. We could even put a purpose-built studio in the grounds for you.'

Poor Huw. Subtlety had never been his strong point, however hard he tried. Rhiannon concentrated on cleaning her brush in the jam jar of water beside her. Maybe it was different with your own children. Maybe there were bonds that bound you tightly, so that differences between you didn't matter. She had tried so hard to love Huw and David equally since they had fallen to her care, all those years ago, even though Huw had made no secret of resenting her presence at Plas Eden from the start.

With a final swirl, she shook a shower of water droplets into the nearest rose bed and wiped the brush carefully dry. 'So that's what you and David were discussing at such length, just now?' She should have known Huw had an ulterior motive for staying the entire afternoon, when usually on a Sunday not even his wife Angela could prise him away from the delights of Talarn Golf Club.

'It was something we both felt needed raising.'

'David agrees with you on this?'

'Of course.' Huw met her eye and turned an uncomfortable shade of pink. He cleared his throat, loudly. 'Well, of course he's not *happy* about it. None of us are, Auntie. But even David can see that the situation is impossible. That leg of his is never going to be as strong as it was before. He's still got months of rehabilitation, and then he's going to need to be careful. He can't possibly lead adventure holidays, let alone the upkeep of Eden. It's simply impossible.'

How very convenient, thought Rhiannon bitterly. Convenient for Huw, that is. Fifteen years ago, when his elder brother had taken over the running of the estate, Huw had never hidden his opinion that David was wasting both time and money in turning Eden's west wing into self-catering holiday apartments and centre for outward-bound courses. Plas Eden sold – Huw had managed to suggest at every turn – would free up huge amounts of capital to invest in far more promising businesses. Such, coincidentally, as the ones Huw just happened to be starting up himself.

While Nainie was alive, selling Plas Eden had of course been out of the question. Within a year, David had managed to make the unpromising holiday venture pay, and Nainie had had her stroke. Huw had stopping his muttering. Until now, that is.

Rhiannon placed her brush with the rest in her little metal case, and set to tidying away her painting materials into their wicker basket, her face hidden. It might be unfair of her, but she couldn't help but note that Huw's renewal of this eagerness to see Plas Eden sold, did not only coincide with David's unfortunate accident. There was now no longer Nainie, needing constant care, with the costs of hiring someone else to look after her, or of a nursing home, a drain on the estate.

Rhiannon pushed the thought quickly from her mind. Huw was, after all, the nearest thing to a younger son she would ever have. David took squarely after his father, and was a Meredith through and through. With Huw, on the other hand, there were times – not often but every now and again – when she could catch a fleeting touch of Marianne in his face. Huw had inherited her sister's brown hair and dark eyes, and that long straight nose of hers, the one that Rhiannon could recognise in her own mirror. Huw was her flesh and blood, alright, however much their respective inner lives remained an anathema to each other.

'Would you like to join David and me for dinner?' she murmured, politely, by way of a peace offering.

'That's okay, Auntie. Must get back, Angela's expecting me.'

'Another time then.' She did her best, but the relief in her voice was not exactly subtle. She picked up her basket and folding stool, accompanying Huw towards the impressively large black four by four sitting squarely in Eden's driveway.

As he reached the car, Huw turned. 'And you'll think it over, Auntie?'

'Of course I will, *cariad*. Give my love to Angela.'

'Yes, yes. She's very fond of you, you know.' Which, thought Rhiannon, was possibly the nearest Huw would come to any statement of family feeling.

As the four by four purred itself down the drive – most probably consuming half an ancient forest before it had reached the gate, she muttered to herself darkly – Rhiannon strode back towards the house.

C

When Rhiannon had first come to live in Plas Eden, the west wing – now turned by David into pristine holiday apartments – had been a vast hinterland of cobwebbed rooms containing the dusty, moth-eaten remains of Victorian beds and Edwardian sideboards.

In those days, the east wing, in all its shabby, cluttered and entirely unpretentious state, had been the family home. It had remained that way ever since. There had been plans, years ago, to modernise the east wing and bring it up to scratch to meet Eden's grand exterior. But after Nainie's stroke, change had been impossible. Both David and Rhiannon had been in agreement: Plas Eden was Nainie's life, the guardian of her memories. While Nainie was alive, nothing in the family part of the house could change.

'Kettle's on,' came a distant voice, echoing through the panelled corridors as Rhiannon pushed open the heavy oak door into the hallway.

'Thanks! Be with you in a minute,' she called back, keeping her tone deliberately light. Rhiannon shivered slightly as she carefully stored her painting materials in a cupboard under the wide sweep of stairs, amongst the collection of boots and old coats half smothering a child's sledge still kept there, just in case. However much she tried to push the fact from her mind, change was unmistakeably in the air, unsettling every part of her.

Rhiannon quickly made her way along the corridors to the large and well-worn kitchen. An ancient Rayburn, battered but still going strong, clicked and whirred gently to itself in the corner amidst the scrubbed pine of the units. A rack for drying clothes hung just above, festooned with dried bunches of rosemary and last year's lavender.

'Huw's gone,' came David's voice from the sunroom that led off from the kitchen. She could hear the strain beneath the attempts to be cheerful.

'Yes I know. Coffee?'

'I was going to make it.'

Rhiannon smiled. The coffee had indeed been ground and measured and mugs set out on a wooden tray. 'So you have, *cariad*. I only need to pour the water. You stay where you are. I can manage that.'

'Hrmmph,' came a grunt from the sunroom. No sounds of David struggling to his feet. Rhiannon frowned to herself. That was unlike David: the afternoon with Huw must have seriously taken it out of him.

On second thoughts, she reached down the tin with the remains of a spiced-apple cake. The topping had turned out far too sweet, but she had a feeling that neither of them would notice. There are times when only serious amounts of sugar will do.

'Hello Hodge.' The sounds of the cake tin being opened brought the arrival of a black Labrador-type dog of uncertain parentage, yawning and stretching as he reached her side. A damp nose butted her nearest hand, feathered tail batting slowly against the table leg in appreciative greeting.

Fitting the cake amongst the mugs, Rhiannon carried the tray down the two steps to the sunroom, Hodge trotting along in adoration – and not a little hope – behind her.

David was sitting in one of the ancient armchairs, his bad leg propped up on a stool. He looked up from scowling at his laptop as she appeared. 'How did the painting go?'

'Not bad. The light was beautiful this afternoon.' She placed the tray on a low coffee table set next to David's chair. His face was drawn and grey, the faint lines at the corners of his mouth tight. She hadn't seen him like this since those first weeks after he'd been released from hospital, when there had been a metal brace running the length of his shin, keeping his shattered bones in place. The attaching rods had protruded from the flesh like an instrument of torture. David had never complained, but she knew him well enough to know when he was in pain.

'Good.' David closed up his laptop and placed it amongst the books and papers on a folding table that had been positioned on the other side of his chair. 'Come over here, Hodge, and stop eying that cake. You always were a dog with a one-track mind.'

Rhiannon poured the coffee in silence, as David concentrated on fussing Hodge's ears. They couldn't put this off forever. One of them had to start somewhere.

'Huw came to see me as he was leaving,' she remarked, placing David's mug within easy reach.

'He did?' David paused, hand half-outstretched towards his drink. The frown was back, deeper this time. 'And what had he got to say for himself?'

'Only to tell me what you were discussing.'

'Damn Huw!' David was struggling to his feet, coffee forgotten. 'He promised me he wouldn't say anything. Not until I'd talked it over with you and we'd had a serious look at all the alternatives.' Grabbing his stick, he hobbled rapidly through the open door of the sunroom, like a man with several hundred demons behind him.

Rhiannon sighed, picked up the abandoned mug and followed him into a courtyard protected on each side by high stone walls. Along the borders beneath the walls, rosemary and oregano spread themselves beneath fragrant arches of clematis and sweet peas, and overhanging boughs from the neighbouring orchard.

David was standing in the centre of the enclosed space, gazing down into the water trickling over a pebble-filled urn into a surrounding pond, filled with the rapid darting of goldfish.

'Coffee,' said Rhiannon firmly, placing the mug in his hands.

'Thanks,' he muttered, not quite meeting her eyes.

'It's not your fault, *cariad*.'

'That Huw tried to make you feel guilty?'

'I'm sure that wasn't his intention,' she lied.

David swore under his breath. 'Of course it was.'

Rhiannon sipped her drink without replying. She could feel fear clenched hard like a ball in her belly. There was no disguising the fact that, whatever he might have promised David, Huw had been determined to get in there first when it came to talking to Auntie Rhiannon.

As far as Huw was concerned, she had no claim on Plas Eden at all. She had seen the way her younger nephew regarded her if she ever mentioned her exhaustion during those last months of Nainie's life. What had she to complain of? All she had to do was sit with an old lady, cook her meals and make sure she was comfortable. It wasn't, his look would say, as if she had to *work*.

Was that his opinion of her for all the time she had been at Plas Eden? Rhiannon hoped he was fair enough to acknowledge that after the accident she had walked away from a good career in the civil service in London, as well as her friends and her life there. As an adult, would it have crossed his mind that there could have been other – even more precious – parts of her previous existence that she had left behind?

But even Angela, who adored her husband unquestioningly, had been heard to complain that he'd never done much with their two sons when they were little and seemed to have some idea that she sat around and did nothing all day. No she had to face it. In Huw's mind, she was a middle-aged woman who had lived rent-free in Plas Eden for the past quarter of a century, occupying her plentiful free time with her little painting hobby.

'We'll work something out,' said David, abruptly. He gave a wry grunt. 'Bloody skiing, eh? If it hadn't been for me stupidly trying to keep up with the others, none of this would have happened. I knew I should never have taken that holiday. Or at least just sat on a beach for a week.'

Rhiannon smiled. 'You'd never have sat on a beach for a week, *cariad*. That's just not your style. You'd have been on the phone to me every five minutes or so to check the guests in the west wing were behaving themselves, and I'd never have had any peace.' She eyed him seriously. 'Anyhow, it was time you took some time off to be with your friends. You haven't had a holiday in years.'

'Not a skiing one, obviously,' he returned ruefully.

'It didn't have to be skiing. It could have been anything. You could just as easily have been involved in a car crash on the way to a business meeting in London. At least you are alive, and you're going to be okay. That's what matters.'

'Yes, I suppose so.' He smiled at her affectionately. 'I couldn't have done any of this, you know, unless you had been here to help me. And I don't know what Nainie would have done without you all those years.'

'You'd have hired a nurse,' returned Rhiannon, stoutly.

'It wouldn't have been the same, and you know it.' He gazed

62

wistfully up at the long roof of Plas Eden, just visible above the courtyard. 'Nainie would have hated the idea of Eden going outside the family. I can't help feeling I've let her down.'

'Nonsense.' Rhiannon was firm. 'Nainie was proud of everything you achieved. She knew Plas Eden would never have survived unless you'd worked so hard to make it a success. She'd understand this is not your fault. It's just one of those things.' She took a deep breath. 'Look, if it helps, I can always take over more of the running of the business…'

'No!' His scowl was fierce. 'No. I can't let you do that, whatever happens.'

'I don't mind.'

'But it's not fair. Not again. That's one thing I swore to myself when I was in that Swiss hospital: that I wasn't going let you pick up the pieces again. You've got your own life to lead, Rhiannon. Eden has taken far too much of it already.' He drained his coffee and began his slow, painful way back towards the sunroom. By the time he reached his chair, his face was white with pain and exhaustion. Rhiannon took his mug as he eased himself down, knowing his pride would not allow him to accept any further assistance.

'It might only be for a while,' she said gently.

'That's what we said when Nainie had her first stroke.' He released his stick and leant back, eyes closed, his whole face tense and lined with the effort. 'How old was I then? Twenty-three? I was only thinking of myself and Nainie and Plas Eden, not of you. You'd just started to get your work into exhibitions again. You could have had a career by now.'

'Or maybe not.'

'Of course you would.' David opened his eyes abruptly. 'That guy in London, the tutor at those night classes you'd been taking…'

'Jason Woodford,' she supplied. Funny, she noted: at last she could say his name without the slightest twinge going through her. After all this time, it was as if she had finally let go and was free. A touch ironic, really, when you came to think about it.

'That's the one. He thought you were good enough to make a go of it, didn't he? And he's world famous.'

'Yes, he did.' Rhiannon turned her attention to pinching out a basil plant on the windowsill. Funny how your children – even when they were not strictly yours – never quite get their heads around the fact that you might once have had a sex life, and a pretty passionate, can't-keep-your-hands-off-each-other one at that. There had always been a part of her that had wondered if it hadn't been the sex that had been the source of Jason's enthusiasm for her work, rather than her painting skills. And, in any case, it all seemed a bit immaterial now.

David, however, wasn't about to let up. 'You gave up one chance when Huw and I were kids, and you gave up another when Nainie became ill. I'm not going to let you give up another one now. You need to do your painting, Rhiannon. I know how much it means to you. Didn't you say once you only felt half-alive without it?'

'I never said that to you.'

'No.' He shut his eyes once more, the frown between his brows increasing. 'I overheard you saying it to someone on the phone, once. I knew it was true exactly because you'd never mentioned it once to any of us. I don't want you to live your life only half-alive. That's not fair of anyone to ask.'

There was a moment's silence.

'The time's drawing on,' said Rhiannon at last. 'I'd better take Hodge for his walk.'

David nodded in silence. Quietly, she fetched a fresh glass of water, which she placed within his reach, hoping he'd give in and take the painkillers next to him on the table. David might not be over-fond of the medicines being pumped into his system, and could prove as stubborn as they come, but there were occasions to just give your body a rest and allow the healing to get on with it. She hoped in her absence he'd see sense and admit that this was one of those times.

'Whatever happens,' he said, as she changed into her walking boots, 'you're not to worry, Rhiannon. You'll always have a home. Huw and I will make sure of that.'

'Yes, I know, *cariad*,' she replied. 'We don't need to think about anything like that for now. You need to get yourself well first.'

She picked up her fleece from its hook next to the door and shrugged it on. 'Find your lead, Hodge.' Hodge's ears, inherited from some collie ancestor and therefore inclined to flop at the tips in repose, stood to attention. He turned his head on one side, eyes bright with all the appearance of the highest intelligence. Rhiannon – who'd learnt long ago that the collie ancestor had been diluted over the dubious generations in between, particularly in the brains department – simplified matters. 'Lead!'

Hodge shot off into the house, returning a few minutes later in triumph, one end of webbing trailing from his mouth, the metal clip bouncing along on the slate tiles behind him in a trail of sparks. The lead was promptly flung at her feet, followed by Hodge vanishing through the door at the far end of the courtyard, to vent mounting hysteria at the magpies lurking with intent on the nearest cherry tree.

'Dinner's in the Rayburn, so don't you dare try to do anything,' called Rhiannon over her shoulder. There was no reply. David, she could see, was completely worn out and had already sunk into an uneasy doze.

The air was cool as Rhiannon reached the ridge of high ground behind Plas Eden. In the distance, lay Talarn, gleaming orange and gold in the evening light, its castle a dark shadow against the sea. Windows of the tall B&Bs along the front sprayed out gleams of brilliance in the sinking rays of the sun. She could just make out the dots of families still on the beach, with a few that might be swimmers braving the water as evening swept away the last vestiges of warmth.

'Come on Hodge,' she called to the rustling amongst the bracken, where a dark shape shot, nose to the ground, deep on the trail of rabbits.

Having reached the highest point, Rhiannon sat down on the single wooden bench placed facing the sea. The bench was new, scarcely weathered as yet, with its feet planted firmly in concrete. The metal plaque, still bright and shiny, bore the inscription 'In memory of Hermione Anne Meredith, who loved this place'. Rhiannon leant back, feeling the comforting firmness of the wood against her.

She should have known that day, she thought to herself, that this would signal the end of things. It had been a bright February morning, with frosts still lurking in the shadows, when Huw and David had trudged up the hill with the bench between them, Rhiannon following behind pushing the wheelbarrow containing spades and bags of quick-setting cement. It had been an unexpectedly cheerful occasion, with even Huw losing his dignity in the effort to dig holes in the rocky ground, followed by the tussle getting the spirit level to keep its little bubble between the lines in all directions.

That had been their own goodbye to Nainie, even more so

than the ceremony later in the afternoon, when the few tattered remains of the Meredith clan had gathered up here for the scattering of the ashes, just as Hermione Anne had decreed.

They had seemed so much a proper family, drawn together by grief; there had been no thought of how much Nainie's death would change them. David had taken over the mantle of Plas Eden in all but name for so long, the question of his not carrying on now had never even arisen. David was the eldest, the one who would take over the responsibility at some point. That was the way it would always be.

Rhiannon shivered, pulling her fleece closer around her. Below, the Eden estate stretched out before her in all its rambling vastness. Plas Eden itself, long and pale between the trees. In front of the house, the lake, with the low cottage of Eden Farm on the furthest bank, surrounded by fields and gardens and the plastic-covered arches of polytunnels. And on the nearest side of the water, the little forest of oak and birch, opening into the neat circle of the glade where the statues lay.

Outside the walls the single road led over an arched stone bridge – reputed to have been there since medieval times – to the little village of Pont-ar-Eden, its slate-roofed cottages clustered around the central square.

'Oh, Nainie,' said Rhiannon aloud. Hodge, who had settled in his favourite position leaning against the warmth of her knee, looked up, eyes large and soft. She massaged his ears, absently. Losing all this would break David's heart, she knew it. Allowing it to happen felt like letting down Marianne, who had loved her sons with every fibre of her being and would have fought tooth and nail for their happiness. And Paul, too, who had welcomed her with gentleness and warmth from the moment Marianne had proudly brought her fiancé for family inspection, and who had spent his days battling to keep the family home intact, just like every Meredith before him.

David might not want her to help directly, but if only there was something she could do. Something she could find that would help; some unique feature that might put Eden on the tourist map and bring in enough income for David to pay for all the help he could need.

Her eyes rested once more on the dark hollow amongst the trees. The statues. Eden's ghosts. Impossible – as she knew all too well – to capture by pen or camera. Beautiful and mysterious in their half-forgotten melancholy.

The statues had always been a part of Plas Eden. Always had been, for as long as anyone could remember. She had been curious about them over the years, but Nainie had never responded to her tentative questions. She could have pressed her, but there had always been so much to do, so many things to deal with. And the statues – being the least troublesome of her responsibilities – had been the least of her worries. But supposing, just supposing, Eden's ghosts held a history that might be the saving of Plas Eden?

'Maybe I'm a fool,' she said to Hodge, who was scenting the air as the breeze began to stir. He laid his muzzle in her lap in a sympathetic manner. 'But it might be worth at least trying.'

She could suggest the statues as a subject to Professor Gwynfor Humphries from the university, and that local history group he was supposed to be starting up in Pont-ar-Eden. He'd written in the local paper only a few weeks ago, extolling the importance of local heritage, and how communities could use it to bring in the tourists, even in these straightened times. She smiled down at Hodge, who was by now gazing at her in a particularly soulful manner.

After all, what harm could it possibly do?

I did not go into the little garden again.

I had learnt my lesson. From then on, I determinedly ate every scrap of food put in front of me. Not that you'd notice. A glance in the tarnished piece of mirror next to Lily's bed showed my cheeks no less pale, or hollow. But at least it kept me strong.

After a month or so at the Meredith Charity Hospital, my legs no longer ached, and I could run up the largest flights of stairs with the best of them, however heavy a burden I might be carrying. And, strange as it might sound, I came almost to enjoy the routine of hard physical work. I could feel myself growing stronger and fitter than I had ever been. I took in deeper breaths – although perhaps not the best of places, with the fumes from the sick rooms and when the winter fog came rolling through the streets, extinguishing everything in its path. But illness no longer seemed to touch me. By day, I scarcely thought at all. At night, I fell instantly into a deep sleep.

But, of course, this oasis of peace could not last long, however much I could have wished it.

It started off innocently enough, just a few days before Christmas Eve. For the first time, I held coins in my hand that had not been given an absolute destiny many weeks before in the direction of soap and underclothes. Not many coins, but enough.

I sat in my little room and eyed them with unexpected glee. This little store of money I had earned with my own hands. I had no one to answer to. I could do with it as I pleased. My instinct was to be careful and to save it. Make a little stash safely hidden away so that I would have a little insurance against wandering the streets all night again. But the other part of me threw caution to the winds.

Poor as I now was, for the first time in my life I could

choose. Suddenly, I was impatient for my afternoon off. Before then, I had felt those few hours of freedom each week as a burden. If I could have simply slept the time away, I would have done. But to have stayed in the safety of the little room under the eaves would have caused notice.

So I had done as expected, taking my way through the iron gates, and through the winding little streets to the river. Walking rapidly, with the air of one on an errand of some urgency, just as I had done in the darkness of that first night, I passed by unnoticed, unmolested, and with scarcely a word exchanged with my fellow human beings until the time came for my return.

Now, however, I had a sense of purpose, and I could scarcely hide my excitement. When the day came, I washed and brushed and mopped at full speed, determined nothing would delay me for even a few minutes. In my mind, I had been through every street, every shop and market place, cursing myself for taking no more notice of such places than as markers for my return to the hospital. And the moment the hour came, I shot out of there, as fast as I could.

It took me some time to find, but by the time I returned to my room that night I had a small precious store of paper and pencils. Colours had been beyond my means, but at least I knew where I could find them.

After all my impatience, I did not know where to begin. I tried a few strokes of the pencil that night, before I heard Lily's voice on the creaking little staircase that made the final journey to the room we shared. It had been a frustrating hour. Something that had once come to me with such ease felt utterly beyond my grasp.

Over the next few days I tried and tried again. Still the pencil would not obey me, and now, for the first time, the strict regime of my working day began to irk. I had no time, and no private space to get back into the old rhythm again. My Uncle Jolyon used to say that women were unsuited to the artistic life. How could they possibly believe themselves equal to the likes of Lord Leighton or Sir Edwin Landseer? Or even Mr Turner in his early works, before the man clearly lost his mind and took to mere washes of colour.

Women lacked the mental capacity, Uncle Jolyon would say. It shrank their delicate feminine organs, I heard him once add, as my aunt and I withdrew after dinner to leave the men to their cigars and the freedom to talk of politics and other such matters likely to offend female delicacy. And where would Society be without the true flowering of womanhood and the appearance of the precious little ones? That's what all this talk of female emancipation and women being given the vote utterly failed to recognise, he added, with particular loudness, and which Aunt Beatrice pretended not to hear.

Uncle Jolyon could keep his opinions. Time and opportunity seemed far more likely culprits to me.

In the end, I gave up the attempt to hide my occupation. Lily watched me as she woke of a morning to find me frowning over scraps of paper, and at night, in a few precious minutes of candlelight as she made ready for bed.

'Is that me?' she demanded one evening, as I bent over a portrait I was attempting from memory of one of the patients I seen walking through the corridors that afternoon.

'No,' I replied.

'Oh.' Her voice held disappointment.

'Would you like me to draw you?'

'Would you?' I might have offered her gold. She pulled a face, tugging at the hair she had just turned up tightly in rags. 'But not like this.'

'No, of course not.' I smiled at her. Lily would be easily pleased and be an uncritical eye to my attempts. The thought gave me a sense of safety. And I knew from the frequency she gazed into her little piece of mirror of the pleasure such a thing would give her. 'I can work quickly. I need only a few minutes each night before you tie up your hair, and I can still work on your face.'

'A real portrait!' Lily's eyes glowed with excitement. 'Like the ladies in the newspapers!' I'd never thought such a simple thing could give so much pleasure. I found it strangely touching.

'A real portrait,' I agreed.

We started the next evening. As I promised, I worked fast. And if I made her lips a little fuller, her eyes a little larger and her hair more luxurious and more curling than in life? What portrait painted for money doesn't flatter the client just a little? And suddenly it had become important to me not to hurt Lily's feelings.

This, I had come to see, was Lily's time of glory. And a poor glory it was, it seemed to me, snatched as it was between scrubbing floors and holidays spent helping her mother in tenements an hour or so walk away. For now, her youth was noticed and courted. Once married, her life would be an endless round of cooking and cleaning, with children to bear and raise, and she would soon become the unnoticed drudge I passed so often in my wanderings. Not necessarily unhappy, but with no time or income to call her own. I swore to myself I would never again pass by such a woman without noting every line of her face and committing it to memory. After all, to the outside world, was not that just as I seemed too?

Absorbed in my task, I had not noticed how Lily had been watching me closely as I worked.

'Who's Judith?' she asked suddenly.

I looked up, the point of my pencil splintering on the page. 'Judith?'

'Yes.' Her voice was hesitant, as if this were a question she had been building up to for some time, and was half-afraid to ask. 'It's a name you call out in your sleep sometimes.'

My pencil was beyond mending, for the moment at least. 'I'm tired,' I said, placing the half-finished drawing on the chest of drawers between us. 'We can begin again tomorrow.'

But I should have known Lily was not to be distracted, not even by the prospect of her emerging eyes and hair on the paper before her. 'And there's other names, too,' she went on, in a kind of rush. 'Ones I can't make out. And you always sound so…' From the corner of my eye I glimpsed her bite her lip. 'So afraid.'

'We all have nightmares,' I replied, pulling the covers tight around me.

'But not like this. I wondered …' She paused, but only for a moment. Lily and her curiosity. Sharp-eyed Lily, who was a born story-maker, who always wanted to make the pieces of a pattern fit to a familiar mould. 'I wondered if maybe Judith might be your daughter?'

I turned my face away from her, toward the hard cold stone of the wall. 'I have no children,' I said.

❦

Despite my fears, Lily did not pursue her questioning the next day. And, thankfully, as her portrait neared completion, her impatience served to distract her.

When it was finished, I was pleased that Lily delighted with the result of my effort. But I should have known her delight would not be contained. First one, and then another of the maids came up to me, shyly, hesitant. Some with a few coins to offer me. I did not take the coins, but I made their portraits, thankful for their momentary stillness and the necessity to please, which overcame self-doubt.

And I had more reward than any coin could have brought me. Apart, perhaps, than paper and the luxury of watercolours. My hand was soon regaining its old fluency. With each portrait my confidence was returning. And with it, I began to see a distant hope of regaining some inner peace.

I should have known better, of course.

'Mrs Smith?' He called to me as I crossed the corridor, with my usual accompaniment of a bucket of dirty water sloshing at my heels. 'If you wouldn't mind just stepping this way, for a moment.'

His tone was even, and not harsh. But I knew it meant trouble.

'Yes, Mr Meredith,' I murmured, setting down my bucket carefully in a nook under the stairs where it would not be tripped over and dirt mar the hard-won cleanliness of the tiles. I followed him into the little office.

'Please sit down.' He was polite. I feared the worst.

'Thank you, sir.' But at least the weight off my feet was bliss. I wriggled my toes, wishing I dared kick off my boots. He turned back to the desk, lifting a piece of paper. I swallowed hard.

'This is yours, I believe, Mrs Smith?'

'I did it in my own time. And Ruby's.' He was watching me. He had an open face. Not handsome, not striking. Pleasant, I think is the word that might be used. Apart from those restless blue eyes of his, that seemed to pierce through to the heart of me. 'And I didn't ask for any money,' I added, for good measure.

'I'm sure you didn't.' He smiled. 'And have no fear, I've promised faithfully to Ruby I shall return this to her before she goes home tonight.'

'Oh.' If anything, this was worse. I cursed myself. Well, and that was the last act of kindness I'd be trying. Virtue definitely did not bring its reward. Quite the opposite, in fact. And I didn't mind standing and saying so in church on Sunday, if I was asked. Or, indeed, ever attended.

'You have quite an eye.'

'Thank you,' I muttered.

'And you always draw faces?'

Without meaning to, I glanced over towards the watercolour of that house of his, Plas Eden, glimpsed between trees, the lavender haze of mountainside sweeping up behind.

'Yes,' I said, firmly. 'It amuses me.' I met his gaze, defying him to ask if I'd been tutored. Which I'd flatly deny, of course. And we'd both know I was lying.

Well, at least, I reflected, as his eyes returned to the portrait in his hands, that show of wilfulness would curtail any interest he might have had for me.

I was wrong.

Those blue eyes were watching me as closely as ever. And I could have sworn I glimpsed a flicker of amusement in his smile. I wished I'd tipped my bucket over his polished, and no doubt highly expensive, shoes, and been done with it. Reference, or no reference. I could see another question arriving. I clenched my fists hard under the table.

'And are you squeamish?'

'I beg your pardon?' He'd caught me on the hop with that one, and no mistake.

'Well, are you?'

'No,' I said. Those eyes of his! 'Well, at least I don't think so,' I muttered. I didn't like the way his smile was going. 'What do you mean by squeamish? I don't faint at the sight of blood.'

'And the dead?'

I gasped before I could stop myself.

'I'm sorry. That was uncalled for, Mrs Smith. I'm not interested in the dead, but in the living.' He hesitated for a moment. 'But when I say 'living', I mean where death is only ever a day or so away, whether it be the very young, or the very old, from accident or pestilence.'

'Oh,' I said, blankly. Did he mean me to train as a nurse? For the most part, my work had not yet taken me deep into the wards. This, I was not ready for. My stomach clenched.

'The charity is undertaking a study of the housing conditions around the hospital. Have you heard of Friedrich Engels?'

'No,' I said. Truthfully, this time. Uncle Jolyon could at least be proud of my carefully cultivated ignorance.

'A translation of his study of the condition of the working class in England was published earlier this year. Much easier reading than my poor attempts at German. It seemed an opportune moment for the Meredith Charitable Foundation to undertake our own study.'

'Oh,' I said, warily.

'It has struck me, in our attempts, that a photographer, although useful, is not always the best way to document living conditions. A camera is such a novelty, it draws attention to itself. But someone with a skill for catching faces…'

'No!' I said. Loud enough to make myself jump. 'My post here,' I added, feebly.

He turned away, so he was looking out of the window into the little garden. 'One of the women on the wards – Alice – has nowhere to return to. At least, nowhere she would care to return, or the charity, in all conscience, could wish to force her to go.'

It was like a blow to the stomach, taking my fragile safety away. 'I work hard,' I protested, suddenly back to fighting for my life once more.

'Yes, I know,' he replied, turning to face me. 'But I take it you can read and write?'

I opened my mouth to hotly deny it. But of course there it was: Eden. The moment I had stepped inside his office on that first morning, I had read the name beneath the painting. I could, I suppose, have sworn blind I knew my letters enough to read the Bible, and it was the Old Testament that had enabled me to recognise the word. But meeting his eyes I saw he wouldn't fall for that one.

'Yes,' I said.

'Then there is other employment here, far more suited to you.' He grinned, almost a boyish kind of grin I had seen once before, warming the customary seriousness of his face. 'Cleaners I can find by the dozen: but the Meredith Charity Hospital is not exactly a hotbed of literacy. So you see I cannot really afford to let any possibility pass me by.'

'I see,' I said slowly. I could feel the temptation, drawing me in. No more ceaseless activity. Time to sit. Time to think. And to earn my living – at least part of my living – by my sketching. I would be given paper and pencils to work with. Maybe, in the future, even watercolours.

Diamonds I could have walked away from. The latest fashions from Paris and the finest shoes money could buy would not have tempted me in the slightest. But now I had the passion in me again, paper and pencils I would die for.

'Think it over,' he said. Like a fisherman who feels the line already taut and ready to reel in.

'Yes. Thank you.'

He meant so well. I could see he meant well. It was the way his mind worked, ceaselessly, in the running of the Meredith Hospital. Another woman they could keep from the streets. And another skill they could use.

I wondered, as I made my way back to my scrubbing brush, if all that working out of his had warned him the danger he was in?

He was a kind man. A gentle, kind man. Not much older than myself, which, for a man, is still young. Still not yet in the prime of life. He was a man who deserved the happy fireside of wife and children, so beloved of the novels of Mr Dickens.

If I had been a noble, self-sacrificing Agnes or Little Dorrit, I would have slipped out of my bed at dawn, and vanished forever into the ether to keep him safe.

Which, of course, I didn't.

Chapter Four

When summer finally arrived, it came all in a rush, as if it couldn't apologise enough for the despair of ice cream sellers along the coast and the shops full of untouched sundresses.

A clear, blazing heat settled over sea and mountain alike. Within days – or so it seemed – the sheep-fields around Plas Eden turned a rich green. In the narrow lanes between Talarn and Pont-ar-Eden, honeysuckle and dog roses climbed high into the hedgerows, sending their delicate fragrance through the open windows of passing cars.

Carys pulled into one of the parking bays in Pont-ar-Eden Square and watched the rays of sun streaming through the village, her mood lifting slightly. It was that clear, early-summer light she remembered so well from her childhood: the kind that always roused the faded blues and yellows of the terraced houses into soft glow, and the dark grey slates of the roofs into a newly-washed smartness.

But there was no time for lingering, not with a car-full of shopping and a million things to be done before Mam's return to Willow Cottage this afternoon. Carys sighed and pulled herself a little stiffly out of the car. She'd intended to have several days in her mother's house before Mam was released from the nursing home. Time to get things in order. Time to adjust. But, somehow, the arrangements in Chester had taken far longer than she'd imagined.

And then there was Joe. Carys grabbed her handbag and zapped the car shut. Joe was making no bones at being unhappy at her choice. The atmosphere in the flat over the past weeks had been unmistakeably that of hurt and resentment. His hurt, her resentment. She wasn't proud of the fact.

It was a subject she had been mulling over all the way from Chester, without coming to any useful conclusions. Carys pushed the thoughts from her mind. That was for another day. For now she had quite enough to be getting on with, what with Mam, in her current emotionally fragile state, to deal with in a few hours and Joe, in his emotionally hurtful state of this morning, to be placated into some kind of peace this evening. If that were possible.

'Good morning,' she said with an appearance of cheerfulness, as she walked into Jones the Grocers.

'Ah, good morning, Carys,' replied Sara Jones, white-haired and round faced, seventy if she was a day, briskly stacking loaves and scones on the wooden shelves behind the counter. A delicious smell of baking filled the air, sending Carys' stomach into a sudden rumble of hunger. 'Today's the day, then,' remarked Sara, as Carys chose Mam's favourite crisp white loaf, still warm from the oven.

'Yes it is,' said Carys. 'And may I have a *bara brith* and a chocolate cake as well, please.'

'Certainly,' replied Sara. 'I know your mam has been looking forward to this day,' she added, as she wrapped the bread and the little rectangular fruitcake in tissue, placing the slightly uneven cake, sleek with icing, into a white cardboard box. 'She'll be glad to get home, I'm sure.'

'Yes, she will,' smiled Carys. With a final choice of a double choc chip muffin (for medicinal purposes only), she put her purchases in her bag and made her way back out into the street.

Despite the sun, there was no mistaking that Pont-ar-Eden high street was clinging onto its existence by a whisper. In between the few defiantly open small shops and the larger Low-Price convenience store lay rows of boarded up and abandoned premises, with several already transformed back into houses or flats.

As long as Carys could remember, there had been something of the spirit of the blitz about the beleaguered *Stryd Fawr*. Mam's *Talarn Herald* was always full of articles on how the big supermarkets were strangling village high streets out of existence, invariably accompanied by the same photograph of Pont-ar-Eden looking particularly rain-swept and bleakly empty. Even the bantering comments of the remaining shopkeepers flying across the street from their doorsteps on sunny days, seemed almost a checking between them of who had survived to battle for customers another day, and who had succumbed to the last rise in council tax and the hike in the electricity bills.

There was, Carys remembered with sudden vividness, more than one reason for that flight of hers from Pont-ar-Eden all those years ago. In fact, if it hadn't been for Mam, she'd have been out of there this minute, bearing Sara Jones' infamous (if you were watching your waistline, that is) chocolate cake home to Joe as a peace offering.

But there *was* Mam. So she made her way into Prydderch's Newsagents instead, in search of Mam's favourite story magazine and usual TV guide, both of which – despite her list – she'd managed to miss in her mad dash around Sainsburys that morning.

Prydderch's was just as she remembered it. The same

cadaverous gloom, crammed full of dog-eared birthday cards and dust-laden boxes of Monopoly and Scrabble. She could have sworn that nothing – not even the faded boxes of after-dinner mints – had moved since she and Gwenan and Nia had piled in there after school for their weekly fix of Love Hearts and Strawberry Bootlaces. Even the smell of newsprint tinged with Parma Violets was unchanged.

Evan Prydderch himself eyed her closely, with the world-weary air of a man who just *knows* half his stock of Pear Drops and a tube of Smarties will have vanished into thin air by the time she left the shop.

'Good morning,' said Carys, brightly. 'Lovely day, isn't it.'

Evan grunted in disapproval at such unnecessary cheeriness. As a child, Carys had been terrified of him, as had even the toughest of self-styled toughs in Pont-ar-Eden Primary, although they would never admit it. She wasn't quite sure she felt at ease in his presence, even now.

Evan Prydderch was tall and stick-thin, bent over at the shoulders as if permanently lifting heavy stacks of newspapers. Like his shop, he scarcely seemed to have aged, having appeared ancient in the first place. Gloom hung about him in the cloud of stale tobacco clinging to his patched tweed jacket and the black, newsprint grubbiness of his fingers. In the early hours of each morning, come rain or shine, for as long as Carys could remember, Evan Prydderch had stalked the village; shopping-trolley of newspapers rattling along behind him, tails of his black trench coat flying, like some retired Nosferatu taking a sniff at the night air for old times' sake.

'Thank you,' said Carys, smiling determinedly against the odds, as she paid for her magazines and placed them into her bag.

'For your mam, are they?' demanded Evan.

'Yes,' said Carys, surprised that he had recognised her after all. 'Yes they are. She's coming home today.'

'Good for you,' he muttered. 'Never let you go, do those places, once they've got their hands into you.' He reached, slightly furtively, under the counter, emerging with a paper bag of sweets. 'Coconut Teacakes,' he stated. 'Mair's favourite.'

'I'm sure she'll really enjoy them,' said Carys, as he impatiently brushed away her attempt at thanks, determining never to yield to temptation and buy her newspapers and treats at Low-Price again.

Those were the last things she needed. All done. Time to get to Willow Cottage. Carys paused as she shut the door of the newsagents behind her, fishing for her car keys. As she did so, the little bell in Jones the Grocers rang out, making her look up instinctively. The dark-haired mongrel now tied to the drainpipe next to the shop door burst out into high-pitched hysterics as David Meredith emerged, loaf and a large carton of milk in hand. Carys stepped quickly back into the shadows behind the carousel of musty postcards outside Evan's shop.

The pain was still there; the deep, twisting pain that always rose in her belly, no matter how many times they had nodded to each other over the years, briefly and wordlessly from opposite sides of Pont-ar-Eden High Street.

He was thinner than she remembered. It made him seem even longer and lankier than ever. His face appeared almost gaunt, with a deep line across his forehead she had not seen before.

'Okay, okay Hodge,' he was saying, bending down to release the lead. He placed the loaf and the milk in a backpack, slinging it onto one shoulder with a practiced air. 'Heel,' he commanded, as the mongrel took off at a hundred miles an hour towards the nearest lamppost. More sedately this time, the two set off away from her, in the direction of Plas Eden, David limping heavily, with all the determination of a man who had been told to use at least one stick at all times, and wasn't about to, not if it killed him.

Well, they always had been a match for each other when it came to stubbornness, if nothing else, thought Carys, with just the faintest of wry smiles, as she made her way slowly back towards the car.

ɛ⌾ɔ

It was the smell of freshly-ground coffee that did for her. As Carys wedged the cake securely for its short ride, the tantalising scent came drifting down the street with a mouth-watering edge of bacon and buttered toast.

In front of her, the Boadicea Café stood newly painted and cheerful, with its striped awning and outside tables topped by the bright splash of hanging baskets still dripping from an early morning watering. Just a quick coffee wouldn't hurt, she decided. She'd still have time to get the most necessary of preparation done before Mam arrived. And besides, wasn't this a chance to check out whether this was somewhere she could bring Mam when she was feeling a little better?

Pont-ar-Eden didn't do busy. It didn't even particularly do thriving. A farmer and a couple of pensioners, that was all there would be. A few curious glances, a few questions about Mam, and she would be left in peace.

'Sod,' muttered Carys under her breath, as the jangling of the Boadicea's doorbell sent an entire sea of faces turning towards her.

The Boadicea comprised of a single long room filled with round wooden tables, and lit by light streaming in from large

84

windows to the side and a huge curve of a bay window at the far end. Every table, so it seemed, was fully occupied. Nearest the door, mothers with pushchairs gossiped over skinny lattes and custard slices. Old men, bent and shrunken, chatted over mugs of tea, or flicked through the newspapers.

The prime position of the bay window, with its comfort of a slightly faded sofa and chairs, had been commandeered by the white hair and wheeled shopping trolleys of Pont-ar-Eden's more fearsome matriarchs – the ones with sharp elbows when it came to the monthly car boot in the church grounds, and a line in haggling that would put a Souk trader from Marrakesh to shame.

Away from the windows, along one side of the café, a further group, of both sexes this time, were gathered around a line of computer screens, deep in animated conversation.

'There's room here, if you care to join me.'

'Are you sure?' said Carys, eying the man in the leather jacket, sporting a ponytail just starting to grey at the edges. She had no intention of spending her last precious free time as a sounding board for some born-again-biker guy's general opinion on life, the universe and everything. On the other hand, this sudden male interest had the Pont-ar-Eden matriarchs returning to their toast. Undoubtedly still watching every move, but at least not trying to get her attention.

Her rescuer, catching the quick slide of her eyes towards the window, grinned. 'I'd quit while you're ahead,' he said, just quietly enough to be covered by the conversation around them.

A fellow traveller amongst the gossips of Pont-ar-Eden, then. Carys smiled, grabbed the free chair folded up against the wall for emergencies, and pulled it across to the little table. 'Okay. Thanks.'

'It's their history day,' remarked her new companion, as the waitress finished taking their orders. 'Professor Humphries will be along in a bit to give them a hand. They all get terribly excited about it. They'll soon forget all about you.'

'I didn't know the Historical Society met here,' said Carys, torn between not entering into conversation and not appearing rude.

'Not just the Historical Society,' he replied. 'It seems everyone is getting in on the act, since the computers arrived. I'd never have thought the village was so proud of its past. I suppose it's like everything: you never really appreciate what you have until you think you might lose it.'

'I suppose.' She was itching to ask what the village might be losing, but that would have led to a more permanent state of conversation, and one for which she was seriously not in the mood. As it was, Mr Biker-man had already returned to the pages of his novel, placed next to an almost emptied coffee cup.

With her companion deep in his book and the matriarchs returned to their previous conversation, Carys let her eyes wander around the café again. While the walls nearest the counter were adorned with a selection of framed paintings, those nearest the computers were lined with boards of old photographs. Undoubtedly scans, rather than originals, the originals being clearly irreplaceable. They had been pinned up carefully, but in haphazard fashion, as if anyone could join in.

Faded 1970s colour, and black-and-white photographs gazed out at her, interspersed with sepia, and even older, almost black with age. Family groups smiling at cottage doors, or under apple blossom in a garden. A man in 1930s loose trousers and cap standing proudly next to a row of broad beans. A Victorian family, stiff, eyes distant, grouped next to a pedestal overflowing with ivy. And a little further away, she could just make out the pale facade glimpsed between trees, that was unmistakably Plas Eden. It was as if the past was there, crowding in on her, making it hard to breathe.

'You're Carys.'

Carys started. 'I beg your pardon?'

The man with the ponytail was watching her. 'You're Carys Evans.'

'Yes,' admitted Carys.

'You're back in Pont-ar-Eden to look after your mam.'

'That's right.'

'I remember you.'

Carys' mind scurried frantically. 'You do?'

'I tried to chat you up once.'

Oh dear. Here we go. So much for a relaxing coffee. 'Really.'

'Mmm. You must only have been seventeen or so at the time. You weren't interested.'

'And I should hope not, too,' came the tart remark from behind them. Carys looked up to find a tray being wielded above her. The next moment three cappuccinos were being placed in the free space in the middle of the table, followed by the owner herself pulling up a stool.

'Five minutes,' said Buddug. 'Before the next rush comes in.' She pushed a cup in front of Carys. 'On the house, *cariad*. Your mam's been a good friend to me when I needed it most. Least I can do.'

'Thank you,' said Carys, feeling herself unexpectedly welling up inside. It had been a long day. She must be more tired that she thought.

'Besides, I can't leave you to Merlin to drive you witless, now, can I?'

'Oh,' said Carys. She should have known. Just before her

fall, Mam had been full of the return of Merlin Gwyn, the only international rock-god to emerge from Pont-ar-Eden. Not quite as big as the Manic Street Preachers or Duffy mind, but he'd once appeared with Bryn Terfel, and that was quite big enough for Pont-ar-Eden.

Carys looked at him, trying to make out in the rounded face before her the lean, Heathcliff spectre in skin-tight leather trousers and jacket, with his statement of stubble and hungry eyes, that had confronted her in the 'Taliesin' pub that night, sixteen years ago.

Merlin sighed. 'Yes, that's just the look you gave me.'

'Look?'

'Searching. As if you could see right through me. And were not impressed. I wasn't used to such a thing. Well, not at that time, anyhow. Sadly, age has taught me a touch of humility.'

'I was a child,' returned Carys, frowning.

He raised his eyebrows. 'A child.'

'You know what I mean. You were years older than me. And you belonged to a world I knew nothing about. Apart from noticing that girls seemed to be either groupies or backing singers, and definitely didn't call the shots. You frightened me.'

'Ouch,' said Merlin, with a rueful grimace.

Buddug paused in stirring her cappuccino. Her grin was mischievous. 'Good for you, Carys. You always did have style, as I remember. Merlin Wyn, sitting with a woman who turned him down, eh? Now that must be a first.'

'Two,' sighed Merlin, gloomily.

Buddug chuckled. 'Very gallant of you, *cariad*. But to be absolutely truthful, you never gave me the chance.' She gave a quick grunt. 'Not that I ever did have eyes for anyone else, once I met Gareth.' She stirred the cappuccino viciously. 'Love, eh? It all seems so simple, when you're that age.'

There was a moment's silence. No one, it appeared, was about to disagree.

'Well, it's outrageous.' Carys looked up at the indignant cry from the far end of the room. Conversation in the Boadicea died to a murmur. The cyclists tucking into bacon butties with gusto paused and turned in faint alarm at the direction of this outburst. The natives, it seemed, were growing restless.

'So it is, Nesta,' came a reply from Edna Williams, once Headmistress of Pont-ar-Eden primary and leader (self-elected) of the matriarchs. 'But what is there to be done about it?'

'Well something should be,' retorted Nesta Pugh, chairwoman of the local Women's Institute, and close rival for Edna's coveted leadership position. 'My mam was right: it was my ancestors who made the bricks that built Plas Eden. Look, see. There are bills showing my great-grandfather was still doing the repairs. The Merediths have no right to sell Plas Eden. Private land: that's what it'll be, you mark my words. And we'll all be shut out like a load of peasants, as if we'd never had anything to do with the place at all.'

'Plas Eden is being sold?' said Carys, putting down her cup with a jolt.

'Maybe,' said Buddug. 'If Huw gets his way.'

'You don't know that we'll be shut out if someone else takes it over,' Nesta's sister Haf was protesting gently, as the outrage in the far corner threatened to spill over into the rest of the cafe. But, all the same, she sighed. 'We used to have such fun in Eden woods, when we were kids, remember?'

'Remember the swing over the lake?' put in one of the older men.

'*Duw,* yes.' Edna's white head nodded, sharp grey eyes softening. 'I'd forgotten about that. It was a log on a piece of rope, if I remember rightly. Old Mrs Meredith put it there for the boys' father, when he was only a boy himself. He was a friendly sort, was Paul. We'd spend half our summers playing with him. You'd swing out, with that swing, right over the lake, and go down with a splash.'

'Remember the tree house?' called a stout, rosy-cheeked matriarch sitting next to her. 'The one old Mr Meredith made like a ship? It even had sails. We used to spend hours and hours in there.' Nods and murmurs showed that the tree house still had the power to stir fond memories.

'I had my first kiss in Blodeuwedd's Garden,' remarked Haf, wistfully.

'You never told me that,' snapped her sister. 'Who was it?'

'Next to King Arthur,' said Haf, with just a twitch of mischief in her wrinkled little face. 'It was *so* romantic.'

Nesta scowled.

'It's our memories they're taking away,' said Edna, frowning severely at this straying from the subject at hand. 'That's what they're destroying. It's not right.'

'Something ought to be done,' added Nesta, not to be outdone in the leadership stakes.

The cowbell chimed once more, letting in a group of walkers, complete with walking poles and a small posse of two black Labradors and a terrier noisily lapping up the water in an old ice cream carton just outside the Boadicea's door. The walkers made their way purposefully to the counter, while outside a second wave could be seen finding tables and settling dogs in the shade.

Buddug rose, gathering empty cups on the way back to relieve her beleaguered assistant at the counter. 'You could always go and talk to them. I'm sure, given the option, David would prefer to see the place remain as part of the village. And I'm certain Rhiannon wouldn't object at all.'

A wave of mutterings rose amongst the tables of the Boadicea as Buddug resumed her place and began taking orders with her usual calm efficiency.

Carys exchanged glances with Merlin. As one, they finished their cappuccinos. Neither of them were children of Pont-ar-Eden for nothing: time to beat a hasty retreat.

As in, now.

'It would certainly be worth a try,' Nesta was saying. 'I'd assist in any way I could, of course. But what with my responsibilities with the WI, not to mention the Guides and the Inner Wheel and the school Eisteddfod…'

With Nesta's abdication of any pretention to be queen of this proposed uprising, all eyes turned, as if one, towards Edna.

'No time for hanging around,' muttered Merlin, under his breath. Carys reached for her bag. 'Edna has a great reputation in the village for getting things done,' he added, rising and shoving his book in his back pocket. 'From what I can see, that usually involves delegating –'

But the time for escape was long gone.

'You know David and Huw better than any of us,' came Edna's voice, shooting straight towards them. Her eyes had fixed themselves purposefully on Carys.

'That was a long time ago,' murmured Carys, dismayed.

'But you were up there at Plas Eden all the time, at one time,' persisted Edna. 'You were such a comfort to them all, Rhiannon used to say.'

Which was a very un-Rhiannon thing to say and a load of flummery. Not that you could exactly say that out loud.

'And besides,' added Haf, an alarmingly (as far as Carys was concerned, anyhow) sentimental look in her eyes, 'weren't you once engaged to David Meredith?'

'No!' said Carys, louder than she had intended, her face

growing hotter by the minute. 'You must be thinking of someone else.'

'Broke his heart,' Haf was already adding, oblivious, in confidential tones to her neighbour. 'No wonder it never came to anything with any of those girls Rhiannon was hoping he'd marry and bring the joyful patter of tiny feet to Plas Eden. Broken heart. Too afraid of having it broken again to try. That's what always does it.'

'That's nothing to do with me!' Carys stared at her, aghast. Trust the gossips of Pont-ar-Eden to make a mountain out of a molehill and end up blaming her for the lack of a new generation of young Merediths. Maybe it wasn't too late to phone the nursing home and inform Gwenan it was all a mistake and she couldn't do this after all, and rush back to Joe. Who'd undoubtedly receive her with forgiveness and more than a little triumph.

Which was possibly worse.

'Don't you think you're being just a little unfair, putting all the responsibility on Carys for talking to the Merediths?' demanded Merlin, gallantly abandoning his own proposed flight, and turning to face Edna. 'I rather imagine she has quite enough on her plate at the moment.'

Edna snorted loudly. Around her, however, several heads were nodding (not too obviously, especially those closest to the matriarch herself).

Edna's eyes narrowed. 'You've got money, Merlin,' she stated, with unashamed bluntness. 'And weren't you saying in an interview not so long ago that you owed everything you had ever done to Pont-ar-Eden?'

'*Sunday Times,*' provided Haf's bird-like little voice, helpfully.

Merlin groaned.

'And really,' said Edna, pressing home her advantage, 'I'm certain you are one of the few people well able to afford to buy Plas Eden. And wouldn't that be rather fitting?'

'Why on earth would I want to buy a place like Plas Eden?' demanded Merlin, his voice echoing in the sudden stilling of every conversation in the room.

'And would you like a jacket potato or chips with that?' came Buddug's voice from the counter.

'Well, isn't it what pop stars do?' put in Nesta, not to be outdone.

'Rubbish,' came Buddug's voice loudly, and clearly not referring to her customers' choice of saturated fat on their potatoes. 'You've been reading too many *OKs*, Nesta. Not every pop star is as rich as sin, or wants to throw their money around. I'm sure if Merlin had wanted that kind of lifestyle he could have found a castle to retire to long before now.'

'Well, I think he owes us *something*,' declared Edna, who had never been known to give up without a fight.

Mutterings were breaking out, spreading from one corner to another.

'You could always try to raise the money to buy it,' said Merlin. 'The village, that is,' he added, hastily, at Edna's sharp intake of breath. 'It's been done before. I think you form some kind of Trust and get people to donate. Do sponsored walks. That kind of thing. It's done for paintings, why not for Plas Eden? I'd be happy to donate for something like that.'

'It's all very well for the rich,' put in Edna, pointedly.

'You don't have to be rich to raise money,' retorted Buddug.

Silence fell amongst the red-checked tables, followed by the resuming of conversations that filled the room as if talk of Plas Eden had never occurred at all.

'So is that it?' said Carys, disappointed.

'That's Pont-ar-Eden all over,' replied Merlin, quietly, settling back down at the table once more, as the entrance of a small, wiry man with bristling white hair and eyebrows to match, heralded the arrival of Professor Humphries to take over the guidance of his little flock.

Carys frowned. 'You make it sound as if nothing can ever change.'

'Chance would be a fine thing. It's why we all left in the first place, remember?

'Yes, that's true,' Carys admitted.

'Exactly. Those who can, get out. That's how it's always been. How it always will be, if you ask me. If you stay in a place like this, you soon learn there's no point in fighting. Nothing ever changes.'

'You came back,' said Carys, glancing at him curiously. 'Why didn't you stay in New York or Los Angeles, if that's how you feel?'

'Ah,' replied Merlin. 'Funny thing about Pont-ar-Eden. It has this habit of drawing you back, in the end.' He met Carys' sceptical gaze, and grinned. 'That and being told if I touched alcohol again I'd most likely be dead within the month.'

'I'm sorry,' said Carys, 'I didn't mean to…' She stopped, overcome with embarrassment at having prompted this confession.

'Not at all.' His brown eyes were surprisingly gentle. 'It's no secret.' His grin was rueful this time. 'Ask Facebook and Twitter. And I'm sure the gossip magazines have my obituary already written. But when it came down to it, I found I wanted to live. And the only way, they say, is to break the old associations and change your life. So here I am.' He lifted the Boadicea's menu from its metal holder, fashioned in the shape of the warrior queen herself, leaning on her spear, clearly eying up a posse of Roman soldiers fit for the trouncing. 'Are you sure you won't join me for lunch? They do an excellent chilli here, the best I've tasted.'

'I'm sorry, I can't,' replied Carys, surprised at finding herself with genuine regret. 'Mam's due back in a few hours, and I'm hopelessly behind as it is.'

'No matter. I quite understand. He smiled. 'Perhaps another time, then?'

'Perhaps,' replied Carys, returning his smile as she made her way towards the door.

We began the next day.

His energy was boundless. The moment I stepped through the office door, a capacious bag was presented to me.

'Well, open it,' Mr Meredith said, seeing me hesitate.

I could have laughed out loud. I, who had once delighted in gifts of any kind, could scarcely bring myself to take the soft leather in my hands. Gifts are a means of purchase, however glitteringly dressed up. I was aware of other eyes watching me from under lowered lids. The photographer stood at one side of the room, ticking off boxes of equipment. A young man with a round, earnest face, and who I later came to know as a student of German and a passionate follower of a German philosopher called Karl Marx, was gathering up writing paper from the desk.

My fingers found the clasp. Heaven knows how he had located them in so short a time, but inside I discovered paper and pencils, along with a selection of brushes and a small wooden box. I opened the box hungrily, taking in the array of colours set in blocks inside.

'I hope they meet with your approval? I know very little of painting, I'm afraid. Let me know if there is anything else you need.'

'They are perfect,' I said, suddenly scarcely able to breathe. 'Thank you.'

'Good, good,' he replied. Job done, he was already turning to his two companions. 'So, gentlemen: are we ready?'

Ready? We never stopped. The energy of the man! Mr Tomsett, the student, could match him easily, step for step. But poor Mr Herring, the photographer, with his cumbersome equipment of boxes and stands, was soon puffing and wiping his brow. As for me, I learnt to bless every stair I had cleaned and every pavement I had walked over the past months that had hardened my muscles and given me the strength I needed.

And the sights we saw? I shudder to think of them, even now. I had never guessed so many people could live crammed in one small, dirty room, in a house so broken-down it was impossible to see how it remained upright, and with so few bits of shabby furniture I couldn't even begin to imagine where they all slept. Sickly babies cried amongst grubby, barefoot children, while an old woman rocked herself, to and fro without ceasing, in a corner. Work-weary men returned to wives worn to the bone with hard work and cares. And everywhere amongst those crammed little alleyways there were signs of disease and the stench of too many bodies – both animal and human – imprisoned together without sufficient light or air.

I soon understood how the charity hospital must seem a paradise to those taken, however temporarily, into its care. And I also saw that there could be worse places than the slums, wretched as they were. Over every family in those tenements I could see hanging the shadow of the workhouse, only ever a few days' sickness, or the loss of a workplace, away, along with the fear that, once parted, they might never see each other again.

After that first day I chose to leave most of my precious new materials behind, taking only paper and a selection of pencils with me, and working on my sketches in colour during the evenings or on a Sunday, the one day we were permitted to rest.

'It's easier, and I'm less noticed,' I tried to explain when Mr Meredith's eyes fell on my simple cloth bag that replaced the leather the following morning. 'I can work fast, and they are less aware of what I am doing. It feels less as if I am intruding, and I'm better working on the rest in my own time.'

He thought about this, nodded briefly, and went away without comment. But when we came home that evening, I discovered a new room had been found for me. A small, quiet room that overlooked the square of the little garden. There was a bed, and a washstand, and, most precious of all, a desk set at the light coming in from the window. There was even an old armchair placed to one side of the desk, also within the light from the window, where I could sketch in comfort.

I missed Lily, who wept loudly at my departure, but who, I was glad to see, soon had as my replacement a maid of her own age with long dark hair for Lily to fuss over to her heart's content. Despite Lily's protests, I had still not permitted my hair to grow beyond my shoulders, and, despite her best intentions, I determinedly pinned the small amount I had back into the severest, most unflattering manner I could find with the aid of her scrap of mirror.

'But you've got *such* a pretty face,' she would sigh, wistfully. 'If you put it like this' – and she would pull my poor bits of hair into all kinds of contortions – 'then maybe one of the doctors, or even some rich gentleman, might see you and fall in love with you. And then you'd be rich, ever afterwards.'

'Not if I'm not rich myself,' I retorted. 'Gentlemen rarely

permit their heart to rule their head. And should they be tempted, you can be certain their mothers ensure they don't forget themselves.' I saw the hurt in her eyes at this breaking up of her daydreams, and smiled. 'Unless you are much, much prettier than I, that is.'

As I said, I missed Lily and her chatter, but I loved the peace of my little room. And, more than that, I gradually discovered as the weeks went by, that the little garden outside my window was not a private place for Mr Meredith and the hospital trustees. I should have known, of course, but it had never crossed my mind.

Often, as I sat at my little desk, I would see Matron, or a little group of nurses, sitting on the benches set along the walls. As winter turned to spring, bringing the yellows of daffodils and primroses, followed by the soft blue haze of forget-me-nots, they began to appear more frequently.

As the evenings warmed and lengthened, I found myself drawn there after my work was done. I tried to time my visits for when I was certain Mr Meredith had returned to his lodgings, although he worked so long and so hard, I could never quite be certain. But if he came across me there, he was always polite and kept his distance beyond the usual pleasantries, and, besides, I would often see him speaking with Matron or the nurses during the day.

Sometimes, as I worked with my paints, or worked in the little offices organising piles of papers into some semblance of order, I would hear a burst of laughter echoing around the little square. It was a peaceful, optimistic sound, welcome in a place where voices were more usually raised in anger or in pain, and where cries of grief came as much, if not more, than murmurings of thankfulness and relief.

For two years, I stayed in that little room overlooking the fountain.

I had been certain, at first, that my inclusion in Mr Meredith's study of the conditions surrounding the hospital would not last. But I continued to be included, and no sooner had the study of one place finished than a new one began.

There might, Mr Tomsett would say, be all the talk about living conditions and the wage of the working man having improved over the past years, but there were still places in London that were a disgrace to man.

Was I happy? I suppose, in my own way, I was. I had my drawing once more; my days were filled with activity, and I had a place where I belonged. Friends, even. I was touched to be invited to Lily's wedding, in the second spring I was there. I even grew my hair for the occasion, much to her delight. I did not have rich men stopping me in the street, or even turning their heads to gaze at me. So I let it grow. Although I still tucked it up as severely as I could. After all, this was a hospital, with no time for vanity.

When did I begin to grow restless? Maybe it was during that first summer, when the letters began. I had not looked for them for so long, I could not entirely hide my joy as that first little packet was handed to me. Or my anxiety. I made my excuses as soon as I reasonably could, and hastened to my room. Whatever news it contained, I knew I could not school my face into indifference, and I had no wish to arouse more curiosity than this sudden appearance of correspondence had already done.

No; those first letters settled me. Made me smile. Left me waiting ever more hungrily for the next one to arrive. Not that

I could keep them, of course. Not even the little drawings placed in between the familiar scrawl of writing. I tucked each one deep into my bodice for as long as I dared, burning them, always, within a day or so.

I wrote letters in reply. Long letters in which I poured out my hopes and my fears. That I was safe and contented. And that, one day, I hoped to be able to earn enough to set up my own establishment, deep in the country, far away, when I, and those I loved, could live as we chose. They were, of course, letters I did not dare to send. And, although it tore my heart in two, I knew I could not return even the simplest form of message. I could but hope that the non-return of that first letter was message enough to its sender that I was receiving them.

Maybe it was the unease that soon began to creep through the cheerful tone that began to unsettle me. By that second winter, they had grown less frequent, the writing more hurried, as if undertaken in brief moments when watchful eyes were not there. And I knew the writer too well not to know the unhappiness that lingered there. And the fear.

By that second spring, I felt my powerlessness more than ever. I was not a fool. I knew well enough that outside the Meredith Charity Hospital I would not be able to earn enough to keep body and soul together, let alone rent a respectable house, or even rooms. And if I was discovered – I dreaded to consider what might happen then.

It must have been about that time my dreams began. I dreamt of the sea, of the clear salt wind tugging at my hair and my gown, and spray shooting wildly over black rocks in a turquoise sea. Sometimes, I was rocked in some little boat, watching the harbour drift away into the distance as we cleared the rocks and caves of a bay, gulls shrieking behind us. And I would wake with the taste of salt on my lips.

I thanked Heaven more than ever for that room of mine, and for no Lily there, to hear what I might call out in my tossing and my turning.

By that second summer, I was close to my wits' end. I had not felt the city to be so oppressive before. Long, hot, cloudless days dawned, day after day, while a more than usually foul stench hung over the capital. Nothing, the older nurses claimed, that could possibly match the Great Stink, before Sir Joseph Bazalgette built his miraculous waste system that had transformed London over twenty years before. But to me, in my restless unease, it seemed foul enough.

'You find pleasure in water,' Mr Meredith remarked, one summer evening, as I sat in my favourite seat, beneath the shade of a trailing vine next to the fountain.

'Like this,' I replied, looking up from my sketching. 'It cools the air.'

'A necessity in this heat,' he returned. It was late. The sun had left the courtyard some hours ago, leaving a reflected golden light hanging above us. The two nurses drinking tea together just beyond the fountain, stretched themselves and gathered up their tea cups, making their way slowly back towards the ward and its long, restless night.

The garden was now deserted. I returned to my pencil, knowing that when I looked up again he would be gone. But not this time.

'May I join you?'

I looked up again in surprise. 'Yes, of course.'

'Don't let me disturb your work.'

'Thank you.' But, of course, he did. I made a show of shading, here and there, but all concentration had gone. I laid it down, after a while, on the bench between us. For a moment, he scarcely seemed to notice my movement. He was,

I found, staring into the waters of the pool, brows knit tight together. His face, I saw, was more drawn and lined than I had seen before.

'I'm sorry.' He stirred himself and looked round. 'I'm interrupting you.'

'The light is fading,' I said, quickly.

He smiled. 'May I see?'

'Of course.' I eyed him. 'It's for my own amusement.'

'I do not expect you to work for me every hour of the day, Mrs Smith.'

'No, sir.'

He looked down at my drawing, as if thankful to have some kind of distraction. 'You have a grand vision of our fountain,' he said with a smile.

I had never heard him criticise my work before. Despite myself, I was stung.

'Grand?'

'An improvement,' he replied. 'I think perhaps if I were commissioning our poor version again, I would take notice of your design.'

I glanced at the paper in his hand. He was right, although I had not seen it before: the rushing water billowing between rocks bore little resemblance to the trickle in front of us.

I swallowed. 'In all this heat, I must have been dreaming of water,' I said. 'Maybe a stream I knew as a child.'

'A stream with statues,' he replied, amusement in his voice. 'Now that, I'd like to see.'

'Statues?'

He looked round at my tone. 'I didn't mean to insult your skill, Mrs Smith. If those are figures…'

'No,' I muttered. The nymph I might have argued away. But not the satyr with his pipe and cloven hooves, and the

102

animals peering out of every nook and cranny. 'It must be a place I saw in my dreams,' I added.

He was watching my face. 'Do you often dream of such places?'

'No.' My tone was harsh, even in my own ears. It had its effect. He placed my drawing into my outstretched hand. I wondered if he knew I would burn it in the flame of my candle that night.

I felt him rise to his feet. 'Good night, Mrs Smith.'

'Good night, Mr Meredith.'

And he walked slowly away. Even in the gathering darkness, I could make out his walk, slow and stiff. Almost like a man who has suddenly grown old.

❧

The next day, I knew I must leave the charity hospital.

Not at that very moment. Not without references. I had not worked so long and so hard to throw my settled life away again. Besides, I was not entirely certain I could begin again from nothing.

I would start that very day, I decided, to look for another position. I had saved a small amount over the past months, and I had experience and a reputation. And, above all, I would have references.

There was no time to lose. I would tell him that morning. After all, it was only fair to give him a longer notice than was required. I would say I was weary of London. That I was a countrywoman at heart, and now had a longing to return closer to home once more.

And maybe, just maybe, I told myself in desperation, I would find a way to return to Cornwall, and the rocky coastline around Treverick Bay that haunted my dreams. And maybe, just maybe, and however impossible, I could find a way…

Meanwhile, Mr Meredith would give me a reference, and I would give him time to find a replacement. What could be fairer? Once I had told him, there would be no going back.

I dressed quickly, and almost ran down the stairs to his office, before I could change my mind. The door, I discovered, was open. I knocked loudly, and stepped inside.

He was not there. Correspondence lay unopened on the desk. I found a strange taste creeping into my mouth, and recognised it as fear.

The girl cleaning out the empty grate jumped up at the sound of my entrance.

'Oh, ma'am,' she said, sniffing loudly. Which didn't exactly help matters. Her face was dusted with soot, apart from two rivulets of clean skin where tears had trickled down her cheeks.

'What is it, Hester?' I demanded. 'Is Mr Meredith ill?'

She shook her head. 'Ruby says there was one of those telegram things came last night. Mr Meredith wasn't here, so they sent the boy on to his lodgings.'

'And?'

Hester, who I knew to be a soft-hearted girl who could not bear to disturb spiders, and squealed at the tail-ends of mice brought in by Gladstone, the hospital cat, burst into tears. 'Oh, Mrs Smith, there's been a terrible accident, and him all alone and catching the midnight train and having to travel for hours and hours. And Ruby says she doesn't think he'll ever come back to London again, ever again. And what'll then happen to the hospital?'

'I don't think the charity hospital depends entirely on one man,' I replied, as gently as I could. 'The trustees will take

104

over, just as they do when Mr Meredith goes away on business or on holiday.'

'Oh,' said Hester, snuffling into her handkerchief, which was growing blacker by the minute.

It was a reasonable question. One that anyone would have asked. So I asked it.

'Did Ruby say where Mr Meredith has gone?'

'Home,' sighed Hester, blowing her nose. 'Some place with a funny name, in the mountains, where they don't even speak English, Ruby said. Hours and hours away, even by steam train, and they go ever so fast. Thirty miles an hour, so Ruby says.'

I glanced over to the painting of the pale house, just glimpsed between the trees. I should have known.

'To Plas Eden.'

Part Two

Chapter Five

Willow Cottage smelt musty as Carys opened the door, with the touch of damp that crept into these old stone cottages when they were left empty for any length of time, even in the summer.

She stepped into the narrow hallway, blinking in the sudden darkness, only just missing stubbing her toes on the coat stand and the grandfather clock that had always been guaranteed to trip up strangers.

The doors to the living room and the old-fashioned parlour had been left open to air the place: all around her light filtered gently in through small, deep-set windows.

They'd certainly known all about insulation two hundred years ago, when the cottage had been built. Forget all that lagging and the stuff they pumped into cavity walls these days. With nothing available to them but the rocks from the mountainside – some almost as large as a horse – and their bare hands, the builders had created walls so thick nothing was getting in or out of there in a hurry.

Even before the double-glazing, Willow Cottage had been toasty warm in the winter and cool in summer. On the hottest days, it was a refuge. Every member of the family would wander back in, Carys remembered, when the heat and the glare of the sun became too much, to feel the delicious chill of the quarry tiles beneath their feet and gulp down Mam's homemade lemonade or ginger beer.

Her eyes adjusting, Carys took the carrier bags of shopping through the door in front of her and into the kitchen. Here it was lighter. Like most of the cottages in Pont-ar-Eden, the kitchen was a modern extension tacked onto the back of the house, with the bathroom directly above, built in the late 1960s to replace the water standpipe at the roadside and the privy at the bottom of the garden.

On the way back to the car to fetch in the rest of her luggage, Carys stepped inside the open door of the living room. Mam's Welsh dresser, inherited from her own mother and dark with years of fire smoke and polishing, stood against one wall, laden with Mam's best plates.

Above the grate of the coal fire, the slate mantelpiece rested in polished splendour, large white china dogs on either side, flanking a reproduction of Michelangelo's Pieta, a bust of Beethoven and another of Schubert, and a seahorse made of shells that she and Gwenan and Nia had brought back from a day trip to Rhyl, interspersed with family photographs in ornate silver frames.

The familiar smell of coal fires and beeswax polish mingled with lavender surrounded her. Instantly, she was a child again, with Mam cooking up a Sunday roast in the kitchen, Dad fiddling under the bonnet of the car or pottering in the old outside loo, which he had turned into a darkroom where he could pursue his passion for photography to his heart's content without interruption from his womenfolk, who didn't understand these things and might do themselves an injury with the chemicals. Gwenan would be out in the garden, organising half the neighbourhood children in some game or other, and Nia would be upstairs, making dresses for her Barbie doll in any material she could lay her hands on.

Where had all that time gone? Carys asked herself, with a sudden ache in her heart. Memories hung in the dust-laden air, as if all those childhood dreams and plans still lingered and were now drawing close around her like ghosts in the silence of the empty house.

Carys shook herself and the moment was gone. She was just Carys again, standing in an empty room, and with the grandfather clock in the hallway warning her she had only a short time before Mam came home.

Her phone beeped loudly in her bag. As Carys grabbed for it another beep followed. Two texts. The first was from Poppy, with instructions to keep smiling, followed by hugs and kisses. The second was an extremely rude joke about sheep from Tanya at work, followed by even more hugs and kisses and three smiley faces.

Had she really seemed that fragile? Carys wondered, as she tapped out her replies. Nothing from Joe. Even though he must know she would have arrived by now. On the occasions she'd visited Mam on her own over the years Joe had always sent regular texts, whatever conference or management course he was attending. It was a weekday, of course. He might be in a meeting.

Carys stashed her phone deep into the bottom of her bag. Up until this morning, when she'd been loading her bags and laptop into the car, Joe had seemed so certain she would change her mind. He'd been charming and helpful for weeks, making sure the bathroom was clean and undertaking more than his fair share of the cooking. He'd even fielded calls from her elder sister, despite his usual determination to avoid Gwenan at all times. But this morning he'd scarcely muttered a goodbye as he left for work, pointedly avoiding her kiss. Joe's hurt and anger always expressed itself in silence. There was nothing she could do about it. She just had to wait until he calmed down and decided to communicate with her again.

She couldn't afford to dwell on that now, not with the practicalities of Mam's return to be dealt with. For all it had appeared the same at first, there were changes to the cottage. Gwenan had had railings put up everywhere and the cloakroom next to the downstairs loo had been knocked through and a shower installed, to make a small bathroom until Mam could get back upstairs again.

Mam's parlour, on the opposite side of the hallway to the living room had always been kept spotlessly clean and tidy at all times in case of visitors. Now it had been stripped of its glass-fronted sideboard, filled with Mam's best Stuart Crystal bowls and wine glasses. The upright piano (never played), and the good-as-new cottage suite from the seventies, that always made visitors nervous with its air of being far too fragile to support any substantial weight, had also vanished.

In their place stood Mam's bed and a brand new wardrobe of stripped pine to replace the large and ancient affair in Mam's room, which would probably not have survived the journey down the stairs, not without giving any who tried an instant hernia anyway.

Mam would be furious. Carys could feel it in her bones. No one had dared to even reposition a chair away from the scorching of the fire for the past fifty years of the parlour's existence. Although Gwenan was right, of course: there was no other choice. At least not until Mam was properly back on her feet again. It was just that Gwenan was not going to have to face Mam's indignation at the sacrilege.

'Curtains,' Carys muttered aloud. The parlour curtains, dark, brocaded affairs to add suitably dignified gloom to the

112

room, were still up. At least if Mam had the soft, flowery curtains from upstairs, it might feel more like her bedroom. And if she moved the bed a little, so that it was more or less in the same position, next to the window, then perhaps Mam might find her way around more easily.

Glad to have a project in hand, to keep the silence and her uncomfortable thoughts at bay, Carys switched on the radio. She fortified herself with a strong coffee, before getting shepherd's pie (Mam's favourite) underway, and then turning to attack the offending curtains.

❧

A few hours later, Mair Evans made her way out of the ambulance and up the short path to the front door of Willow Cottage under her own steam. She was slow and careful and leaned heavily on her stick, but she made it without the help of the accompanying ambulance man, her lips set in the thin line of determination Carys knew so well.

'Cup of tea, Mam?' said Carys cheerfully, as she closed the door behind them.

'A *paned* would be lovely, *cariad*,' replied Mair, breathing heavily as if she had just made it to the base camp of Everest. The effort had clearly exhausted her. She took a step forward, looking wistfully up the stairs towards her bedroom.

'In here,' said Carys quickly, taking her mother's arm and guiding her into the parlour. 'We've arranged everything in here for the moment. Just until you're feeling a bit stronger.'

Mam scarcely seemed to notice the desecration of her best room. She sank into the armchair and closed her eyes. Carys hesitated a moment, unsure whether to stay with her or go into the kitchen to make the tea.

Mam looked frailer than ever in her own surroundings, where she had always been the driving force of the household. When Carys had last seen her in this room, Mam had been a strong, healthy woman, her face tanned from hours spent working in her garden and glowing from the organic vegetables diligently bought and cooked into delicious soups and stews. Now the chair engulfed her, while her fragile fingers groped for the controls on the arm, as if she had forgotten how to use them.

'It's this one,' said Carys, gently, placing her mother's fingers on the electronic button that set the chair whirring its way into a half-lying position. 'Is that far enough?'

'Lovely, dear.' Mam sounded half asleep already. Her eyes had closed and her mouth had gone slack. A clench of fear knotted itself in Carys' belly. The reality of looking after a woman who seemed so old and fragile, and so totally unable to do anything for herself, overwhelmed her.

I'm not a nurse, she thought, in panic. Supposing Mam became really ill, all of a sudden? She eyed the clear plastic bag of medication, with notes, horribly aware that she had no real idea what any of it meant. Gwenan had spent half an hour explaining each drug last night, when Carys' mind had been too swamped with Joe, hovering impatiently in the background with plans for that brilliant Arctic Adventure he'd spotted – a total last-minute bargain if they booked it for two weeks' time – to take things in. Supposing she made a mistake, and gave Mam the wrong ones, or in the wrong order?

Mam seemed to be scarcely breathing. Supposing she fell, or had a heart attack? Or couldn't make it on her own to the loo or into bed? Supposing she did it all wrong, and Mam died and it was her fault?

'Get a grip,' Carys told herself firmly. 'Just get a grip.'

Worse things happen at sea, and a lot of other places, come to that.

You cope. That's what Poppy had said, when Carys had exclaimed in awe at the sheer logistics of trying to feed and change two small babies, neither of whom appeared to choose to sleep at the same time as the other, not to mention trying to keep a business afloat

So, said Poppy: you count two hours sleep a good night and you can never even sit on the loo on your own, and you grunt vaguely to your husband in passing on the stairs, who grunts vaguely back, each of you frazzled and covered in milky sick and chocolate. Sex is something you don't even dream of any more. And, in any case, you'd both swap passion for a straight eight hours kip … no, Poppy couldn't have imagined it either, but when it happens, survival mode takes over and you cope.

Maybe looking after your aging parents was not unlike looking after your children, it struck Carys. It isn't a subject you get taught at school, and nothing prepares you for the reality. It's still 'women's work', whoever actually does it. Not college stuff. Not what successful, important, real grown up people do. They're your flesh and blood, and you're just left to get on with it. Guided by instinct, most probably.

She had a sudden desire to break into nervous giggling. All her working life, she had been through endless training sessions, complete with PowerPoint presentations, flipcharts, flow diagrams, SWOT and SMART analyses and evaluation sheets. But she'd never had training sessions (on a full day's pay and buffet lunch, with generous breaks for 'networking') to prepare her for being in sole charge of a fragile old woman.

Carys had never considered looking for any such thing, and she wasn't sure it existed, even if she had. She didn't even remember seeing manuals on the subject, along the lines of the piles of *A Child's First Year* Poppy had collected by the time the twins arrived.

'So, are you making that *paned*?' demanded Mam, eyes still closed.

Carys smiled at her. This time, Mam sounded more like herself. Maybe the return home had done her good, after all.

Sod Joe and his bloody dog-sled safari and snow-mobile excursions. Had he really thought ten days of wall-to-wall ice and the off-chance of seeing the Northern Lights would be enough to make her change her mind? And if he thought his silence was about to browbeat her into crawling back for his forgiveness, he had another think coming.

If she was ever to demonstrate to Joe that she meant what she said, she had to carry through with this to the end. If she caved in now and went back to Chester, she would be giving him permission to assume that, when it came to the crunch, he could always alternate charm and the silent treatment until he got his own way. Carys hastily shut her mind to the possibilities of where that thought was taking her. One thing at a time. And she'd enough to deal with, right now.

'Just going now, Mam,' she said.

They'd cope, she swore to herself. Between them, she and Mam, whatever happened, they'd cope.

Chapter Six

For Carys, the next few weeks passed in a daze. There always seemed so much to do, interspersed with the visits of the nurse to keep an eye on Mam's progress.

They were all simple, mundane things she felt she should be able to do in her sleep, but which somehow seemed to take on vast dimensions when combined with constantly keeping her emotional antennae tuned towards Mam's needs.

At least Joe had stopped giving her the cold shoulder. They had only spoken briefly on the phone, but texts and emails began to arrive after the third day of silence. Joe was cheerful and affectionate as if nothing had happened. There was no mention of ice safaris or the Northern Lights. After the second day without any contact, Carys wondered if he might go without her, possibly dragging along a few of his mates into the bargain, to bombard her with photos and links to YouTube demonstrating just how much fun they were having. Thankfully, he appeared to have forgotten the idea and was busy at work instead.

She was relieved that he was talking to her, but she couldn't quite help the sliver of unease that remained. Joe might insist on behaving as if this was simply an extended weekend and she'd be back at the flat before long, but they couldn't go on like this forever. There was a discussion looming, one they couldn't put off.

For now, Carys did her best to push such thoughts from her mind. She'd quite enough to keep her on her toes without trying to work out how to tackle Joe. Mam had been a proudly independent woman, coping with whatever was thrown at her ever since Dad died, and hated asking for anything. Carys soon gave up asking, given how much it embarrassed them both, and found herself trying to gauge from the smallest of clues if Mam was too hot or too cold, or if the cushion at her back had slipped.

She soon learnt to recognise the slight frown of anxiety that meant Mam had forgotten yet again how to work the DVD remote and was worried that the next bit of the film might turn nasty with no way of sending it back into oblivion.

Then there were Mam's struggles to regain her independence. Even when she was watching TV or snoozing (or, more usually, both at the same time) Carys found she could never quite relax.

Her ears were always listening for the creakings and the whirr of the chair that signalled Mam getting herself upright and setting off to trudge round her room, practising her walking. Or (more alarmingly, from Carys' point of view) setting off towards the toilet with its step and endless possibilities for tripping over. She had even caught Mam balancing cups and plates precariously in her free hand as she hobbled towards the kitchen to 'do the washing up'.

Of course she wanted Mam to get better and be able to do things for herself again. What terrified her was the thought of Mam falling and injuring her newly replaced hip, or, even worse, breaking a wrist or an ankle. At times, it felt like being in charge of an overgrown toddler. Except this toddler was the parent of the household who most definitely saw Carys as the child and was fond of telling her where to put the dishes when they were wiped and which bits of washing went with what and at which temperature, if you didn't want them all to come out a uniform shade of grey.

'You'd think I'd never had a house of my own,' Carys muttered to herself, trying her very best not to explode with irritation as Mam supervised the changing of the bed.

'If you make a fold at each corner, it'll be much neater,' said Mam, frowning at Carys' efforts to smooth down the sheet.

'It's a fitted sheet, Mam. It's got elastic at the corners, see? Saves you doing all that.'

'That's not mine.'

'No, Mam. It's new. And so's the duvet cover. Isn't it pretty? Gwenan bought them for you. She knows you love roses.'

'What a waste of money! Those old sheets were perfectly good. I hope she hasn't thrown them away.'

'I shouldn't think so,' replied Carys, who knew perfectly well that Gwenan had stuffed the offending articles in black plastic bags months ago. She could hear the process taking place when Gwenan had phoned her, outraged at the lack of decorum in Mam's bedding.

'And half of them are so thin, you can see your hand through them,' she had exclaimed.

Carys realised that such things didn't matter to Mam any more. The main thing was the familiar. Mam, as she got older, was like a cat, bonded to territory even more than to her loved ones. Her old things, the ones she had seen and felt about her since before Dad died, were her territory, marking her safe boundaries on this earth. She didn't want the new. It confused and alarmed her and spoke to her of a brave new word that felt alien, one that was increasingly moving away and beyond her, towards a future in which she had no part.

Above all, Carys had discovered, there was Mam's routine.

Toast and cereal at eight in the morning, tea and biscuits at ten, soup and sandwiches at midday, a snooze until *The Archers*, just after two, followed by a cup of tea at four and a cooked meal at six. All rounded off by a glass of sweet sherry and a piece of cake just before bed.

Mam had always baked delicious cakes: lemon sponge, sharp as could be, dusted with icing sugar, and a dark, rich chocolate cake with a hint of cherry liqueur. Carys, who'd always had a passionate relationship with her microwave, hadn't the first idea how to go about making a scone, let alone a full-blown cake. Feeling a little furtive, she ordered them with the groceries from Sara Jones instead. Along, it had to be said, with half the village. Nobody could make a cake quite like Sara Jones. Whatever Nesta Pugh and her WI coffee mornings regulars might think.

Carys understood the routine kept Mam feeling safe and knowing where she was in the day. But for her it was like an iron prison, keeping her constantly watching the clock and unable to get a good run at anything she tried to do. So much for any starting up as a gardener idea. She was finding it hard enough to keep up with the accounts Tylers were sending her over the internet between all the cooking, cleaning, washing and finding a plumber who would actually answer her calls to fix the leak that had developed under the bathroom sink. Not to mention shooting out to drop the grocery shopping list in with Sara Jones and pick up a few necessaries from Low-Price and the butchers while she waited for Mam's prescription to be made up in the chemist. Everything was undertaken at top speed, before Mam's next cup of tea was due, or in the two precious afternoons she was whisked off to her physiotherapy session or Pont-ar-Eden's little social club.

Full, as Mam grumbled each time, of *old* people. 'All they

do is play bingo,' she muttered, for at least the third time that week.

'And scrabble, you said, Mam.'

'I hate scrabble.'

'You used to like it when we were kids.'

'Did I?' Mair frowned dismissively. 'That was different.'

Okay.

Carys counted to ten, and refrained from banging her head against the wall. Her own, that is.

Mam, who had always filled her days with activity, had a low boredom threshold. What she needed was something to engage her brain. Bingo and scrabble clearly weren't doing it. Projects. That's how Mam occupied herself when she was well. Pruning the roses, washing the windows. Helping with the church fete and meals on wheels. Those were the kinds of things she always talked about. What Mam needed was a project.

'What about history?' suggested Carys, over tea that evening. There had been no word from Joe all day and she was beginning to feel a little jumpy. He always kept his phone on at work, and they hadn't argued, so there was no reason for him to be giving her the cold shoulder again. She'd even swallowed her pride after her second text hadn't been answered and resorted to ringing him, just to check he was okay. But Joe, it seemed, had vanished into the ether. Which was very unlike Joe.

'History?' Mam's tone was not encouraging. But there was possibly just the slightest glint in her eye.

'Didn't you say you'd been meaning to join Professor Humphries' group at the Boadicea?'

'I can't possibly go there.' Mam was looking alarmed.

'No, of course not. Not yet. But we could make a start here.

121

I've got my laptop, and didn't you say there were loads of old photos in the attic?'

'Well, yes. But nobody's going to be interested in that old stuff.'

'Oh, I don't know. They're always starting with old photos on *Who Do You Think You Are?* We could at least go through them. And then we could put anything that looks as if it might be interesting together, and take it along for Professor Humphries to look at, when you're feeling better.'

'Well…' said Mam. The thought of venturing somewhere new was clearly giving her the heebie-jeebies.

'There might be photos of Plas Eden,' persisted Carys, doggedly. 'Didn't you say Granddad used to take photos when he was head gardener there? Maybe they show how the gardens used to look. You've always loved gardens. Those would be interesting.'

'Well, yes…' Mam allowed. Her face relaxed. 'Your Granddad was so proud of that garden. Blodeuwedd's Garden. That's what they called it, you know. Except we used to call it the Whispering Garden. When we were kids, that is.'

'Oh?' prompted Carys. Mam's eyes had brightened. Her face had lost its little-old-lady look and seemed a little more like Mam.

'Mmm.' There was a definite gleam to Mam's eyes this time. 'Whenever the wind blew through the leaves, it was like voices, whispering. Whispering secrets you could never quite hear.'

'That sounds a bit spooky,' said Carys, to humour her. Trying not to notice the slight shiver down her spine. She'd never been good with ghost stories.

'Oh, you know what imagination kids have.' Mam's eyes were far away, lost in memory. 'I suppose it *was* a bit spooky. But I don't remember ever feeling afraid. Sometimes, you know, it used to feel as if somebody was there. Watching over us. And the statues. Keeping us safe.'

'A guardian ghost,' said Carys, smiling for her mother's benefit.

'Beautiful, it was,' her mother murmured. She appeared to be drifting off once more. Suddenly, her eyes shot open. 'It was always such a pity, so it was. You and David Meredith. Such a pity.'

Carys blinked. All these years, and not a word on the subject. Mam had seemed so relieved when she and Dad had waved Carys off at the train station, on her way to take up her place at Manchester University, without a trace of David Meredith in sight. Surely she wasn't about to change her mind now?

It was bad enough, thought Carys, having the prospect of bumping into David in the village every time she ran an errand, without Mam singing his praises. Did Mam – who had never been exactly subtle when it came to matchmaking – really think so little of Joe?

'And him such a nice boy, too,' said Mam, as she drifted off into a doze.

&

Later that evening, Carys left Mam happily installed in front of her favourite film and made her way into the kitchen, retrieving her mobile on the way.

There was still no text or 'missed call' message on the little screen. Carys put the kettle on and reached for the teabags with a feeling of emptiness opening up inside her. It was these moments, the few moments of stillness in her day when Mam was dozing or watching TV, that she missed Joe.

123

It was strange: from the beginning of their relationship, they had agreed they would each keep their separate interests and social life and not always do things as a couple. In Chester, she had spent several evenings a week – sometimes whole weekends – alone in the flat without ever once feeling lonely. Time on her own to slob around, not do the washing up and watch every girly programme she could think of, had seemed a luxury. But that was knowing that soon Joe would be appearing through the door, and their life would pick up its threads once more.

She tried ringing him again. But the phone in the flat was on answer phone, and Joe's mobile was still switched off. England must be playing, she told herself. Or maybe in his current bachelor state he was fitting in a few more games of pool. He felt far away. Almost as if he didn't exist any more. She ached with missing him: his voice, the clean-shirt smell of him, and the smile that lit up his face when she came through the door.

Her fingers paused over 'create message'. But she didn't want to irritate him unnecessarily, or provoke him into suspecting her of keeping a watchful eye on him. Or, heaven forbid, nagging. Joe didn't do nagging. He was always complaining of being nagged by his mother and sisters even though their fussing over him seemed to Carys well meaning and very mild. And it wasn't as if he actually lived with any of them any more.

She made the tea, aware of an uneasy clenching in her stomach. Maybe Joe was right. Maybe she was being unreasonable, expecting him to accept that she could abandon him for a couple of months. She began arranging bourbons next to custard creams and a fan of chocolate fingers on one of Mam's favourite side plates decorated with roses. And that being so, maybe she was even more of a fool to think she could change him.

She couldn't entirely put the blame on Joe. From the very beginning he had been clear about never wanting marriage, or children and the whole family thing. Each Christmas had been just the two of them. Popping in briefly to see his mother on Boxing Day and popping up to see Mam, equally briefly, on the day before New Year's Eve. Carys swallowed, hard, the wobbles in her stomach redoubling themselves. Maybe, in his own mind at least, Joe had every right to be so hurt and so irritable with her.

Carys placed the tea and plate of biscuits on a tray. She couldn't bear this uncertainty. She and Joe needed to talk about this. Not via email or text, but face to face. With complete honesty. All cards on the table. And then deal with whatever that might bring. At least the air would be clear between them. Tomorrow, she would ask Gwenan or Nia to make good that promise to look after Mam for a few days so she could go back to Chester.

A swell of strings made its way from Mam's room, filling the entire house with sounds of lovelorn anguish. Mam, being slightly deaf, always had the sound turned up to an ear-splitting level that was inescapable in any room of the house. And her taste in screen heroines, being of the old-fashioned self-sacrificing kind, could seriously do Carys' head in at the best of times.

Before she could make the arrangements to go back and see Joe, Carys realised, she needed to be clear what she was going to say to him. And for that, she needed to know in her heart exactly what it was she wanted.

Yesterday, this morning, an hour ago even, she could have said what she wanted without a moment's hesitation. Now she found she was not so sure.

'There you are, Mam,' she said, placing the tray with tea and biscuits on the table at her mother's side.

'Thank you dear,' said Mam, who had tears in her eyes and was clearly enjoying herself hugely. 'Aren't you having one?'

'We're nearly out of milk,' said Carys, slightly hesitantly. 'I thought I might just pop along to Low-Price, so we've got enough for the morning.'

'Of course, dear,' said Mam, her attention back on her film, with the aid of a custard cream and two chocolate fingers.

'I won't be long,' said Carys. But already Mam was well away, vaguely waving a chocolate finger in her direction in reply.

Relieved, but still feeling slightly guilty (and hoping Mam didn't investigate the contents of a fridge awash with cartons of milk), Carys grabbed her coat and bag and shot out into the fresh air. The streets of Pont-ar-Eden might not be the same as a walk on the beach, but at least she could be alone with her thoughts for a while. Time to clear her head, make her decision, and set herself on the course she must follow for the rest of her life.

Not that, Carys had a sneaking suspicion, this was going to prove easy. Especially with the familiar outlines of the Plas Eden estate looming over the village, everywhere she looked.

Chapter Seven

Halfway down Plas Eden's long, tree-lined driveway, David Meredith paused, set down the barrow of slate chippings next to another pothole, and stretched his aching back.

This definitely felt harder than it used to be, he considered ruefully. Just a few hours ago, he had felt full of energy. His leg hadn't given him a single twinge as he'd made his way down to the kitchen to join Rhiannon for breakfast. Things, it seemed, were taking a turn for the better. He'd set to with a vengeance, tackling the list of the most urgent jobs with the exhilaration that he was at last returning to normal. Life could go on the way it always had done.

But he was only halfway through his first task, and already the exhaustion was creeping back. His bad leg felt as if a dozen red-hot pokers were stabbing inside the bone. Maybe Huw was right; maybe it really was time to call it a day, face the facts and let Plas Eden go.

David tipped the load from the wheelbarrow into the pothole, took hold of the ancient rake, and set to work again. It wasn't just his accident. Long months of enforced inactivity had brought him face to face with uncomfortable realities that could be so easily buried beneath a busy life.

There was no escaping that he was no longer the boy who had taken over the running of Plas Eden. He was only five years away from forty. No great age nowadays, but he had to admit that even before he took to that ski slope, he'd been aware of his body slowing down. Only a little, but in the world of outward bound and adventure courses, a little was enough. The guys he had first worked with had long since moved on to less physically demanding roles in management, leaving the up and coming twenty-somethings to take their place.

David grimaced. Maybe it had been that sense of being left behind, of something to prove, that had sent him flying so recklessly down that Swiss ski slope in the first place. That, and impressing Rachel. God, just how clichéd could you get?

He paused in his raking to glance up at Eden, just visible between the trees. There had been other women, of course, over the years. But none who had shown the least enthusiasm for burying themselves in a family business in the back of beyond, where a trip to Tesco, some twenty miles away, was the height of local shopping.

So much for the lord and master of his own country pile being the object of every woman's desire, he thought, placing the rake in the waiting wheelbarrow. At least not when the grand house turned out to be shabby and falling apart – unless inhabited by paying guests – plus one aunt and one disabled grandmother already firmly installed.

With Rachel, he'd thought it might be different. For one thing, she'd worked at the outward bound centre in Talarn and thrived on country life. He'd loved her energy, her laughter and her amazing ability to persuade the most terrified schoolboy to take that step backwards over the cliff and abseil to the ground. At twenty-five, Rachel had seemed unfazed by anything, even the endless attention that Plas Eden required.

But then Rachel had been offered the job in a Swiss ski centre. It was the chance of a lifetime, and only for a year or so. There had been a slight feeling of hurt, but he had hid it well. After all, they had the rest of their lives before them, what was the hurry? He should have known that long-distance relationships rarely work, and how quickly they would grow apart during the year. In the days before his accident, they'd scarcely been on speaking terms, his long-anticipated holiday a disaster even before true disaster struck.

David quickly pushed the thought out of his mind and gave the pothole a good stamping under his boots to bed in the slate.

'Impossible,' he muttered, shaking his head. It wasn't only Rachel who had moved on. The friends he had kept in touch with from school and university had scattered far and wide, some in England, some in Europe, with at least one in Dubai. They had carved out careers and businesses for themselves, settling down with wives and children. A few were even divorced and on their second family. He'd been, considered David, to endless weddings in the past five years. But take away Plas Eden, and what had he achieved? Even Huw had built up a business empire of his own, with a smart new house, a wife and children and a holiday cottage in the south of France.

His leg was becoming unbearable. David cursed under his breath. He'd been warned that overdoing things too soon could set his recovery back. He just hadn't believed it. He took the handles of the wheelbarrow and slowly began to make his way back towards the house. Without the responsibility of Plas Eden, he might at least be free. But to walk away would leave him with a terrible sense of failure: of having betrayed Dad and all the Merediths before him who had brought Plas Eden back from the brink, whatever it had cost them personally.

Besides, the thought of not being here, of never being able

to come here again, left a deep emptiness inside. Even now, he couldn't imagine life without the house and the tangled melancholy of the gardens. The statues whispering gently to each other in their little glade. And he would miss the silence. The lack of rush. The kite now circling round the hill on the seaward side; the owls calling to each other through the woods at night. The hedgehog that snuffled its way across the lawn after the cat food Rhiannon put out once the cats were safely ensconced indoors.

He paused as the distant gate clanged open, followed by the purr of an engine making its way ever so gingerly towards him.

'Damn!' The Adamsons were out for the day, heading for the top of Snowdon by train, and the next set of guests weren't due to book in until this evening. The last thing he needed was Huw, back for another assault on the future of Plas Eden. Sure enough, a black four by four came into view and swerved around the worst of the potholes with a practised air, before drawing up beside him.

'There really is no point,' remarked Huw, lowering his windows with an impressive whirring sound. 'The entire thing needs resurfacing.'

'Well, at least this will ensure it doesn't get any worse, for now,' returned David, trying not to bristle at his younger brother's tone.

'The trouble is, as I've been saying for years,' replied Huw, heavily, 'just about everything needs to be re-done. The east wing really is falling apart at the seams, you know.'

'It needs some work,' conceded David.

'A major overhaul, if you ask me. You said yourself, the number of guests in the holiday apartments has dropped off dramatically this year, which means you can hardly carry on as you are.'

'I'm not intending to.' David's temper was not improved by the shooting pains now rippling up and down his bad leg, making him slightly nauseous. 'Those were hardly normal circumstances.'

'But they're the circumstances we find ourselves in now.' Huw pulled his Land Cruiser onto the verge beneath the trees and left it there, as if to emphasise the dire state of Eden's drive.

The drive, thought David, doing his best to squash mounting irritation, might be suffering from the ravages of last year's hard winter, but the Adamsons, at least, were viewing it as part of Plas Eden's old-fashioned charm. And surely that's what Land Cruisers were for?

He took a deep breath. 'Things might change again. There was always going to be a drop-off in the holiday lets while the building work on the east wing was taking place. It might just be that it's a good time to start upgrading the east wing.'

'To do what? You said yourself the adventure holiday side of things isn't possible for now. You've already ruled out going down the B&B road, and just continuing with straight holiday lets doesn't made good business sense.'

'There might be other possibilities. Solutions none of us have thought of yet, because we haven't been looking.'

Huw was frowning. 'There's a recession on. It's hardly a good time to start taking risks. Beddows are a reputable firm, and they know me. But they won't hang around forever. And who else is likely to see the potential of a place like this? Especially in this economic climate.'

'We've agreed we'd discuss it,' said David. 'All of us,' he added, pointedly. He had still not forgiven his brother for his insensitivity towards Rhiannon. At least, he noted, Huw had the grace to turn an uncomfortable pink around the ears.

'I'm just saying, there might not be much time.'

'And Rhiannon?' David demanded, rather more sharply than he had intended. 'Don't we at least owe her some consideration? Where do you think you and I would have ended up, if Rhiannon hadn't come to look after us?'

'There was Nainie.'

'Nainie had just had her first stroke. Don't you remember? It wasn't bad, not like the one she had later. But who knows if the stress of having to cope with us two and Plas Eden might not have brought on a second stroke much earlier? Especially with that idiot Edmund ranting on at us every week or so. Without Rhiannon, you and I could have ended up Lord-knows-where, and Nainie could have spent the rest of her life in an old people's home. We can't just take everything from under Rhiannon. Especially not so soon after Nainie. She needs a bit of time to adjust and get her life back together again.'

'I didn't say she should just be thrown out. We can always buy her a cottage. There are plenty for sale at the moment in Pont-ar-Eden. Or even Talarn.'

Why did Huw make it sound as if this was a bargain hunt? A case of let's pay off Auntie Rhiannon by beating down the price of a house to the lowest amount possible? And what, exactly, did he have in mind? Some pokey two-up, two-down terrace, with a cheap 1970s extension on the back and the smallest of gardens?

Despite being in the midst of a recession, the offer Beddows were proposing was astounding. Even when divided between them, it was still an eye-watering sum. And it wasn't as if Huw had done badly out of the estate by being the second son, as it was. There had been a considerable amount set aside in their father's will for Huw, more than enough for him to set up his first business and buy a substantial house.

For all he loved Plas Eden, there had been times over the

years – particularly in the throws of a hellishly knotty problem with difficult tenants in the estate's cottages, or attempting to keep control of builders – that it had crossed David's mind that Huw had been given the better deal. The thought never lasted long. Given all the money in the world, he would still not exchange it for Eden, with all its problems.

David looked at his brother. Huw had been staying with a pen-pal in France, the day Rhiannon came to tell them about Mum and Dad. It had been hard enough, David remembered all too well, being in the familiarity of Eden, with Nainie and Rhiannon a constant presence. Heaven knows what it must have been like for a seven-year-old boy among strangers having to make the flight back on his own, knowing that Rhiannon, and the whole reality of the thing, was waiting for him at Manchester airport.

No wonder, David acknowledged to himself, Huw had buried his feelings ever since. Until maybe even Huw no longer knew what his deepest emotions really were.

'I'm sure we can sort something out,' he added, in a slightly gentler tone. 'Come on, Rhiannon's painting Buddug's portrait in the courtyard. They'll both be ready for a cup of tea by now.'

❧

'You really think I should apply?' said Rhiannon, her pencil pausing in its scurry across the half-finished portrait in front of her, as she eyed her subject thoughtfully.

'Of course. Don't think; just go for it,' replied Buddug Parry, taking this pause in proceedings to give her shoulders a quick wriggle and stretch the arm resting on a large, plastic, and decidedly un-picturesque, plant pot.

Dressed in loose trousers, a light-blue linen jacket and a straw sunhat, her brown curls riotously loose around her shoulders,

Buddug was seated on the steps leading up to the fountain in Plas Eden's little courtyard, surrounded by pink and blue sweet peas and the ramblings of purple clematis. The pot was, in fact, perfectly in place, having been pressed into service as a temporary substitute for Hodge, who had grown tired of gazing lovingly into Buddug's eyes some twenty minutes ago (when the mini gravy bones ran dry) and was sprawled out in the last of the sunshine, excitably dreaming of squirrels.

'Artist-in-residence in an American college is bound to be popular.' Rhiannon put down her pencil and took a thoughtful sip of water. 'And with people who've got far more experience and reputation, both as painters and teachers. I can't see me having a chance in hell, to be honest.'

'Just put in your application and forget about it. Even if you only get shortlisted, it's good for the CV. If you don't try you'll never know, and with things as they are, and if Huw is still so set on selling the house, then you need to take any opportunity you can.'

'Yes, I suppose you're right,' said Rhiannon, with a rueful smile. 'I can't just sit here and wait to see what happens.' She glanced at her watch. 'Ten more minutes, if that's okay with you? Then I'll have enough to be able to get on with this.'

'Okay by me,' said Buddug, resuming her position. Hodge opened one eye at this movement, in case he was missing something. Something not appearing, he returned to The Mysterious Case of the Vanishing Squirrel, nose twitching furiously.

'I'm not convinced portraits are my strong point,' said Rhiannon, after a few minutes of rapid brushstrokes, standing back and eying her work critically.

'It looked good to me last time I saw it. And at least I don't have three heads or triangles for my nose.'

Rhiannon laughed. 'You're safe. The idea is to sell as many pictures as I can. Talarn Festival is hardly a hotbed of modern art.' She grimaced. 'But perhaps it was rather foolish, trying out something new, with my first big exhibition coming up.'

'You'll be fine,' said Buddug, firmly. 'People love your work. The craft shop in Beddgelert sold out of your watercolours within weeks, remember? They said they couldn't get enough of them.'

'That's true.' Rhiannon smoothed a harsh edge with her thumb, mind clearly elsewhere. 'If Huw does manage to persuade David, maybe Merlin Gwyn will buy Plas Eden after all, and turn it into a recording studio. I have a feeling Paul would have quite liked that idea.'

'I don't think he will,' said Buddug, frowning.

'From what I've seen, he seems pretty keen on developing that band he's starting with the village kids. The basement of his dad's old electrical shop isn't all that big. Somewhere to expand might be a logical next step.'

'Merlin has only promised he would provide investment if the village set up some kind of fund to take on Plas Eden. He would back a project to help the village but I really don't think he wants to have any closer involvement. It's a case of been there, done that, and wanting to lead the quiet life from now on. And besides it's not exactly the right atmosphere if your doctor has told you to stay off the drink and drugs. I really believe he means to leave it to the village to get on with the actual responsibility.'

'Oh.' Rhiannon put down her pencil. 'I think that's enough for one day.'

'May I see?'

'Of course. It's only very rough, remember.'

Buddug joined her in an instant. 'Oh!' she exclaimed.

Rhiannon eyed her uncertainly. 'That bad, eh?'

'Don't be daft Rhiannon, it's beautiful!' Buddug leant closer. The sketch showed a woman smiling out of the picture, an unmistakeable Hodge at her side, and a tangled profusion of flowers all around them. It could easily have been chocolate-box goo, but there was an energy to the rambling of the clematis and sweet peas, and – though Buddug said so herself – a down-to-earth, wrinkles, hips-and-all vitality to the central figure that made it simply, gloriously, a moment caught in time. 'And very you,' she added. 'You've got a distinctive style, you know. I'd know that was a Rhiannon Lloyd anywhere.'

'Mmm,' said Rhiannon, examining her work critically, and itching to have another go at getting the thing nearer to the perfect image in her mind's eye.

But at that moment there was an excited yelp from Hodge, who had abandoned dreaming at the sound of the front door opening and footsteps inside the house.

'Come on in!' called Rhiannon, as David and Huw arrived through the sunroom. No conversation; both with hands deep in pockets, Rhiannon noted. Never a good sign.

'I've put the kettle on,' said David, attending to Hodge, who was greeting him with the slow-swinging tail of abject adoration.

'Thank you, *cariad*,' replied Rhiannon, with a warm smile. 'Hello Huw, nice to see you. Come and sit down.'

'Hello, Auntie,' muttered Huw, kissing her in a slightly embarrassed fashion.

'How's the portrait going?' asked David, as they waited for the kettle to boil.

'Fine,' said Rhiannon.

'Absolutely brilliant,' added Buddug, watching the two men closely.

'Better than drawing the statues?'

'Definitely,' replied Rhiannon. 'I love them, and they are good to practise on, but portraits of portraits are never quite the same as making your own attempt from the original.'

'I like your sketches of the statues,' said David. 'I still think you should include them in the exhibition.'

'Maybe.' Rhiannon hesitated. 'And I suppose it was the statues that got me drawing again after I came to live here.'

'There you go,' said David, with a slightly forced cheerfulness that nobody could quite miss. 'They need to be included. Don't you think, Huw?'

'Of course,' murmured Huw.

Rhiannon sighed. 'It feels a bit disloyal, I suppose.'

'Disloyal?' Buddug asked her.

'Nainie never approved of Dad's obsession with the statues,' explained Huw, shortly.

'Really?' Buddug paused in removing her sun hat. 'Did she ever say why?'

Rhiannon shook her head. 'She never wanted to talk about them. At least, not after Paul and Marianne.' She glanced briefly at David who was bent over Hodge, fussing his ears, his face hidden. 'She almost seemed to blame the statues in some way.'

'Which is ridiculous,' snorted Huw under his breath.

'Eden's ghosts,' said Buddug, as if she hadn't heard.

'Exactly,' said David, without looking up. 'Plas Eden's ghosts. It seems there are plenty of those.'

❧

Night was beginning to fall as Rhiannon waved goodbye to Buddug at the edge of Plas Eden's grounds, where the lights of the village began.

'Come on, Hodge,' she said, taking a side path that led through a rusted gate and down into the little woodland next to the house.

All the time she had lived there she had never felt unease being alone within Plas Eden's grounds, even in darkness. Ancient pathways criss-crossed the estate, sending out a sense of security from the passing of many feet over the years. Those feet had not only belonged to the workers from the present house, but farmers from medieval villages making their way to market in the larger settlement on the banks of the Eden, more-or-less where Pont-ar-Eden stood now.

And before that, as Professor Humphries was fond of informing her, there had been centuries of more ancient travellers following trackways between clusters of roundhouses, each tiny, extended-family sized village, held within protective stone walls. Those trackways would have been old even then, was Gwynfor's guess, stretching back to hunter-gatherers on their long migration out of Africa, rippling out to form the human nations of the world in all their sameness and diversity.

And all of those people, Gwynfor was convinced, would still be able to recognise the landscape within Eden as their own. The woodlands, which had once covered the entire coast and the mountains up to their summits, had been cleared from the land around, but still remained within Eden's grounds.

Even the lake was a natural feature. It had been widened and deepened by David's great-grandfather, who had greatly improved the estate in the early part of the twentieth century, providing much-needed employment in the village after the ravages of the Great War. The widening had uncovered numerous Celtic swords and brooches and tiny figurines in the mud below, all long-ago offerings to forgotten gods, sent sinking beneath the waters with a memory or a prayer, like the flicking rows of tea lights left before the altar of a church. One particularly fine brooch was still on display in the British Museum in London, with the rest scattered around the National Museum in Cardiff and smaller collections.

A night breeze stirred the air as Rhiannon set off through the old stone arch, down past the fountain with its Venus just about holding her own amongst the moss and the ivy, to the glade where Eden's ghosts stood waiting. Around her the leaves shivered now and again as if waiting for something. Which was, as Huw would say, ridiculous. Maybe it had been the talk of Nainie that had unsettled her tonight. Along with the older ghosts of Paul and Marianne.

As they reached the little glade, Hodge growled, deep in his throat. A low, warning growl. Jolted from her thoughts, Rhiannon came to a halt. The breeze came again, stirring the leaves around her into a quiet, sighing rustle.

Down amongst the statues, something was moving. Hodge – never known for his bravery – let out a brief whine and pressed himself hard against her knee. The movement came again. A shadow next to Blodeuwedd, bending closer, as if to remove the trail of ivy from the statue's hair.

This time, the shadow stopped and seemed to turn towards them. Maybe Hodge's cowardice had been heard above the rustling of the leaves.

'Can I help you?' said Rhiannon, loud and bold. Humans she was not afraid of. And as for Eden's ghosts…

'Oh!' The woman's voice sounded just as freaked as the beating of her own heart. And reassuringly mortal. 'I'm sorry. I didn't mean to …'

Talk about ghosts.

'Carys?' said Rhiannon.

He did return, but I knew it could only be for a few days. One morning, as I approached the little office, he was there, sorting through papers. An advertisement had already been sent out to fill his post; it could well have been filled already. Nothing would be the same again.

He must have sensed me there, hesitating in the doorway. 'Good morning,' he said, looking up with that familiar smile of his.

'Good morning,' I replied. He was pale, and drawn. I had never seen anyone age so quickly. 'I am so sorry,' I said.

'Thank you.' He saw me still hesitating, not certain whether he wanted company or not. 'Come on in. There is so much to be done, and I'm rather in need of assistance.'

'Of course.'

The painting of Plas Eden had been taken down from the walls, I saw. It lay on the desk, already half wrapped in a soft cloth, ready to be packed away in the trunk at one side of the room.

He followed my eyes. 'My poor mother,' he said. 'She made that painting for my grandfather when she was a girl.' He sighed. 'She had been worried about my brother and his reckless actions this past year or more, but we never thought it would end like this. It's why I have to return,' he added, eying me earnestly. 'It's not just Plas Eden Caradoc put in jeopardy, but our business interests, too.'

'You mean the hospital?' I couldn't help it. Selfish alarm spread through me. I cursed every moment of my restlessness, as if it had of itself caused this.

'I'm afraid so. When we finally could make some sense of his affairs, it seems Caradoc had been reckless with more than just racing these new automobiles along mountain roads 'til he missed that corner. My poor mother has never taken much of an interest in the business side of the Meredith fortune. She has always been shut away in her own world, if not with her studies, then with her garden.' He caught my enquiring eye. 'My mother is a passionate student of ancient mythologies, when she is not working on ideas for her garden. Her father was a well-known scholar of Welsh folk traditions. He was even consulted by Lady Charlotte Guest when she was translating the Mabinogion.'

'Oh,' I said, blankly, Lady Guest and her subject being equally unknown to me.

'So, you see, I have no choice.' He had, it seemed, forgotten me once more. 'Either I return and take charge of the business and the house, or both the hospital and Plas Eden will be lost.' He rested his hand on the pile of papers in front of him. 'Although Heaven knows it is not a choice I would have taken. I hate the thought of starting something and not finishing it. Our observations will, I'm sure, help Mr Booth in his surveys of London life and labour, but there is so much more I would have wished to do.'

'There are poor and needy in the countryside, as well as in London,' I offered.

'Yes, that's true.' He gave a wry half-smile. 'Since nearly all the families in the village next to Plas Eden have someone or other working on the estate, I could hardly concentrate my energies here and leave them to their fate.'

'Oh,' I said. I had, it seemed, not given comfort, after all. Quite the reverse. I determined to say nothing at all.

We worked for the rest of the morning in silence, ensuring everything was tidy for the new inhabitant of his office.

'And what will you do?' he asked, suddenly.

I looked up from wrestling with a particularly dusty file. 'Do?'

'You seemed unsettled the last days I was here. I wondered …' The dust must have caught in his throat, as he coughed and bent over the letter in front of him. 'I wondered if you had tired of city life?'

'Me?' I knew I should have spun my story of returning to the countryside and my family and asked for a reference, there and then. 'Oh, not at all.'

'Good,' he muttered, still bending over his file. 'Matron – we all – value your work here.'

I looked at him curiously. I had been acting as under-housekeeper for the past year. Was Mrs Reevers about to retire and they were considering offering me the post? I could not imagine Mrs Reevers leaving, certainly not at such a moment, any more than Matron.

'I'm glad,' I murmured, for want of anything else to say. 'I don't know what I would have done had I not found this place,' I added.

He smiled. 'It seems we both did each other good.' His smile took my breath away, like a blow to the stomach.

'Yes,' I muttered, trying not to gasp for air like a drowning woman. I met his eyes briefly, and I knew I could not stay in that room another moment. Not while I still had enough sense to know that I would only add to his troubles.

And for me? I couldn't tell him, and especially not at that moment, that the Meredith Charity Hospital had given me back my taste for life. A broken heart I can live with. I've survived worse. And, despite what they tell you in stories, the breaks mend. Uncle Jolyon had been so busy telling me that the female sex was delicate, and always in need of guidance and protection, that he forgot to mention that women are the great survivors. I had survived. And since I had been at the Meredith Hospital I had seen women of all ages survive more pain and anguish, both of the body and the mind, than I could ever, in my former life, have imagined.

And besides, from what I had heard, Aunt Beatrice was surviving her widowhood in positively spectacular fashion, travelling the world on the proceeds of his estate. I hoped there was a heaven for Uncle Jolyon to look out of and take note.

And, whatever it cost me, I was not about to take that long, lonely road towards the river once more.

Chapter Eight

♣ 'I didn't mean to intrude,' said Carys, stepping hastily away from the statue of Blodeuwedd, mortified at being discovered lurking in Eden's grounds this way. And by Rhiannon, of all people.

Carys could feel herself growing hot. Rhiannon probably saw her as some mad stalker, on route to peer through Eden's windows, desperate to throw herself at David Meredith and end up as mistress of Plas Eden at last.

'You're not intruding.' Rhiannon's voice was cool, but not unfriendly. 'You're always welcome to Eden, Carys. Why don't you come up to the house? Come and join me in a cup of tea. Or a glass of wine, maybe?'

She was just being polite, Carys told herself. It was the sort of thing people said but didn't really mean. Especially not to potential stalkers.

'I'm so sorry,' she murmured, 'but I'm afraid I can't. I only left Mam for a few minutes, to get milk. I must get back before her film ends.'

'Of course.' Rhiannon's voice was even, showing no sign of either relief or disappointment. 'And how is Mair?'

This, Carys thought, was decidedly surreal, standing in the near-dark having a slightly stilted social exchange with Rhiannon, while the statues loomed up around them.

'Oh, she's okay. Getting better slowly.'

'And driving you crazy?' Rhiannon's tone warmed. She had, Carys recalled, looked after an old lady for years and must know better than most just how exasperating it could be. And that didn't mean you didn't love your charge, or feel for her pain and frustration. But the accompanying sensation of your own life being irrevocably sucked away could, at times, be unbearable.

There was so much about her life with Mam that Carys couldn't quite explain to anyone. Not to Gwenan, who took her periodic exasperation as a sign she wasn't coping and instantly offered all kinds of long-distance advice. Not to Nia, who took Carys' worries about Mam trying to get up the stairs when she wasn't looking, completely to heart and burst instantly into tears.

At least with Rhiannon she didn't have to pretend everything was just fine, and her halo was growing by the day, for fear of sounding like an undutiful daughter and an utter bitch.

'Totally,' she replied, with feeling.

Rhiannon gave a sympathetic chuckle. 'Tell me about it. Don't get me wrong, I loved Nainie to bits, but there were times she completely did my head in. It's being locked together in a small space going over the same things again and again with someone who's bored and frustrated, and often a little frightened. It'll be better when your mam can get out more. I always used to find that Nainie was much better when there was something to occupy her, and take her out of herself.'

'That's true.' Carys smiled. 'I was thinking of taking Mam along to the history group in the Boadicea. She's never been much into family history, but I thought she might enjoy it now.' She cleared her throat. She liked Rhiannon, for all she had always been slightly unnerved by the older woman's bold dress sense and her directness. She didn't want to be thought some sad woman still obsessing about Plas Eden and the past. 'That's what made me come here, when she started talking about the statues.'

'Oh?' Rhiannon's voice was tense in the encroaching darkness.

'Just her memories of them,' explained Carys hastily. 'I suppose it just got me thinking that she might enjoy finding out more about them.'

'There's the new history group that meets in the Boadicea,' said Rhiannon, the wariness easing just a little. 'They're concentrating on the history of the village for now, but Professor Humphries has been talking about doing more about the statues in a couple of months' time.'

'That's good to know, it might help Mam to start going. I'm sure if they begin to find out more about the statues…' From inside her bag, Carys' mobile rang out its tinny little jingle. 'Hell.' She scrabbled for it amongst the depths. Her mobile number was the first in the speed dial on the house phone, and was stuck in large figures to the wall.

But it was not Mam. The little screen announced that was Joe's mobile. Carys allowed it to go onto voicemail, and stashed the phone in her pocket. 'I'm sorry, Rhiannon, I really have to go.'

'Why don't you come up one day, and bring Mair with you?' said Rhiannon, as Carys turned to go. 'It would be nice to catch up again while you're in Pont-ar-Eden.'

'That would be lovely, thanks,' murmured Carys, awkwardly. Was this Rhiannon being polite again?

'How about this weekend?'

Carys blinked. 'I'm afraid it's Mam's birthday. Gwenan and Nia are coming down. We're taking her out for a meal.'

'Oh, right.'

They could leave it like that. A vague friendly overture of an invitation that in reality didn't have to be taken up by either side.

The breeze was stirring again, setting the branches swaying with a gentle, almost melancholy sighing. Around them, the statues loomed in the darkness, silent and still.

'But they'll be gone by Sunday night,' added Carys, without quite meaning to.

'Okay.' At least Rhiannon didn't sound dismayed or instantly start finding her own excuses. 'So why don't you come to supper next Thursday? That'll give Mair a couple of days rest in between. Why don't you come around four, say, then you can have a good look around, and Mair can get herself settled. We can eat early, and you can get home before she gets too tired.'

'That sounds great,' said Carys. 'Thank you. We'd like that.' There had been no mention of David. Maybe he was away. Maybe she wouldn't have to meet him. Carys found her heart doing a quick back-flip, followed by a sinking sensation, just like a stone. Neither of which, she told herself firmly, made any sense at all.

'I'll look forward to it,' Rhiannon was saying, clipping the lead on Hodge, to prevent any following of the visitor.

'See you on Thursday, then,' replied Carys, making her way hastily back along the little track, towards the village.

❧

'I got it!' cried Joe, picking up immediately she returned his call. He must be in a bar. The beat of music and the sound of laughter made its way in from the background.

'What did you get?' asked Carys, making her way as fast as she could through the half-deserted streets of Pont-ar-Eden.

'The job,' he returned, just slightly impatiently.

'The job?'

'The partnership. Constantine and Hutchinson.' The triumph in his voice was unmistakeable.

Constantine and Hutchinson? They were huge. International. Global, even. She didn't know they had an office in Chester. 'Congratulations,' she said, slowly. 'When did this happen?'

'Today. This afternoon, in fact. We're going out to celebrate. They're paying for me to stay over.'

'Over?' Her brain seemed to have stopped working.

'Hotel.' He was practically purring. 'Big one. Posh one. Just off Oxford Street.'

'Oh.' A couple of drunks pushed past her, swaying in a good-natured manner as she turned off the High Street and towards Willow Cottage. Her heart was beginning to beat fast, and there was a strange taste in her mouth. 'So it's based in London then?'

'Yes, of course. They're like, massive, Cari. A real step up.' He lowered his voice. 'Pay's not that bad, either. Housing's expensive, of course. But, despite the downturn, we'll still have made a bit on the flat. That'll help.'

'What?'

The disbelief in her voice seemed to have got through to him. 'Yeah; right mate. Coming now,' he said, loudly, in his manly 'we're-all-mates-together' tone, that always irritated the hell out of her, to someone in the room behind him. Whether this was a fictional someone or not, Carys was too blindingly on a mission to throttle him to care. 'Sorry, Cari, got to go. The restaurant's booked for half an hour, and you know what the traffic's like.'

'You can't just–'

'Sorry. Got to go. Love you. Speak soon.'

And, with a click, he was gone.

Cari's fingers itched towards the redial, and a no-holds-barred, just-what-do-you-think-you-are-playing-at text. Although apart from the word 'bastard' she couldn't at this moment think of anything else to say. Besides which she had reached the door of Willow Cottage to the closing music of Mam's film sneaking between the double-glazing.

'I didn't know you'd been out,' said Mam, emerging from the loo, with much flushing, as Cari pulled the front door closed behind her.

'Remember, I was going to get milk, Mam.' Carys waved the carton, thanking heaven she had at least had the presence of mind to shoot into Low-Price before talking to Joe.

'Oh. Right. That wasn't a criticism,' said Mam. 'Nice walk?'

'Lovely, thanks,' said Cari, trying to sound cheerful. This was not self-sacrifice. She and Mam had never been particularly close, and definitely not close enough to share all her inner secrets with.

Besides, Mam was of the old school. A man is there to do his thing, and it's a woman's lot to compromise, was Mam's idea of a long and successful union. She might not entirely approve of Joe, but that was probably only because he hadn't placed a ring on her daughter's finger and swept her off to Hawaii for two weeks' honeymoon. She would certainly take Joe's part now.

Mam's idea of marriage was fine for someone born in the 1940s, but it had been enough to put Carys off the subject for life. Which was possibly why she had taken it as a reassuring trait in Joe that he had never particularly been into marriage either. At the time it had seemed like the meeting of minds.

Now it unmistakably held the hollow sound of options being left open.

'I've had a call from work,' she said. Which was easier than the truth.

'Oh?' Mam looked nervous.

'Nothing serious,' Carys reassured her hastily. 'I just need to go back to Chester for a couple of meetings this week. How about if we see if Gwenan can come a bit earlier for your birthday and stay with you, while I'm away?'

'Don't worry about me, dear. I'll be fine on my own.'

Yeah. Right. Like leaving the gas on unlit and deciding now was a good time to try those stairs.

'I think Gwenan would feel happier,' replied Carys. 'And Nia. And we don't want them to think I'm not looking after you, do we?'

'Oh, no. Of course not.' Mam patted Carys' hand in a comforting manner. 'You've been wonderful and looked after me so well, *cariad*. And I know you have your own life, and you can't keep on doing this forever.'

'I'll only be away for a day, Mam.'

'Right.' Mam looked relieved.

'I'll go and phone Gwenan then,' said Carys, before Mam could change her mind.

ে৩

The return to Chester was disorientating. Not least because over the past few weeks Carys had grown so used to organising her life around Mam that just being in the car on her own threw her completely. Even though her mind was filled with thoughts of Joe and what she was going to say to him, she found herself automatically glancing at her watch to see how

150

much time she had left, or checking the passenger seat to see if Mam were comfortable and not feeling tired or sick and not saying anything.

And when it finally sank in that Mam wasn't there, she began to make lists. Shopping. Which bits of cleaning to be fitted into Mam's next nap. Which accounts for Tylers were the most urgent to be tackled when Mam went to bed, and really she should make the spare room into a proper office so she didn't waste time trying to find things. What on earth was she going to cook that didn't include cod and parsley, and was a mild curry just too exotic, and how did you make a curry anyhow, and could she find a good recipe on the internet as Mam's cookbooks came from the dark ages (Marguerite Patten and Delia excluded, of course), and hadn't she ever heard of Jamie Oliver?

It was only as the Polo made its way up the twisting little road from Beddgelert and past Snowdon – Carys having taken the scenic route in the hope it might calm her down and give herself time to think before facing Joe – that it finally sank in she had no responsibilities for Mam for at least twenty-four hours. In a spirit of rebellion, she stopped at the viewing point at the side of the road. She bought an ice cream from the van waiting patiently for passing tourists and sat on a rock for a few minutes looking out over the curve of Snowdon rising high above her.

Despite her dread of what the next few hours might bring, it was nice just to be herself, with no demands made on her at all. A precious luxury, in fact. 'I'll never, ever take this for granted, ever again,' she promised herself, as she crunched the end of the cone, and, with a heavy heart, set off once more.

☙

She had promised herself that she would be calm and reasonable. Well, that didn't last long. She hadn't been back in the flat for an hour before the arguments began.

'Of course I'm pleased for you,' she found herself saying, in uninhibited exasperation. 'And it's a brilliant opportunity, and of course you have to take it. I just wished you'd discussed it with me first.'

Joe was frowning at her. 'So it's okay for you to swan off to spend a couple of months with your mother, but not for me to have a career.'

'No, of course not! I've never said that. And anyhow, we discussed me going to look after Mam.'

'Not that it would have made any difference.'

Ouch.

'But she's my mother,' said Carys, feeling her temper rise. 'She was in trouble. It's what human beings do for each other. And anyhow, she's much better already: it's only for a few more weeks.'

'But you were quite happy to put her first.'

Carys stared at him. Was that what this was all about? Was this some kind of punishment for her perceived disloyalty? 'For a few weeks. Not for the rest of my life, Joe.'

There was a moment's silence. At last Joe looked up, the warmth back in his eyes. 'It'll be brilliant, Cari. A new start.'

'But I thought the idea was to move out of the city, into the countryside. Set up our own business.'

'Oh, we can still do that.' Joe was pleased. He'd obviously thought this through. 'Look, on what I'll be getting, we'll be able to afford a flat in London and a holiday home in the countryside. Sorted.'

'A *holiday* home?' Not a smallholding. Not a business. A playground. A Marie Antoinette playfarm to keep the little woman happy while he got on with his brilliant career in the real world. He'd got it worked out, all right. 'I'm not sure I want to live in London,' she added slowly.

'Oh, you'll be fine once we're there. Just you see.'

Carys watched him, feeling a huge gulf open up in front of her. This wasn't about her at all. This was what Joe wanted. And what Joe wanted, she must want too. He was listening to her words, but he no longer heard. It was like coming up against a brick wall. The wall of Joe's vision for their future. The world according to Joe.

Panic shot through her, catching her unawares. An old, strangely familiar panic. A feeling of standing on a precipice, about to be absorbed into someone else's life, someone else's passion. And knowing that if she did so, however much she struggled, she would have no existence at all.

'I'll put the kettle on,' she muttered, making her way into the kitchen. Her hands were shaking.

Maybe this moment would always have come. And better now, than when they had children between them. She'd known this in her heart for months – maybe years. Why had she never fully faced it before? She'd heard some of her married friends complain that it was always they who made the compromises, and been impatient at their lack of backbone. So she could hardly complain now she was faced with her own choice.

This time she was a woman in her thirties, not an eighteen-year-old girl whose life was about to begin, with a university to go to, who could just pack her rucksack and run.

'So you'll give it a try?' Joe said, making his way over to the fridge to get milk.

'I thought you liked the idea of living in the country and setting up our own business.'

'It was a nice idea.'

153

'Was?'

'Things change, Cari.'

She glanced at him. When she'd first met Joe, they'd been fresh out of college, raring and ready to go with their new careers. They'd both escaped backgrounds of few prospects and few choices. A good life had been their mutual ambition. A nice home, along with money for theatres and concerts and the ability to jet off on a whim to see places their parents had never even dreamed of.

They'd worked hard and played hard, and it had worked so well for all the time they had been together. Of course, during the past couple of years there had been less money, with a last-minute booking for a few days in Tuscany and Morocco, rather than weeks spent scaling the heights of Machu Picchu or the jungle temples of Angkor Wat. But that was only a stage and an investment in a more personally rewarding future, so temporary and worth it.

Now she could see that forty had begun to loom over Joe's horizon. The skinny youth she'd first known had gone, settling down towards a more solid middle age. Why had she never noticed before the way the flexibility had eased from his face, defining itself into more permanent lines?

Was that what was happening to her, too? Was she just being inflexible and settled in her ways? The comfort of a long weekend in the hotel in Florence last September had seemed so much more appealing than a trek through yet another heat-steaming jungle, or balancing on overcrowded trains with a basket of chickens at her feet and her rucksack on her back, for all Joe had complained of a weekend in a 4-star hotel being 'tame'. Was that her getting old? More tied to her creature comforts? Less adventurous? Or maybe she was just a woman who always ran when faced with difficult decisions.

She took a deep breath. 'And if I don't like the idea of living in London?'

'You haven't tried it.' His logic was immoveable. 'How can you reject something you haven't even tried?'

'Do you think I don't know my own mind?'

'Well, how can you tell unless you've tried it?'

'But I do know. I know I don't want a city life. That's why I changed career and went back to college. We discussed it, remember? Living without all the backbiting of the management structure. Being our own boss, so we don't have to work our guts out just so someone else can get rich beyond our wildest dreams. We discussed it. We thought it through. We were prepared to make sacrifices. I thought that's what you wanted, too.'

'It was a nice idea,' he repeated. 'But this is the real world, Cari.'

The real world. Power lunches and bonuses. A guided tour of the Taj Mahal each summer and a new Porsche every year. Was that the real world?

And her world? Her world at this moment? The world with Mam, working out the intricacies of relationships; the looking back at your own childhood and the things that made you. Finding a way to face the future, the future of old age that lies ahead for all of us, one day, with courage and dignity. The things that make you human. Was that truly nothing to do with the real world at all?

Not for Joe. Finally, she understood. That was the world Joe's sisters would always take care of. The world that Joe would never have to face at all. The world he would never acknowledge even existed.

A desperate sense of loneliness filled her.

'It can be more lonely being with someone than being on

your own,' Poppy had once declared, one drunken night, long before Stuart, when yet another disastrous relationship had crashed and burned, in Poppy's usual spectacular fashion.

The choice was hers, Cari knew. She could try, yet again, to make him see her point of view, and attempt another compromise. But they'd been through that before, and she'd sworn to herself that if it failed she would not do it again: there was no point. That left her with only two choices: to go with Joe's world, or walk away.

Logic said there was only one choice. Her sense of self-preservation said there was only one choice.

But her heart said it didn't want to make a choice at all.

Chapter Nine

Willow Cottage was out-and-out spotless by the time Carys made her dispirited return from Chester in time for Mam's birthday.

'Go okay?' asked Gwenan, as Carys let herself in.

'Fine,' replied Carys, trying to sound cheerful.

'Nice trip?' said Mam, eying her with unusual sharpness.

'Lovely,' replied Carys mechanically. 'Happy Birthday, *Penblwydd Hapus*, Mam.'

'Well, I don't see what the fuss is about,' said Mam, who had always made a virtue of never putting herself first. 'When you get to my age, every birthday is much like the rest.'

'Nonsense,' said Gwenan, who had a habit of taking things literally. 'This is *your* day, and we're all going to spoil you. Nia phoned as they were leaving Oswestry, so they should be here any minute. The table at the Llewellyn isn't booked until half past one. We've plenty of time. Presents first.'

'I'll just go and change,' said Carys, escaping upstairs as quickly as she could.

Nia and her family arrived shortly afterwards, bearing an oversized card and a large parcel wrapped in glossy pink paper. The parcel contained a fluffy dressing gown, with matching slippers, along with a large box of Mam's favourite chocolates.

'Lovely, thank you, darling,' said Mam, stroking the softness of the dressing gown as she placed them on top of the sets of towels and duvet covers given to her by Gwenan, along with several bottles of her favourite sherry.

Carys handed over her own offering with a slight feeling of trepidation. The two large black folders, under a box of chocolates, sat for a moment in their mother's lap.

'Photograph albums,' said Mam, slowly riffling through the pages.

'They're empty,' said Gwenan, frowning slightly.

'They're for Mam to fill up herself,' explained Carys.

'Ah, how sweet,' sighed Nia. 'I keep on telling Sam we shouldn't just keep ours on the computer. We hardly ever look at them. A proper photograph album is much better.'

Mam looked up. Her eyes were twinkling with more life than Cari had seen in ages. 'I meant to sort out our pictures ages ago, but somehow I never had time. And I never did like going up into the attic, even when your dad was alive.'

'You should have said,' exclaimed Gwenan. 'Charles would have gone up for you, or one of the boys, if only you'd asked.'

Mam smiled. 'There's really no need, dear. Carys has been marvellous. She's been looking out the old photographs up in the spare room. You found a whole lot more the other day, didn't you, *cariad*? It's so nice to see them all again. Lots of them I'd totally forgotten about. They're in the boxes next to the sofa. We're still sorting them out. Bring that top one over, Carys, I'm sure your sisters would like to see.'

'Yes, Mam.'

'Some of those look really old,' said Gwenan at the appearance of an ancient shoebox. She turned back from the window that opened out into the garden, where the men-folk had been left entertaining four slightly grumpy teenagers for whom terminal boredom had already – and loudly – set in. 'Half of them are falling to bits.'

158

'I'm going to scan the really fragile ones into my laptop,' explained Carys. 'And I'll be able to touch up the worst ones.'

'Well, if you've got the time. Sounds like a big job to me,' said Gwenan, dubiously. 'No you can't go to the shops,' she snapped to her offspring through the open window. 'I told you; we're going to take Grandma out for a birthday lunch in a few minutes.'

'I think it's a really sweet idea,' said Nia. 'Are there lots of us when we were little?'

'Quite a few. We're sorting them out at the moment, aren't we, Mam? The three of us when we were small will go into one book, and then we're going to put any really old ones, before we were born, in another.'

'Oh,' said Nia. 'Where are the ones with the three of us, then?'

'Here, in these.' Carys handed her a box that had once held reams of paper, now stuffed to the brim with curling prints.

'I bet we look funny,' said Nia, sheafing through. 'Oh look! Mam, how could you wear a coat like that?'

'They were all the rage,' said Mam mildly.

'Here we are.' Nia pulled out a small selection in triumph. 'Oh my goodness, wasn't I just so fat!'

'Nonsense, dear. You were a lovely looking little girl. Everyone said so.'

Nia smiled and turned to the rest of the photographs. 'I remember those picnics on Talarn beach, Mam. My goodness, don't we look wrapped up! Dad used to love taking photographs, didn't he?'

'Your grandfather had a photographic studio, you know,' said Mam, smiling down fondly at the dog-eared prints. 'The Merediths set him up with it, when he retired from being head gardener.'

Carys looked up in surprise. 'I didn't know that.'

'Oh, yes. On Pont-ar-Eden High Street, it was. There used to be so many shops there. You could do all your shopping without leaving the village, and everyone was so friendly. Not like going to the supermarket today. Your dad used to work there when he was young, when he wasn't working at Plas Eden. Of course, I didn't know him then. He was so much older than me, you see. He still did weddings and portraits, on and off, when you were all small, when he wasn't driving the taxi.' Her eyes took on a faraway gaze. 'I think he'd have liked to have been a famous photographer, like David Bailey, or Lord Snowdon. But he had us to support, and times were hard in those days.'

'There aren't any really old ones here,' said Nia, who had reached the bottom of the box. 'I'm sure there used to be some ancient ones Dad used to show us. People in really old clothing. And there was a carriage, a proper one, with horses, right in front of Plas Eden.'

'Yes, that's right, *cariad*,' said Mam. 'I'd forgotten about those. They must still be up in the attic. There are lots of things up there of your dad's. I always meant to sort them out,' she added, a little sadly. 'I expect your grandfather's photographs are still there. Photographs were really special things, in those days. Your grandfather took up photography when it was out of the reach of the pockets of most people.'

'Exactly,' said Gwenan, nodding. 'Being head gardener would have been a really good job in those days. The butler and the head gardener were the most important members of staff in places like Plas Eden. The equivalent of senior managers in a large firm today.'

'Would they really have been that important?' Carys, who hadn't given the matter any thought, was dubious.

'Oh, yes.' Gwenan was firm. 'The head gardener would have had dozens of men under him. They didn't just grow flowers in those days, you know. He'd have been responsible for making sure Plas Eden had enough food grown throughout the year. And things like pineapples and grapes that were really exotic and hard to grow. Dad used to tell me about it.' Her face had softened with memory. 'He was really proud of the connection, you know?'

'Oh,' said Carys. Silence had fallen in the little room.

Gwenan cleared her throat. 'Time to think about moving, don't you think? Or we're going to be late for that booking.'

℘

By the time Gwenan and Nia left for the hotel in Talarn that evening, families dutifully in tow, Mam was completely worn out and fast asleep in her armchair in front of *Coronation Street*.

Quietly, so as not to disturb her, Carys hooked down the ladder to the loft and clanged her way upwards, the biggest torch she could find in her hands. She was tired herself, after a few fitful hours of sleep on Poppy's sofa last night, followed by the drive home and then keeping up the appearance of cheerfulness throughout the day. But Mam hadn't half perked up since the appearance of those first photographs, so probably best not to lose momentum now.

And besides, she'd done enough thinking and feeling for half a lifetime over the past twenty-four hours. Time to keep herself busy. That's how Mam had dealt with grief when Dad had died. Joe wasn't dead, of course: but after that last sniping, warts and all row, there was no going back to the way things had been before. Some things can be said that clear the air and make a relationship stronger, Cari had discovered. After some, there is no way back. Last night was definitely the no-way-back variety.

Tomorrow, she would pick herself up, dust herself down, agree with Joe that the only thing that could be done was to put the flat on the market as soon as possible, hold her head high and get on with her life. Wherever that might take her. Which was mightily scary, starting off from scratch once more.

'This time, I'm in charge. And I'm going to do things my way,' she muttered to herself, placing the torch on a rafter and pulling herself up into the attic.

It hadn't changed since she was a child. She could swear some of the boxes were the same. Once she located the switch in the darkness, a shadeless bulb illuminated the long, sloping space. Bare rafters rose above her, with equally bare rafters below her feet. Taking care not to put a foot wrong and end up through the ceiling below, Carys made her way to the centre of the light, and looked around her.

Dad had been a hoarder and Mam had never had the heart to throw anything away, instead adding items of her own bit by bit. For a good twenty minutes, Carys was waylaid by cardboard boxes filled to overflowing with school reports and exercise books. A tin trunk opened to reveal games and toys she had almost forgotten, but which now came back to her with memories of sitting round the fire at Christmas, or up in Gwenan's bedroom on wet afternoons, obeying Gwenan's ordering of the doll's house Dad had made from bits of plywood, with the Sindys and the Barbies and the Tiny Tears all marshalled into their respective positions.

She peered through old curtains, a complete tea set that had never seen the light of day (and thank goodness, the psychedelic sixties pattern in brown and orange was enough to make your

162

stomach churn), along with glass ice cream dishes, old pots and pans and broken bits of table, and a truly hideous vase, of the kind that never breaks however hard you try.

She paused for a few minutes over her old rag doll: bald, threadbare and with one arm hanging off. Suzie was placed on a select pile of 'don't let Gwenan or Nia get their hands on this', along with her own school reports and the medal she'd won for swimming.

Grasping the torch and feeling her way gingerly along the rafters, Carys made her way into the deepest, darkest recesses of the loft, where logic told her the oldest of Dad's hoardings were likely to be found. The first box she came across held magazines, old and yellowing. The next, ancient copies of the *Beano*. Probably worth a small fortune to a collector.

The third was a shoebox stuffed full of old photographs. Carys peered at the first few in the dim light given out by the electric bulb and the beam of her torch. They were black and white, and definitely older than the family ones taken by Dad that she had found in the spare room. These had been taken in the thirties or the forties, judging by the clothes.

Some were of aunts and uncles Carys faintly remembered, with a whiff of egg mayonnaise sandwiches and salad cream on long, crisp sheaves of Cos lettuce, brought in straight from the garden. Others bore a family resemblance to herself that made the hairs on the back of her neck begin to stir. All people who had lived their lives in a time that looked straight out of a history book with its ancient cars and empty roads, and the formal cut of suits and coats of a way of life unimaginable to Carys now.

And yet each one was part of her. Shared blood flowed through their veins. It was a belonging to the world that Carys had never felt before.

Weird. Very weird. It gave her a sudden hunger to know more.

'So that's the fascination of family trees,' she said aloud, the excitement at the Boadicea suddenly falling into place, along with all the books, DVDs, magazines and TV programmes. All that geeky, trainspotting, hunting down of birth certificates and death certificates and middle names that told one John Jones and one Jane Williams from another.

Very Important People have history: that was the history she had been taught at school. From the Bible downwards, come to that. All that begetting that went on for pages and pages to prove a bloodline and who's dad did what to whom. All politics and battles and poisonings, as far as Carys could see. And – Queen Elizabeth and Boadicea apart – nothing for girls at all.

This kind of history – real history – that was another matter. In the hope that this was only the start, Carys put them to one side, and moved on towards the wall at the far end.

The full-sized pram parked there was of the boneshaker variety, and probably a collector's item too. It was filled with more magazines, more shoeboxes of tin cars and broken necklaces.

'Dratted magazines,' she muttered in exasperation, lifting them up and placing them with less than her usual care on an adjoining rafter. 'Ouch!' Something square and wooden that had been sitting patiently beneath the pile toppled off its rafter and banged on the board of the ceiling. Carys caught at it quickly, terrified the edges might break through into the room below. It looked like a box made out of shiny dark wood. A medium-sized rectangular box. And yet not a box.

'Bloody hell!' Carys' mind cleared in an instant. It was a camera. A very old, very precious camera. It was a folding box

164

camera. Of the wet collodion method. Or was that the dry? Carys' idea of early photographic methods was a tad vague. She was more of the digital variety herself. But Dad had hauled them around enough museum cabinets showing the history of photography for her to recognise this as one of the first portable cameras. The kind that ladies and gentlemen of Victorian and Edwardian times could take out into the field to take photos on the spot without dragging an entire studio with them.

She lifted it up, slowly. Even in the light of the distant bulb and her torch, she could see it was beautifully made.

'Carys? Carys, are you up there?'

She jumped, nearly toppling over. 'I'm just in the loft. Down in a minute, Mam,' she called.

'Well, you be careful, *cariad*. There are all sorts of things up there.'

'Yes, Mam.' Carys flashed the torch carefully in the corner of the eaves where the camera had been wedged. She pushed aside a pile of papers and placed the camera as far back as she could under the narrowest part of the eaves. Sure enough, there was something else in the far corner. A wooden box. Another camera, maybe?

'I'll put the kettle on, then, shall I, *cariad*?'

'Yes please, Mam. I'm coming now.' She lifted the box until it was resting next to her. A small catch held it shut. Carys opened it. Not a camera, then. Just a box. A strange musky smell with a sharp chemical edge, almost like vinegar gone stale, floated up towards her. Even in the light of the torch she could see the prints were sepia in colour, rather than black and white. It was of a group of men and women posed rather stiffly on the front steps of Plas Eden. From their dress, she guessed it was Victorian, or Edwardian, at the latest, and not the ladies and gentlemen of the family, but the servants who kept the place running.

Underneath, there were more. A young girl in a maid's uniform bending to smell a rose. A horse and carriage, with the driver standing to attention at the side of his horse. A young man posing with a wheelbarrow. Carys' heart began to race. Despite the ominous sounds from the kitchen of cupboards being opened and the kettle boiling furiously, she couldn't resist pulling out another, this time of a group in the garden. Young men, old men. And right at the centre, smartly dressed and looking very conscious of his status, Carys looked down into features that had just a touch of Dad about the eyes.

'Mam!' she called. 'Mam, you've just got to see what I've found!'

'Very well, *cariad*. Have we got any of those teacakes left?'

'We finished them yesterday,' Carys called back. 'But I'm sure there are some in the freezer. Second shelf, I think? I'll come and get them now. And there's the rest of the birthday cake Gwenan brought.'

She pressed the photographs into the box and began fitting on the lid. In her haste, she missed a couple. One was a postcard, tucked in amongst the larger prints. Cary grabbed it as it fell. It was old, like the photographs. A square, rather forbidding-looking mansion looked out from between a formal arch of trees. The other was a print, which was floating down to the rafters at her feet, where it landed, face up.

It was the eyes that caught her attention. Sharp, arresting eyes. Carys crouched down and shone the torch on the image. It was a woman with her hair piled on the top of her head, wearing a long skirt and loosely swathed in a kind of apron that appeared to cover her from chest to ankles. Not a beautiful face. Not even a handsome face. Much, much too well lived-in and too striking to be called either. Skin settled tight over the prominent bones, sculpturing her features around the large eyes. She looked out at the viewer, clear-eyed, as if to challenge any who might choose to judge. Her right hand was resting on a wooden table, fingers curled around an instrument of some kind, the other resting lightly on the shoulder of a small child.

'Kettle's boiled.'

'Coming!' Carys stared at the photograph. The photograph stared back at her. The woman she had never seen before, but the child – Carys' scalp was prickling, as if she had landed, head first, on a bed of sea urchins. She knew that face. Given the age of the pictures, the woman must be long dead. Most probably the child, too. And yet she knew the smile on that impish little face, and the eyes that gazed out boldly at the viewer, displaying none of the wariness of the adult. The feeling was so vivid it seemed to take Carys over completely.

'Have you seen the bread, *cariad*?' Mam must be getting really hungry.

'In the breadbin, Mam.'

'Oh, so it is. Silly me. I'll put some on, then, shall I?'

'It's okay: I'm on my way. It'll only take a second to find those teacakes.'

Carys placed the photograph back in the box, pushed the camera hastily behind a stash of magazines until she had a chance to retrieve it and, tucking the photographs under her arm, made her way back downstairs.

There was one more day to live through, and then he would be gone and I would never see him again.

We were all quiet that day, I think. He was well-liked among the staff, and he was the familiar face of the Meredith Charity

Hospital. And for more than one, the fear of the unknown was creeping in at the prospect of the new manager starting tomorrow.

For me, I wished that day gone as quickly as it could be. Parting might be such sweet sorrow for Juliet in the play, but I had no wish to prolong the pain. I wanted it finished. Now. So that he could go to his new life in Plas Eden, and I could lick my wounds in private. I'd live. Heaven knows how; but I'd live.

As the day drew to its end, I kept myself employed, waiting for the inevitable summons. He had made time for a personal word of farewell with all the members of staff. I had watched them going in, and coming out again, with tears in their eyes and clutching a small gift. I was speaking to Matron in the hallway, when the message came that Mr Meredith wished to speak to me.

'Well, then. Hurry along,' said Matron, watching me with a smile. A knowing kind of a smile: one that had me flustered as I made my way towards the familiar office. This was not exactly what I had intended. Calm. Professional. Grateful. Full of good wishes for his future. Not with my blood banging in my ears like a drum.

'Come on in,' he said, looking up with a smile as I knocked on the open door.

I don't know what else he said. The usual things, I imagine. How he had appreciated my work for the hospital and wished me well for the future. I just knew I had to get myself out of there, as quickly as could be. And finally he reached into a drawer at one side of his desk, and brought out a large wooden box.

'I wasn't certain what kind of supplies you might need,' he said, a little awkwardly, placing the box on the desk. 'So I have given you the best selection I could find. Brushes. Pencils. Colours. And paper, of course.'

'Thank you,' I said. My voice sounded reasonably steady. Now I could make my escape. 'I will make good use of them.' I reached towards the box, my hands resting on either side, my head bent as the blinding of tears finally came.

'Don't go.' His hands were suddenly warm, resting on mine.

'I must,' I said, quickly. 'Matron–' But his hands tightened, extinguishing the lie.

'I should have found the courage before,' he said.

'Courage?' I looked up at him.

'To beg you to come with me. To Eden.'

I pulled myself free. I should have played outraged virtue and fled, knowing his dignity would not allow him to chase me through the hospital for all to see. But instead, like a fool, I wavered. 'I can't,' I muttered, feebly.

'Now I've offended you.'

'No.'

I saw him flush slightly. 'I didn't mean – you must forgive me, I'm not accustomed … how could I have been so clumsy?'

His distress caught me off my guard. Before I could help myself, I smiled. And that was enough. He was at my side in a moment, my hands clasped once again in his. 'I'm not very good at this. But I can't let you go. Not like this. I love you. And I cannot face the thought of a life without you. And I thought, I hoped, and especially during these past few days…'

I murmured something, trying to pull myself free. But his grasp was firm. 'No, please hear me out,' he said. 'What I am trying, in my poor clumsy way to say – to ask – is for you to marry me. To return with me as my wife. As mistress of Plas Eden.'

I shut my eyes. Every part of my being willed to say 'yes'. To be with him forever.

'I can't,' I whispered. 'You don't know me. You don't know who I am.'

'I know you,' he replied, in a voice so gentle it nearly broke my heart. 'I know all I ever need to know about you.'

I shook my head.

'Then tell me.'

I looked at him. How could I tell him?

How could I tell him that I could not bear to watch the love die from his eyes and his face turn away from me? How could I tell him that it was not my life alone I was keeping safe in my silence? And that I might be careless of myself, but there was one I would kill to keep from harm, and that the hands that had thrust those coins so carefully deep into the safety of my pockets, and had given me life when all hope was lost, were ones I would never betray.

How could I tell him?

'You don't know me,' I said. 'You don't know who I am, or what I have done. You don't know what I am capable of. You don't know me.'

And I fled, leaving him, and the kindness of his gift behind. I fled deep into the hospital, up to the tiny room I had once shared with Lily in those first days of my being there. To where I knew he would not follow.

❦

I never saw Mr Meredith again.

Or, at least, that is where my story should have ended. But I was not born for virtue or willing self-sacrifice. I was not born to let go when there was one, last, desperate hope still whispering there in my heart.

Besides, hadn't I been told often enough already that I

would not, under any circumstances, be joining my Uncle Jolyon in Paradise? One more transgression hardly seemed to make a difference to my fate. And when I occasionally made my way to the back of the congregation of St Catherine's, where the staff and more able-bodied patients of the hospital worshipped each Sunday, the Reverend Peters seemed to speak with a less mean-spirited creator.

So later that day, as the dark curled around the hospital and rain dashed itself against my windows, I pulled on the battered old coat I had arrived in, a lifetime ago – or so it seemed – and made my way out silently into the night.

Chapter Ten

A burst of laughter echoed around the Plas Eden terrace, drifting outwards over the still expanse of lake.

Rhiannon turned back from the water's edge, where an overexcited Hodge was engaged in saving his squeaky from a faintly outraged audience of ducks, with a good deal of splashing and barking.

'It feels good to have life back in poor old Eden, once more,' she said to Carys, who was watching Hodge's confrontation with a particularly large mallard that was clearly under the impression the squeaky was a duck's lunch, and nothing whatsoever to do with a dog at all.

'So it does,' she replied, returning Rhiannon's smile.

Carys and her mother had arrived shortly after Gwynfor Humphries, fresh from his history day in the Boadicea. He had been press-ganged into the occasion by Rhiannon with the irresistible promise of yet more old photographs of Plas Eden.

Mair had been a little nervous of venturing out onto the uneven gravel and into the heat of the sun. But, with a little encouragement from Gwynfor (who had a way with elderly ladies) she stepped out determinedly, one arm supported by the professor, walking stick tapping on the stones, to be installed in a comfortable armchair set up beneath the shade of a parasol.

'Here's Huw,' said Rhiannon, at the heavy crunch of wheels on gravel. 'I knew he wouldn't be long.'

Moments later, a grey-suited Huw made his way across the lawn to join them, his wife following rather breathlessly in the wake of his rapid stride.

'Hello Carys,' he said, in a stilted tone, shaking her hand in his best management-lunch-with-networking manner. 'You know Angela, don't you?'

'A little,' replied Carys.

Angela, however, had none of the formality of her husband. Round-faced and pretty, with a mass of short blonde curls, she kissed Carys firmly on both cheeks. 'Nice to see you again, Carys. What a lovely top.'

'Thank you.' Carys beamed at her. After a few passing meetings in Pont-ar-Eden High Street, she had not been quite sure what Huw might have told Angela. But Angela, who was a Harlech girl – and so beyond the gossip of back-of-beyond Talarn, let alone Pont-ar-Eden – was quite clearly oblivious to any undercurrents to the visit.

'David not back from his meeting, then?' she was asking Rhiannon.

'The train was delayed, I'm afraid. So he missed his connection.'

Angela clucked, gently. 'Oh, what a pity. It's so nice to have all the family together.'

'He knows the London line always has delays,' remarked Huw, frowning. 'I don't see why he didn't take the car.'

'Huw!' Angela eyed him in exasperation.

Huw blinked at her. 'What?'

'Darling, I don't think David finds it easy driving long distances. You know? After his accident?'

'Oh,' muttered Huw, flushing slightly. 'I thought, after all

173

that physiotherapy that driving wouldn't be a problem any longer.'

'You're hopeless,' said Angela, laughing with gentle affection. 'Aren't men just hopeless? Of course David isn't going to *say* he still has trouble, or when he is in pain. But you can see it in his face when he gets tired. Just like you always carry on with your golf when your knee plays up and never say a thing. You two are as bad as each other you know.'

'Hrmph,' grunted Huw, who could bluster his way through the trickiest of board meetings, but clearly knew better than to argue now.

'I'm sure he'll be here soon,' put in Rhiannon, with a quick glance towards Carys, who had turned back to watching the antics in the pond once more, face hidden. 'It's only a short drive from the station. Come and see Mair. She's got some fascinating photographs of Plas Eden to show us. I think we might get her to join your group in the Boadicea yet, Angela.'

Angela shot off, with Huw following in a slightly awkward fashion, uncertain whether his duty was to follow his wife or engage in polite small talk with Carys. He settled down in a free chair at the table with a brief nod in the direction of Professor Humphries, safe in the knowledge that Angela, at least, would fill any awkward gaps in conversation. Within minutes, he found himself left in peace as Angela plunged headlong into discussions with Mair about the wonders of trawling the online census on the web from the comfort of a proper chair and a pot of tea at hand.

'I hadn't realised your grandfather had taken so many photographs of Plas Eden,' said Rhiannon, as they followed slowly behind Huw.

'No, I didn't, either,' Carys replied. 'There are loads of them. I didn't bring them all, just the ones I've managed to scan into the computer and copy. I can't see any signs of negatives, so these must be the only copies. It would be horrible if anything happened to them.'

'Well, I'm really looking forward to seeing them,' said Rhiannon, cheerfully. 'Although, perhaps we ought to eat first. I'm sure Mair must be getting hungry.' She cleared her throat. 'And it'll give David time to get here before we start properly on the photographs.'

'Yes,' murmured Carys, even though she did not believe this, any more than Rhiannon.

She had braced herself so much for this meeting. For the first conversation, the first time they had spent any time in each other's company since that day amongst the statues. It seemed the hurt and wounded pride she had seen in his eyes each time they passed in the street still ran deep in David, even after all these years. Far too deep to do anything else than avoid her. She should have known. After all, hadn't she spent at least half the past week trying to think of good reasons not to come with Mam to Plas Eden?

A sense of deep sadness enveloped her. It would have been good to have at least made peace. Especially now. For what was probably the last time she would ever come here.

Carys paused, looking out over the still expanse of lake, with the green of fields and hillsides beyond. If Eden was sold and Rhiannon gone, David would not come back to Pont-ar-Eden, she knew it. For all she knew, he could already be planning a future away from here. It could even be what the meeting in London was all about. He had years of managing Plas Eden under his belt, there must be plenty of careers in tourism and management that would open up to him. He might even go abroad. As far away as possible.

And as for herself – she frowned, trying to push the

inevitable conclusions of the last few days to the back of her mind. Joe had already contacted an estate agent. The Chester flat would be on the market within days. This was reality facing her slap-bang in the face. Even with her savings, and the money they would get from the flat, she would struggle to afford the smallest of places on her own. If she tried to keep on at college, she'd have no chance at all. And anyhow, what was the point? The dream of the smallholding and the good life had been for her and Joe. For their future together.

Funny how things can change in a moment. Suddenly, there was the whisper of a management position coming up in Tylers, and the word was if she went for it they'd snap her up, no question. At least then she might be able to keep on the property ladder, even if it took all her savings and mortgaged her to full-time accountancy for the next twenty years. After all, it's what other people did. What her friends were doing. She had been living too long in a dream world of her own. It was time to wake up. And be grateful she still had the prospect of full-time work at all.

She looked round as Rhiannon joined her.

'I was wondering what you think Mair would prefer? I've made things easy, so that we can eat inside or out.'

'She looks really settled,' replied Carys, glad to return to immediate practicalities. 'It seems a shame to move her, if that's okay with you.'

'Perfect. We've had so few fine evenings this summer, it seems a crime to waste them. Everything's ready. You go and join your mam, Carys. I'll just go and put the kettle on.'

'I'll help you,' said Carys, on impulse.

'Oh, you don't have to. You're a guest. Enjoy the sunshine.'

'But I'd like to.'

'Of course,' said Rhiannon, smiling as Hodge emerged

triumphant from the water, to shake himself in a rainbow of spray. 'In which case, you'll be very welcome.'

They turned to make their way up the short flight of steps to the terrace, passed by a soaking wet and highly excitable Hodge, who seemed to have already got the scent of dinner in the air.

'Where's your squeaky?' demanded Rhiannon. Hodge paused; ear alert, eyes bright and intelligent. 'Squeaky?' Hodge blinked, expectantly, as if the object of his obsession was about to appear at any minute. 'Well I haven't got it.' She pointed. 'Go on, Hodge: go and fetch your squeaky. Fetch!'

Hodge shot off, back towards the lake.

❧

'It hardly seems to have changed in here at all,' said Carys, as she followed Rhiannon into the kitchen.

'Poor old Eden. Nothing much changes, I'm afraid, only age and dilapidation.'

'I rather like it like this.'

'To be truthful, so do I.' Rhiannon opened the fridge door and reached inside. 'But Huw is right: things can't stay the same way forever.'

'No,' murmured Carys. With Rhiannon occupied in bringing out plates of sandwiches covered in cling film, Carys found herself free to look around with more open curiosity.

She'd been wrong. The kitchen *had* changed. Or maybe it was just that her adult, home-owning eyes noticed the damp patch on the ceiling, the broken door to the unit next to the fridge and the peeling of paint at the corners of the ceiling.

It had never been a neat room. Too much the centre of busy lives to ever be that when the boys lived there. Carys had loved its overflowing qualities, so very different from Mam's scrupulously clean and tidy kitchen, with everything washed up and tidied away out of sight as soon as it had been finished with.

In Plas Eden's kitchen, there were always piles of opened letters and junk mail flung into a glass dish on the sideboard, as if the household were far too busy to deal with them straight away; along with half finished sketches of Rhiannon's, and Nainie's hot water bottles.

And the shoes! Carys smiled to herself. They'd thinned out now, of course, but there were still a stash of wellies by the patio door of the sunroom, surrounded by miscellaneous sandals, the odd trowel or two, and a perilously stacked pile of terracotta plant pots, with a slouch to rival the Leaning Tower of Pisa, all ready for action.

This part of Plas Eden had always been a place of things happening. It had been full of noise, from Nainie's TV to Rhiannon's cassette player – liable to send out anything from Bach to Dire Straights to Joni Mitchell, with a Welsh folksy bit of Dafydd Ewan and the odd panpipe or so, depending on her mood.

Now the house was silent, as if all the life had oozed out through its pores and left just a shell behind.

'It's never easy,' remarked Rhiannon, a little sadly, arranging plates of cucumber sandwiches alongside salmon, cheese and pickle and the slightly more exotic selection of brie and avocado, and chicken with wild rocket. 'Change, that is.'

Carys began placing bowls of olives and small, fragrant tomatoes straight from the courtyard on a faded wooden tray with well-worn handles. 'No.'

Rhiannon lifted a homemade cake from out of its tin, releasing the sweet sharpness of lemons into the air. 'Change happens, throughout our lives, whether we like it or not. But I think that's the hardest lesson, when you first begin to realise that things can't always be as you might choose.'

Carys paused, her hand on the cheese board with its array of camembert and stilton interspersed with round Welsh cheddars, each in their waxy rinds of green and dark orange, set amidst the Mediterranean sunshine of black grapes. 'Do you ever regret it?' she asked, abruptly. 'Leaving London and coming here, I mean.'

Rhiannon paused. A look of pain passed briefly over her face.

'I'm sorry. That was thoughtless of me. I should never have asked.'

'No, you're okay. It's perfectly natural. You just caught me a little by surprise, that's all.' Rhiannon gave a wry smile. 'It's something that's been occupying my mind rather a lot recently.'

'You mean, with Plas Eden…?' Carys left the question hanging in the air.

'Yes.' Rhiannon rearranged cups and saucers on a tray, even though they had been perfectly neat in the first place. 'To be honest,' she said at last, 'when I was first here, I'd have put Eden on the market myself, given the chance.'

'Really?' Carys felt her eyes widen.

Rhiannon's gaze was far away. 'Life seemed so short, at that age. There was so much I wanted to do. A career. Marriage. Children.'

'Marriage.' Carys looked at her. How self-absorbed children are, she thought. Even more when they are teenagers. Rhiannon had always been Rhiannon. Even now, it had never crossed her mind that Rhiannon had once had a life that had nothing to do with Eden.

A memory stirred. She had come down from the old nursery one snowy afternoon, on a mission to get supplies for the video cassette marathon of the *Star Wars* trilogy, given to Huw for Christmas that year. She had found Rhiannon, sitting in the dusk, her hands that were never still resting silently in front of her. She hadn't stayed, she remembered. She hadn't even let Rhiannon know she was there. She had run back to the safety of the ice-cold rebel planet of Hoth empty-handed, glad to find David and Huw too absorbed in Luke Skywalker's light sabre to notice her failure. But the sadness had remained with her: a forlorn sadness, more frightening than tears, that finally, after all these years, made sense.

'There was someone,' she said. Rhiannon looked up, slightly startled. 'Sorry,' said Carys. 'I didn't mean to pry.'

'That's okay.' A faint smile appeared on Rhiannon's face. 'There never was much that could be hidden from you, Carys, *bach*.'

'Yes, there was,' muttered Carys. 'There still is, come to that,' she added under her breath.

'And of course you're right,' said Rhiannon. 'There *was* someone. One of my tutors at art college in London, as it happens. He'd won a major prize for his work that year and had the offer of going to work in New York. Fame and fortune beckoned. He'd just asked me to go with him, when the news came through about Paul and Marianne.'

'Oh,' said Carys. A vision of Joe, his face filled with hurt and disappointment floated in front of her eyes. And hadn't he, with his offer of the holiday cottage in the country, at least tried to compromise? 'I'm sorry.'

'Oh, don't be.' Rhiannon looked up. 'It took me years, but after a while I realised going with him would have been the worst mistake of my life.'

'The worst?'

'Oh yes.' Rhiannon's voice was certain. 'It was the right time for Jason. Not for me. He was much older than me, you see. He knew exactly what he wanted and he'd worked for years to get there. I think I knew at the time – even though I'd never have admitted it to myself – that I would always have lived in his shadow.' She gave the faintest of smiles. 'He's semi-retired now, but still hugely successful. And onto his fifth wife.'

'Ouch,' said Carys, without thinking.

'Quite.'

There was a moment's silence.

'Funny thing is,' said Rhiannon at last, 'I think maybe even Jason can see it now.'

'Oh?'

'Not that I've spoken to him. But he sent a message through the publishers of that book I illustrated, giving me details of an artist-in-residence post in an American college. Apparently they're keen on having someone from the UK. The publishers forwarded another email from him a few days ago, asking if I'd put in my application yet and offering to give me a letter of recommendation, if I applied.'

'Wow.' Carys was impressed. 'And he's mega-famous? That's amazing.'

'I suppose it is,' said Rhiannon.

Carys frowned at her. 'People would kill for contacts like that. Which means you've got to apply.'

'It would mean leaving here.'

'Oh.' Carys hesitated. 'But if Plas Eden is being sold, anyhow …'

'I know.' Rhiannon turned away to fiddle with something in the sink. 'It just feels a big step, that's all.'

Rhiannon was still hoping David would stick it out, find a

way through and keep Plas Eden, thought Carys. She probably hadn't told David about the application at all.

'How long is it for?' she asked.

Rhiannon turned back, a collection of newly washed teaspoons in her hand. 'Six months. Initially, that is. Part of the brief is to set up a permanent exchange with a college over here. So it could mean a lot of travelling.'

'But it doesn't have to be forever. Something like that could lead to all sorts of things. It would give you so many openings. So many choices. Even if you only do it for a year, or even a couple of years. Any decision about Eden might take months, years even. You can't miss an opportunity like that.'

Rhiannon smiled. 'It is tempting. And, to be honest, I suppose I feel ready for it now. When I was younger, I thought that life was so short.'

'Isn't it?'

'Well, yes it is, in one way. And especially if you are a woman and desperately trying to cram in everything before you are forty-five and suddenly become invisible, as if you don't matter any more.' She grimaced. 'It wasn't until I hit forty myself that I realised it doesn't have to be that way. Life doesn't just stop when you have children, or when they grow up. As far as I can see, many women nowadays only start their careers later in life, when their responsibilities are at least lessened.'

'I suppose,' said Carys, slightly dubiously. That seemed an awful long time to wait, from where she was sitting.

'And if you think about it, these days I might be only halfway through my life. That's a long time. To be honest, I was exceedingly boring when I was twenty: self-obsessed, arrogant, and about as shallow as can be. Although I say it myself, I'm much more interesting now. And freer.' She gave a mischievous grin. 'It doesn't half sort the men from the boys, having a fifty-something face, I can tell you. The boys – whatever age they are – try to pretend you don't exist, because really you scare them witless. So you can forget about them, for starters.'

Carys eyed her, not entirely sure if she was being serious or not. 'And the men?'

'The men.' Rhiannon smiled. 'Real men never see just youth or age. They see the human being that was always there.' Her eyes ran fondly round the old kitchen. 'I learnt so much, being here in Eden. If I'm honest, I had a bit of a talent, and little else, when I came here. All the experiences I've had in my life, these are the things that give me real passion for my work. So it was no longer about my ego, and being admired and famous. I suppose you could say this is where my painting really began.' Her eyes focused as they rested on the shadow of the doorframe, and she straightened up, abruptly. Carys turned instinctively in the same direction.

'David!' A look of pure pleasure had come over Rhiannon's face. 'You made it, after all.'

'I managed to get the next train,' muttered David, sounding more than a little embarrassed. Almost like a man who had changed his mind at the last minute and wasn't about to confess it. 'I came in through the garden. Angela said you were in here. I thought you might like some help.'

'We're fine,' replied Rhiannon. 'Although you can certainly help to carry things out, if you like.'

'Okay,' he said, stepping into the kitchen. 'Hi, Carys.'

Her eyes met his, briefly. They were as blue and clear as she remembered, with that tinge of brown around each iris that always sent her stomach into full kamikaze dive. Time, she discovered, had not changed the kamikaze part. Not one little bit.

183

'Hi.' Her mind had gone blank. Her insides had just squelched themselves into tight knots. Frantically, Carys searched around for something to say. Something calm, cool, collected and polite. It was all she could do to breathe.

David reached hastily for the nearest tray of sandwiches. 'I'll take this one, shall I?'

'That'll be great,' smiled Rhiannon, as if she hadn't in the least noticed the abrupt silence hanging in the air. 'Smells as if the flans are cooked,' she added to Carys, as David vanished as fast as his damaged leg could take him. 'I've kept to the mostly unadventurous, I'm afraid. I thought your mam might prefer it that way.'

'Thanks,' muttered Carys, retrieving plates from the draining board to give her face a chance to cool down a little and her heart rate time to get back to something near normal. 'I'll make another pot of tea, shall I?'

Okay; so they could get through tea and the showing of photographs, and then go home, and it would all be over and done with. She would never have to venture within the grounds of Plas Eden, or speak to a Meredith, ever again. And the past could remain where it belonged: buried forever, without trace.

Chapter Eleven

The meal on the terrace was, in the end, an unexpectedly cheerful affair.

Getting out and about, Carys could see, was doing Mam no end of good, despite her slight panic beforehand, and her tendency to drop off to sleep at any significant lull in the conversation. But in between, her eyes had regained much of their old brightness. Even her mind seemed to be recovering from its institutionalised dependence on others and was up and running again.

'Maybe I could try and come to the café,' she admitted, as they finally reached the stage of cake and leisurely cheese and biscuits. 'And bring the photographs. Although I expect they've got lots of them already.'

'Not like yours,' Gwynfor assured her, eyebrows on alert. 'There aren't many of Eden itself. At least, not of the servants. There are plenty of the family, of course.'

'Really?' said Carys, looking up from the crumbs of cake she was chasing absently round her plate. She didn't remember photographs from the time she came regularly to Eden. But then, when you came to think about it, you wouldn't. Not with the past, hanging there in each silent corner of the room. Not when it was still so raw and painful. Photographs, in those days, were the last thing that were needed. She carefully avoided David's eyes. Which, since he had spent the last hour or so carefully avoiding hers, was no big deal.

'Well, not plenty, exactly. But a few,' Gwynfor corrected himself. He smiled encouragingly at Mair. 'Although I have to say – present company excepted – I find those of the servants considerably more interesting.'

'Oh!' Mam looked slightly bemused at this. 'Well, I suppose there were some characters in Pont-ar-Eden, in those days.'

'And not just in those days,' smiled Gwynfor, eying her over his thin-framed reading glasses, in true professor style.

Laughter went up around the table. Hodge, who was sitting at Carys' feet, on the principle of having tried everyone else for the odd sandwich or three that might go missing in action under the table, looked up in alarm. Human laughter and human tears, being almost indistinguishable at times, always unnerved him slightly. And especially when there was more than one human in need of his comfort and general sympathy, which left a dog uncertain of where to start.

'You're okay, Hodge,' said Carys, spotting his dilemma, and massaging the nearest ear. Hodge forgot the comforting and went on full cheese-morsel alert. Things were looking up at last.

'Leave Carys alone, greedy,' David said, who seemed to have become aware of this performance, despite not looking in their direction. 'You know the rules: no food from the table.'

Hodge gave a deep sigh and settled down again. Not too far from Carys' chair. Just in case. Carys found herself smiling at his antics. She looked up, just in time to discover David watching her.

'Labrador,' he remarked, as if to cover the fact of him looking at all. 'Stomachs-R-Us.'

Carys laughed. 'I remember.'

'Ah, yes. Nainie and her labradors,' he replied, with just the faintest of smiles. His eyes held hers for a moment, then looked away.

She looked older. A woman with defined cheekbones and a wide, expressive mouth, rather than the gentle, round-faced girl he remembered. It was a lived-in face; one browned by sun and weather and moulded over the years by experiences he had not been there to share, and would probably never hear of. She was older and sadder, with unmistakeable lines of strain at the corner of her eyes. But she was still Carys.

David discovered the old hurt, that he had managed to keep up as a barrier from even thinking about her over the years, had eased a little. 'May I see these photographs?' he asked.

'Of course you can.' Carys pulled out the plastic folder, where it had been placed out of harm's way on a bench along the house wall. 'There are others at home.'

Including the one of the woman and child. It still sat, in a folder all of its own, amongst her socks in her bedroom at Willow Cottage. She hadn't even shown it to Mam, yet. The more she looked at it, the more there was about the woman's face that unnerved her, with its lines of a life of fierce emotion, and mouth that – even in a smile – was a line of utter determination.

'That's the cottage,' said David, his surprise breaking in on her thoughts.

'Cottage?' Huw, who had kept himself a little apart from the conversation, as if so much tittle-tattle was beneath his notice, looked up from slicing a particularly fine Caernarfon brie.

'Eden Farm.' David pushed the photograph towards his brother. 'Funny; we were just discussing that.'

'Pity,' muttered Huw, a crease of annoyance appearing

between his brows. 'If you'd given the Sullivans notice straight after your accident, when I suggested, Beddows might have considered taking it as part of the estate. As it is, they're not interested.'

'That wasn't why we were discussing it.' David scowled at Huw, who seemed to have conveniently forgotten that the conversation as they'd made their way up the drive had centred around Eden Farm being a far more suitable home for Rhiannon than a cottage in Pont-ar-Eden, and the least they could do. Since Huw would have equal rights if it came to a sale of the estate, nothing could be done without his agreement. Huw, it appeared, was not about to agree. At least not without a fight.

And just how long had his brother been in discussions with Beddows? David asked himself, grimly. From the moment the call came through from Switzerland to tell Huw and Rhiannon about the accident? Was this an opportunity Huw had been waiting for all these years? No wonder he had been so against a long lease to the Sullivans. David cursed himself. He'd been the fool who'd listened, believing his brother, with all his business acumen, was thinking of a more profitable solution for the farm. Just how naïve can you get?

'It was such a lovely place,' came Mair's voice, breaking into David's inner beating up of himself. She was nodding and smiling, her eyes misted with memory. 'That used to be the head gardener's house, Carys, dear. Where your dad grew up. He took us there to see it once, before the new tenants came in. You could only have been about five or six. I don't expect you remember.'

'I remember,' said Carys, slowly. 'At least, I'd forgotten I remembered. But I remember.' She had always thought it a dream, or a place they had visited, that childhood memory of

Dad taking her to see a house with yellow roses round the door, rows of fruit and vegetables and the little orchard of wind-blown apple trees, and the arch of peas and beans that led to the tiny, self-contained, walled garden. 'I thought it was still being run as a farm?'

'It was.' Angela was peering closely at the photograph. 'The last tenants, the Sullivans, were brilliant. They were supplying veg and eggs to quite a few of the houses in Pont-ar-Eden. And to the Boadicea. Didn't they just move to a place in the Midlands?'

'Shropshire,' said Huw. 'Better growing conditions.'

'But I bet no walled garden,' returned Angela, pointedly.

Just for a moment, a flush of discomfort passed over Huw's solid features. 'Their choice,' he muttered.

'And our loss,' retorted Angela. 'Local produce is the in thing at the moment, as well as being more environmentally friendly, and all that. I miss my veg box. Even those squash thingies no one seems to know how to cook.'

'And Jerusalem artichokes,' added Rhiannon, with a shudder.

'Oh, I rather like Jerusalem artichokes,' said Mam. 'In moderation, of course.'

'There, you see,' said Angela. 'The Sullivans' farm was just what is needed in Pont-ar-Eden. I don't see why you want David to sell it off for a housing estate at all, darling.'

'Oh!' said Mam, to whom this was clearly news. Her eyes rested on Huw, who was looking less at ease by the minute.

'Well, something has to be done,' he growled defensively. 'If David had given them the ten-year lease they'd wanted, we'd quite likely have been stuck with the farm, whatever happened in the future. Given the way things have turned out, I was quite right to advise against it.'

'Nothing has been decided yet,' put in David. 'Especially about Eden Farm.'

There was a moment's silence. 'Such a pity,' said Mam, at last. 'I'd have liked to have seen the old cottage again. Your dad had such happy memories there, Carys, especially of your grandma and granddad. It would have been nice to see it again.'

'Is it empty at the moment?' asked Carys. David nodded. 'Well, in that case, would you mind if Mam and I went over to see it, one day?'

'That sounds like an excellent idea,' said David. 'In fact, Mair, why don't you let us take you round one day next week?'

Mair beamed. 'Thank you, dear. You always were a thoughtful boy.' A sudden sharp gleam appeared in her eyes. 'But I'm afraid it'll be a bit too rough for me, *cariad,* especially with that track. You could always take Carys, though, and she could tell me all about it.'

'Mam!'

'Well, I don't see why not, dear. You could take a camera and take pictures for me. That sounds like the best solution.'

'I'm sure the estate agent could show me round,' muttered Carys, hoping there was such a thing.

'No, you're okay.' David cleared his throat. 'I'll take you there. It's no problem.'

'In fact,' said Angela, who had been watching the two of them closely, 'why don't you go now, Carys?'

'Now?' Carys blinked. 'Shouldn't we be getting back soon? I mean, Mam…'

'Nonsense, dear. I'm fine,' said Mam, who was all of a sudden as alert as could be.

'We can move inside in a bit, if it gets too cold,' said Rhiannon, who seemed quite unaware of the soft and wistful

190

look that had appeared in Angela's eyes. 'We've still got Nainie's chair. It gets nice and warm in Nainie's old room, and the TV still works.'

'And we can stay for as long as you like, can't we, Huw, dear?' added Angela. To which Huw grunted in the resigned tones of a man who knows his place in the domestic scheme of things. 'You can take my camera, Carys,' she added, fishing out an expensive-looking pink metal affair. 'It's got an amazing zoom lens, and there's still lots of memory on the card. I can email you the pictures tonight so you can show Mair straight away.'

'Sounds like a good plan to me,' put in Gwynfor, who was still shuffling through the photographs and had missed this little scene entirely. 'And we've got plenty more of these to get through, haven't we, Mair?'

'Okay,' said Carys, feeling decidedly stitched up.

'I'll row you across,' David said, with the abruptness of a man who knows he'll think better of this, given half a chance to think it over. 'That'll be the quickest way.'

This was getting complicated. 'There's no need.'

'It's fine. I need to pop over and check kids haven't been lighting fires in the apple orchard again. It's time to give Hodge a bit of a run anyhow, and he can run for miles over there. Rabbits,' he added to Hodge, who was already alert and on his feet in readiness at the sound of his own name. The tail banged furiously against the nearest chair leg in appreciation.

Carys looked round at the faces watching her. Apart from Huw and Gwynfor, whose minds were clearly elsewhere, and Rhiannon who was busily tidying plates, each gave her the message that resistance was futile, and might just make her feel even more of a fool than she did at this moment. She willed herself to keep her last shreds of dignity and not blush.

'Okay,' she conceded at last, bowing to the inevitable. 'That sounds great. Thanks, David.'

'You're welcome,' he replied, smiling faintly. Almost as if he were glad the ice had been broken between them. Carys firmly squashed the tendency for her heart to go racing off again. If David could be all grown up about this, then so could she. It was nothing personal: they were both doing this for Mam's benefit.

'That's not Eden.' She looked round at the sharpness of Gwynfor's voice. He was peering closely at the little postcard in his hand.

'Yes, I know,' she replied, thankful for the distraction. 'That's a real puzzle. It was in amongst the others, but I don't know where it is. Mam didn't recognise it, either. Did you Mam?'

'No,' said Mam, shaking her head.

'No writing. There isn't even a stamp on it,' Gwynfor said, disappointed, as he turned the card over.

'We used to do that, all the time,' said Mam. 'When we were young. Before we could afford a camera. We'd bring postcards back as a reminder, instead.'

'The writing on the front is really faded,' said Carys. 'That's why I brought the original, rather than a scan. We've been trying to make out the name.'

Mam nodded. 'It starts with "Tre". And then it's faded away.'

'We thought it might have something to do with Trefriw, further north in the Conwy Valley,' said Carys.

'Only I don't remember it at all,' put in Mam. 'And there wasn't a house like that near Conwy or Trefriw, or anywhere I remember as a child. In fact, I don't remember ever seeing the postcard before. So it must have been one from your dad's side of the family,' she added to Carys. 'And anyhow, it looks as if it ends with an "i", "c" and a "k". And then "Hall". That's not Welsh.'

'Treverick,' said David, slowly. He sounded as if he had been punched right in the stomach.

'It can't be.' Huw's voice sharp. 'You must have read it wrong.'

David held out to him. 'See? It has to be.'

'Bloody hell,' said Huw.

'What is it?' demanded Angela, watching her husband's face.

'Treverick,' said David, peering down at the postcard once more. 'It's a village in Cornwall.'

'Surely not?' Rhiannon had risen, and was looking over David's shoulder. 'I didn't know there was a Hall there.' She gave a slight shudder. 'What a forbidding-looking place.'

Gwynfor, who had also risen to peer over David's shoulder, looked up. 'This was in amongst your Dad's photographs, Carys?'

'Yes,' said Carys, watching them uneasily. Huw, she saw, had turned away, as if to block out the conversation.

'How very strange,' said Rhiannon.

'You know it, then?' asked Carys.

'Not exactly,' said Rhiannon. She glanced at David, who was still gazing down at the picture, a deep frown on his face.

'It's where they were going,' he said, at last.

'They?'

'Mum and Dad.'

Carys blinked. 'I thought they were on their way to London?'

'They were,' said Rhiannon. 'They'd told Nainie they were going to stay a few days with me. I think they didn't want her to know. Or maybe they thought she might stop them. We were going to the opera that night, and then they were going on to Cornwall the next morning.'

'Did they say why?' asked Carys.

Rhiannon shook her head. 'They didn't even tell me where they were going. They were both very mysterious about it.'

'But then how do you know –' Carys came to an abrupt halt. The answer was so horribly and blindingly obvious. She felt, rather than saw, Angela place a protective hand on Huw's arm.

'They were amongst Dad's things, when they gave them to us,' replied David quietly. 'A train ticket to Cornwall. And the confirmation of a booking for them to stay overnight.'

'In a hotel?' said Carys, eying the postcard dubiously. Anywhere less like a hotel she couldn't possibly imagine.

David shook his head. 'No. B&B. Sounded more like a pub. The Treverick Arms. In a village called Treverick. There was nothing about a Hall.' He looked down at the postcard once more. 'But that must have been where they were going.'

I made my way quickly between the flickering street lamps, passing unnoticed as I had done that night years before.

The rain had begun in earnest as I left the hospital, pounding on my coat and soaking through the leather of my boots. But the gusts that threw drops harshly against my face, hard as hailstones, had stirred my blood. There was no turning back now.

When I was a girl, I had too much decorum to escape to the beach outside the village where the pebbles were tossed to and fro in the surf and great waves broke over the black rocks of the headland. I would sometimes watch from my window, when the turquoise sea was turned to grey and the fishing boats rattled in Treverick harbour, as if straining to break free and join the dance of the storm. But I always turned away, back to the fire and the piano I was supposed to be practising, or watching Aunt Beatrice as she taught me the finest embroidery.

I knew even then that the wild dance was calling to me far more than the Mendelssohn Etude I was perfecting (for even at that age I was determined to outdo the other girls in our social circle). Let alone the tedious embroidering of Aunt Beatrice's firescreen, with its endless shrubbery and more than its fair share of fully clothed and simpering cherubs.

It was only later, much later, that I understood where my cowardice, and my self-satisfaction had led me, satisfaction in the small triumphs I had over half-a-dozen equally ill-informed girls who, like me, knew nothing beyond our small circle and a brief parading of ourselves in London Society.

And by then it was too late. Far, far too late. My shallow pride and my vanity had already sealed my fate.

I paused for a moment in front of Mr Meredith's lodgings. I knew well enough where to find them, of course. I had not been quite able to resist passing them more than once as I made my way to the park nearby on my afternoon off. Although I never told anyone – and I made sure I hurried by, my face hidden – I could not always fight my curiosity to see where his life beyond the hospital took place.

I raised my hand to the knocker, and again my courage failed me. But only for a moment. I could see movement behind the door, in the lights of the hall. It was too late to go back now. I knocked.

I had expected a housekeeper. I'd braced myself. Spun a story about some urgent question concerning the hospital. But instead, I stepped back a little, as Mr Meredith opened the door himself.

For a moment, he stood there. Boxes and a large trunk stood ready behind him. The house, I knew immediately was silent. The staff had already gone. I half expected him to close the door, or at least shoo me back to the hospital to keep my reputation intact. And, for once, words failed me. I did not know where to begin.

He smiled that old, familiar smile.

'You had better come inside,' he said.

Chapter Twelve

'Ready?' said David, as Carys emerged from settling Mam safely in Nainie's old room, with Angela in full attendance and the photographs spread out on a table.

Carys glanced at the terseness of his face. 'Are you sure about this? We can leave it to another time, if you prefer.'

'No, it's fine.' He cleared his throat, awkwardly. 'Rhiannon's found you this.' Carys found herself presented with a purple mohair cardigan that reached down to her knees and was most definitely Rhiannon. 'The air can be cold out there on the lake.'

'Thanks,' she murmured, taking possession of the fluffy softness.

The boat tied up at the jetty was not exactly inspiring.

'I hope that isn't the same one we used to use as kids,' said Carys.

'It's okay,' he replied, with a grin. 'Rhiannon made me get rid of that one years ago. In you go, Hodge.'

The rowing boat was larger and more substantial than it had first appeared. Carys stepped in, followed by David, as Hodge settled himself into what appeared to be a practised routine of curling up under the nearest bench.

David detached the oars hidden in a shelf beneath the jetty. 'Just in time,' he remarked, as Carys unwound the rope keeping the boat in place, allowing him to pull away into deeper waters. 'Here comes trouble.' He motioned towards a perfectly white swan which, used to the appearance of humans heralding food, was sailing majestically in their direction, snackering with his beak at any moorhen who got in his way.

'Why, is it dangerous?' asked Carys, trying not to sound wimpish. Swans could break your leg with their wings. She'd read it once. And a broken leg was the last thing she needed in her life just now.

'Hallelujah? No, he's not dangerous. Rhiannon's been feeding him along with the rest of them.' His voice was wry. 'He just needs a girlfriend. Swans mate for life, and no one seems to fancy him. I don't blame them: he's a bad tempered old bird.'

'Poor thing.' Carys smiled sympathetically at the swan, which was watching them expectantly, but with a faint air of knowing disappointment was around the corner.

David manoeuvred around to the right direction and began pulling away, setting them slipping gently through the waters. Soon they were in the middle of the lake and heading for the small island at the very centre.

Near-to, it could scarcely be called an island at all. Not even a duck island. Just a scrub-covered mound really, filled with nest boxes. A sign carved in slate, with an intricate surround of mistletoe and oak leaves proclaimed 'Ynys Afalon'.

'"The Island of Apples",' translated Carys. 'I'd forgotten about that. Avalon. That's where King Arthur was supposed to be buried, wasn't it? I thought that was on Snowdon? Unless you're from Glastonbury, of course.'

David paused, allowing the boat to glide silently forwards under its own steam. 'That was Dad's joke. Calling the island Avalon. He roped in Huw and me to put that sign there, when we were little. Dad always had this thing about King Arthur.'

He cleared his throat. 'It's where we scattered the ashes. It seemed kind of appropriate.'

Sod.

Cary could have kicked herself. She should have remembered. 'Oh,' she said.

David began rowing again, slowly, one oar, then the other. 'I think Dad would have just loved to have lived in a time when there were knights and heroes. That's probably why he loved cowboy films so much, when Huw and I were kids. They always had great social causes, did the Merediths. Not just in Eden, either. They set up charity schools and hospitals all over Wales in Victorian times. Even a couple in London, Dad used to say. Nainie's father, my great-grandfather, was one of those really passionate philanthropists.' He smiled. 'Dad always hero-worshipped him. I suppose that's why I was called after him. I think Dad would have liked to have been just like him. But Dad wasn't really a brilliant businessman himself, so he never did earn the vast amounts it took to keep all the Meredith charities up as well as the estate. And besides, I think the welfare state rather took the wind out of his sails.'

'Oh,' said Carys, this being the only tactful thing she could think of to say. Now, she felt, was not the time to point out that the Merediths could hardly be classed amongst the poor, and there was always someone, somewhere in the world, in need of help.

David rowed on in silence, apparently lost in thought. Carys turned her face away, as if absorbed herself in the bound of startled rabbits in the fields alongside the water's edge, and the distant rise of mountains behind.

Freed from the need to keep up a cheerful face in front of Mam, she could feel the hollowness opening up inside. Her mind, after its first rage and grief at the split with Joe, seemed to have gone numb. She had been through it over and over again so many times, her body wide-awake and crackling with betrayal at four o'clock each morning, however early or late she went to bed. She hadn't even the energy to be angry any more.

Tylers had returned an attachment of the job description and application form within minutes of her sending her email. She had made a start, even though her heart wasn't in it. With the flat already on the market and Mam showing signs of getting stronger, she had no choice. With so many people out there who'd die for such a chance, she could hardly complain. But it still felt like a step backwards. As if she had wasted so many years and left it too late even to aspire to the life she really wanted.

'Won't you miss this?' she said, abruptly. 'If it's sold, I mean. I can see why Huw might want you to get rid of it, but Eden's always been your life.' David's oar missed a stroke. He swore softly under his breath. 'I'm sorry.' Immediately she was contrite. 'I didn't mean to pry, and it's none of my business. I just can't imagine you without Plas Eden, that's all.'

'I might surprise you.'

Now she had offended him. Bloody men. Fragile egos, the lot of them. Why on earth did she bother? Carys took a deep breath. Her head had begun to ache with lack of sleep and if he was under the illusion she was nice, sweet, understanding Carys of years ago, he had another think coming. 'I didn't say it was some kind of failure,' she returned, trying not to sound irritable. 'Just that it seems a pity. Not many people have a chance to make a place like this their life's work.' She gave what she hoped was a suitably placating smile. 'And be their very own lord of the manor.'

'You make me sound like some medieval robber baron.'

'Well, that's probably how your family got the land in the first place, isn't it?' she retorted.

He turned to her. 'Still with that chip on your shoulder?'

'I do not have a chip on my shoulder. That's the way the world works, hadn't you noticed?' Even in her own ears she sounded bitter. 'At least the Merediths ended up with a sense of responsibility,' she added, deliberately softening her tone. She didn't want to fight with David. They had parted all those years ago with so much left unsaid: there was no point in arguing now. 'I just meant that at least here you are in charge of your own destiny. It's not like that when you're working for an organisation. However high you climb, you are still working for somebody else. Here you can choose what you do. Within reason,' she added, as he appeared about to dispute this fact. 'Anyhow, as I said, it's none of my business.'

David rowed on in silence, his face hidden so that she couldn't make out his expression. Which was fine by her. This was beginning to feel like one big mistake. She should have insisted on the estate agent and avoided having anything to do with the Merediths at all. They'd only brought her heartache, last time around. Why have anything more to do with them now?

Carys returned to watching the fields and the mountains once more, blinking unexpected tears from her eyes. She was being unfair, she knew it. It wasn't David's fault she had messed up her life. He wasn't responsible for her current problems. Her anger was with Joe, and with herself. At least she still had her health and her strength. Heaven knew what the prognosis was for a full recovery for David's damaged leg. The last thing he needed was her sniping at him.

'Wow, that looks pretty,' she said in the friendliest tones she could muster as David expertly brought the boat alongside a rickety wooden jetty, definitely in need of repair. 'I didn't realise Eden Farm was so big.'

'Not a mud hut for the servants, then,' replied David, dryly.

She shot him an apologetic look. 'Of course not.'

They set off along a well-worn path, Hodge racing in front of them. Eden Farm consisted of a traditional cottage of huge grey and brown stones under a dark slate roof. Yellow roses climbed up over the stones and around the small, square windows. On the reasonably flat ground between the cottage and the lake, before the ground swept up towards the mountains behind, neatly kept barns and greenhouses appeared, along with orderly beds containing the faded remains of vegetables and herbs, and a row of three large polytunnels.

'That looks amazing,' exclaimed Carys, who had finally worked out how to use Angela's digital camera, and was busily photographing the outside of the cottage before the light went. 'Your tenants must have done a lot of work.'

'They did.' David was watching Hodge, who was racing round in a state of mad-half-hour enthusiasm, with the odd hopeless dash towards instantly vanishing rabbit tails. 'The Sullivans did miracles. It's surprisingly sheltered, which I suppose is why the Estate's kitchen gardens were put here in the first place.'

It was a strange feeling, thought Carys, to realise that this was, in some way, part of her. She could almost see the gardeners working their endless routine of ensuring there would be fruit and vegetables all year round for the family at Plas Eden and their guests. The polytunnels apart, it must have looked very like this when her grandfather had held the responsibility for feeding the big house, and even for his father before him. She could almost smell the autumn burning of leaves and the spring richness of freshly dug earth. It gave her a slight shiver in her spine to think of their eyes looking out on very much the same scene as she was seeing now.

'Can we get into the kitchen garden?' she asked, tentatively.

'Yes, of course. Not that there's much to see. We tend to keep it locked now there's no one living in the cottage. Kids from the village don't usually make it this far, but after that incident with the apple trees last month I'd rather not take any chances.' David pulled a large, old-fashioned iron key from his pocket, and they made their way along a path of slate chippings to a painted wooden door.

'Wow,' breathed Carys, as they stepped through. A wilderness greeted them. An untamed wilderness of dock and grasses, surrounded by high stone walls, with a tantalising hint of distant apple trees and broken-down greenhouses between the jungle greenery. 'The Sullivans didn't start on this, then?'

He shook his head. 'I know they pruned the fruit trees and a vine in one of the greenhouses, but I don't think they did anything else. This was the next project.'

'You could grow so much in here.' Carys bent and parted the thick covering of couch grass. 'I bet the soil is incredibly rich from all the care it must have had over the years.' Nettles and docks stretched out on either side, leading to a rampant bank of raspberry canes. 'It would need a hell of a lot of clearing, though.'

'You're telling me,' said David, gloomily. The walled garden had drifted so far down the seemingly endless to-do list of the Eden estate, it had practically fallen off the bottom decades ago.

'I bet it's rabbit-proof, though.' Carys was rapidly taking in every detail of the garden. 'That wall looks pretty intact.'

'There's supposed to be a pineapple pit on the far side,' David volunteered. 'Where all those brambles are.'

'Oh, so that's where it is! Dad used to tell me about that.' Carys sighed, wistfully. 'He always said that was where they used to put in loads of manure to get the temperature right to grow pineapples, way before they had any other kind of heating. It was like a status symbol if you were posh,' she added with a smile.

'I'll never dine without one again,' he replied. His eyes met hers. Apology for her previous bad temper had been given, and accepted. Carys felt a sense of relief flooding through her. She didn't want bad feelings between them. If this really was the last occasion they would spend any time in each other's company, it would be better for both their sakes to end on some kind of peace.

David bent down to pat Hodge, who had completed a quick investigation of every possible corner of the garden and in the absence of rabbits had returned to lean gently on his good leg, gently nudging a dog-biscuit pocket. 'I've been thinking it would be only fair to keep the cottage for Rhiannon, whatever happens with the rest of the estate. She wouldn't be able to cope with all the land, of course, but a couple of people from the village have been asking about allotments. Which might be a possibility.'

'That sounds a brilliant idea,' said Carys enthusiastically. 'Allotments are amazingly popular. The ones in Chester have something like a five-year waiting list. And apparently that's nothing, nowadays. I'm sure once a few started, plenty of others would join in.' She hesitated. She wanted to say something nice, but it seemed whatever she said came out the wrong way. 'I'm sure Rhiannon will appreciate not having to move completely away,' she said, slightly awkwardly. 'And having somewhere to come back to.'

'Hrmph,' he grunted, sounding like Huw. He gave Hodge

an encouraging pat on his haunches and strode off towards the wooden door. 'Come on, I'll show you the house.'

Carys turned and looked back over the neglected wilderness of garden. She was glad she had made this visit. If nothing else, just seeing the places Dad and her grandfather had loved and worked in had told her that it had been real, that sudden passionate enthusiasm of hers for growing. That dream of a smallholding, at least, had not come out of nowhere, or been an excuse for going back to college, reliving her twenties and avoiding adult responsibilities. At least that had always been real.

She wasn't sure if something like gardening could exactly pass down the genes, but the enthusiasm had been there, all around her, all her life. Dad might have stuck to his lines of regimented beans at the bottom of the garden at Willow Cottage, while Mam indulged her passion for roses and a cottage garden flow of colour around the borders, but it was the love of watching things grow that had brought Dad and Mam together in the first place, and, she suspected, kept their marriage solid, despite the differences in their ages.

Stuff Joe. If she was offered that management job at Tylers she would rent the cheapest place she could find and save like crazy until she could afford her own plot of land. She wouldn't mind living in a caravan or a yurt until she had saved up for a house. Or even the prefabricated eco-build she had wanted all along, which Joe had scoffed as being hopelessly new-age hippy with off-grid power and compost toilets.

Well now she could have all the compost toilets she liked, thought Cary defiantly. And nobody could stop her.

Chapter Thirteen

Inside, Eden Cottage was quaint and old-fashioned with low beams and sash windows set deep within its thick, whitewashed walls. It was probably, Carys thought, still very much as it had been when her grandparents lived here.

As David and Hodge had disappeared to inspect guttering and check the outbuildings for signs of raves, dope-smoking dens and any other illicit goings-on, Carys was free to roam as she wished. She made her way through the house, Angela's camera clicking away.

A neat little bathroom had been fitted into one of the rooms on the first floor, the roofs of the two remaining bedrooms sloping under the eaves. Downstairs, there was a large kitchen with a long, solid wooden table that looked as if it hadn't moved in a hundred years or more.

The kitchen had been the centre of Eden Farm, Dad always said. Carys didn't really remember her grandmother, and the only photographs were of a very old lady, small and wrinkled, but bright-eyed and beaming with pride as she held Nia in the family christening gown, with Gwenan and Carys on either side.

But Dad, especially as he grew older, had talked of a younger, vibrant woman. One whose kitchen always smelt of baking bread, and who kept a kettle permanently on the go on the range for the stream of visitors who filled the kitchen with conversation and laughter. Each Christmas, Dad said, the cottage had been stuffed to bursting with children as well as adults; even that time there was snow up to the lintel of the door and it was so cold half the village went skating on Eden lake.

The range had gone, replaced by a cream-coloured Aga, but the kitchen still had the feel of a place just waiting to be filled once more. David was right, thought Carys: this was a Rhiannon kind of place. All ready and waiting for life to come bursting through the doors.

From the kitchen, she made her way into a living room, with a huge inglenook fireplace set off to one side. This in turn opened out into a sunroom, not unlike the one at Plas Eden, although on a much smaller scale.

A key hung on a little hook to one side of the French windows. It turned easily in the lock, allowing her to step onto a small patio area overlooking the lake. In the distance, across the water, she could just catch a glimpse of Plas Eden.

Carys sighed wistfully. Over the hedge surrounding the cottage, she could make out the roof of the nearest polytunnel and the wall surrounding the kitchen garden. It was all very well being practical and resigning herself to working for Tylers fulltime for the next ten years or so. *This* was what she wanted to do. Right here, in front of her.

Plas Eden might be the Meredith's family inheritance, but hadn't her ancestors helped create the garden? Plus kept it flourishing for a hundred years or more. Probably as long as Plas Eden itself had existed, in fact. In the days before supermarkets and the freezer, Plas Eden couldn't have survived without its kitchen garden to keep its inhabitants supplied with fresh fruit and vegetables all year round. No wonder the older inhabitants of Pont-ar-Eden felt themselves entitled to have a say: after all, if it hadn't been for generations of Evans working away, the Merediths would have all died out from scurvy long ago. Not that she expected a Meredith to see things this way, and she was certainly too proud to beg. Especially where David Meredith was concerned.

But there was another option. From the nearest barn she heard the sharp buzz of a ring tone, quickly silenced, followed by the sound of David's voice. She wasn't looking for an inheritance or a stake in a grand house, but a business. One that she could start now, while Mam still needed looking after and that she could grow as Mam – hopefully – became more independent.

A business idea. Wasn't that what Merlin had said he would support? A business idea that would help the village. If David was already looking at allotments, he might well be open to considering other ideas as well. A Victorian kitchen garden brought back to life and providing locally grown food to homes, hotels and restaurants could be just the kind of enterprise that Pont-ar-Eden needed, whatever might eventually happen to the house.

It would of course mean staying in Pont-ar-Eden for the next few years, if not more. Carys frowned to herself at the distant crunch of approaching footsteps over gravel. Her stomach gave a wobble: Devon and Cornwall had always been the destination of choice when she and Joe had been discussing a smallholding. Not that she was familiar with the south coast, but Joe had family in Taunton and hadn't she spent half her life trying to get away from Wales?

Then there was David Meredith. Mam and Angela would no doubt be ordering wedding cakes and planning marquees and rose arches for Plas Eden's grounds at the mere hint that she was staying.

But not if Plas Eden itself were sold. Anyhow, Carys told herself firmly, what did it matter? She was over David Meredith. She'd been over him a long time ago. The kamikaze stomach and the tingling all over her finger ends were just hormones. And hormones didn't get you anywhere. They only brought heartache, and wasting years of your life with idiots like Joe who were only ever going to do what they wanted to do in the first place.

She was over David Meredith. She was over men in general, in fact. All she wanted now was to get on with creating a life for herself. And she could do that fine on her own, thank you very much. You didn't even need a man to have children nowadays, if it came to that. It had been a storyline on *The Archers*, so even Mam must be aware of the possibility. From now on, she was going to live her own life, and no one could stop her.

'That was Rhiannon,' came David's voice. Carys jumped. He was closer than she imagined. His eyes, she discovered, were scrutinising her face, almost as if he could read her thoughts.

'It's not Mam, is it?'

'No, you're okay. Mair's fine. She's just having a nap. Rhiannon was asking if we're on our way back. It'll be dark soon.'

'Oh.'

He was still standing there, eyes on her face. She knew that look. It was David Meredith gearing himself up to say something. Heat shot through her, taking her by surprise and knocking the breath from her body. She didn't want to know what he was going to say. She didn't care. She was over David Meredith, and she didn't want to give that treacherous heart of hers any excuse to think otherwise.

'I'll lock up, then.' She turned briskly back towards the French windows. 'This has been great. Thank you so much for bringing me.' She sounded stiff and formal in her own ears, which was fine by her. 'Mam will just love all these photos. They'll bring back happy memories that she can keep forever.' She could feel David still hesitating behind her. 'I'll meet you at the front door, shall I?'

That finally seemed to do the trick. 'I'll find Hodge,' he muttered, limping off back towards the barns.

There was a nano-second when she was tempted to go after him. But it was the briefest of nano-seconds only. Carys concentrated on locking the French windows, placing the key on the little hook set to one side of the door. As she did so, a swirl of greenery caught her eye. Not real leaves, but painted ones, emerging from a wash of white paint. It looked as if somebody had been cleaning away the top layer of paint to uncover them. The leaves were decidedly those of a vine. Bunches of dark grapes were half uncovered at one side. A butterfly appeared a little further down, and below that the blue-green of a kingfisher sat on a branch, staring eagle-eyed at some invisible patch of water below.

There was such exuberance in the colours and the lines of the drawing, she couldn't help but smile. Further down the wall she could see another patch had been cleaned, revealing a riotous profusion of harebells and poppies, interspersed with camellias and tall yellow iris with nodding clusters of lily-of-the-valley at their feet, surrounded by deep orange wall flowers and spikes of blue stock. All of which had been interwoven with the delicate ramblings of a dog rose.

Whoever had painted those, she thought, had had such a zest for life, it was catching. It was obviously old. Dad had never mentioned there being a painter in his family. Plenty of gardeners, but no artists. Too busy earning a living, no doubt Dad would have informed her, roundly. But the painting was there, all the same. And painted by someone with skill and verve, who could catch the arch of a swallow's wing with the merest flick of a brush.

'Ready, then?' called David from the front door, his voice echoing through the house.

'Just coming,' she replied.

❧

The light had softened as evening crept around them, leaving the sky an impossible, fragile blue, and the summer-evening smell of autumn in the air.

'I'll row,' said Carys, as they made their way back to the boat. David might be setting up a fine speed, but he had spent the day working in London, followed by a long train journey, and nothing could disguise the increased limp in his damaged leg.

'There's no need.'

'Oh, so you think I'm not capable?'

'Of course not,' he replied, on his dignity. 'I'd never even suggest such a thing.'

'Good.'

Just for a moment he hesitated, but then he grinned. 'Bolshie women, eh?' he muttered under his breath to Hodge. 'Story of my life.' He settled a slightly bemused Hodge underneath the passenger seat and sat down. 'There,' he remarked, with only a touch of irony. 'Happy?'

'Very,' conceded Carys graciously, settling the oars into the water.

David smiled to himself. It was good to see that Carys had

relaxed a little and regained her sense of humour. There was something troubling her. It wasn't just her mam: something deeper, more raw. Something that had been eating at her on their earlier journey, taking the smile and the life out of her.

He was glad, after all, that she hadn't given him the chance to ask just now. It was none of his business. His concern might have appeared horribly intrusive, and he could feel anger simmering deep inside her, just waiting to be unleashed. She was keeping a lid on it, but only just. Whatever it was, he sensed, this was something Carys was going to have to work out for herself. But there was still a dull ache inside him, wishing he could help.

Carys had pulled them away from the jetty and was now manoeuvring the little boat to take a wide berth around Avalon. They'd been too young, he acknowledged, watching Carys, her face turned away from him as she concentrated on avoiding the treacherous mudflats around the little island. Too young, too naïve. Too innocent of life and the unexpected places it can take you. What they'd once had was in the past. He admitted the fact to himself. Maybe he'd always had a fantasy that one day they would meet up again and the old feelings would be there, just as they'd always been. Maybe, he admitted with an inward cringe, he had had – especially in the early years – a vision of Carys returning contrite, admitting she could not live without him, and of him forgiving her. Graciously, of course.

After today, he would always know that the Carys of this dream, the Carys he remembered, was gone forever. It was a new Carys in front of him, handling the oars with an inner confidence he had not noticed before. A Carys who was older, sharper, with a new edge to the gentleness he remembered so well. She had thrown off the constriction of Rhiannon's

212

mohair jumper when she sat down to row, allowing him to see that the soft arms he remembered had hardened into muscle; not the vanity variety of bicep gained from slavery to a gym, but the strong healthiness of someone accustomed to hours of physical work.

This was a Carys he didn't really know at all. It was like losing her all over again.

As they cleared the island, the facade of Plas Eden, with its encroaching ivy, loomed up on the far shore. Carys brought the boat to a halt, steadying it gently with a touch of the oars.

David gazed over Eden lake, its waters turning an indigo sheen as the sun began to leave the sky, to where the house glowed pale amongst the shadows of hills and trees.

'Beautiful, isn't it,' sighed Carys, a little wistfully.

'Yes, it is,' he replied. Across the little boat, his eyes sought out hers. She met his gaze for a moment, then turned to look over her shoulder as she prepared to set off once more.

David watched the water drip from Carys' raised oar, splashing into the dark water, sending countless ripples out towards the shore.

He still couldn't imagine his life without Plas Eden. But then once he could not have imagined his life without Carys. Maybe it was just simply time to let Plas Eden go. Start his life again, freed from the estate's all-consuming responsibilities. Lead a normal existence, whatever that might be. There was one person, at least, who would be seriously disappointed.

David grimaced. So far, he'd managed to keep the emails and phone calls away from Rhiannon and Huw, but that couldn't last. They'd all been so certain the periodic stream of vague threats and innuendo had finally been left behind several years ago when notice had come of cousin Edmund's death in a nursing home in Patagonia.

213

But now there was Edmund Meredith's son, Edmund Jnr, who had, it appeared, taken up his father's sense of past injustice. David had hoped meeting Edmund Jnr during his latest business trip to London would allow them to settle the matter, once and for all. One look this morning at Edmund's sharp, well-oiled face, along with his boasts of numerous high-placed contacts in Russia and the Arab Emirates, had put that particular hope to rest.

David sighed, wearily. Whatever Edmund Meredith was up to, it was bound to involve a battle, one that could last for years. He wasn't certain he had the stomach for a fight, not any longer. Maybe the price of keeping Eden had just become too much.

This could be the sign that the time had come to concentrate on other things. He'd done his best, but there came a point when it was just time to let go. He raised his eyes to watch Carys, still absorbed in directing the rowing boat towards the jetty. He rather liked this new Carys. She was intriguing. Getting to know her, even a little bit more, would definitely be a challenge, if nothing else.

David smiled wryly to himself. With the rest of his life falling about his ears, he could do with such a challenge.

They were now approaching the shore, following a trail of ducks and geese heading for an evening share of seed and the odd stale crust or so, trailed by Hallelujah, sailing slowly and deliberately behind them.

As they reached the bank where Rhiannon was waiting, a shadow in the encroaching dusk, Hallelujah directed a swift peck at an inattentive mallard daring to cross his path. The mallard shot off in a flurry of spray and shrieks of indignation, sending the rest of his kind into a panic. Raucous cries and the flapping of wings filled the air, echoing into the silence and the vast spaces of the mountains, and then dying away.

Above the nearest peak, a point of light flashed across the sky, flaring up into blues and greens as it swept above their heads, and then was gone.

'Wow,' breathed Carys.

'Spectacular,' said David. 'I haven't seen a meteor like that in ages. We've still got Dad's telescope, you know. There's so little light pollution here, you get amazing views of the skies. Rhiannon and me have turned into proper stargazing geeks, when we get a chance.' He cleared his throat and tried to sound casual. 'You'd be really welcome to join us one night.'

He could feel the hesitation. He could positively hear her mind working, searching around for some credible reason why she couldn't possibly. Then the resistance went out of her.

'I'd love to,' she murmured, as she guided the little boat to the shore.

Chapter Fourteen

Carys paused at the bottom of the steep flight of stairs, blinking in the darkness, not quite sure where to go next.

As her eyes adjusted, the basement of Wyn's Electricals opened out into a vast cavernous space. Thick sheets of grey sound insulation hung from the walls and the ceiling, like the insides of giant egg cartons. Not exactly pretty, but no doubt it did its job in preventing half of Pont-ar-Eden high street writing to the council and marching down here to protest at the noise.

'Hello?' called Carys tentatively. Her voice echoed around her. In the centre of the dimly lit space, she could make out a drum set and microphone stands, surrounded by several abandoned electric guitars and a full-sized harp, like a land-locked Marie Celeste, its performers spirited away halfway through a verse.

A door opened, letting light flood out. A woman in her early thirties, her short curly hair revealing a pair of intricate dangling earrings, emerged from a room crammed with computers and sound desks, and which was full to bursting with boys of all shapes and sizes.

'Hi Carys,' said Mari Lewis, making out the visitor. Since almost everyone in Pont-ar-Eden knew everyone else, any introductions were unnecessary.

Mari was one of those who had stayed in Pont-ar-Eden,

leaving only to gain her teaching qualification and a couple of years' experience teaching music in a tough inner Manchester comprehensive, before bringing her energy and enthusiasm back to Talarn Secondary. She was the first to volunteer when Merlin Gwyn got himself police-checked for working with youngsters.

'Hi, Mari.'

'Looking for Merlin, are you?'

Carys nodded. 'They said in the shop he was down here.'

'He was.' Mari Lewis peered around in the gloom. 'The band are just on a break at the minute, but he'll be around here somewhere.'

'He isn't really expecting me,' said Carys, hastily. 'I should have phoned first. I can come another day.'

'No, no that's fine.' Mari gestured towards a small room in the depths of the basement, whose partially open door revealed a desk containing a computer and printer and an 'in' tray overflowing with papers. 'He must be on the phone. He'll be out in a sec.'

As if in reply to this, the door to the office was pulled wide open and Merlin himself, cordless handset clamped to one ear, waved a biro in her direction in a gesture of welcome.

'Organised chaos,' said Mari, with a grin. 'Sorry, got to go. It's my job to see this lot don't find their way round the internet controls and start accessing porn. Or smoke in the loos,' she added. 'Nice to see you, Carys. Good to see your mam looking so much better.'

'Sure, sure,' Merlin was saying as Mari vanished and Carys slowly made her way towards him. 'Tuesday? Yeah, no problem. I'll be here all day.' He began scribbling furiously on a pad of paper. 'No problem. I'll email directions to you. The SatNav can take you round some pretty windy roads, if you don't keep an eye out. Pont-ar-Eden,' he said, in answer to some question, annunciating each word of the name carefully. 'Yeah, it is a long name. Means "Bridge over the River Eden".' He waved for Carys to follow him back inside the little office. 'Yes, there are apples. No, no snakes.' The biro was put down. 'Look, sorry mate, got to go. Visitors.' His eyes went skywards. 'Yeah, they had clothes the last time I looked. Might get arrested, otherwise. Thanks, mate.' He put down the phone. 'Wise guys, eh? Why is it they never can resist the old jokes about paradise and the Tree of Life? Wait 'till he finds there's a "Nazareth" and a "Bethlehem" just down the road and half the chapels have Old Testament names.'

In the office, the phone rang again.

'Look, if you're busy …' Carys began.

'It can wait.' He was watching her closely, an unmistakeable question in his eyes.

She looked around the basement, playing for time and to steady the wobble in her stomach. 'Amazing place you've got down here. I didn't realise it was so big.'

A pleased look crossed his face, replacing the question. 'This is the sort of place I dreamed of when I was a kid. Pont-ar-Eden can't keep on living in the past, or there'll be no one left in twenty years or so. I'd like to think I was helping towards taking it into the future.'

'I'm sure the kids love it.'

'Yes, they do. And they give so much back, too. All that energy and creativity. It's good to be reminded, sometimes.' He gave a rueful smile. 'The music business is not always a nice one. It's easy to get jaded at times and forget what it was that got you there in the first place. Come on, I'll show you around.'

By the time Carys had peered into miniature studios stuffed to the gunnels with recording equipment and admired the room flanked with computers, the musicians' refuelling break was over.

As Carys followed her guide back into the central space, figures could be seen moving in the semi-darkness. A cymbal chimed on the little stage, followed by a drum roll. There was a high-pitched squeal of microphone feedback, instantly cut.

'I know what you mean about this being the kind of place you'd have dreamed of as a kid. Even though I can't play a note, I'd have loved this when I was their age,' said Carys, wistfully, watching the group of teenagers getting themselves together.

'It's always been a dream of mine, making a place for the kids in Pont-ar-Eden,' replied Merlin, quietly. 'I never quite thought it would come true. It was slow at first, but looks like we're going to need a waiting list at this rate.'

She watched him. 'Plas Eden would make an amazing recording space.'

'I'm sure it would.' He met her eyes. 'I haven't changed my mind, though. This is small, and manageable. My days of wild ambition are over. I don't want to be responsible for loads of hormonally challenged teenagers, and I don't want any media attention and the whole thing turned into *The X Factor*, thank you very much. This way, I can keep small. Do things on my terms.'

'Oh.' More figures were appearing. A spotlight was switched on, sending a flood of colour into the gloom. A girl appeared in the spotlight. She was wearing a loose cotton dress with bits of emerald velvet let into the skirt, the kind you get from ethnic-type shops that smell of incense and faraway places. Her skin was pale, with just a faint scattering of freckles, set off by a long sweep of dark chestnut and copper hair, most of which had been brushed away from her face and twisted behind her head, to be held in place by a blunt pencil with a rubber at one end.

219

'That's Buddug's daughter, isn't it?' said Carys, as the girl sang quietly, half under her breath, picking out chords on an acoustic guitar in an experimental fashion to go with her tune.

'Yes.' Merlin's voice was thoughtful.

'Buddug said she had a good voice.'

'She does. A real haunting quality. Very distinctive. And she's a good little songwriter, too.'

Carys frowned, suddenly uneasy. Merlin seemed to have mellowed into a nice guy with time, but that predatory figure of twenty years ago could still be there somewhere. Did people really change that much?

She discovered Merlin watching her, as if reading her mind. 'Yes, I know,' he said. 'Hannah would be a publicist's dream. And maybe one day, when she's older and has more experience, and knows who she really is and what she wants and can understand what she's getting into if she goes into the music business …' He gave a wry smile. 'It's not just the girls who are exploited, you know. I learnt that the hard way, when I left Pont-ar-Eden for the bright lights of fame and fortune.'

'You seem to have done okay.'

'Not half as okay as a couple of our managers,' he retorted. 'At least in the financial sense. Me and the band were properly screwed at least twice before we learned the ropes. In those circumstances, you learn fast or you sink.' His voice softened. 'I wouldn't willingly put anyone else through that. And especially not someone that vulnerable. I can't imagine the guts it took for Buddug to get those kids free from their dad, and I know she worries about the damage done just by the violence they must have witnessed. To be honest with you, she isn't entirely a hundred per cent about Hannah being here at all.'

'I see,' said Carys. She met his eyes. In the instant, her mind was made up. She smiled.

'Did I pass the test?'

'Test?'

'The 'not-a-complete-bastard-after-all' test.'

Carys felt herself blushing furiously. 'I didn't – I wasn't…' She flustered herself to a halt, and grinned. 'Possibly,' she retorted. She used to be good at this. It was one of the things she missed about being in an office, part of the week, at least; the quick-thinking, edged-with-flirtation banter, covering only thinly the serious negotiations going on beneath. Her brain needed a pencil-sharpener taking to it, most definitely. She could feel the old adrenalin begin to stir.

'Possibly?' It was Merlin's turn to be uncertain.

'Okay; almost certainly.'

'Almost certainly. That'll do me. So? What was it you came to see me about?'

Carys took a deep breath. 'I came to sound you out on something.'

'Brilliant.' He rubbed his hands in anticipation. 'I knew you'd be the one to come up with ideas for me to invest in. Ask away.'

'How do you feel about allotments?'

His eyebrows shot up at that one. 'Allotments.'

'Yes. On Eden Farm. For people of the village to grown their own fruit and veg.'

He scratched his head. 'Well, sure; it might not be quite what I was expecting, but it sounds a good community project. If you think anyone in Pont-ar-Eden would bite.'

'It only takes a few to start with then others will follow. Allotments are such a big thing, and there aren't any available near Pont-ar-Eden. I asked. And everyone is saying they miss the Sullivans' veg boxes.'

'True.' He was still sounding less than convinced. 'But won't that take custom from the existing shops in the village, if people are growing their own?'

'Well, that would only be part of it.'

'Aha.' There was a gleam in his eyes. 'I had a feeling there might be more. Besides, you don't strike me as a woman whose ambitions stop at a single allotment.'

'Thank you,' said Carys, not quite able to hide her pleasure in the compliment. She took a second deep breath. Any more of this, and she'd be turning dizzy. 'I was thinking of part of it being run as a business. My business. I'd take over the polytunnels and the old kitchen garden, and try to carry on where the Sullivans left off, providing local veg to local businesses for people who don't grow their own. If Plas Eden is turned into some kind of hotel or tourist centre, I could try and supply them, too. I'm not asking you to invest in me,' she added, hastily. 'I wouldn't have the cheek. I don't have much experience behind me, and I'd have to drop my college course, so I wouldn't have any qualifications. I'll have some money to invest in the business, and to support me for a year, maybe eighteen months. By that time I should know if I can make some kind of an income, or if I need to apply for my old job back again.'

'That sounds like a risk.'

Carys swallowed, hard. She had spent all night wide-awake, her mind rushing feverishly through every possible permutation of disaster, edged with the tempting safety of a full-time job back at Tylers. She had spent the morning trying not to think about either, on the principle that safety might win.

'This could be my one chance,' she said, at last. 'I don't want to spend the rest of my life regretting that I never even tried. Okay, if I fail, at least I'll know I've tried, and I just have to grow up and get on with my life. I've done a business plan,'

222

she added, fishing a folder out of her shoulder bag. 'Financial projections, cash flow. Marketing strategy.'

'You don't hang around,' he remarked, smiling. 'So, if you don't want me to invest in your business, what do you want me to invest in?'

'The land. Oh, not for me. But for the people of Pont-ar-Eden. That way, a bit of Plas Eden would always be a part of the village. A place where people can grow food, keep chickens. Where the kids could learn, too. Besides, I can't afford to buy the land around the farm, and any allotment holders would need some kind of stability.'

He was watching her thoughtfully. 'You don't want to buy the whole farm, then. Be a part of Eden?'

She shook her head. 'No. And, in any case, David was talking about not selling the cottage, so Rhiannon can have a home.'

He nodded. 'That makes sense. And if Rhiannon is going to be living so close, you don't think she would object to your plans?'

'No. At least, I don't think so. Obviously she'd need to be consulted first, if David offers her the cottage. The allotments would need to be at a distance, and the kitchen garden and the polytunnels don't overlook Eden Cottage, in any case. If David doesn't want to sell the land, he might agree to some kind of lease.' Her nerves were beginning to jump again. 'Even a ten-year lease would give me a chance to establish something and see if it might work.'

'So you'd be a tenant, along with the rest.'

'Yes.' She frowned at him. 'I know it couldn't be mine. I don't really want it to be mine. I'd pay rent, of course. That's only fair. And if I can make a go of it, I could save up and buy somewhere of my own, when I'm ready.'

'Ah. So not necessarily in Pont-ar-Eden.'

She met his eyes. 'No. I'd originally thought of Devon or Cornwall, when I was considering setting up a business.' Merlin, she felt, was studying her closely. 'I'm still going to go and have a look around. But it's going to be expensive down there. I know I couldn't afford anything just now.'

'You're still thinking about settling there eventually?'

'Maybe. But not for a while, at least. I've got Mam to think of, and I know I've loads to learn first.'

'Hmm.'

'You'll think about it?'

He nodded briskly. 'Oh, definitely. And I'd like to look through that business plan of yours. Do you have time now?'

'A bit. I'm taking Mam to the history morning at the Boadicea in an hour. But I'm okay until then.'

'You'd better come into the office in that case. I'm afraid I can't offer you the hard stuff, like they do in *The Godfather*, on account of kids and my liver, and this being an alcohol-free zone. But I make a mean cup of tea, though I say it myself.'

'Sounds perfect,' said Carys with a smile, as she followed him inside.

⁊

A few hours later Buddug delivered her tray of soup and rolls to the table nearest Pont-ar-Eden's history club's latest – and most excitable – gathering to date, and wiped her hands carefully. 'Those look very old, Carys.'

'Old? They're historic,' exclaimed Sara Jones, her wrinkled face flushed with excitement. 'Look, the woman in the centre: that looks like a cook's uniform. If this is the 1920s she must be your grandmother, Buddug.'

'She looks a bit fierce,' replied Buddug, just a little dubiously.

'More like determined,' said Carys. Buddug smiled at her.

'Exactly.' Sara was nodding vigorously. 'Didn't you say she brought up nine children on her own? That would certainly take determination in those days.'

'That's what my mam always said,' replied Buddug. 'I know my grandfather was killed in the First World War, leaving her with nothing, but she managed to work her way up to cook at Plas Eden, and I know she was there for years.' She peered closer. 'It does look like her you know. I've got some old photographs upstairs. I was starting to look them out for you. She does look like the photos of my grandmother, but I'd need to have another look to be sure.'

'I've made several copies,' said Carys, reaching into her shoulder bag and bringing out a plastic folder.

'Thanks.' Buddug took the print. 'It's amazing to see them like that. Makes them real, you know? I'm sure this will have plenty more people in Pont-ar-Eden rushing to trace their ancestors.'

She grimaced as the doorbell clanged, letting in a rush of new customers, drawn in by the promise of smoked bacon and mango salad, and the aroma of courgette, garlic and wild rocket soup. 'I'll let you know as soon as I can,' she called back, picking up the empty tray she had stashed by the old sofa which divided the computers from the café, and returning to rescue Alison on the till, who was a new recruit for the summer season and beginning to look faintly flustered as the Boadicea's lunchtime rush hit its peak.

'One of those gardeners looks rather sad,' said Sara, abandoning the photograph of the servants to glance at the young men with their spades and wheelbarrows. 'Lots of men left, you know, when the First World War was declared. They thought it would be something new. An adventure. A way of escaping being stuck in such a rigid society.' She shuddered. 'I hate to think of what most of those poor boys were experiencing only a few years' later.'

'Most of them never came back,' put in Gwynfor, joining them. 'Many of these are probably names on the village memorial. Hopefully we can match some of them up.'

'It's like looking into the end of a world,' added Haf, abandoning the single portraits to join them.

'I think it was, in a way,' Gwynfor replied. 'Life would have gone on very much the same from medieval times. If not before that. And then it all changed.'

'It must have been horrible,' said Carys, joining Mam, and looking down at the face of Dad's grandfather, proud in his role as head gardener.

'And frightening,' replied Mam.

'True,' said Gwynfor. 'But then if things had stayed as they were, we would never have had the chances we've all had in life. Rights for women, for one,' he added, as Edna began to protest. 'The world these people were born into had few chances for change.'

'And Victorian women had no legal status of their own, remember,' put in Sara Jones, white head nodding vigorously. 'They belonged to either their father or husband. No divorce, no property rights. For years, even if your husband divorced you, you lost your children and any income you earned still went to him.'

'Typical,' muttered Edna, feelingly.

'It is still quite extraordinary, having such a clear picture of the past,' Gwynfor was saying thoughtfully. 'I'm sure we could get heritage organisations interested. This could really make a difference to Plas Eden, you know. People flock to places like Erddig, that National Trust estate near Wrexham where you can see how ordinary people lived. David and Huw might at least consider it.'

Conversation started up again around them as the heads grouped round different prints, exclaimed over the total lack of cars in the high street, and look, there was Pendragon's Hardware shop, didn't it look smart, and look at that one of the kitchens at Eden – could you ever imagine cooking huge dinner parties on a range like that?

'It's the blacksmith's that gets me,' said Gwynfor, picking up a photo of a shadowy interior, complete with furnace and anvil, and the blacksmith looking up as he replaced the shoe of a huge shire horse. 'That's my grandfather, you know. Blacksmiths had a special status in the past. Goes back to the sword in the stone from the King Arthur story. That's where the story came from: blacksmiths working with metal when it was a new and magical material. They'd pour the liquid metal into a stone mould, and when it cooled the mould was broken open and bingo – there you have it, a sword pulled from a stone. So forget that white beard and flowing robes malarkey: Merlin the magician was probably a blacksmith.' He rubbed his hands in enjoyment. 'I like it.'

'Dad's mother must be amongst the servants on the steps,' said Carys, seeing Mam was beginning to grow drowsy at this talk of the village and blacksmiths. 'I'm sure Dad said she was a maid at Plas Eden before she was married. We were trying to work out which one she could be, weren't we?'

'Yes, that's right, dear,' said Mam, growing alert again. 'But she doesn't seem to be there. There don't seem to be any photographs of your grandmother when she was young, which is such a pity.' She smiled. 'Your granddad always used to say

227

when you were little that you were the spitting image of her, Cari. Never mind, I expect we'll come across some, one day. I'm sure there are all sorts of things hidden in that attic still.'

'I'm sure there are,' replied Carys, smiling affectionately at her mother. It was good to see Mam entering so wholeheartedly into the spirit of things. Mam's walking still might be a bit of a struggle at times, but at least her mind appeared to be speeding back into full working order.

And talking of things hidden…

Carys hesitated a minute, then reached into her bag once more. 'There's this photograph, too,' she said, placing the picture of the woman and child on the table. 'We weren't quite sure about who they could be.'

There was a murmur of conversation, as the little group gathered around. Mostly, Carys saw, they were shaking their heads as if none the wiser.

'May I see?' Across the table, Sara Jones reached out her hand for the photograph.

Carys turned the image to face her. 'We wondered if anyone might know who the child is?' she ventured.

Sara shook her head. 'I'm not sure. I'd have to ask my Alun about that one. He might have more of an idea, being older. But I know who the woman is, all right.'

'Really?' said Carys, eagerly.

'Oh yes. I remember her, from when I was a girl. Scared the living daylights out of me, she did. Not a woman you'd ever want to cross. There's no mistaking her. That's Blodeuwedd.'

'Blodeuwedd?' Carys stared at her. Sara might not be in the first flush of youth, but there was nothing doolally or fey about her, and she'd never claimed to know a character from the *Mabinogion* before. All the same…

'Nainie's mother. Hermione Meredith. The one who made the statues.'

'A woman made the statues!'

'Oh yes,' said Sara, nodding vigorously. 'Didn't they tell you about her in Pont-ar-Eden Primary?'

'No,' admitted Carys.

Sara clucked. 'Memories are so short, nowadays. So short. Taught herself, she did. Sculpting from stone that is. To make the statues for the garden. That's what she's holding in her hand, see. That chisel thing of hers. You used to see her with her hands all bandaged. That's what my mam used to tell me. Until she got the hang of it, that is. But Mam said you could still see the scars on her hands, years later. One determined woman, that one. She could do anything she set her mind to, they used to say.' Sara grinned, impishly. 'She could show the men a thing or two and all, if you ask me.'

Edna was peering down at the photograph with a frown. 'Yes, of course. That's her all right. David and Huw's great-grandmother.' She lowered her voice. 'And not quite the lady she made herself out to be, according to your mam.'

Sara clucked, louder this time. 'Mam had very definite ideas of what a lady should be.'

'Well, she wasn't from London, like she claimed,' returned Edna, primly. 'My aunt Alice was brought up in Whitechapel, and she always said that was no London accent she'd ever heard of.'

'Well, Hermione Meredith was hardly likely to have come from the east end, was she?' said Sara, with a rare flash of irritation.

Edna took a step back. 'I was only saying. And then there was that detective.'

'Detective?' Carys stared at her.

'Oh, yes.' Edna was clearly enjoying herself. 'Private detective he said he was. Well, at least, that's what my mam always said.'

'Oh, so it wasn't recently,' said Carys, disappointed.

'Oh, no. Mam was a little girl at the time. 1912, it must have been. She remembered it, because it was the time when the newspapers were full of all the stories of the *Titanic* sinking. And there was this man, asking questions. And all the children were told not to say anything to him about Mrs Meredith. Not a word. Mam said it was because of the Children's Hospital.'

'David's great-grandmother *did* build a Children's Hospital in Pont-ar-Eden,' put in Gwynfor, who had left the rest of his charges and was listening intently. 'It's still there. It became the community centre after the last war.'

'Well, there you go.' Edna was triumphant. 'And there always was something. You remember Mair, when the boys were small: that producer from the BBC who wanted to make a film about the statues?'

'Oh, yes,' said Mam, who had been watching this exchange with a faintly bemused expression on her face. 'So there was. Marianne was full of it, for weeks.'

'Until Paul put his foot down,' said Edna, darkly. 'The boys' mother always got her own way, but not that time.' She looked around at her watching audience. 'Haven't you seen *Who Do You Think You Are?* Things like that always turn out to have some truth in them. I bet those statues have quite a story to them, somewhere. If you really looked, that is.'

Chapter Fifteen

In the little glade, the statues stood quiet and still under the last flickering of sun. A breeze stirred the leaves now and again, sending shadows racing and the branches into life, with a dry rattle of dead leaves.

'They are beautiful,' sighed Carys, gazing round at the blank-eyed faces with their air of neglected melancholy.

'Whoever made them was certainly skilled,' David said. Carys glanced at him, hearing the unease in his voice. Maybe she shouldn't have said anything. Or at least not that bit about the private detective and David's great-grandmother having something to hide in her past. It had seemed quite an exciting possibility at the time. A real detective story all ready to be uncovered with a bit of hunting through Ancestry.co.uk. But if it was your family, and you suspected your parents hadn't wanted anyone to know about it and had rushed off in secret to prevent anyone ever finding out... Carys bit her lip, hard.

'She certainly understood human nature, too,' added Rhiannon, who was gazing round at the faces intently. She tugged at a bramble that was daring to arch over Ceridwen's cauldron, revealing the fiercely exultant face of the old woman. 'I wonder just how deep that understanding went. And how she came by it.'

'I'm sure the private detective thing was just a story,' said Carys. 'And it was a long time ago. It could hardly matter now.'

'I'm sure you're right.' Rhiannon, however, sounded unconvinced.

There was a moment's silence. Squirrels dashed to and fro above their heads, pausing every now and then to chatter angrily at Hodge, who was busily engaged in trying to work out where his latest quarry had vanished to, and was dashing from tree to tree as if there just had to be a solution to this mystery somewhere.

'Except that Mum and Dad were obviously trying to find out something. Something they felt might upset Nainie and wanted to keep secret,' David said at last. He was frowning into the face of King Arthur. 'Suppose it really was something to do with Great-Grandmother Hermione and the statues?'

'I suppose it could be,' said Rhiannon. 'Although I don't see how we are ever going to find out now.'

'I suppose.' He seemed lost in thought. 'D'you know, I never thought about it before, but looking at all those old photographs, that looks so like Dad.'

Rhiannon jumped slightly. 'What does?'

'King Arthur. Dad when he was young, I mean.'

She joined him and peered at the face. 'I suppose he does. Funny how you can look at a thing for most of your life and not really see it. But I can't see how it could be. Unless it was a portrait of your grandfather when he was young, of course. Or maybe even your great-grandfather, come to that.'

'So could any of the others be portraits of the Merediths too, in that case?' said Carys.

'I suppose they could.' Rhiannon frowned. 'I'd need to have another look at the family photographs. I met some of the family at Paul and Marianne's wedding, and later, of course, but I can't say I really knew any of them well.'

'It would be fascinating if they were,' said Carys.

David stuck his hands in his pockets. 'Unfinished business,' he muttered, under his breath. 'That's what Nainie used to say sometimes, after that last stroke, wasn't it, Rhiannon? I always felt she was trying to tell us something.'

'Yes,' replied Rhiannon, quietly. 'But Nainie struggled with her speech and her memory during those last years: we don't know for sure she meant anything to do with the statues.'

Carys cleared her throat. 'Look, I started this.'

'You didn't set out to,' said Rhiannon.

'But I still started it, when I went looking for the photographs for Mam.' She took a deep breath. 'Gwenan's coming to stay with Mam next week. I need to go back to Chester for a few days. Work stuff,' she explained to two faintly enquiring, too-polite–to-ask glances. A girl has some pride, and the split with Joe was too recent, too viscerally painful, to open up to others' scrutiny. And especially not when David Meredith was about.

David, she noticed, was watching her rather too closely for comfort, almost as if trying to read her mind. She pulled herself together. 'Anyhow, the thing is that I was thinking of going to Devon for a few days after I've finished. Clear my head a bit, you know? A couple of days in Cornwall, doing a bit of private investigating, sounds good to me.'

'You mean, find this Treverick place?' said Rhiannon.

Carys nodded. 'That seems to be where the answers might lie. Or at least, that's what the Merediths thought. And isn't it weird that neither of you had seen a photograph of Treverick Hall until I found the postcard in Mam's attic? Surely the postcard should have been in Plas Eden, not at Willow Cottage at all.'

David toyed with a cluster of fallen leaves around his foot. 'Yes, I've been wondering about that. There might be something in Eden, I suppose.'

Rhiannon shook her head. 'There was nothing amongst your Dad's stuff, or Nainie's. You're right, Carys; you would have expected at least something.'

Carys walked over to gaze at the statue of Blodeuwedd. She wasn't more than a girl, she thought. A teenager. Sixteen, seventeen? Eighteen, at the most. That moment – if you're lucky – before life touches you at all. Innocent.

A double-edged sword, innocence. Sometimes it can mean being so protected, so open to the world, you've no idea there is pain and suffering, or how cruel your fellow human beings can be. Carys found herself shivering.

'It might not have anything to do with this Treverick Hall,' David was saying dubiously. 'And nobody seems to have been able to find out anything about a Treverick Hall on the internet.'

'Except Treverick was where your Mum and Dad were going.'

'Yes.' David sounded thoughtful. 'Dad did go to serious lengths to find out something, and not to let Nainie know he was looking at all.'

'Looking at Treverick Hall,' said Carys.

David met her eyes. Something was troubling Carys and he knew for a fact this return to Chester wasn't anything to do with her work. It couldn't be. Not with that fragile, deeply wounded feeling he sensed wrestling inside her. No, this was far more personal. She obviously needed company, he told himself. Someone to look after her, if she needed it. As a friend, of course. And who better than someone she'd known for most of her life?

It was the least a friend could do, David told himself. Just be there for her. The fact that it might give the two of them a chance to get to know each other again, far away from the looming distraction of Plas Eden – well, that was purely coincidental. Nothing to do with it at all.

He took a deep breath. 'Are you really sure you want to go?'

She nodded. 'You bet.'

'Then I'd like to come with you.' He caught the look of dismay that crossed her face. Not exactly flattering. His pride told him to walk away and just let her get on with it. The rest of him dug its heels in. This was, without doubt, a last chance. Let her go now, he sensed, and he'd be letting her go forever. Even if, at the end of the time, they both knew that they had grown too far apart for it ever to work, at least then the question would be answered, and they could both get on with their lives. Besides, he was a Meredith, and a Meredith never gave up that easily.

Carys cursed inwardly. She knew he probably meant well – and it was his family, after all – but this was the last thing she needed. Why had she opened her big mouth in the first place?

It had been hard enough persuading Gwenan to take charge of Mam for a week, and even harder persuading Mam to accept the arrangement, but Carys – feeling horribly guilty – had persisted. She wasn't ready to tell either of them the sordid failures of her personal life, or face the inevitable questions. First, she needed to retrieve her things from the flat and make the final break with Joe. Most of all, she needed time to herself to get her head back together. A bit of space, a bit of time on her own to do some wound-licking and regain a bit of self-esteem in the process.

A few days investigating the realities of finding affordable land in Devon had seemed a good project. Looking to the future. One step closer to deciding where her ultimate destiny lay. The last thing she needed was David Meredith. Not to mention any sentimental view of the past he might have lurking in the background. He was a man, after all, she muttered to herself, and she was seriously off all men: now, and forever. Unless Hugh Fearnley Whittingstall happened to be passing, of course.

'Don't feel you have to,' she said, knowing she sounded horribly stilted. She didn't dare glance at Rhiannon, who was probably viewing the whole thing as some deep plot to get David on his own, away from Plas Eden, just so Carys could lure him into her lair with who-knows-what feminine whiles and return, ring safely on her finger. The mere thought sent her scarlet with mortification.

'I'd like to,' replied David. 'If it really was something about the statues that Mum and Dad were trying to find, then I feel I'd like to finish it, if you see what I mean.'

'Oh.' There was no argument to that. 'In that case, yes, that's fine.'

'Great,' said David quickly, before she could change her mind again. 'Why don't I meet you in Chester? It seems pointless to take two cars. We can book rooms at the Treverick Arms. At least that still exists.'

'Um, yes. Of course.' Carys had an uncomfortable sensation of being swept along, despite herself. Oh, what the hell. At least he seemed to have got the point: 'rooms' was unmistakably in the plural. She hoped Rhiannon had noted this, too.

She discovered Rhiannon was watching them both intently. 'What about Huw? What are you going to tell him?'

'He doesn't need to know,' replied David, firmly. 'Not unless we really find something. He'll only disapprove. And what's the point of upsetting him if there's nothing there?'

'So you're intending to keep this a secret?' Rhiannon sounded uneasy. 'Like Paul and Marianne, all those years ago.'

David blinked. 'But that was an accident. Everybody said it was an accident. Wrong time, wrong place. One of those things. It couldn't have been anything else.'

'No, of course not.' But the unease was still there in Rhiannon's voice.

The last of the light was by now fading from under the trees.

'I'd better get back,' said Carys. 'Mam'll start to wonder where I am.'

'I'll walk back with you,' said David. 'I want to get to Low-Price before it shuts. Milk, wasn't it, Rhiannon. Anything else?'

'Not unless you spot anything particularly exciting for tea.'

'Okay. Do you want me to take Hodge?'

'No, you're fine.' Rhiannon bent down to stroke the head resting quietly at her knee. 'He had a good walk this morning. I'll take him back with me and get him and the cats fed, so we can have peace and quiet when you get back.'

'Fine by me,' said David. 'And the company is never of the best outside Low-Price this time of night. Might lead you into bad habits, Hodge.'

❧

For a while, David and Carys made their way in silence.

Then David cleared his throat. 'Your mam seems much better, when I've seen her in the Boadicea?'

'Yes, she is. It seems to have taken a long time, but it feels as if she's beginning to turn the corner. She's started washing up and peeling potatoes. I think she's determined to get back to being independent.'

'Still, I expect she feels better having you here.'

'Yes, I suppose she does.' Carys gave a rueful smile. 'Although I'm not sure we'd last very long in the same house

237

once she's well enough to take charge again. And Gwenan's finally persuaded her she needs a permanent home help. So, for the moment at least, she should be able to cope on her own.'

'Right.' He eyed her sideways in the faint orange glow of the nearest street lamp, as they approached the village. 'Merlin was mentioning about leasing the land around Eden Farm.'

'Oh?' murmured Carys. Merlin was nothing if not a fast worker, then.

'Mmm. He said something about you maybe renting part of the land for a bit? Setting up your own business?'

'Yes.' Carys avoided his eyes. Damn. This hadn't given David the wrong idea, had it? That she was staying in Pont-ar-Eden to be close to Plas Eden and to him? 'I'm considering my options, that's all. Setting up a business of my own is what I've wanted to do for years. My first choice was Devon, before Mam got ill. It still could be. I was just exploring possibilities up here in case Mam needs me for a bit longer.'

'Oh.' They walked on in silence again until they reached Low-Price, where they came to a halt. 'I'd better go in and get my milk.' David's eyes travelled over the small group of hooded youths and scantily clad girls, who appeared to be holding an impromptu party on the bench outside the convenience store. 'Will you be okay?' he asked.

'I'll be fine,' she smiled. 'They're pretty harmless.'

As a teenager, she'd itched for the freedom of the kids who didn't have to be in doing their homework, or for the family meal. Funny how you didn't spot until much later that the kids who roamed the streets unchecked and hung around Low-Price were the ones who, in the end, had the fewest choices of all. At least Mam and Dad had always pushed the three of them. Made sure they had the means to support themselves and made sure they knew they had more choices than to end up with a child to raise before their own life had really started.

'See you then,' David muttered awkwardly. There was so much more he wanted to say. But, despite never having been a man who was stuck for words, he now didn't know where to begin.

Carys fished out her mobile. 'Give me your number. I'll ring you back and you'll have mine. Then I can text you when I know what I'm doing.' It was her turn to sound awkward. 'It might not be easy to ring, especially once I get to Chester.'

'Of course. Here.' Numbers exchanged, they hesitated a moment, neither of them quite sure what to say again.

'Good evening!'

Carys turned to find Nesta and Haf trotting down the street in their Sunday best. 'Hello,' she replied.

'Good evening,' said David, with the hunted look of one who wished nothing more than to dive behind the frozen meals counter in Low-Price until the coast was clear.

'Lovely evening, isn't it,' said Nesta, watching them both with eagle eyes.

'Going anywhere nice?' smiled Carys.

'It's our scrabble night,' said Haf, who was clutching a shopping bag bulging with the unmistakable outline of a wine bottle.

'Best night of the week,' added Nesta, who was holding a box of German biscuits, hot from the shelves of Lidl on Talarn High Street.

'Have a good time,' called Carys, as the sisters set off on their way again, heads suspiciously close together, deep in conversation.

David groaned.

'Charming,' said Carys, prepared to see the funny side. 'Is that all the thanks I get? I've just made your reputation as the village Lothario. They'll be treating you like the real lord of the manor now. I'm the one who's going to have to spend my days as a low-down hussy.'

'I'm not the ...'

'Okay. Heathcliff, then.'

He struggled with his dignity for a few moments, but she could see the old familiar twitch of his mouth. 'Don't be daft,' he said. But he was laughing, all the same.

It was the laugh that did it. That warm, rumbling laugh of his when he was trying his best not to. Carys swallowed as her stomach leapt instantly into one of those familiar high-dive somersaults and her toes began to tingle.

Oh no. Definitely not. Not again. Not ever. The last thing she needed was complications – and particularly complications of the David Meredith kind – in her life.

'See you,' she said hastily. And with a wave, she was off, careful not to look back once.

This was definitely not the time to prompt any of the old oops-they-only-had-a-double-room wheeze. She wasn't born yesterday, thank you very much. And, besides, she had a heart to keep safe.

❧

Rhiannon sat for a while amongst the statues after David and Carys had gone, until there was scarcely any light left under the trees.

She couldn't quite get rid of the sense of unease that hung around her. But surely that was only natural, with the recent conversation bringing back memories, and the ring of the

240

doorbell of her London flat all those years ago that had changed her life forever.

The statues seemed closer in the darkness. As if they were gathering around her, stone faces flickering into life. Was that hostile, or sorrowful? She had always been certain of their mood before. But not tonight. A night breeze stirred, sending a sigh of leaves around the little glade. Tonight, she would not have been surprised if a stone hand had appeared on her shoulder, like the commodore in *Don Giovanni*, dragging her down to hell for her sins.

Through the gentle sway of trees the lights of Eden flickered, its shape rising like a ghost through the darkness. Houses were like people, thought Rhiannon: living, evolving beings, formed from their past and always being reformed for their future. And nothing can stay still forever.

'I've changed, too,' she said aloud, the realisation flooding through her. Her memory of Nainie was still as strong, but now it was the good memories that were surfacing above the painful ones: as if, over the past months, a healing had finally taken place.

She missed her like crazy, of course she did, along with the precious moments when they had giggled together like schoolgirls for no particular reason at all, and even the long hours of listening to the same stories over and over again that, at the time, she had felt would drive her mad.

But at ninety-seven, Hermione Anne had simply had enough. She had lived through most of the twentieth century and seen it turn into the twenty-first. She had outlived her only child and most of her friends. Her hearing was failing, her sight was almost gone, and once she no longer had the energy to potter round the courtyard of an evening sipping her 'gin and it' (a lethal combination of gin and dry white

241

Martini, without hide nor hair of tonic water to soften the blow), she didn't see much point any more.

Much as she loved her, Rhiannon could not wish her back. It would have been like torture to the gentle, delicate woman who had been the centre of Eden from before the Second World War to punk rock and the iron lady. An agony to the woman who, even in her seventies, had wandered her beloved gardens daily, and every evening, sunshine, rain or hail, had taken generations of Labradors up to the rusting iron bench overlooking the bay.

She would not, Rhiannon knew, have missed those final months, not for the world. They might have drained her and left her with a hollow in her heart, but for Hermione Anne it had been a gentle closing down, a pulling of her life around her, like a shawl, closer and closer, until there was a shell that looked like Nainie, but wasn't her at all.

It had been a time when Rhiannon had seen that nature can have kindnesses as well as cruelty, making her feel she would never be afraid of the fact of death again. It was a time when every brief flicker of the old Hermione Anne had been unbearably precious, urging Rhiannon to take every moment as it happens and not waste a second regretting the past or worrying about the future. And it had been a time when life had been stripped down to its simplest, its most straightforward, when nothing else had mattered outside the easing out of a life well lived.

Rhiannon took a deep breath, steadying herself. Time to let go, she acknowledged. Time to move forward. Nainie would always be with her, as the boys were. As Marianne was. As all the people she had ever known and loved were still alive and with her, and would always be, for as long as she lived.

But now, she finally understood, it was time for her to move on beyond Eden, into wherever life might take her. 'This is my time,' she told herself.

Eden's future was for David to sort out. Rhiannon could feel the responsibility finally falling away from her. She would love Plas Eden until the day she died. But it had already slipped into the part of her life that was memory, along with her life in London and the boys' childhood. It would never again be the centre of her life.

Her application for the artist in residence in Vermont was still on her computer desktop, unfinished. The closing date for online applications was midnight tonight. With strong coffee and a good dose of adrenalin, she could just about get it in on time.

Rhiannon took a deep breath. Even if she didn't succeed with this application, she would keep on trying, pushing away at any opportunity that came her way. At her age, an opportunity might only come once. No second chances. If she was going to be serious about this, she needed to focus on the future. Her future. And that meant freeing herself to take up any chance – any sliver of a chance – that came her way.

At her side, Hodge raised his head, a low growl rumbling in his throat.

'It's all right.' Rhiannon bent to stroke his head in reassurance. 'It's only Tash.' A black shadow slunk beneath the statues, leaping up onto the rounded head of the giant and mewing a plaintive greeting.

If David moved from Plas Eden too, heaven knew what would happen to Hodge and the cats, she thought, as she felt Hodge lean himself lovingly against her. But between them, they'd find a way. There had to be some solution that would keep them all safe and contented. Animals, like people, did move, too. Even to the other side of the world. They'd cross that bridge when they came to it.

She gave Hodge's head a brisk pat. 'Come on then, you two: let's get you back and fed.'

Hodge wasn't one to pass up the allure of dog biscuits topped off by the remains of last night's stew, but there was the little matter of checking whether this cat really was his cat and not some interloper who needed marching firmly off the premises. Rhiannon waited as he reached up gingerly to touch noses, while Tash graciously bent down from her advantage to return the greeting, claws sheathed.

The darkness was by now almost complete. Rhiannon pressed the button on Hodge's night-time collar, setting a ring of crimson lights flashing into the blackness. Then she fished out her torch and switched it on. The statues retreated, eyes blank, as she swung the beam around.

Just in case.

'Come along, Hodge.' The circle of flashing lights trotted obediently at her side. Up ahead, Tash's eyes fluoresced in the beam of the torch as she turned to check they were following her lead, tail held high.

Slowly, they made their way up towards the patchwork of lights in the distance, where Eden lay waiting.

There was a fire burning in the grate. I stood there for a moment, feeling its warmth on my skin in the glow of candles on the mantelpiece.

'You must be soaked to the skin,' he said.

I shook my head. 'Just my coat,' I murmured, shrugging myself out of the damp sleeves. He took it and draped it over a chair next to the fire, where it steamed gently. My hat was in an equally sad state, dripping water down the back of my neck, so I removed that, too. But not my boots. For all I could feel the rain seeping through my stockings, chilling my feet. My coat I could grasp in a moment, or – at worst – leave without. But not my boots. Not without the first policeman I met arresting me for a vagrant. And the questions that might then be asked.

'Can I offer you a cup of tea?' He sounded a little uncertain. As well he might, with an unattended young woman arriving at his door in the middle of the night. I shook my head. 'A glass of wine, perhaps?'

'No! Thank you,' I added, hastily. For all the fire was warm, I could not stay still. I paced the room for a few moments. The hem of my dress and petticoats were heavy with rain and London mud, I could feel their weight slapping hard against my ankles as I walked.

He watched me in silence. Patiently waiting. I could see the faint enquiry on his face. And the concern. It was the concern that nearly undid me. But it was too late for me to go back now.

'I came to tell you … to explain about myself,' I said. 'And to tell you why you can't – why you mustn't…' I turned away from him. I could hear the crackle of the logs in the grate and the rain tapping rhythmically on the windowpanes. 'I never was a widow,' I said, at last.

I heard him move. Take a step closer to me. 'And do you think I didn't know? I didn't guess?' He grasped my hands, and pulled me gently back towards the warmth of the fire. 'How many "Mrs Smiths" do you think come through the door of the hospital each year? Do you think I don't know their stories, and the suffering they have been through? And do you think such a thing matters to me? You matter to me. Nothing else.'

'You don't know me.'

'Yes, I do,' he said, very gently, holding my hands tight. His lips were warm on the back of my hand. 'I know you. You as

245

you are now. And that's all I ever need to know.'

I shook my head. 'No,' I said. 'You don't understand.' I kept my eyes on my fingers, still held close within his. I swallowed hard. But it had to be said. 'There was a child…' My voice was a whisper. I waited for the hands to fall away from mine. If anything, they held me tighter.

'Any child that is yours is part of you,' he said. 'I never aimed to pick and chose what I loved. I love everything about you.' I looked up at that, and met his eyes. They were clear and untroubled. And I knew at that moment just how much I loved him. And how much it was I would lose.

He released one of his hands, reaching up to brush the wet hair from my face. 'Plas Eden is a lifetime away from London. No one knows you there. No one need ever know. I'm not the only man to marry a widow –' His finger rested on my lips, stilling the protest with a smile. 'Or to adopt her child and love it and raise it as his own.'

I said nothing. I could not speak. But he must have seen it, there on my face. 'Oh dear God,' was all he said. 'Oh my dear God.'

I don't know if his hands drew away from me, or not. All I knew was that I held him, tight as a drowning woman, and I rested my cold, cold forehead on the warmth of his hands, so that I could not see his eyes as I spoke.

Part Three

Part Three

Chapter Sixteen

Very little was said on the drive down to Cornwall.
Carys was tired after two days pulling apart the pieces of
her life in Chester, and thankfully David appeared to be in a
similarly uncommunicative mood. They were both happy to
let the radio do the talking as they took it in turns on the long
journey south.

Of course she would go back to Chester. Her friendship
with Poppy was as strong as ever, and she would almost
certainly keep in touch with her other friends. Besides she was
lucky Tylers didn't want to lose her, even if in the end she
decided not to apply for the full-time post. To her relief, they
had been understanding about her commitment to Mam and
agreed to her taking on more clients while working from
home. This meant that even if she stayed in Pont-ar-Eden, she
would be travelling back to Chester at least once a month for
meetings. But it wouldn't be the same.

But at least she didn't have to go back to the flat ever again,
and her contact with Joe – quite obviously painful on both
sides, during their brief but necessary, conversations – could
now be mainly via a solicitor. It wasn't that she hated him, but
it had amazed her, how quickly they had grown apart in just
a few months, until there seemed to be no point of contact at
all.

She hoped that one day they'd be able to return to a

friendship like the one they had shared before. But somehow she doubted it. Joe was already the high-powered businessman. She felt like a slightly shabby hippy at his side. They were already at opposite ends of a spectrum with utterly different aims for the future. And a whole lot of hurt feelings caught in the middle.

Now the remains of her life in the flat were sitting in Poppy's office at the top of her house. She had left the big items, like furniture. There was nowhere to store them and too many reminders. And anyhow whatever her future held she had a feeling it would not fit the clean, minimalist lines of the pieces she and Joe had chosen together. There seemed very little left of a shared life. The thought was depressing.

By the time they left the motorway at Exeter, heading for the north Cornwall coast, Carys was relieved to relinquish the wheel to David again.

'Not long now,' he said, following the reassuring tones of the SatNav as she directed them along the dual carriageway, then smaller, winding roads.

At last, over the brow of a hill the rocky coastline appeared, the calm afternoon light gleaming on a wide expanse of sea.

'We're here,' said Carys, as 'Welcome to Treverick' appeared at the side of the road, along with a request to drive carefully.

'Great,' muttered David, who was beginning to look tired, and more than a little strained. His bad leg had clearly been bothering him for the past hour, which only made him more stubborn in his refusal of Carys' offer to take over. She resisted the urge to kick him for his pigheadedness. It definitely wouldn't help.

A steep street and a few more lanes between pretty cottages, and the SatNav finally announced that they had reached their destination.

'Oh, charming,' muttered David irritably, gazing round at the deserted village square with a network of roads leading off in several directions.

'Over there.' Carys indicated an illuminated sign in the far corner of the square. 'It's the village pub as well, remember.'

'Right. I hope there's parking.'

'Bound to be.'

They followed a tiny lane and arrived in a large gravel parking space next to a busy pub garden, where drinkers were enjoying the last of the warmth.

Yawning and stretching, they stumbled stiffly out of the car.

'Well, we made it.' David limped round to the boot to lift out their luggage.

'Why? Did you think we wouldn't?'

'No. No, of course not.' He zapped the locks on the car. 'But I promised Rhiannon I'd let her know as soon as we arrived. I think she was feeling – well, a bit superstitious?'

'Oh, I see,' murmured Carys, slinging her bag over one shoulder, and following him inside.

The Treverick Arms had low, dark beams and comfortable, slightly battered-looking chairs. A warm smell of chips mingled with the pub smell of beer. Carys found she was ravenous.

Having booked in, they were shown up creaking wooden stairs to their rooms, along the same corridor, but discreetly distant from each other.

'Fancy seeing if there's somewhere open in the harbour?' said David.

Carys nodded. 'Sounds good to me. Meet you in the bar in half an hour?'

'Perfect.'

Her room was small but pretty, tucked under the eaves at the back of the pub, with a view towards the sea. It was immaculately clean, with a flowered bedspread and a bale of fluffy white towels in the bathroom. She was hot and sticky, smelt vilely of car fumes and ached all over. A quick shower and a change of clothes later, and she at least felt human again.

Making her way down to the bar, she discovered David deep in conversation with the owner, Mr McIntyre, as declared on the website and alcohol licence.

'Treverick Hall,' Mr McIntyre was saying. 'I can't say I've heard of it. There's a Treverick Gardens, just outside the village. You'll see the signs at the harbour. I haven't heard anyone mention a Hall. But then I'm not from around here.' As Mr McIntyre sounded unmistakeably Scottish, this revelation came as no surprise. 'I don't suppose you've tried Google?'

''Fraid so,' David replied with a smile, as Carys joined them. 'No mention of Treverick Hall. Or any gardens, come to that.'

'Well, they're not exactly gardens. More like overgrown scrub really. Been a bit of an eyesore for years, until the council decided to do something about it earlier this summer.' He eyed them both with mild curiosity. Young man and young woman, not obviously related but not sharing a room. Carys could see his point: not exactly twenty-first century stuff. Treverick was probably just as bad as Pont-ar-Eden when it came to gossip, she considered, hiding a grin. This one would no doubt keep the villagers spinning stories around them for weeks. 'On holiday, are you?'

'Sort of,' David replied, slightly warily.

'Plus a bit of research,' added Carys. Mr McIntyre might not know every detail about Treverick, but he must have regulars who did. 'We're part of a family history project.' Almost true, without going into details.

'Really?' He looked up from pouring a pint. 'And was that where you came across this Treverick Hall, then?'

'That's right.'

'Thanks, Will.' Mr McIntyre handed over the finished pint to his customer and scattered coins into his till with a thoughtful air. 'Well then, it's my wife you need to talk to. She's into local history.' He grinned. 'Mary's a proper Treverick girl, see.'

David caught Carys' eye. Change of plan? Scampi and chips and a pint, and save the harbour for later? Carys nodded.

'Might she be around at all?' David enquired.

Mr McIntyre shook his head. 'Off with our daughter in Port Isaac. Being a grandmother,' he added, with unmistakeable pride. 'But she'll be back in time for tomorrow's breakfasts. You can certainly speak to her then. I'll mention it to her, if you like.'

'Thanks,' said David. 'That would be great.'

'Thanks,' called Carys, as, scampi and chips abandoned, they made their way out into the village.

❧

It was only a few minutes' walk down to the sea, past neat rows of cottages painted in soft pinks, blues and yellows. Seagulls chattered from the rooftops, taking off every now and again with a raucous shriek, or swerving down towards the sea, while cats stretched out on any convenient piece of wall, yawning in the warm evening sun.

Built within the curved rocky bay of a natural harbour, the little quay was buzzing by the time they arrived there. Tourists mingled with the beautiful surfing dudes among the outdoor tables of restaurants and a small kiosk selling 'award-winning' pasties 'as seen on TV'. The tide was high, and in the harbour a small collection of fishing vessels rocked and swayed, sending a decidedly fishy aroma rising from the waves.

'Treverick Gardens,' said Carys, pausing at a small, rather roughly made tourist sign and forgetting her empty stomach and the delicious smells overpowering the sea when the wind was in the right direction. The arrow pointed away from the harbour, towards one side of the village.

David glanced at her. 'Fancy a quick look? We can have a proper nosy tomorrow morning. Unless you prefer to eat.'

'It'll be dark before long. How about going to the gardens first?'

He grinned. 'Sounds good to me.'

They followed the sign along the paved walkway in front of the harbour. After a while, the walkway became a path, leading them up a small rise.

'Wow, beautiful,' sighed Carys, as they reached the top of the small mound. Behind them they could see the harbour, full of life, while in front, the rocky coastline opened out. Ranks upon ranks of sheer cliffs stretched into the distance. Dark rocks rose up from a clear turquoise sea, now touched with a glow of orange light as the sun began to set. Despite the stillness of the evening, rollers crashed every now and again, sending up wild sprays of foam.

'This must be it,' said David, indicating a stone wall half hidden in ivy and undergrowth, which ran the length of the ground rising up from the sea. 'I don't know about a garden, but if I was going to build Treverick Hall, I'd certainly build it here.'

Sure enough, a few minutes later a simple, decidedly temporary-looking sign set next to an archway in the wall, announced 'Treverick Gardens'.

'That looks like the illustration on the pub sign,' said Carys. 'Except it's honeysuckle, not clematis.' There was no gate to bar their way, and they stepped, slightly gingerly, inside. 'Oh, wow.'

There were no two ways about it; it was like walking into a magical landscape. Warmed in the soft evening light, the gardens opened up into intricate swirls of flowerbeds between gravel pathways, framed by a small woodland. Immediately the noise from the harbour vanished, leaving only the chatter of sparrows and the clear song of a blackbird.

'There's a fountain,' said Carys, hearing the quiet ripple of running water between the birdsong. It took a moment to work out the direction, but eventually they made their way into the trees.

'They must be still working on this,' said David, as they paused at newly dug earth.

'It has to be a fountain of some kind.' Carys peered into the shadows, trying to make out the source of the watery sounds. The sun had finally vanished, bringing dusk to the little gardens. She hesitated, torn between curiosity and being ever so slightly spooked.

David had followed a path to one side between newly – and severely – restrained rhododendrons. 'I think it's a waterfall.'

He was right. They ducked beneath a second arch, heavily entwined with clematis and heady with an exotic scent that vaguely hinted at spiced chocolate. There a waterfall meandered down among rocks, with bright little alpine plants glowing on either side.

'That doesn't look natural.' Carys had her gardening head on. 'The ground doesn't look steep enough behind to bring down that amount of water. It looks like one of those Victorian water features. The ones that are supposed to look like wild places. I bet this is another part of the garden design.'

'You're right.' David was crouched down, peering at a small sign that was no more than a laminated piece of A4 tacked to a post. 'It says here that this is the wilderness area of Treverick Gardens, which is still in the process of being restored.'

'It is pretty.' Carys made her way onto the stone bridge over the stream where the waterfall ended in a small pool, and then vanished underground. 'I've seen some that look really tacky, but this is almost natural – oh!'

David looked up at her sharp intake of breath. 'What is it?'

'There's a statue. Up there, amongst the gunnera.'

'The what?'

'That massive leafy thing.'

'Oh. Right.' He sounded wary. There were statues, and statues. And even he knew that old gardens like this were likely to be littered with all kinds of follies and classical-style ornaments. 'What kind?'

'Not sure, I can only see an arm.' Carys was already picking her way up by the side of the fountain, careful not to disturb the plants. Just for a moment she hesitated, then she pushed aside the huge green leaves of the gunnera plant. 'It's a nymph. The ordinary kind.'

'Ordinary?'

'Not like Eden.'

'Oh, I see.' She couldn't tell if he were disappointed or relieved.

'She's rather sweet.' Carys wasn't ordinarily a fan of mock-Grecian garden ornaments. But although the nymph might not have been carved by the skilled hand that had created Eden's ghosts, she had a livelier face than the usual round of urn-bearing goddesses. 'There are more here, as well.' Now that her eyes had adjusted to the gloom beneath the trees, she found stone creatures hiding beneath the undergrowth. A fox slunk through the silver feathers of a santolina. A tiny dragon reared on its hind legs, stone fire rising into the air from behind a tangle of nasturtiums. A family of rabbits sat as if listening to a decidedly Victorian-looking fairy sitting on a toadstool.

'It's like the statue of Peter Pan in Kensington Gardens,' said David, joining her. He pointed to the far side of the waterfall. 'No wonder that nymph is smiling.'

Carys laughed. Sitting on a stone, hooves and all, a satyr was grinning with decidedly lustful intent at the smiling nymph, who didn't appear to object. 'Someone had a sense of humour,' she said.

'No gnomes, I see.'

'Definitely no gnomes.'

'You're right; they aren't a bit like Eden's statues,' said David.

'No,' replied Carys. 'And the Victorians did love this kind of thing.'

They glanced at each other. 'Still weird,' said David, at last.

'Mmm,' said Carys. It was growing decidedly dark by now. Her spine began to tingle.

Without warning, there was a rustling of the bushes and a creaking of broken sticks above them.

'Shit,' muttered David. He grabbed Carys' hand, and in a moment they were out of there, back down into the formal gardens and out through the arch onto the cliffs.

'What the hell was that?' whispered Carys, breathing hard, as they finally came to a halt at a safe distance from the gardens.

'Poachers, most probably,' he replied, doing his best to sound rational.

Behind them rose the high-pitched meowling of one serious catfight.

It was Carys who gave in first, bursting into laughter. After a moment of trying to keep his dignity, David joined in.

'What a pair of idiots,' said Carys, at last. Her hand, she discovered, was still being held. David appeared to realise this at the same moment. He released it hastily.

Carys glanced at his face in the semi-darkness. But it was turned away, as if trying to find the path once more. Hurt shot through her, taking her by surprise and sending her stomach into a tight knot.

The silence was becoming decidedly awkward.

'I don't know about you,' she said, 'but I'm starving.'

He turned back. An emotion passed briefly over his face. Relief, most likely, that she hadn't taken the unintended gesture seriously, decided Carys. At least, she told herself firmly, she hoped so. That feeling of rejection just now was her being silly. A shadow of something they had lost long ago. It was being physically close to him again, stirring up all those old emotions, that was all. It was a memory. It didn't mean anything. How could it? She should be glad David didn't appear to want anything more than companionship on this journey. That's exactly how she wanted things to be.

'Me too,' David was saying.

'Come on, then.'

They found the path, a strip of pale gravel in the dark, and made their way back towards the street lamps. The quay was still full of visitors, but they managed to find an outside table at a café overlooking the harbour.

To Carys' relief there was no question of being lured into a secluded candle-lit supper among these crowds. David didn't appear to mind, but chatted easily away as if they had never been anything other than childhood companions and their fish, when it arrived, was fresh and delicious. Carys found herself

258

relaxing. They'd been such good friends, she and David, when they were kids. They'd spent hours in each others' company, just talking or swimming in Eden lake. Maybe friendship was all it should ever have been, she thought to herself, a little sadly.

The decision to return to the Treverick Arms for a drink turned out to be a wise one, as they were both falling asleep before they had half-finished their first glass, the eight-hour drive finally catching up with them.

'Night!' called Carys, making her way to her room deliberately without any lingering. The moment the door was shut, she felt she could hardly stay awake long enough to crawl into bed. But by the time she had cleaned her teeth and changed into her nightshirt, she was wide-awake again. She wrapped herself in a dressing gown, and made herself a cup of tea and sat by the open window for a while.

From nearby came the quiet murmur of voices, interspersed with laughter. There was a smell of salt in the air, and the rush of faraway rollers. In the distance, under a starlit sky broken with cloud, she could make out the sudden flash of white as the waves broke, making their way towards the dark shadows of the cliffs.

She hadn't thought about Mam once. Just for a moment she felt guilty for such betrayal. But Mam was safe and no doubt obeying Gwenan without protest. At least without any outward protest. Gwenan was more than capable of keeping Mam well fed and out of trouble, even if she did disapprove loudly of *Coronation Street* and *Britain's Got Talent*, making Mam feel hesitant about watching them, even in the privacy of her own room. But that, thought Carys, was for Mam and Gwenan to sort out among themselves. You can't live someone's life for them and you can't protect them. And sometimes, out of nowhere, stuff happens.

Until she had looked after Mam, she had never really appreciated her own life. Free. Independent. With a career, and all things possible. Choices Mam had never had.

Mam had always put her family before herself. She'd never said whether she minded being the one who supported Dad, and made sure her three daughters passed their exams and didn't linger with the latch-key kids around the off-licence (the precursor to Low-Cost) after school. Mam had always had part-time jobs that didn't pay well, but could be fitted around looking after her own parents as they grew older and call in on Dad's sister, Aunt Menna, when she was ill. She'd never said if once, when she was younger, she'd dreamed of another life. It had never occurred to Carys before to wonder.

She didn't want Mam's life. Merlin was right: that was exactly what passing exams and getting out of Pont-ar-Eden had been about. Carys didn't even want her sisters' lives. They might be sisters, but they were very different. And the future? Carys sighed. One day, no doubt, she would get over the pain and sense of betrayal that still ground at her insides. One day she would be able to forget Joe and move on.

The sound of a sash window being pulled up close by made her jump. Was that David? Silently, she wriggled off the window seat. Being so close to him in the darkness felt uncomfortably intimate. How little she knew about his personal life, it struck her. He hadn't mentioned a girlfriend or a fiancé, any more than she'd talked about Joe. There was bound to be a woman, somewhere in the background. He was a nice guy, even without being lord and master of his very own Downton Abbey, and there weren't many of those to go around.

What was she thinking of? Carys shook herself. An entire queue of women camping outside the gates waiting for the chance of becoming mistress of Plas Eden would be nothing to do with her. Maybe being this close to David Meredith, even after all these years, wasn't such a good idea. His physical presence was confusing her, stirring up long-buried emotions and preventing her from thinking straight.

But it was only for a few days. Tomorrow they would find what they could about Treverick and the demolished Hall, then move on to North Devon and her original plan of looking at possible smallholdings. That would clear her head and get her brain back in focus again. Maybe David coming along on this trip had demonstrated just how impossible she would find it to live anywhere near Plas Eden if he remained there. It might be the very thing that pushed the balance towards staying with the Devon plan.

Exhaustion and sea-air finally catching up with her, Carys crawled into bed and was instantly sound asleep.

Chapter Seventeen

David was already seated in the little dining room. The rest of the guests were still in their rooms and he was talking with a tall woman in her early fifties, with a well-defined face – of the kind that advertises no nonsense tolerated in this pub, thank you – and a mass of curling brown hair, holding an empty tray in her hands.

'Oh, I know; they're charming, aren't they,' she was saying, with a smile. 'We couldn't believe it when we did a bit of exploring and found they were still there. There are loads more of those animals. One of the volunteers is repairing the ones that can be saved, and we've been talking about raising money to make reproductions of the rest.'

'Hi,' said Carys.

'Morning,' said David, smiling up at her. 'I was just telling Mrs McIntyre about our adventures in Treverick Gardens last night. They've just started doing a local history project here in Treverick, too, as it turns out.'

'Really?' This was a stroke of luck.

'Yes.' Mrs McIntyre, she discovered, was eying her closely. No doubt, like her husband, trying to fathom their relationship. 'Of course,' she continued, 'they're all the rage, nowadays, and it's really taken off over the past six months. I suppose that's what prompted the council to look at renovating Treverick Gardens. Plus making an extra tourist attraction of course.'

'Of course.'

Mrs McIntyre smiled. 'You must be Carys. I'm Mary. Can I get you tea? Coffee?'

'Coffee would be lovely, thanks.'

'Right you are.' Mary McIntyre disappeared into the kitchen.

'Sleep okay?' asked David.

'Like a log. And you?'

'The same.' He grinned, slightly sheepishly. 'Nothing like scaring yourself silly to wear you out.'

Carys laughed. 'I don't think we'll ever forget that.'

He sipped his coffee in silence as she sat down. The awkwardness was suddenly back again, an invisible gulf between them. Carys drank the glass of fresh orange juice next to her plate and frowned at the menu without really seeing it.

Within minutes, Mrs McIntyre had returned with an individual cafetiere of fresh coffee on a tray, plus a small jug of warm milk and a bowl of chocolate-brown sugar lumps.

She took their breakfast orders – bacon and eggs, naturally – transferring them in a low murmur to her husband, who set to work straight away.

'So it was Treverick Hall you were interested in, Rob said,' Mrs McIntyre remarked, rejoining them in the dining room.

'Yes,' said Carys. 'We couldn't find anything about it.'

'There was a Hall.' Mary McIntyre was tidying small sprays of freesias and carnations at each table and paused next to them. 'It's got rather a sad history, I'm afraid. It was pulled down just after the Second World War. It had been going to ruin for years.'

'Oh.' Carys met David's eyes. So that was that, then.

'Did you find some mention of it, then?' Mary scrutinised them both with open curiosity. 'When you were doing your history project, that is. Snowdonia, wasn't it, you come from? Long way. Maybe someone came here on holiday?'

'That's probably it.' Carys reached into her shoulder bag. 'I found this postcard in my mother's attic. That's what started it all.'

'Really?' Mary took the postcard with eager hands. 'We've been trying to find a good photograph of the Hall. They're really hard to come by. I had no idea there were postcards. I never thought. This must be the Hall in its hey day.' She peered closer. 'Ugly great thing, isn't it.'

Carys eyed her with surprise. Mrs McIntyre sounded almost angry. 'But those gardens are beautiful,' she said, uncertainly.

'Yes, the gardens are.' Mrs McIntyre's face relaxed. 'The Trevericks were known for their gardens. There were some quite famous garden designers among them, down the ages. Amateurs, of course.' Her tone was dry. 'The rich have to have something to fill the hours where earning a living should go.'

'So "Treverick" is a family, as well as a village?' said David.

'Yes. Well, it was. The immediate line died out with William Treverick at the beginning of the twentieth century. He left no heir, and no one in the family seems to have wanted to take on responsibility for the place. All sorts of relatives came out of the woodwork to fight over the money. But not the Hall. I suppose they knew no one would even want to buy a place like that after the First World War. No one wanted to be servants anymore, and that way of life had gone. Apart from a very few. Treverick Hall just fell into rack and ruin until it was requisitioned by the army in the 1940s. There's a cousin in St Ives. Jon Phelps. He might know more. I can ask him, if you like?'

'That would be great. Thanks,' said David.

'Although I should warn you, he might not be prepared to

share much with strangers. He's a bit protective about the family, is Mr Phelps. Personally, I don't see why. Dig deep enough, and there are tragedies and scandals in most families, I think you'll find.'

'Tragedies?' David's voice was sharp.

Mary McIntyre looked up from the card. 'Yes.' Her eyes were back to scrutinising his face closely. 'Treverick Hall seems to have been one of those places that just attract tragedy. There's a story in the village, you know, that when the tide is high in Treverick Bay, you can hear the sound of someone weeping if you listen carefully.'

'Really?' Carys had never been convinced by ghostly goings-on, but she felt a finger of ice edging down her spine.

Mary nodded. 'It's quite true. I've heard it myself, once or twice. It's the way the wind blows through the rocks, of course, but it's quite eerie, all the same.' She looked up. 'It's all part of the local tradition that the house and the family were cursed. But then I expect they say that about a lot of these old houses.' She turned her attention back to the postcard, turning it over in her hand. 'Pity there's no writing. I don't suppose you've any idea who it might be from?'

Carys shook her head. ''Fraid not. There isn't even a stamp, so it couldn't have been posted.'

'Oh, yes. So I see. How very curious.' There were creaks on the stairs from the bedrooms, accompanied by voices. In a moment, Mary was back to being a landlady once more. 'Well, I'm sure Jon Phelps will be eager to hear all you have to tell him. I'll phone him as soon as breakfast is over.'

'Thanks,' said David.

'Not at all.' Mary grinned. 'To be honest, you'll be doing me a favour. My history group have been trying to get Jon to let us see family photographs and find more information about the old Hall. With this postcard, he might just open up a bit. Good morning,' Mary called brightly to next group of guests as they appeared, bending under the low beam of the doorway. 'Mr and Mrs Johnson, isn't it? I'm Mary McIntyre. There's a table for you over here, by the window. Now, what can I get you. Tea? Coffee?'

❧

Jon Phelps was a small, wizened man in his mid seventies. His house – once they found it after several scenic tours of the higgledy-piggledy back streets that comprised St Ives' one-way system – was a 1920s-style whitewashed bungalow, set on the southernmost outskirts of the town.

'This craze for family history,' he remarked disparagingly, as he led David and Carys onto a small balcony overlooking the coastal path and the cliffs. 'History was history, in my day.' This wasn't exactly a promising beginning.

They sat down at a wooden table in the centre of the balcony, where a slightly built woman in her early sixties – who might possibly have been a nurse, but who had been firmly introduced as Mr Phelps' housekeeper – was pouring tea.

'It's very kind of you to give up your time, Mr Phelps,' said Carys.

He grunted. 'Yes, well. Persistent woman is Mary McIntyre. Women never give up, do they?' As if to prove his point, he directed a severe glance towards the housekeeper. 'Yes, that will do, Mrs Boscawen. Thank you. I'm sure we can manage now.'

'There's plenty of tea in the pot,' said Mrs Boscawen, taking not the slightest bit of notice of his tone. 'And I'll be in the kitchen if you need anything. Just give me a shout. And no more than two sugars, Mr Phelps. You know what the doctor said.'

'Yes, yes,' muttered Mr Phelps, irritably. He placed two chocolate biscuits in his saucer, with an air of defiance. Mrs Boscawen shook her head with indulgent despair. Carys caught her eye, and a look of silent understanding passed between them. Mrs Boscawen grinned, picked up the empty tray, and made her way back inside the house.

'Mary said you might know a bit more about Treverick Hall,' said David.

Jon Phelps stirred his third sugar lump into his tea and reached with silver tongs for a fourth. 'It was my sister Laura who set them all off on this. Leaving all those bits and pieces to the Treverick Historical Society in her will. Can't see why. No one had ever shown much interest before. Very proud of the Treverick connection, was Laura.' He eyed them severely. 'Leave well alone. That's what I say. No point in raking up the past. And people love it, of course, poking over other people's misery. I mean, that's all you see on television these days, isn't it? If it isn't those dreadful game shows and so-called celebrities climbing Everest.'

There was a moment's silence.

David cleared his throat. 'Mary mentioned that the house seemed to attract tragedy,' he persisted.

Mr Phelps drained his cup in one fell swoop and set about demolishing the biscuits before Mrs Boscawen could reappear. 'Mmm,' he said. His eyes were sharp. Carys had a feeling he was playing for time. Almost as if he wanted to come to a decision. 'Mary said you had some photographs you might like to show me.'

'Yes, that's right,' said David, sounding deliberately hesitant, so that Carys had to turn away to hide her smile. 'We wondered if there might be some link to Treverick Hall. Not that we want to put you to any trouble.'

The old man finished his second biscuit and placed another two on his saucer, as if the first ones had never moved. Mission apparently accomplished, he sat back in his chair. 'So where are these photographs, then?'

John Phelps went through the photographs of the statues and Plas Eden without any particular interest. He paused for a fraction longer on the greening Venus poised in the midst of her fountain. A slight frown tugged at his brows. But then it was gone, and the photograph placed at the back of the selection in his hand. The postcard of Treverick Hall, on the other hand, remained on the table in front of him.

'Magnificent,' he muttered, shaking his head. 'Travesty, that's what it is. Requisitioned by the army during the war, you know. Then it was abandoned and pulled down in the 1950s, like so many of our great buildings.'

For a few minutes he sat deep in thought.

'Mary told us about the last of the Trevericks,' said David, at last.

The old man roused himself. 'William Treverick, you mean?'

David nodded.

Jon Phelps shook his head. 'Tragedy, that was. Old William was the very last of the Trevericks. The proper Trevericks. Laura and me, we were just second cousins.' A wistful look came into the faded blue eyes. 'He died there, you know. In Treverick Hall. Wouldn't leave it, not until the last. There are letters from him. The Historical Society's got them now, I suppose. You'd have to ask them. He hoped right until the end that someone would come and take it over. Look after the place. Restore it to its former glory. But of course they didn't.'

'Who were the letters to?' prompted Carys, as he seemed to lapse back into thought once more.

'Oh, he never sent them. Left in the house, they were. He had a younger sister. Judith Treverick. Pretty little thing. The family always said he got mightily confused before the end. He was continuously writing letters to poor Judith, quite forgetting that she was long gone.' He clicked his tongue disapprovingly. 'Long gone.'

'I'm sorry,' murmured Carys.

Jon Phelps sniffed. 'You'd have thought the National Trust would have taken the Hall and the grounds over. Would have been a great thing for Treverick. Tourist attraction. That's what it might have been. But now, of course, it's far too late. Far, far too late.'

'But if they restore the gardens…' began Carys.

'Oh, the gardens.' The old man was dismissive. Carys glanced around the little garden below the balcony. Mostly green lawn, bordered by a regimented privet, with roses placed the same distance apart, and alternating red and white.

Okay. Point taken: not all Trevericks were heavily into gardening, then.

This was getting them nowhere, decided David, trying to hide his impatience. A total waste of time, in fact, despite Carys' skilful attentiveness toward their host. He smiled to himself. Carys had never been fazed by Nainie, unlike so many of his other childhood friends. Her ears had attuned quickly to the old lady's slightly slurred speech and she had not seemed to mind listening to an elderly woman reminisce about her childhood in Plas Eden. Along with how much of a struggle it had been for them all during the Second World War with the food shortages and the blackouts. And stories of the planes that came over – often lost bombers about to jettison their

269

cargo in a desperate bid to get home, or heading for destruction on the mountains.

He would never have expected her to look after Nainie. David frowned, remembering that accusation of hers, all those years ago. Here he was, feeling guilty enough that Rhiannon had put so much of her life on hold and determined to make sure she had a stab at making a career for herself, however late in the day it might seem. He swallowed. But at least Rhiannon had spent years studying before she came to Eden, and still had managed to develop her skills in her brief free hours. With no time to develop a career and with children thrown into the mix…

He watched Carys smile at Jon Phelps, nodding understandingly at his complaints. Now Carys had her mam to look after. David remembered Gwenan and Nia well enough to have no illusions that either of them would ever come riding to the rescue. And Carys could no more have dumped her mam in an old people's home than he could have ousted Nainie from Plas Eden as a drag and a nuisance. A youth spent caring for the elderly and infirm didn't strike him as much of an existence. Especially not when you had dreams and ambitions and a zest for embracing life and all that it might bring.

'I don't suppose you have any family photographs yourself, Mr Phelps?' he asked abruptly, pushing the uncomfortable conclusions to one side.

'Mmm.' Jon rose stiffly and went back inside the house, returning in a moment with an ornate silver frame. 'I got rid of the photographs when Laura went. Didn't see much point in keeping them myself. All those dead people. But this…' He held out the photograph with an air of pride. 'William Treverick tried his best to keep the Hall going, you see. When he was a young man. That's what caused it all. This is him.'

Inside the silver frame there was a faded sepia print of a slightly stiff-looking man in a long coat and waistcoat. One hand rested on a waking stick, the other was placed on an outsized Grecian urn as he gazed in what was intended to be a noble manner, across a landscape that was plainly some kind of painted backdrop. The original effect might have been impressive but to twenty-first-century eyes, it looked faintly ridiculous.

'Very nice,' said Carys, politely.

Jon eyed her over the half moon of his reading glasses, his gaze softening a little. 'I've a daughter your age,' he said. 'Lives in France. I don't see her often.'

'I'm sorry,' Carys murmured, not entirely sure what to say.

'Yes, well,' he grunted, looking out over the sweeping curve of the town.

'It's very beautiful here,' said Carys, following his gaze. 'I can see why St Ives is famous for attracting painters. It must be a very special place to live.'

'Used to be real artists here, of course,' said Jon, savouring the last of his chocolate biscuits with a melancholy air. 'The kind who live off little and dedicate themselves to their art. It's all changed now, of course. All designer shopping and galleries and those young people who spend their energies surfing instead of getting a proper job. You don't get people like William Treverick any more.'

He began to get to his feet. This was definitely a dismissal. Carys glanced at David across the table. So they were none the wiser, after all. But the old man's mouth was set in a stubborn line, while his eyes were suddenly ringed, his skin pasty with exhaustion.

'Thank you for your time, it's been very interesting,' said David, taking the hint and rising to his feet, shaking the old man's hand.

Carys stood up and pushed her chair neatly under the table.

Maybe the postcard had just been a red herring. Maybe there really was no connection at all. As she looked up, a movement caught her eye. Mrs Boscawen had appeared silently in the doorway. Across the room, Carys met her eyes.

'Um, excuse me, Mr Phelps,' she said, quickly. 'Do you mind if I use your…?'

'Yes, yes of course,' he muttered, embarrassed at the mere suggestion of such an activity, especially in a female. He turned helplessly towards the doorway, as if about to attempt directions. 'Ah,' he said, his eyes falling on Mrs Boscawen with relief. 'My housekeeper will show you the way.'

'Of course.' Mrs Boscawen deposited an empty tray on the table. 'If you'd just like to come this way.'

Carys followed along a straight corridor as Mrs Boscawen strode rapidly towards the back of the bungalow. At the door of the neat white bathroom they paused. Carys eyed the housekeeper in silent enquiry.

Mrs Boscawen glanced back towards the balcony and the sound of voices as David chatted away to Mr Phelps while they made their way into the living room.

'Proud man,' said Mrs Boscawen. 'And we all like to keep our little illusions, don't we?'

'Yes,' replied Carys uncertainly.

Mrs Boscawen took a piece of paper from her pocket and thrust it into Carys' hand. 'Ketterford Museum,' she said. 'That's where you need to go. I've written down the postcode for you. You're using a SatNav, I take it?' Carys nodded. 'It's a bit of a way inland and there aren't many signs yet. That'll take you there.' Her eyes were sharp on Carys' face. 'Ask them about Ann Treverick.'

Carys blinked. Something strange was prickling at the back of her scalp. 'Ann Treverick?'

272

'Yes.' Mrs Boscawen hesitated, then began to say something. But at that moment Jon and David appeared at the far end of the hallway. Carys shot into the bathroom.

'Ask them about Ann Treverick,' she heard Mrs Boscawen repeat, as the door closed behind her. 'That'll lead you to what you want to know.'

❧

'This is ridiculous,' grumbled David, as their electronic guide took them down yet another network of country lanes, lined on by tall hedgerows bursting with pink campion and fading stalks of frothy cow parsley, intertwined with the first unripe blackberries. 'That was a sign to St Michael's Mount back there, we'll be halfway to the Lizard before you know it.'

'Only a little longer.' Carys peered at the more conventional variety of map, trying in vain to locate anywhere by the name of Ketterford. 'It looks like we'll be there soon, from that flag thing on the SatNav. Aren't you curious?'

'Wild goose chase, if you ask me,' he muttered. 'I can't see what this has got to do with the Trevericks. Or what the Trevericks have to do with us, come to that. No one seems to have heard of the Merediths or Plas Eden here at all.'

'Well, that postcard was in my attic, so it's got something to do with me too,' said Carys, stubbornly. 'And now we are here I want to know.'

At that moment the road opened out into scrubby moorland, high and windswept, with a distant view of the sea.

'Who on earth would want to live up here?' said David, turning the car out of the latest lane and into a wider highway. 'It must be bleak in winter.'

'There, that must be it!' Carys pointed excitedly at a tall, sparse building of pale-coloured stone up ahead.

Sure enough, the SatNav guided them up to a turnoff, with a sign declaring 'Ketterford Museum'. David eased the car along a rough lane, until it opened out into a car park.

'That's even worse than Treverick Hall,' he said, pausing at the entrance and peering up at the small, regimented windows. 'I thought Cornwall was supposed to be full of pretty places?'

'It looks almost industrial,' agreed Carys. 'Weren't there lots of tin mines here? Remember *Poldark*?' David looked blank. But then he'd never been glued to repeats of Ross Poldark as he rode dashingly along the Cornish cliffs, dark hair blowing in the wind. So Carys forgave him. 'Come on then,' she said. 'Let's go in.'

David didn't appear to hear. He had turned, and was gazing intently through the open window at a sign just inside the entrance.

'What is it?' demanded Carys.

'It's not industrial,' he replied, his voice strangely hollow. 'Ketterford was a lunatic asylum.'

Chapter Eighteen

Inside, Ketterford turned out to be dark, gloomy place, with few windows and large, empty rooms.

Much of the building had been turned into a museum of local history, from Stone Age megaliths and stone circles to Iron Age hill forts and more recent copper mines and tin smelting. Just the small entrance hall had been left to explain the origins of the building, and that gave very little information, apart from the bare facts of Ketterford House having originated in the nineteenth century as a private female lunatic asylum. A few dingy pictures of women who looked more downtrodden than raving accompanied a small amount of text.

'There aren't any records kept here,' explained the elderly volunteer behind a table next to the front door, whose badge read 'Margaret Tyack'. 'We don't get many people asking about the asylum,' she added. 'Researching asylums, are you?'

'Not really.' Carys gave a quick glance at David's face. 'We're doing a bit of family research, and someone suggested we come here.'

'Oh?' said Margaret Tyack, green eyes alert with irrepressible curiosity. 'And who might that be, if I may ask?'

'Mrs Boscawen. She's, um, she works for Jon Phelps from St Ives? I think his sister left something about the Trevericks to the Treverick Historical Society,' ventured Carys.

'Oh, yes. Ursula,' said the guide, nodding wisely. It was not only Pont-ar-Eden where everybody knew everybody else. 'And she suggested you come to Ketterford?'

'Yes,' said Carys, quickly. David, she could feel, was itching to get out of there. 'We're trying to find out more about Treverick Hall, but we don't seem to be getting very far. Mrs Boscawen suggested we ask here about someone called Ann Treverick.'

'Ah, Ann Treverick.' Margaret looked at them intently: first Carys, then David and then back to Carys once more. 'Now that's an interesting request.' She shuffled some leaflets on the desk. 'Family tree, is it?'

'We're not sure,' replied David. 'We seem to have found a link somewhere between my family and Treverick Hall, we're just not sure what it is.'

'Ah, that's the beauty of tracing your own history.' Margaret Tyack was clearly an addict. 'It can lead you down all sorts of roads you never expected to take.'

'I'm not sure about this one,' said David, gloomily.

'Mmm,' said Margaret, who also appeared to have a taste for the dramatic moment and left the subject hanging in the air with no signs of taking it any further.

'So there *is* an Ann Treverick,' Carys prompted her at last.

'Oh, yes,' Margaret's tight white curls bounced as she nodded. 'Well, at least there was. Unless you've found one now, that is?'

'No.' Carys, tried to hide her impatience at this verbal mystery tour. 'So who is – I mean was – she?'

'Just one moment.' Margaret – who was definitely enjoying herself – disappeared into a room behind the desk, returning in a few moments with a battered case of soft leather, complete with rusted zip. 'Laura Phelps gave some things to the trustees,

276

when they were raising money to turn Ketterford into a museum. They are quite fascinating. She asked that none of them be returned to her brother.' Margaret's eyes were gleaming with intrigue. 'I suspect he doesn't even know we have them.' She carefully undid the zip. 'There's been so much to do, getting the displays up, and volunteers are so hard to come by these days, we are only just getting round to cataloguing them. I take it Jon told you about the last Treverick?'

David looked blank, and even more eager to go. Carys nodded vigorously enough for both of them.

'Yes, I thought he might. What he might not have told you is that the Hall and the gardens had drained the family finances by the time William Treverick inherited, in the mid 1880s, and all the Treverick land had been sold off. He married the daughter of a local businessman. No connections, but very wealthy. Very beautiful. Very accomplished. She must have seemed the answer to his prayers. Ah, here we are.' With a flourish, Margaret brought out a sepia print, curling at the edges, and laid it on the table. 'There she is. This is Ann Treverick.'

Carys peered at the faded photograph. 'She looks very young.'

'Eighteen when they married, I believe.'

'She was very beautiful,' said David politely.

Even with her stiff clothes and even stiffer pose, the young woman standing in full Victorian regalia of wide skirts and a tightly fitted bodice, before the painted backdrop of a ruined Roman temple, was unmistakeably stunning. A neat figure with an impossibly tiny waist. Curling fair hair caught up behind her head. Large eyes and regular features. A classic kind of youthful beauty.

'And doesn't she know it,' said Carys, before she could help herself. The eyes looked boldly into the camera, while a complacent smile curved the wide lips.

'Yes, quite,' said Margaret drily.

Carys met David's eyes. It was not Blodeuwedd. At least, not the Blodeuwedd of the statues in Eden's gardens, with her eager glance and her passionate desire to experience the world. This young woman could not possibly be further from the photograph of the sculptress Hermione Meredith, with her bold, direct gaze and her hand placed so protectively on the shoulder of a child. Carys was sure this was a young miss who had reached the highest pinnacle of her ambition: bagged the local lord of the manor and was set up for life.

Carys handed the photograph back to Margaret. She was glad it wasn't Blodeuwedd. There was something about that self-satisfied smile that it was very hard to like.

'So Treverick Hall was saved,' she prompted.

'Oh, yes. At least so it must have seemed. For a while. There's just one photograph of the family. The rest were apparently destroyed. I think that's why Laura Phelps wanted these ones safely out of the way here. That's what she told the trustees anyway.' Margaret pulled out a second photograph.

'They had children,' said David, showing signs of interest. He frowned down at the family portrait, posed as stiffly as the rest.

Carys peered over his shoulder. It was the same young woman, this time even more ornately dressed, gazing towards the camera and holding a baby almost extinguished in lace and ruffles, at arm's length on her lap. Obviously just been dumped there by the nanny, or nursemaid, or whoever actually did the looking after of children in Victorian times, thought Carys wryly. The proud husband sat bolt upright in a vaguely

278

military-style jacket, both hands resting on a walking stick, as if about to stride out to inspect his lands. Between them, a young girl, who appeared to be around twelve, bent over the baby, apparently trying to keep it amused.

'They had just one child,' said Margaret. 'A son. The girl is Judith Treverick. She was twenty years or so younger than her brother, so she would have still been quite a child when he married.'

David looked up. 'I thought Mr Phelps said there was no one to inherit Treverick Hall after William Treverick died?'

'That's right,' said Margaret. 'There wasn't.' She looked down at the photograph. 'Not exactly a happy family, even then, I'm afraid.' Her voice was thoughtful. 'Where was it you said you come from?' she demanded. 'Not round here, is it?'

'No,' said Carys.

'North Wales,' said David.

'North Wales.' The guide's eyes were alight with what could only be described as the joy of intrigue. 'That's a fair distance to come looking for someone. Like going to Australia for people in Victorian times.'

Carys caught David's eye. She hadn't thought of the logistics like that before. Driving down in a twenty-first-century car plus SatNav had taken long enough. Horse drawn carriages and steam trains. Not to mention an alien language and culture. Margaret was right: it would have been another world. This looked like a wild goose chase, after all.

'So why are they here?' she asked. 'The pictures of the Trevericks. Is the museum going to put up an exhibition about them?'

'Oh, no,' replied Margaret. 'Nothing like that. Jon Phelps would be mortified. She died here, you see. In the asylum.'

'Who did?' demanded David sharply. He had suddenly

acquired the look of a man considering a rapid tramp over the next hill and down to Penzance, possibly following the coastal path right round to Plymouth at full pelt for the next few days.

Carys shoved the car keys deep into her pocket. Personally, she was staying put, whatever a Meredith chose to do in the cause of avoiding any issue that might be around the corner.

'Ann Treverick,' said Margaret. 'She was confined here for most of her life. She went missing for a short while, according to the records, but she was brought back. And she died here. She can't have been very old, poor thing. There's a plaque to her in Treverick Church, but she's buried here in the grounds.'

Carys shivered slightly. She looked again at the young woman holding the baby so stiffly. Maybe it was her imagination, but there seemed to be a blankness to the eyes that had previously gazed out with such self-assurance. And surely it had to be her imagination, but as she looked, it seemed as if the features of the young woman's face began to resolve themselves into something that was, after all, familiar.

'She was an accomplished artist, you know. Ann Treverick,' said Margaret.

'Oh?' said Carys, meeting David's eyes again.

'Oh yes. That was a usual young lady's accomplishment in those days, of course. But Ann Treverick was something a little more. Or at least she became so, in her time here.' Margaret disappeared into the back room again, this time returning with two flat parcels protected in bubble wrap. 'These were amongst the things brought in by Laura Phelps. Of course, no one can be absolutely certain, but Laura always swore they had been made here, in the asylum, by Ann Treverick.'

'Wow,' breathed Carys, as the bubble wrap fell apart to reveal sheet upon sheet of pencil-drawn portraits. As Margaret spread them out on the table, women's faces of all ages looked out at them, some fierce, some resigned. A young woman, hair cropped short around her head, stared vacantly into space. An old woman with a face networked with fine lines and huge gnarled hands looked out at the viewer, a challenge in the direct gaze.

'Pretty stunning, eh?' said Margaret, proudly.

Carys nodded.

'Ceridwen,' muttered David, who was frowning intently at the portrait of the old woman.

'What was that?' demanded Margaret.

'Oh, nothing,' said David, sounding embarrassed. 'It just reminded me of something. But it can't be. It must be a coincidence.'

Carys followed his gaze. He was right; there was a slight resemblance to the statue of Ceridwen. But there was nothing of the wise woman's exultant expression as she stirred her potion. And didn't all old people tend to have a similar look to them, to young eyes, at least? The same sharpness of features and crumpled skin? The sketches of the inmates of Ketterford Lunatic Asylum did indeed have the same step-out-and-talk-to-you qualities as the statues in the little glade, but that didn't mean they bore any other relationship to each other.

'Would it be okay to take a couple of photographs?' she asked.

'Yes, of course, dear. I don't see why not. You'll be able to photograph the drawings when they eventually go up on the walls in the entrance here, so there's no reason why you shouldn't now.'

'Thanks,' said Carys, fishing out her camera.

David was still frowning at the portrait of the old woman. 'Why was she put here?' he asked, at last. 'I mean, surely someone who was capable of making these couldn't have been completely insane. At least not all the time.'

'Now, that I don't know,' confessed Margaret. 'People were placed in asylums for all kinds of reasons in those days. There are several stories among the older people of Treverick. The ones whose parents would have remembered her. But they're all a bit ghoulish. Oh, I wouldn't take much notice of them,' she added, as David looked up at this. 'Treverick Hall had been falling apart for more than a century. All kinds of stories grow up around places like that. It's only human nature. As I said, we've only just had the time to start looking at these. I think someone from the Treverick Historical Society began to have a look for some real information, but didn't get very far. And most of the records seem to have been lost from the asylum itself. It was a reform school for boys for years,' she added, with disapproval. 'Much of the old place got trashed, as my grandson would put it.'

'Oh.' Carys put down her camera. She had only photographed a few drawings, but it seemed more and more like another dead end, anyhow.

'You might find some more information in the Celtic Studies Library in the Cornwall Centre in Redruth,' suggested Margaret. 'It's not far from here. Between here and Truro,' she added, as Carys and David looked at her blankly. 'I've a leaflet here that'll give you directions. Anyone can use the library, and they're very helpful. They have most of the local newspapers for the past hundred and fifty years or so on microfilm. You might find something there.'

'Thanks,' smiled Carys. David was looking dubious again.

Margaret's eyes gleamed once more. She bent forward in a slightly conspiratorial manner. 'And, whatever they say, there is another Treverick, you know,' she added, in a low voice.

'Really?' said Carys.

'Oh, yes. Been in New Zealand. Only came back a couple

of years ago. Didn't half put Jon Phelps' nose out of joint. Someone who still had a claim to the family name, that is.'

'Oh, you mean someone *now*,' said David, who was feeling slightly Victorianed-out, and had been waiting for a dark tale of murder, complete with Jack-the-Ripper and Sherlock Homes hanging over some boiling sea, as a group of smugglers brought in the brandy down below.

'Oh, yes.' Margaret nodded. 'She came here once. Left her card.' Margaret lifted a brightly coloured business card down from a notice board. 'Runs one of these new local-grown-flowers businesses over near St Austell. Just outside the Lost Gardens of Heligan. Ethical flowers for weddings, that sort of thing. She doesn't seem to have shown much interest in the family history, but she might have something that's been handed down. You never know.'

'Thank you.' Carys reached in her bag for a pen.

'No, no, it's fine. Take it with you,' said Margaret. 'She left a little pile of them. In fact, I'm not sure that wasn't her main reason for popping in here. No one seems to remember her asking any questions about the family.'

'Thanks.' Carys smiled, placing the little card safely into the innermost compartment in her bag.

'Well, and let me know if you find anything,' said Margaret, as she turned to help a newly arrived family with two small boys, who were heading firmly for anything remotely related to Vikings, pirates and smugglers.

'We will.' David took a last look at the drawing of the old woman as Carys finished photographing the sketches.

With the family happily sent in the direction of 'The Smugglers of St Ives Bay' for the children, accompanied by 'Daphne du Maurier's Cornwall' for their mother, Margaret turned her attention back to the drawings. 'Wales, eh?'

She began to put the sketches back in their folder. 'Funny that.'

'Oh?' said David.

'Someone was asking about Ann Treverick, not so long ago. On the phone, they were. Didn't say where they came from, but I could have sworn the accent was Welsh. We used to stay with my aunt in Betws-y-Coed when I was little,' she added in explanation. 'It was nice, hearing the old accent again. Never gave a name, and I never thought to ask. You never do, at the time, do you? Rather strange, it was. Something to do with statues,' she added, folding bubble wrap around the folders once more and tearing off new strips of sellotape from the roll on her desk to secure it. 'Ring any bells?'

'When was this?' demanded David.

'Some time ago.'

'Twenty years?'

She laughed. 'Good Lord, no. Whatever made you think that? A year or so ago, maybe. No; maybe not that long. It was just after the museum opened. I'd only just started as a volunteer. Six months, perhaps? A year, at most.'

'And they definitely mentioned statues?' said Carys.

'That's right. It seemed such a funny thing to be asking about.'

'Oh?'

'Well, it wasn't just *about* them. It was about the making of them, and if there were any in the grounds. Of course, there are no statues here. I mean, I can't see any of the women here being allowed anywhere near a hammer and chisel, can you?'

'No, not at all,' said David slowly.

☙

'It could be someone just researching statues,' said Carys, as she followed the SatNav's directions to the Cornwall Centre. 'Ketterford doesn't exactly advertise that it was once a lunatic asylum, and people ask museums all sorts of things.'

'Bit of a coincidence,' David muttered.

'Just because someone speaks with a Welsh accent doesn't mean they live in Wales now.'

'Yeah. Right,' he returned. 'You don't believe that either.'

Carys grinned. 'Let's say I'm keeping an open mind. And, anyhow, don't you find it just a little bit exciting? I could get into this chasing down of clues, like a proper history detective. I don't care if this Ann Treverick has nothing to do with Plas Eden at all. Now we've started, I want to know what happened to her.'

David smiled. He'd been vaguely irritated by traipsing from one place to another without it seeming to lead anywhere. And especially with blue sky and miles of cliff waiting there, all ready to walk. But this was Carys on a mission. Carys on a mission, he remembered, had always shown an unexpectedly stubborn streak.

He'd believed that side of Carys had gone, banished by the grown-up duties of career and mortgage. And he was, he had to confess, as he watched the green roll of the Cornish countryside pass by, rather enjoying having it back again. When Carys got the bit between her teeth, it was best to just lean back and go along for the ride. David relaxed into his seat feeling strangely liberated by the prospect of not being responsible for once. It felt almost like being a teenager again.

With the SatNav determined to take them down the narrowest and most winding lanes it could find, and an alarming tendency to go round in circles in the cause of following the shortest route, Carys concentrated fully on driving. This was more like it. She'd forgotten how much fun they'd had, the two of them, before hormones and the seriousness of life had kicked in.

When they'd been kids, the lawns and the cherry trees around the house – where Rhiannon could keep an eye on them – had become a jungle of dens and secret encampments. The neglected part of the house had been a world of mystery in itself. In summer this had expanded to major expeditions in the rowing boat, discovering dragons and America in equal measure, while remaining within shouting distance of home.

They'd tried their best to include Huw, but he'd squirmed at their more outrageous flights of imagination, preferring instead to build dams in the stream feeding the lake.

She missed that sense of life being an adventure. It was probably a sign of getting old and viewing the past through rose-tinted spectacles, she told herself with an inward sigh. She should get a grip before she landed herself into all sorts of trouble. Grown-up trouble. The kind that doesn't go away with a sticking plaster and a slab of homemade chocolate fudge cake.

ဆ

Once in the safer territory of urban streets, the SatNav came into its own, locating the Cornish Centre without fuss. David and Carys soon found themselves in the Cornish Studies Library, in possession of adjacent microfilm readers.

'So what, exactly, are we looking for?' whispered David, as they scrolled their way through separate years of the *Treverick Times*, captured for eternity on microfilm.

'No idea,' replied Carys. 'Anything to do with the Trevericks, I suppose.

'They seemed to have judged plenty of flower shows and opened their fair share of fetes,' he complained.

'Trust you to go straight to the Lord of the Manor stuff,' she retorted, forgetting to whisper. A couple of fellow researchers looked round at this, but appeared more amused than irritated. Clearly taking this exchange as a lover's tiff, thought Carys, fighting the sudden colour down from her face. She glanced at David. But he was deep in the petty thievery and advertisements for tooth powder of Victorian Cornwall and seemed not to have noticed. Apart from the faint smile on his face. Male vanity, thought Carys, trying to be indignant.

Just for a moment, her mind went back to Joe. A subject she had been almost-successfully keeping out of her mind since they had left Chester. She could just see him settled into his new office in central London and already at the centre of things. And no doubt smiling that gentle smile of his at the young women around the water cooler.

Damn all male vanity. Even if it was nothing to do with her any more. It was still close enough in her memory to be personal.

She turned back to the microfilm, determinedly focussing on scanning the lines of newspaper print and grainy photographs. They would, they had agreed in the car, work in opposite directions from the date Margaret had told them Ann Treverick had been first admitted to Ketterford Asylum. Carys had bagged going backwards, on the principle that it was her idea in the first place and there was more likely to be information before the time of Ann's committal. Apart – as David had pointed out – from the fact that she was supposed to have escaped from the lunatic asylum for a while, and that sounded like a story in itself.

Several hours of fruitless searching later, Carys was feeling decidedly cross-eyed, and not a little hungry. The centre was busy, and once in possession of a microfilm reader, it seemed uncharitable to abandon it for more than a quick dash to the loo.

'Anything?' she murmured to David.

He blinked and shook his head. 'Not a dickybird. There's plenty of mention of William Treverick, and a couple of his sister opening things. But nothing about anyone called Ann. Or the asylum. I suppose they wouldn't exactly have broadcast the fact that she was there. Or that she had left. Or escaped, for that matter. Especially not if she escaped. And definitely no mention of paintings, drawings, or statues. What about you?'

'The same. Apart from nothing really about Judith Treverick. I suppose she'd have been too young in these ones to open things. It's weird. It's as if Ann Treverick didn't exist at all.'

David yawned. A couple of students, of the vaguely Goth variety, had walked past the now fully occupied microfilm readers at least twice in the past ten minutes, with meaningful glares in the general direction of the occupiers of the chairs. Tough. They were probably local and could come back tomorrow, and anyhow there was a sign telling all and sundry of the need to book your reader to be assured of one. All the same, the glares were a reminder of just how long they had been sitting there.

'Ten more minutes?' he suggested. 'Then perhaps we should go and get something to eat. I don't think my eyes will take much more. We can always book a couple of readers and come back tomorrow.'

'Okay,' agreed Carys. Her brain had stopped taking in

information she realised, as she came to the end of yet another year. She began to scroll through faster, trusting her eyes would pick up any mention of the Treverick name, or that the image of the Hall would catch her eye. She could always go through more systematically tomorrow.

When it came, she nearly missed it. She shot several pages forward before she could stop and retrace her tracks, not quite certain where the headline had been. Or even if she had read it correctly. Then there it was. 'Dreadful Events at Treverick', accompanied by the familiar view of Treverick Hall. Carys settled the page in front of her on the microfilm and began to read.

She was still sitting there, unmoving, when David finished with his reader and came to join her.

'Carys?'

'I've found her,' replied Carys, her eyes still on the screen. 'Ann Treverick. It's all here, in the article.'

'That's good, isn't it?'

Carys shook her head. 'No it isn't. Not at all. Poor woman: no wonder she lost her mind.'

I found him in the dawn, where the tide had brought him.

There was a cruel illusion of life from the water lapping at his coat sleeves, and the wind stirring the fairness of his hair. But even as I ran towards that tiny, lonely figure stranded in the vastness of the beach, I knew he was gone. He had always been a timid child, afraid most of all of water. Even I knew he would not have lain so long, rocked by the incoming waves, had there been any life left in him to drag himself out of their reach.

The sea clung to my skirts as I knelt down beside him,

pulling me down. The chill of that November morning had taken everything but the very last warmth in his small body as I lifted him into my arms, and rocked him, as I had never done in all those few short years of my son's life.

I never knew love, you see, until I lost it forever. What did I know of children? He was brought to me each evening as I dressed for dinner: clean and polite, blinking at me shyly and only too eager to return to the familiarity of his nursemaid. His chatter amused me for a while, until it delayed my preparations, with his fat little fingers so eager to clutch at the jewels in my ears and disturb the careful preparation of my hair.

I was happy enough to leave him to the nurse. And, as he grew older, to his father, who showed off his heir with pride, but grew impatient to take his son with him in his favourite pursuits of hunting and sailing his boat, the 'Princess Beatrice', around the headland, mastering the fiercest of tides.

My husband, I had soon come to understand, was a man who had always had his own way and never allowed that things might be otherwise. His ambitions were of the noblest. To have the finest Hall in all of Cornwall, a wife all those in his circle would envy, and a strong, strapping son to follow in his footsteps.

I gave him everything but the last. I knew that, as I cradled Charlie in my arms for that first and last time. It was as if the surf of last night's storm had crashed in on the barriers of my self-absorption. Those long hours of lamps bobbing amongst the cliffs in the darkness and the voices calling had broken me apart.

I had been asleep all my life. As the pale light eased across the sea, I felt I had lived my whole life in a dream. A dream in which the world had been made for me, and had been waiting, breathless for me to grow into womanhood. That once there, it would remain unchanging. Where I was a chosen one, who would never alter now I had reached perfection. I had despised Aunt Beatrice for the lines beneath her eyes, the slight sagging of her jaw, and looseness of skin where her ivory arms and shoulders should have been. That would never happen to me. I would not allow it. This was my time.

As the waves surged around me, I understood what an utter fool I had been. I was no chosen one. No princess. No queen. And certainly no angel soaring down from Heaven. I was just another woman, who would grow old and whose life would pass, unnoticed in the endless stream of existence. And, in my blindness, I had allowed the one thing that was truly precious in my life to perish in fear and loneliness. I had not lifted one idle finger, or disturbed my comfort one iota, to attempt to plead for him.

I held my son tight. I knew I could never let him go. Not again. Not forever. I thought of every mother who had lost a child, and I could feel their grief searing through me, along with mine.

The tide had turned. Out in the calm of the bay I could see the tide race, just beyond the rocks, that would sweep anything that entered it out into the wide-open sea. I rose, slowly, and taking my burden with me I made my way through the waves towards that welcome oblivion.

I was already waist high, with the surf catching at my breasts, when I heard my name. I pushed it away, but it came again, followed by a rush of water, and the warmth of a hand reaching my cold arm, staying me.

'Don't,' she said. 'Please, Ann. Don't.'

I tried to pull myself free, but her grasp was firm. She had always been a stubborn child. William could not control her, and she had certainly never once given the appearance of listening to me.

'Go back,' I commanded, turning towards her.

I saw Judith shake her head, with that set to her lips I knew so well. 'No,' she said. 'Not without you.'

She was lighter-built than I was, still little more than a child. I could see her already shivering in the icy chill, the waves pulling at her, ready to sweep her off her feet.

'Go back,' I repeated.

She shook her head once more. And this time I saw the fear in her eyes. 'Don't leave me,' I heard her say, as I turned my face once more towards the open sea, as the surge caught us and began to pull us out towards the tidal race. 'Please, Ann. I couldn't bear it. Please don't leave me.'

The next wave broke into a wall of surf, and came rushing down toward us.

Chapter Nineteen

'She's preparing flowers for a wedding, today,' said Carys, placing her mobile back in her pocket. 'But she says she'd really like to learn more about her family, and she can meet us tomorrow. Any time after 10.30.'

'Perhaps it's as well,' replied David watching her closely. That sad little story in the newspaper article seemed to have got to Carys for some reason. She'd appeared distracted ever since they had obtained their print-out of the page and escaped back out into the warmth of the afternoon, and in the sunshine he could see the pallor of her skin and the lines of strain beneath her eyes.

It wasn't just the Trevericks, which was, after all, a story about people who had lived over a hundred years ago, however tragic. And they were not even family. Well, at least not for Carys and most probably not for the Merediths, either, by the looks of things, postcard or no postcard.

That return to Chester had nothing to do with work: he'd put money on it. If the accountancy firm was giving her a hard time she'd tell them to stuff it and find something else. He'd put even more money on Carys being the kind of employee no firm in their right mind would want to lose to a rival. No, it had to be something else. He'd a pretty good idea what the something else was.

He'd taken an instant dislike to that boyfriend of hers. Not that he'd spoken to him. One glimpse across Pont-ar-Eden High Street had been quite enough. Then there had been the lack of texts arriving on Carys' mobile, apart from a couple from Gwenan to say their mother was fine. Unless, of course, there was a flurry of messages at midnight. Only Carys didn't seem to be expecting them. There had been no looking at watches, no hasty excuses. David had brought his iPad, just in case they needed it, but Carys hadn't once asked to use it to check emails and they hadn't been anywhere near an internet café.

David frowned to himself. It was, of course, none of his business. Besides, Carys didn't do sobbing or fainting. She'd always dealt with things quietly, in her own way. Only those who knew her really well understood how deep her feelings went.

He hated seeing her like this. If only there was something he could do. He was hardly in a position to ask her to bare her soul, he admitted gloomily. Knowing Carys, he'd probably get his head bitten off and, given their past, he could hardly blame her. He could try distraction, though. It might not solve her problems, but when his leg was at its worst the few pain-free hours after he'd taken his medication at least made him feel human again and ready to face the next onslaught.

'Come on,' he said firmly. 'We're in Cornwall. It's a gorgeous day. I don't know about you, but I've had enough of all this for one day. St. Michael's Mount is only twenty minutes away. How about we forget the detective work and become proper tourists for the rest of the day?'

To his relief, Carys smiled. Her eyes brightened and her shoulders relaxed a little. 'Sounds perfect to me.'

છ૭

They climbed the narrow steps of St Michael's Mount and

made their way back across the causeway to the mainland before the tide raced back across the sands.

With the SatNav safely removed from duty, they explored the winding roads along the south Cornish coastline. Afternoon tea in the quaint surroundings of Porthleven was followed by walking along small sections of the coastal path above rocky cliffs, and sitting on wide sandy beaches watching the surfers parade tanned and honed bodies before donning designer wetsuits and driving the bleach-haired lifeguard (who was definitely more Australian than Cornish) to distraction by straying too near the rocks.

An afternoon of sunshine and sea air, complete with the deliciously decadent cream tea (photographed on David's iPhone and sent winging to Rhiannon with a promise of a pot of real clotted cream, if it survived the journey), left them sleepy and relaxed.

'That sun's getting awfully low, I suppose we ought to start making our way back,' said David, regretfully, as he took over the wheel after their last stop.

'I suppose,' agreed Carys. They looked at each other. 'We're very near the Lizard,' she added, consulting the old-fashioned paper variety of map.

'It's too far.' He met her eyes. 'We'd have no chance to look around if we're to get back to Treverick tonight.'

'I know.' She hesitated. 'Look, I know we're already paying for the Treverick Arms, and it seems silly…'

'But we've driven hundreds of miles to get here, and it's not like we can pop down every weekend,' he finished for her. 'And we'd only have to come back again this way tomorrow.' They grinned at each other like schoolchildren playing truant. 'I think I've had enough of anything to do with Treverick and Treverick Hall for one day.'

'Me too,' said Carys, feelingly. 'I don't even want to talk about them. If we can find rooms, that is,' she added, quickly, emphasising the plural, just so that there was no misunderstanding over this.

'Of course.' David concentrated on the road. 'Let's see if we can find a place to stay, and then we can phone the McIntyres and let them know we haven't just driven over a cliff.'

Carys sighed wistfully. 'I'm going to have to come here again. There's so much of Cornwall I want to see, and not just the Eden Project and the Lost Gardens of Heligan.'

'I hope you're not proposing those tonight? They're miles away.'

'Definitely not,' she replied with a smile. 'We can do those tomorrow, on the way back.'

ღ

In the spirit of making the most of this afternoon of truancy, they followed the signs to the Lizard Point. After meandering their way through the huge, eerily futuristic, skyward-watching dishes of Goonhilly Downs they arrived at the wild beauty of the Lizard coastline, warmed to a soft orange glow in the evening sunshine.

In the end they managed to book the last two rooms in the Paris Hotel, in the tiny harbour village of Coverack, a short distance away from the main tourist spot of the Lizard. After a day filled with visitors and sightseers making the most of the sunshine, Coverack felt like a quiet hideaway. They wandered up the steep little road past thatched, whitewashed cottages to the stretch of land above, with its view of the undulating coastline. As the sun began to sink, they made their way down again to sit in the last of the evening light on the harbour wall, drinking the wine that had somehow found itself amongst their essential supplies along with a couple of plastic tumblers.

After the rush of the day they were both happy to sit in companionable silence, watching the surfers ride the waves inside the small rocky bay until little more than the white of the surf could be seen.

'They must be mad,' said Carys drowsily, as the encroaching darkness finally forced the wetsuited figures to tuck their surfboards under their arms, heading presumably for the nearest shower and bar.

'Mmm.' David was lost in thought. 'I can see why you were thinking of moving down here,' he added after a few minutes.

Carys sighed. 'Like plenty of other people trying to escape the rat race. I can see why the price of land here is astronomical.'

'There's always a way.'

'Possibly.' She sounded unconvinced.

David's heart did a couple of handsprings while he wasn't looking. 'So it might have to be Pont-ar-Eden, after all?'

'Maybe.' Her face was a shadow in the dark. 'It would make sense. Plus I don't have any connections down here. At least not now.'

'I see.' That was definite sadness in her voice. A definite saying goodbye to something. Or someone. David found the handsprings in action once more. Perhaps if he approached the question very gently, very tactfully, this might be where Carys would open up a bit. His mind searched for the best place to start.

But already it was too late. As if reading his intentions and determined to head them off, Carys was already speaking. 'And what about you? Have you decided where you'll go? If you do sell Plas Eden, that is.'

Damn. He'd forgotten that part. Why did life have to be so complicated? 'I don't know. To be honest, I havn't really thought that far ahead.'

'I suppose you could go anywhere.'

'Yes.' There was no disguising his lack of enthusiasm.

'If you really don't want to move from Eden, there's always a way,' said Carys.

Ouch. He deserved that. 'Touché.'

'No. I mean it. Seriously. The whole adventure holiday thing might not be practical any more, but hasn't it struck you how many different ways people are tapping into the tourist trade down here in Cornwall? Successfully, too, by the looks of things.'

'I suppose so.' He had noticed, but without thinking of relating it to Eden. Funny how you can get stuck in a rut after so many years. Lit by her energy, a flicker of excitement began, deep inside. One he couldn't quite trust yet. 'There are a lot more tourists here, though.'

'That doesn't mean they won't go to Snowdonia as well. Especially if you give them something worth visiting. Look at all the people who go up Snowdon and visit Portmeirion! Then there's all the cycling that's taken off in Coed y Brenin over the last few years, that's bringing in families, too. I think we should at least have a look at the Lost Gardens of Heligan and the Eden Project on the way back to Treverick and see what they do to bring the visitors in.'

'Okay.'

'Plus anything else we come across.'

'Sounds good to me.' This was a project. Something he could get his teeth into. For the first time since his accident, David could feel his passionate do-or-die commitment to Plas Eden returning. Maybe, after all, there might be a way to silence Huw and create a new future for Eden.

He smiled into the dark. Carys always used to have this effect on him. How could he ever have forgotten her energy and that creative, quick-fire brain of hers? As kids, he'd been the one blundering on ahead, but he'd learnt to ignore Carys' acerbic comments at his peril. And when they'd come across a particularly knotty problem she'd been the one, often as not, to come up with the solution and spur him on. How could he have forgotten?

The truth was, he hadn't. Not ever. The realisation was like a pressure growing inside him until he could scarcely breathe. Carys had turned her head away to watch the lights along the sea front, apparently lost in thought. Her profile was as familiar to him as his own heartbeat. He leant a little closer. He could smell the salt in her hair, with vanilla undercurrents of the lip balm that was so very Carys. The urge to kiss her was becoming irresistible. He caught the glint of the streetlight in her eye just in time. Carys, he saw, was crying quietly and pretending not to.

A feeling of helplessness swept over him. He ought to be able to do something. But that was the thing with grief: there was nothing anyone could do, just be there.

'I'll get rid of this,' he muttered, limping off towards the nearest recycling bins with the wine bottle and tumblers to give her time to blow her nose and get herself together.

By the time he limped back, Carys was tucking a tissue into her pocket, with her bag slung over one shoulder and ready to go.

He tucked her arm firmly through his, in companionable fashion, as they turned back towards the hotel. 'Quite a day, eh?' he remarked, keeping his tone deliberately light.

'Yes,' replied Carys. 'Yes it was.' He had noticed, she realised, but he was tactfully leaving her in peace. He wasn't expecting conversation or demanding anything of her. The strength of his arm holding hers and the warmth of his body stealing through her jumper was surprisingly comforting.

'Makes you wonder what tomorrow might bring,' David said, as they made their way past the surfers – still beautiful, even in the dark – downing pints on the sea wall, talking surf, the wave that got away, the relative merits of the south and north Cornish Coasts, and was Watergate Bay, like, the Most Awesome Place Out There?

'Mmm,' replied Carys, too drained and exhausted even to think, as they finally reached the hotel.

Chapter Twenty

'Karenza's Field of Flowers' said the sign, as Carys pulled up the next morning outside a low, whitewashed building set amongst the rolling green countryside just inland from Mevagissey.

She had woken up with a thumping headache and puffy eyes, but a couple of painkillers and breakfast with strong coffee had soon chased them away. Now she felt calm and energised, as if last night's tears had washed away the raw edge of her hurt, enabling her to begin moving forward at last.

'Rhiannon would love this,' David remarked, looking round at the brightly coloured hanging baskets overflowing with the hot reds and pinks of geranium and busy Lizzies, intermingled with the bright blues of lobelia. Reaching up towards the hanging baskets, late delphiniums stood amongst a riot of orange and yellow nasturtiums, with the green heads of sedum just turning to their autumn russet.

'Rhiannon's idea of heaven,' Carys agreed, with a smile. Through an archway of jasmine and honeysuckle, she glimpsed row upon row of late summer flowers, bordered by greenhouses at the far end.

'Hi, you must be Carys.' A woman with dark hair, caught away from her face by a green silk scarf, looked up as they stepped through the door. She abandoned her row of coleus and aloe vera plants next to a large reception desk, and came towards them, wiping her hands on her jeans. 'And you must be David Meredith. I'm Karenza Treverick. Pleased to meet you.' At which point, the phone rang, temporarily ending all possibility of conversation.

'It's okay, Karenza. Got it,' called a young man in a stripy jumper of the hand-knitted and every colour of the rainbow variety, appearing and settling himself down at the reception desk. 'Karenza's Field of Flowers. How may I help you?' he declared into the mouthpiece, ready to lead any bride – or mother of bride – gently but firmly down the path to Karenza's door and nowhere else.

'Come through,' mouthed Karenza, leading them through an archway divided from the reception area by a curtain screen made up of strands of tiny shells. 'Sorry, it gets a bit hectic in there,' she added, as they made their way through a room with two stone sinks side by side, and shelf upon shelf of rolls of wire of every thickness imaginable and every colour of ribbon. A higher shelf contained jars of beads, tiny bows and sequins, swathes of silk, a vase bursting with peacock feathers and a papier mache pumpkin that grinned at them in a slightly vacant fashion, as if embarrassed to find itself there at all. A heady scent of freesias filled the air.

'I hope we're not interrupting,' said Carys, feeling a little foolish. Had she really forgotten that it was all very well for those on holiday to go around asking questions about a family from long ago, but in the real world everybody worked, and anyone running their own business was usually rushed off their feet.

'No, not at all.' Karenza smiled. 'Ed loves being in charge. I set up Field of Flowers a couple of years ago, so I've only recently been able to afford to take on staff. Growing the flowers and helping people choose the look they want is the bit I love. Ed was a real find. He's a born salesman, and he's worked with plants since he was sixteen so he really knows his stuff.' She grinned. 'It gives me the luxury of a bit of free time. I'll make a cup of tea, and then we can sit out here, and you can show me this article.'

She led them to a gravel area overlooking the banks of flowers and the greenhouses. A large round table surrounded by chairs stood just outside the door to a small kitchen.

'My consulting area,' Karenza explained cheerfully, leaving the kettle to boil and returning to join them.

'It's beautiful,' sighed Carys, just a little wistfully, gazing out over the sea of flowers in front of them. The gravel area was edged with a low hedge of lavender that sent up its rich fragrance in the warmth of the sun.

'It was a mess when I bought it.' Karenza gave the grimace of hard work well remembered. 'The previous owners had kept pigs and chickens and a few goats. Most of the back there was completely overgrown. I'm sure I've still got the scars of brambles in places.'

'Did you clear it yourself, then?' asked David. After yesterday's adventures, he had expected Karenza Treverick to be a white-haired lady pushing seventy-five at least, not this tanned, energetic young woman, of about thirty-five.

Karenza nodded. 'Every single last bit. I'm not sure I'd do it again. But at the time I reckoned I could do brute force and ignorance myself, and save my cash for stuff like the building work and putting up the greenhouses.'

'Was it something you always wanted to do?' asked Carys.

Karenza's dark eyes rested on hers for a moment. 'Yes. I suppose it was. But I thought it was a childhood dream. Funny, really. I always thought my life was in New Zealand, not here. But then when my husband and I split, it seemed like a new start. It might have been different if we'd had kids, but I didn't really have ties back there. Apart from friends, of course.' She smiled at Carys. 'I suppose, deep down, I knew it was my only chance to do what I really wanted with my life.' Her eyes rested on the green of the fields on either side, with the distant hint of the sea. 'And maybe home is always home, after all.'

'So you grew up here?' said David.

'Not here exactly.' Karenza smiled at him. 'I lived in Treverick until I was fifteen. The village, not the Hall,' she added. 'Then my parents emigrated to New Zealand.' From inside came the click of the kettle as it boiled. 'It seems a lifetime ago,' she added, as she went inside, returning a few moments later with a tray containing a teapot and cups, which she set down in the middle of the table with a practised air. 'When you called, you said you were researching the Trevericks,' she reminded them, pouring tea.

'Yes,' said Carys.

'In a way,' said David.

'Oh?' Karenza handed them their cups. 'So you think we might be related in some way?'

'Not me,' said Carys. 'But the Merediths might be.'

'Really?' Karenza's eyes searched Carys' face. 'You're not a Meredith, then.'

Carys blinked. 'No. We're not related.' There was something in Karenza's glance that was making her slightly uneasy. 'Well, apart from the fact that my family were David's family's servants, that is,' she added lightly, to break the mood.

'Head gardener hardly counts as a servant,' David retorted.

'No, indeed,' said Karenza with a smile. 'I'd never call a gardener a servant. I thought I recognised a fellow plant addict,' she added to Carys. 'So it runs in the blood, then.'

'My grandfather,' Carys explained. 'My dad too, for a while. And my mother swears there was always an Evans running the gardens at Plas Eden, ever since Roman times. Although I'm not sure Celtic tribes had head gardeners.'

Karenza laughed. 'So does this mean you found a Treverick in your family tree?' she asked, turning to David.

He shook his head. 'Not a name,' he said.

'I found this postcard of Treverick Hall in my mother's attic,' said Carys, pulling out the postcard. 'No one had ever mentioned it before.'

Karenza fished out a pair of purple-rimmed reading glasses, with a jaunty leaf motif etched down each arm, and peered at the photograph. 'Oh so that's what it looked like.' She pulled a face. 'Dad always said it was a monstrosity. I can see why they all fought over the money and wouldn't touch the place. Thank heaven for the British inheritance rules. I'd have hated to have ended up responsible for keeping an old mausoleum like that in one piece. The men are welcome to it.' She looked up again. 'So this was what started it?'

Carys bit her lip. She glanced towards David, aware Karenza was following her every move.

'No,' he said, slowly. 'It was my parents who seemed to think there was a connection, years ago. We're sort of following in their footsteps.'

'So they didn't find anything?'

David shook his head. 'They didn't have the chance.' He cleared his throat. 'There was an accident. Their train was derailed. They were both killed outright.'

'I'm so sorry.'

'It's okay,' said David, awkwardly. 'It was a long time ago.'

Karenza gazed down at the postcard in her hand, as if lost in thought. 'Rhiannon,' she said, at last.

Carys jumped. David set his cup down a little too hard, spilling tea over the table, where it ran in milky rivulets away from them and dripped bit by bit onto the gravel. 'How do you know Rhiannon?'

'I don't.' Karenza looked up again. 'At least, I've never met her. Who is she?'

'My aunt,' said David. 'My mother's sister. She looked after my brother and me when our parents were killed.'

'That makes sense.' Absently, Karenza reached for a cloth and mopped up the spilt tea. 'I did wonder after Carys phoned me. It was her mentioning the Meredith name. But of course it could easily have been a coincidence.' She let go of the cloth. 'My parents ran the Treverick Arms, when I was a child. I used to help them sometimes after school, unofficially of course, when things were really busy. I was the one who took the call, you see.'

'The call?' said Carys. 'From Rhiannon?'

Karenza nodded. 'I still dream about it sometimes. I suppose it made quite an impression, I must only have been eight or so at the time.'

'So what happened?' asked David.

'It was a particularly busy weekend for some reason. Mum was run ragged with the B&B. There were phone calls every half hour or so with people wanting to book. She was furious that two of the guests hadn't turned up that Saturday night. No message. Nothing. She could have let the room five times over, you see. The phone rang, and I picked it up.' Karenza began to fold the cloth carefully into tiny squares. 'I don't suppose it registered that she was speaking to a child. She was so calm, I remember. That was the worst bit. Hearing her voice keeping so steady and practical and trying to explain something so terrible and sort everything out, and all the time you could tell that inside she was falling apart. She offered to pay for the room. Mum wouldn't take anything, of course.' She looked up at David. 'So that was your aunt.'

'Yes.'

Karenza's eyes searched his face. 'You can't have been very old at the time.'

'I was nine. My brother's a couple of years younger.'

'What an awful thing to have happened.' She placed the cloth carefully on a spare chair, and smoothed it gently. 'I lost my parents within six months of each other when I was in my late twenties. That was hard enough. I can't even imagine what it must have been like to lose them both so instantly like that, and so young. I'm sorry.'

'You okay?' It was Carys, her voice low as Karenza returned to the kitchen, murmuring something about more tea.

'Fine,' he replied, smiling at her. 'It just brought it back, that's all.' He traced the pattern of veins in the botanical drawing of a Morning Glory bloom on his mug with one finger. 'Huw and me, we lived such privileged lives in Plas Eden. Big house. Money. The best education money could buy. Nothing to worry about. But it doesn't matter who you are or where you live when something like that happens.' He brought out the copy of the newspaper article from his pocket with a slight shudder. 'I can't imagine what it must have been like to lose a child like that.'

'No,' agreed Carys, quietly.

'Is that it?' said Karenza, returning with a fresh pot of tea. 'The article you were talking about?'

'Yes,' said Carys. 'We made several copies while we were there. This one is for you.'

'Thank you. That was really thoughtful. I'll read it properly later. I'm not very good with things like that. I'm just bound to cry.' Karenza looked down at the article. 'No wonder there were always stories about the Trevericks being cursed. I suppose that's what got to Dad in the end. He'd always rubbished that idea of a curse. But I think it must have been your parents being killed like that, David, on their way to find out more about the family that finally got to him. He started talking about New Zealand only weeks afterwards, I seem to remember.'

'So did they say what they were looking for, then?' asked David.

'They must have done. They must have spoken to Mum about it when they made their booking.' She frowned, searching her memory. 'In fact, I'm certain. I can remember Mum and Dad talking about it afterwards.'

'It was definitely something to do with the Trevericks?'

Karenza nodded. 'Oh, yes. I remember Dad saying they must be mistaken, and they must be thinking of the satyr and the nymph in Treverick Gardens.' She watched them exchange glances. 'I take it you've been into the gardens?'

'Yes,' said David.

'And got ourselves well and truly spooked,' added Carys.

Karenza laughed. 'I can believe that. I've been meaning to go and see them now they're restored. But somehow I never seem to have the time. You know how it is.' She frowned. 'Or maybe I didn't want to spoil the illusion. We used to play there when we were kids,' she explained. 'Me and my friends from the village. It was massively overgrown. A proper jungle. The Lost Gardens of Heligan when they were still lost had nothing on Treverick in those days. We used to scare ourselves silly at Halloween. Not that there was anything there, of course. At least, I don't think so. And anyhow, I always felt that if there were ghosts, they were family and were unlikely to want to hurt me. It was Judith Treverick who is supposed to have designed that waterfall bit and had the nymph and the animals made.'

'But …' Carys looked down at the article, puzzled. 'I thought from this she died as a child.'

'Oh, no. I'm pretty sure not. I've got a picture of her somewhere. I think it must be still amongst the boxes I haven't unpacked yet. Dad always loved it, because the photograph was taken by the waterfall in Treverick Gardens. She's definitely a young woman. Dad always said it was the last one of her ever taken. The real end of the Trevericks, he called it.' She met two pairs of enquiring eyes. 'Sorry, he never explained, and I never thought to ask. Family history never really interested me, I'm afraid. At least, not until it was too late and I had no one left to ask.' She considered for a moment. 'I think I know roughly where that photograph is stashed. I'll try and find it later, if you like. Are you staying long in Treverick?'

'We have to get back to Wales tomorrow,' said Carys.

'Okay. Well, if you give me your email address, I can always send a copy to you. You never know, it might be useful.'

'Great, thanks,' replied Carys, with a smile.

For in the end I could not leave her.

And I could not take her with me, into the disintegration of the ocean. Somehow, even in my despair, I could not take life from this child who had irked me from the day of my engagement, with her watchful eyes and her wilfulness, and that dogged determination to lead her life as she chose.

She held on tightly as I kept her steady with the weight of my body and the heaviness of my clothing, while the surf clawed at us, the undertow boiling around our feet. Then, as the wave passed, I turned and led her back towards the shore.

I did not know we had been seen. Not until the voices called to us, and I saw shadows come racing along the beach.

Judith was immediately swept up and taken back to the house. She went, unwillingly enough, but less able to resist now half the household was surrounding me on the shore. Besides, even I could see that her lips were blue and the core of her was chilled, almost beyond redemption, certainly beyond protest.

I knew what would come next. Their voices were kind. But, released from Judith's gaze, I sank down to my knees on the sand, and I could not let him go. After a while, I felt them step back, defeated. One of the valets was sent for my husband. The other for a priest. And then they fell silent.

I felt a perfect dawn rise around us. A winter sun streaked along the beach, clear and fragile beneath a cloudless sky as the sea drew back to a gleaming turquoise, leaving a sheen of wet sand shimmering in its wake, and a scattering of shells.

'I'll take him now, shall I?' It was one of the grooms. An elderly man, reaching the end of his time at Treverick Hall. I had not spoken to him once in all my time there. I did not even know his name. But his eyes were kind. He had lost a son in the rebellion in the Transvaal, I remembered. I had seen him, standing deep in thought in front of the gravestone each Sunday, as we went to church.

Slowly, I nodded.

He knelt down beside me. 'I'll take him now.' His voice was gentle, as were the hands that reached around my burden, waiting to take its weight.

My arms were cold and cramped. I could scarcely feel the lessening of pressure as I let go. But I heard the cry that went up along the beach. A wild, hard cry of an animal dying. I did not understand until later that the sound was the one vibrating through my body. And that mine was the throat from which it came.

Chapter Twenty-One

It was almost dark by the time David drew into the car park of the Treverick Arms that evening. After he'd cut the engine, they sat for a while in silence.

'I'm not sure we're any the wiser,' said David, with a grimace.

Carys shook herself. Her mind was rushing with ideas from wandering for most of the day through the Lost Gardens of Heligan, following paths through the palms and giant ferns of the jungle, and sitting amongst the green peace of the Lost Valley woodland. She was quite certain she had bored David half-senseless with her lingering over the flower and vegetable gardens and her wild excitement over discovering the melon yard, despite him busily taking notes on the ways the Lost Gardens attracted visitors.

'But at least we know that your dad thought there was some kind of connection between Plas Eden and Treverick Hall. And that was why he was trying to get here that day. Maybe it doesn't matter if we never know what he thought the connection was. Maybe this was just about laying that part of the past to rest.'

'Yes, I suppose.' He turned to her with a smile. 'I'm glad I came. Even though it has stirred up lots of memories.' He cleared his throat in a hesitating sort of a way. 'And I'm glad you were with me.'

'Me too,' said Carys, returning his smile.

David took a deep breath. He'd been working on this for the entire drive, but it still didn't seem any easier. 'Look,' he began tentatively. 'I don't suppose –'

'Have a good day?' It was Rob McIntyre, watering can in hand, making his way back from the line of hanging baskets at the side of the car park, and the moment went winging away over the horizon.

'Lovely, thanks,' called Carys. 'We managed to fit in the Lost Gardens of Heligan and the Eden project all in one day. It's beautiful down here. I'm never going abroad on holiday again!'

He laughed. 'People who come to this part of the world are usually smitten. You'd be surprised how many come back time and time again.'

'Well, I hope that includes me,' Carys replied.

'Great stuff.' He turned back towards the outside tap. 'Mary's around. She said to pop in and see her when you're back. No hurry though, if you're going into the village for a meal.'

'We rather thought we'd eat here,' said David, as they made their way out of the car. 'We decided we'd had enough rushing around.'

'Great stuff,' said Rob again. 'I recommend the sea bass. Chef's speciality.'

'Is that with or without chips?' returned Carys, keeping the bantering tone.

He laughed. 'Red wine reduction and a rhubarb jus, naturally. Got to practise for my appearance on *MasterChef*, whatever the punters really prefer.'

'I think he was joking,' whispered Carys, seeing David looked like someone heading straight for the harbour and a good dose of cod.

'Oh, right.' He looked faintly embarrassed. 'You're not into all that fine dining stuff, are you? I was looking at the leaflets earlier: Rick Stein's restaurant in Padstow isn't that far away.'

'Don't be silly.' Carys watched a faintly hurt look pass over his face. This wasn't David Meredith asking her out on a date, was it? Surely they'd known each other a bit too long to be doing first date stuff? Besides, it was far too soon after Joe to even think of anything like that, and especially with David Meredith. Bound to end in trouble. On the other hand... 'I mean, I'd love to.' She cleared her throat. 'Only, I'm sure you have to book ages in advance.'

'Ah.' He grimaced. 'I've a feeling that's probably the case. But they might have a cancellation?'

Carys bit her lip. But she was determined to start as she meant to go on, and that meant being honest. 'Would you mind if we did that another time? I've a feeling Mary will want to hear about everything we've found, and I'd quite like to leave early tomorrow with such long drive ahead, if that's okay with you.'

'That's fine. No problem.'

She smiled. 'And besides, we might be seen as casting aspersions on Mr McIntyre's cooking skills if we hear the menu and immediately up sticks and head for a celebrity chef instead.'

David laughed. 'Well seeing as my cooking is generally confined to beans and omelettes, I'm hardly in a position to judge.'

'You used to be a good cook. Rhiannon taught you and Huw well, I remember. You were both much better than me.'

'Were we? Well, I'm out of practice, I'm afraid. I'll have to try and be more adventurous in future.' He cleared this throat. 'When you say another time ...'

'Don't you want to come back?'

'Well, yes…'

'Great,' said Carys. 'We didn't see half of the Eden Project, and I definitely want to go back to the Lost Gardens. Didn't you just love those figures rising out of the ground? That giant's head was amazing, and weren't you just blown away by the woman lying there asleep? People loved them.'

'And the estate was in far worse a state than Eden, when they started, according to the book we bought,' added David.

'So that's why you were so quiet on the way back.'

He smiled. 'Well, it did cross my mind. Wales has got its own Eden Project, but it doesn't have a lost garden. At least, not in the north and not like Heligan. It might at least be worth looking into. Especially with Plas Eden's statues. There's nothing like those at all.'

'So maybe it wasn't a waste of time coming here, after all,' replied Carys, as they made their way into the pub.

The Treverick Arms was quiet when they arrived, with only a few drinkers sitting in the bar. As Carys made her way back down twenty minutes later, after a quick wash and change of clothes, Mary McIntyre was chatting to an elderly couple who were also guests in the B&B.

'Enjoy your evening,' Mary called to her guests, who appeared to be heading to the quay for a meal and a touch of genteel nightlife.

'Have a good time?' enquired Mary.

'Fascinating,' said Carys. 'And we've lots to tell you.'

'Not exactly what I'd expected,' said David.

'There are always surprises when you look into the past, I've found.' After handing over to the young man who appeared to be her assistant for the evening, she turned back to David and Carys.

'Come in here,' she said, beckoning them behind the bar. 'We won't be disturbed.' She led the way into a whitewashed courtyard surrounded by pots that overflowed with the reds and blues of petunias and lobelia, mixed in with dark green sprays of rosemary, the long, slightly purple-tinged leaves of sage, clumps of chive and several varieties of mint. At one side of the courtyard a door opened into the kitchen, where they could hear the banging of pans and the murmur of voices as the preparation for the evening meals began.

'Yes, that makes sense,' said Mary, as they finished and Carys placed the copy of the article from the *Treverick Times* in front of her. 'I suppose that's where the story of the sound of a woman's grief among the rocks on Treverick beach must have started.'

Carys shivered. 'I'm glad it was calm when we went to see Treverick Gardens.'

'And you still have no idea if there is any connection with your family at all?' asked Mary.

David shook his head. 'Nothing for definite. As Ann Treverick died in Ketterford, I can't see how there can be. I just wish Dad hadn't felt the need to keep whatever it was he was trying to find a secret. Then at least we might have known where to start. I suppose it was the madness thing. People are funny about that, aren't they.'

'If she was mad,' remarked Mary, looking up from the article.

Carys blinked. 'You mean, you think she might not have been?'

'I think the loss of a child might drive you to the edge. But those drawings you showed me looked like the work of sanity to me.'

'Didn't Margaret Tyack say something like that, when we

315

were at Ketterford?' said David. 'It never really struck me at the time.'

'Yes, you're right,' replied Carys. 'I didn't think much about it either.' She frowned at Mary. 'But why…?'

'Lots of reasons. Mental illness wasn't really understood in those days. From what I've read people – especially women – were sent to asylums for all kinds of reasons. Postnatal depression. Menopause. Depression itself. And sometimes just for being inconvenient. Good way to get rid of a wife. Victorians didn't get women at all. They didn't even have a legal existence in their own right. They belonged to their father, then their husband. You didn't even have any rights to anything that belonged to you before you were married until the divorce law was changed in the 1880s. As far as legalities was concerned before then, married women were the same as criminals, small children, and the mad. Charming, eh? Even after a law is changed, old attitudes die hard.'

'I'm glad I live now,' said Carys.

'Absolutely.' Mary smiled at her. 'The world might not be equal still, but at least we aren't classed as children.' She shook her head. 'There were supposed to be safeguards against people being incarcerated in places like this just because they were inconvenient, but if you were ruthless and powerful enough – and had enough money – you could usually get around anything.'

'But that's horrible!'

'Well, from what I've seen in the letters and newspapers of the time, William Treverick didn't exactly stay at home grieving. He tried to marry again after Ann died. Several times. All of them young and very wealthy.'

David frowned at her. 'But he didn't?'

Mary gave a wry smile. 'This is a small community. Word

gets about. I'm sure even then there were men who loved their daughters and cared for their happiness above the chance of good connections. Or had wives who made damn sure they knew their lives would be hell if they tried. I don't think getting rid of an inconvenient wife in Ketterford did the Trevericks any good at all.'

'Poor woman,' sighed Carys.

'I don't expect we'll ever know,' said Mary. 'Not if so many of the records at Ketterford have gone missing. He might not even have put her there under her own name in the first place. Not a thing people tend to broadcast, even nowadays. It's fascinating, isn't it, to see how someone begins, and how they end. Especially women. All you hear about them usually is when they are young. Hit middle age, and you vanish. As a woman, that so annoys me still. It's experience that interests me, and how that creates someone.'

'So when did she die?' asked David.

Mary considered for a moment. 'In the Edwardian era. Early nineteen-hundreds? About then, I think. To be honest, I can't exactly remember. It's a bit late tonight, the church will be locked. But if you've time tomorrow before you go, I'll take you to see the plaque her husband put up to her.' She smiled at the raised eyebrows. 'Oh, it's quite spectacular, I can assure you. Money is no object when you've plenty, and want to look good for the neighbours,' she added, dryly.

'Okay,' said David, glancing at Carys. 'I suppose, if nothing else, we should at least find out the end of the story.'

Carys nodded. 'I'd like that. It's funny; when I saw that first photograph of her, I never thought I'd grow quite fond of Ann Treverick. I suppose following her story is like getting to know her. Seeing the end would be like laying her to rest, in a way.'

Mary looked up enquiringly as her husband appeared in the

doorway, phone in hand. 'Oh dear. I knew I wouldn't escape for long.'

Mr McIntyre coughed delicately. 'I'd have taken a message and asked them to ring back, but she was terribly insistent that she spoke to you and our guests straight away.'

'Oh?' said Mary.

'Karenza Treverick,' said her husband. 'She's saying she's found something, she won't say what, she wants to come over tomorrow morning, and she wants to make sure it's before David and Carys leave.'

'Really?' Mary's eyes were suddenly gleaming, as she reached for the handset. 'Well, it looks as if you might find some answers, after all.'

For a while, they left me alone to do as I pleased.

I think maybe the servants were a little afraid of me. While William dealt with his loss in his own way, which meant attending to the Treverick estate more diligently than usual. I scarcely even laid eyes on him for more than a few minutes at a time as the first frosts of winter came.

It was an unusually hard winter. In other years, being so close to the sea, Treverick had rarely been visited by snow and ice. But as I finally emerged from the listlessness that hung over me, I found myself wandering aimlessly, hour upon hour, amongst the ice-clad ponds and frosted trellises of Treverick's garden.

Strangely, of all of them, it was Judith who chose to spend time with me. At her age, I remembered with shame, my own chatter had been about ribbons and the lace for my next dress, and whichever of the young men was handsome – and most definitely rich – in the neighbourhood.

Judith, on the other hand, was full of plans for the coming

318

spring. For the plants she was raising in a corner of the smallest greenhouse, and for creating a wilderness for the waterfall, so that it appeared to be in truth a rushing mountain stream. She sketched her plans, endlessly. Changing them, this way and that, filling her paper with drawings as she did so.

There was a sculptor in the village. A young man with high ambitions, I believe. A passionate follower of the Pre-Raphaelite brotherhood – much to the outrage of Uncle Jolyon, who still cornered the vicar most Sundays on the subject of Filth Allowed to Corrupt Young Minds, and Where Would it Lead To? Although for now at least, young Mr Pawley – having been born into respectability rather than wealth – was dedicating himself to the trade of creating garden ornaments in the no less honourable pursuit of keeping a roof over his head and his belly reasonably full.

I watched for a while as Judith made her plans for Mr Pawley to follow. The nymph I thought he might enjoy. While the satyr, I had a feeling, might just get out of hand, and be banished forever into the furthest undergrowth.

I could still smile, I found. Still laugh at times too. And, strangely enough, never had the gardens seemed so beautiful. It was as if my senses had been woken. I saw, as I had never seen, the lacing of spiders' webs across the grass, bejewelled with mist. The frost flowers icing the windows had never seemed so intricate and so marvellous. And before long my fingers were itching, Until, one day, I took up Judith's abandoned pencil and paper, and I began to draw.

Until then, my painting had been for show. As I worked, I had heard the words of admiration that would flow once it was displayed. But now it became a passion. My existence. My way of being in the world. Each day as my confidence grew, and I became more ambitious in my attempts, I found an inner peace returning. My sorrow was still there. I saw it would be there, as part of me, for as long as I lived. But I had found a way to live again.

I should have known my peace would not last. I suppose they told him I was recovered. That I had left my room and returned to some semblance of the woman I had been before.

Whatever it was, he appeared one night at my door. I blinked at him in surprise. I had never particularly enjoyed his attentions, and since our son's death I had been left well alone. I could not be as I had been before. I could not smile. I could not please. I could not be what he wanted me to be. At first it had stabbed me to the heart that he could not even seem to bear the exchange of a few words with me. That my lack of smiles and silly chatter seemed to disturb him. But then I had welcomed the peace his absence brought.

I looked at him in bewilderment. He seemed a little embarrassed. I'll give him his due, my husband was not entirely lacking in brains; he had sense enough to know that I was no longer the girl he had married.

He muttered something. Something about a child. And how it would be good for me.

'It's too soon,' I said quickly. Suddenly I was afraid. I could not have a child. Not now. One day, maybe. Or maybe never. But not now. Not with my grief so raw. Not with this new creature I was becoming still struggling towards life inside me. For some it might be the answer. But not for me. I knew, as clear as daylight, I would truly lose my mind.

He smiled and reached for the fastening of my nightgown. 'You will not think that when you hold our child in your arms,' he said.

I looked at him, this man I had married. And it was as if the final illusion fell away. I saw that for all the years we had

320

been man and wife, I did not know him at all. No more than he did me.

I had married seeing only the envious eyes of the other girls in my circle. I had lived my life in their imaginary gaze. And he? A brutal clarity hit me at that moment. I saw without doubt that he had not chosen me for my father's money alone. Had I not seen myself that there were heiresses in London with more dowry to bring, and far more beauty and accomplishment than I could ever boast?

No; William was a man who arranged the world according to his own comfort. He had seen that I would not demand of him, or create any disturbance in his life. He had chosen me above all others because in my indolent emptiness, he had recognised his own.

He stroked my face, his eyes soft and sentimental. As if somehow that was enough. Panic began to rise inside me. I had not seen the memorial he had had placed in Treverick church to his son, but I had heard that it was a fine one. The best money could buy. Like clothes packed away into a trunk, he had already placed Charlie in the realms of things gone by. Our son's death was God's will. Nothing to do with his parents' actions, our mutual selfishness and lack of care. God had called Charlie to him, and there Charlie sat in Heaven as an angel, smiling down at us. Life could go on, just as it had done before.

Had I remained quiet, the moment would have passed, as it had always passed before and, child or no child, my body would have dragged itself on a little longer in my gilded prison. Had I struggled, he might even have shown some enthusiasm for the task. But instead, I think for that minute at least, I was truly mad. I laughed. It was a bitter laugh, but a laugh.

He paused. No longer the amorous Knight wooing his

Lady. He looked affronted, clinging to his dignity like a schoolboy who had lost his footing on ice and gone sprawling headlong in the mud. There was a foolishness about him that made me laugh all the more. Wildly now, unable to stop myself.

He turned on his heels and left. Stillness descended into my room. After a while, my laughter died. Desperately, like a drowning woman, I took up my pencil and began to draw great ships sailing the oceans, their sails in full flight, until my mind settled and sanity came creeping back. This time to stay.

I thought I had defeated him. I thought I would be left alone for a little while longer at least. I thought I had time to find myself again, so that I would be ready to face this life I had chosen so blindly, and now wanted nothing more than to escape. Even though it might be to a life in poverty and disgrace, at least it would be a life.

Fool that I was I thought he would let me go. I knew so little of the world, then, and I knew nothing of pride. Of saving face. And I did not understand the power he had been given, the moment I married him, to decide my fate.

જી

For many months William ignored my presence. Guests came and went. I heard their talk and laughter below, but I was never summoned. Judith would often escape and join me in my lonely state in my rooms. She would watch me sometimes, her eyes full of concern.

'Could you not make your peace with William?' she asked one evening, as we watched the sun sink beneath the horizon. Summer was in the air, with a smell of roses on the warm breeze.

'One day, maybe,' I replied. I had no wish to hurt her feelings. And to tell the truth, this estrangement from my husband had begun to weary me. His life was the one that continued as it had done before. For all I knew, he had taken a mistress. He would not have been the first. I was the one who remained a prisoner within Treverick Hall. By then I had given up even trying to order the carriage, or even Guinevere, my mare. The servants, I could see, had their orders. I was too proud to stamp my feet and scream. I soon grew tired of their embarrassment at my requests, and the way they avoided my eyes now, at all times.

'Maybe soon?' she persisted. I was surprised to see the glint of tears. 'It's just that sometimes, when he talks of you…'

'He talks of me?'

'Oh, it's nothing,' she replied. 'I'm sure it's nothing.'

It seemed I had no choice. As that perfect summer wore on, with day after day of cloudless skies, so life returned with it, making me restless. He would not let me go. I had understood that by now. That was not how the world worked, and for all the raging against it within me there was nothing I could do to change it.

I began to understand Aunt Beatrice a little more. I had never seen her gainsay my uncle, at least not to his face. But looking back now I could see that her life was at its fullest when Uncle Jolyon was not there. She had her friends, her charities, her occupations. She had no children of her own, but she had spoilt me to her heart's content from the moment I had arrived, a bewildered five-year-old child, when the typhoid fever killed my parents and my baby brother.

As the summer wore on to autumn, it seemed to me that such a bargain was the only way open to me. At least it would be some kind of life. Who said that our next child would be a boy? With a girl, maybe, I reasoned to myself, at least I could find some meaning to my life again. And so I swallowed my pride and resolved to fight my husband no longer.

My first opportunity to demonstrate my new acquiescence came the very next day.

'You ordered the carriage,' said William. He was standing at one of the tall drawing-room windows, watching Judith making her way down the drive in the company of her cousin, Arabella Phelps, stalwart of the Treverick Widows and Orphans Society.

He had not spoken to me in so long I eyed him in surprise. 'No,' I replied.

'Well, you should,' he returned. 'The sea air will do you good. I will order it for you now.'

'Thank you,' I replied, grateful that he had made this first overture of peace between us.

'Good.' He was turned away from me, pulling the bell cord to summon the servants, so I could not see his face. 'I shall accompany you, as Judith is otherwise occupied.'

I kept my pride firmly in check. 'Thank you,' I replied, in the humblest of tones. 'That is very kind.'

'There is no need for you to change,' he added, as I made a move to return to my room. 'We should go directly, before the rain comes.'

It was a beautiful, clear September day. I felt the sun on my face as we drove past Treverick Harbour and along the coastal road. I tried to speak to him, to demonstrate my gratitude and my wish for us to be friends again. He made little reply. But then, I reasoned to myself, he had his pride, too. He could not choose but hear. And, after all, had I not charmed him once? Surely, over time, I could charm him again. So I settled back on the cushions and watched the green fields pass by as the carriage began to take the road inland, away from the turquoise swell of the sea.

We took a road I did not know. A small, winding road that led onto a broad expanse of moorland with a distant glimpse of the ocean. I had eaten little for months, and I was growing tired by now, and dizzy with the movement of the carriage and the heat. I shut my eyes. I must have dozed a little, for the next thing I knew we were passing through high iron gates. For a confused moment, I thought we had returned to Treverick.

'We are here,' said William. The carriage door was opened. Puzzled, but thankful for the motion to have stopped, I followed as he stepped out, handing me down. A group of people were waiting for us. As if they had been expecting us, I suddenly saw, with the first stirrings of alarm. I looked up at the grim bricks of the building. The bars at every window.

'William –' I turned, fear rising inside me, strangling my voice. But already it was too late. He had already stepped swiftly back inside the carriage, and was impatiently calling to the driver to move off.

I was stunned. I stood there, unable to understand what was happening to me. Then I ran, as fast as my weakened legs could take me, towards the only link with my life, now vanishing rapidly out of the gates.

I did not get more than a few paces. 'There, there, Mrs Adams.' My arm was grasped firmly by a large, burly woman. 'No need to fret. You'll be safe here. No need to distress yourself.'

I stared at her. 'I am not Mrs Adams. I am Ann Treverick. I wish to return with my husband. Let me go! I am not Mrs Adams.'

'Of course you're not, dear.' The woman's voice was cajoling. As if speaking to a child. A child who might protest, but would have to give in at some point. 'You'll be quite safe here.'

She was holding me easily, but securely, so that I could not even struggle. A woman accustomed to restraining those in her charge. I do not know if it was anger, or terror, that held the upper hand in me, as I was marched, helpless, towards the house.

❧

I fought them. For hours, days, months, I fought them. I fought them every inch of the way. But there were too many of them. And they were accustomed to the strength that desperation can give a woman.

When I had no more fight left and they released me to be with the other inhabitants of the place, I was terrified. Every moment of the day and night I waited for a knife to be put to my throat, or wild, insane eyes to look into mine as clawed hands reached for my throat.

'You won't escape,' the staff told me that from the start. I looked up angrily one day as an old woman approached the chair where I was sitting. I had no need of a fellow inmate to tell me so again.

'I will,' I replied to her. 'I will. One day. Or I'll die trying.'

Faded eyes watched me from a face wrinkled and worn with cares I could not imagine. 'Then make it seem that you've given in,' she replied.

'I wouldn't give them the satisfaction,' I retorted scornfully.

'Maybe not. But at least that way you will slip out of their notice. They will leave you alone.' Her eyes rested on mine. 'Sometimes being invisible can give you the greatest freedom.'

I stared at her. 'You're as sane as I am,' I said, astonished. I had thought my fellow inmates to watch the world with vacant stares, or to be raving.

326

She laughed, a low hollow laugh. 'What is it to be sane?' she replied. 'They say you lost a child, and that drove you to lose your mind. I'd say you were truly mad if you hadn't been crazed, at least for a little while.' She held my hands for a few minutes. 'Fight them,' she said. 'All of us in here, we make for ourselves what lives we can. They are not all cruel, you will find. Some like to lord it, of course, others are indifferent. But there are a few who understand that their work here is keeping a place for those who are troublesome, or inconvenient.'

I stayed quiet all that day. Obeyed every order. And at the end of the week I was led to a small room of my own. Bare, furnished with a simple bed. But it was, I soon learnt, a mark of privilege. Of my husband's wealth. Or rather, I thought bitterly, whatever still remained of my dowry.

Would I have lost my mind? Maybe. There were many women there who had, even though they had arrived saner than I. Sometimes I thought just being shut up inside with little company, no occupation for my mind and no hope would be enough to send me mad, staring out as winter faded and the spring flowers began to open in the gardens beyond the bars.

But then one day I heard a commotion outside my room. 'I'm sorry, Miss. You cannot disturb her. It could do untold damage to Mrs Adams' state of mind…'

'Nonsense.' I looked up at the familiar voice. 'Did no one tell you I am now a patron of this place? I can do as I please.'

It was Judith, bristling and furious. She had pushed past those attempting to block her way, and had made her way into my room, deaf to all their protests. Thank Heaven they were a little afraid of her scorn and of offending a patron, and the money that might be lost should she take her patronage elsewhere. We were left alone.

I think we both wept as we held each other tight.

'I'm so sorry.' Judith brushed away her tears at last. 'I'm so sorry. I couldn't find you. William wouldn't tell me where you had gone. He told the servants you'd gone abroad for your health, and he tried to convince me of that, too. I never thought he could be so cruel as to put you in a place like this. Not until I made your Aunt Beatrice tell me, only a few weeks ago, what he had done. I've tried to reason with him, but it's as if he doesn't hear. Or won't hear. He's forbidden me to see you.' She smiled. 'But he can't dictate what good works my allowance supports. It's wicked,' she added, growing passionate again. 'Utterly wicked. But I'll find a way to free you.'

She did not stay long, but she was back the next day, this time bringing with her my drawing materials. Now I had an occupation and a means of escaping, in mind at least, from my confinement. And hope. Most of all, I had hope. Though what I would do with myself should Judith enable me to escape in earnest, I could not even begin to consider.

◈

For the next few weeks, Judith came as often as she could. William, she said, was watching her, but he couldn't neglect his duties to the estate every hour of the day. I should have tried to dissuade her. Told her that I was resigned to my lot. But she was my one source of hope in this new dark world of mine. I clung to her, as one might cling to life itself.

The last time Judith came, it was as night was falling. She appeared in my room silent as a shadow, a finger to her lips.

'William is sending me away,' she said. 'I'm to go tomorrow to my Aunt Elisabeth in Florence. For my education,' she added, bitterly. 'Much William has ever cared about my "education".' She fell silent as footsteps passed outside my door. 'I had to see you this one last time,' she whispered. 'William doesn't know I'm here.' She placed a bundle on the bed beside me. We looked at each other. 'I had hoped to have more time to make arrangements to get you out of this place. Now there will be no other chance.'

'Where will I go?' I looked at her in despair. 'Not to my uncle. I know exactly what he would do.'

'I know.' Urgently, she was undoing the bundle, uncovering a dark dress that looked as if it had belonged to one of the serving women. 'It will fit,' she said, quickly. 'My charity work has more than one use. And I know of a place you can go. In London.'

'London!' I gazed at her, suddenly frightened. I had been captive, one way or another, for so long the mere thought of the outside world terrified me.

'They are good people,' she said. 'And it's a place William knows nothing of. You will not be easily found.' There were tears in her brown eyes once more. 'Please. This might be your only chance. I can't leave you here. Not in a place like this.'

I knew what she meant. I would most likely be alive in body when she returned, but in mind… I hesitated only for a moment. Judith helped me change my clothes, and then shrugged off her coat. 'It's an old one. William will be none the wiser, and at least it will keep you warm.' Finally, she placed her own hat over my shorn locks.

We made our way quietly and quickly down the staircase, slipping into the shadows of doorways whenever footsteps approached. I think she must have bribed the doorkeeper, for no one was there to hinder our passing. In the yard she took my arm, sweeping me hastily onto the floor of the carriage, where I was covered with a shawl.

I don't know which railway station she took me to. It was a large one, bustling with passengers. As far away from Treverick as she dared, I think.

'I'll write,' she said, as we hurried onto the train, only moments before it prepared to leave. She pressed a ticket and a purse into my hands. 'As soon as I get back to England, I'll write to you.'

I turned as she prepared to step back down onto the platform. 'But if William ever finds out…'

'He won't.' She hugged me tight. 'The coachman is a good man. He won't say a word. Anyhow, it is not easy to find someone, once they are in London.' I scarcely felt her place a handful of coins deep inside my pockets. 'Just in case,' she said, watching me anxiously.

Suddenly I was fearful. I held onto her, as the train prepared to leave. 'You must tell me,' I said. 'If you are ever in trouble. You must tell me. I'll find a way to help you, whatever it takes.'

'I know you will,' she said, smiling at me as she stepped down onto the platform at the first movement of the train. But she knew as well as I that any help I could bring was impossible. Should I ever return, William would know what she had done. I could never speak to her again. Never see her. She had saved my life, and all I could ever bring her, from this day forward, was harm.

She looked so young. So slight. For all her determination and her confidence, she knew so little of the world. She believed nothing could ever stem that free spirit of hers. Certainly a brother couldn't. But William understood the power of a husband to curb a wife, where there could be no escape.

If there was one thing I had learnt in Ketterford, it was that in the end, when all hope is gone, the strongest of spirits can be broken.

'Tell me,' I called, as steam enveloped her, leaving a pale shadow on the station as the train pulled away. 'You must tell me.'

But my voice was lost in the crash and whirr of machinery. I watched her waving until I could see her no more, as the train took me into the darkness of the night, away from my life, and into the unknown.

Chapter Twenty-Two

Karenza arrived shortly after breakfast the next morning, her eyes gleaming with suppressed excitement.

'I knew there was something,' she said, hugging Carys. 'I just knew there was something. Stupid of me not to think, really.' She paused, took a breath, and looked around the comfortable sofas of the little sitting room. 'My goodness, this hasn't changed a bit. And you've kept the open fire!' she exclaimed to Mary, who had pressed her husband into duty on reception and followed their visitor with undisguised curiosity.

'It was so lovely when we came to see it, and this room in particular, it seemed a shame to change it,' replied Mary.

'Wonderful!' said Karenza. The mission that had brought her there so hot-footedly seemed to have been forgotten as she gazed at her old home. 'I should have come here before,' she sighed. 'I'd love to look around.'

'Of course,' said Mary. 'You'd be very welcome. It would be nice to hear what it was like when you lived here. After all, that's history, too, nowadays.'

'Yes, I suppose it is,' replied Karenza. 'That makes me feel old.'

'You said you had found something?' prompted David, before their visitor could be completely distracted by a tour of the pub.

'Oh, yes,' said Karenza, her focus back on the matter in hand. 'You were quite right: there is a connection between Treverick and Plas Eden. A huge one, in fact.'

'Oh?' said David warily.

'Although not quite the one I'd been expecting,' added Karenza. 'But exciting, all the same.'

'And you've found something that will show us what it is,' prompted Carys, trying not to sound impatient as their visitor appeared to drift off into thought again.

Karenza grinned. 'Oh yes,' she said. 'First, I'm just going to have to dash to the loo after all that driving. Then you can take me up to Treverick Gardens. That's where the answer lies, you see.'

☙

The fire had burnt low as I finished speaking, and finally found the courage to lift my eyes to his.

Mr Meredith's face was turned away from me, into the darkness. I should have expected no less. I should have been grateful he did not recoil from me. Gently, I pulled my hands free from his.

But they would not come free. He held them tight. And when he turned his face back to mine, I saw the glint of tears in the orange glow of the flames.

'I must go,' I said. 'The gates of the hospital will be locked within the hour, and I will be missed.'

'Yes. Yes of course.' But his hands still held mine fast. 'Marry me,' he said.

I had steeled myself to show no emotion as he dismissed me. But at that, I gasped. 'It's impossible,' I said. 'I don't ask for your pity, and you cannot marry a mad woman. A lunatic.

333

One who has fled from her place of legal confinement. And I have no wish to end my days in your attic,' I added tartly, 'while you find yourself a quieter bride.'

At that, he laughed. 'If you think Plas Eden is half as grand as Thornfield, you will be sorely disappointed, I'm afraid. Much as I admire Miss Bronte's novels, I have no wish to be Mr Rochester. Far too much glowering, for my taste.' His eyes became serious once more. 'As for madness: you are the sanest creature I know. You forget: I have just returned from being with my mother after she lost a child. I saw what grief did to her.' His smile was gentle this time. 'I think that maybe grief makes us all a little mad, for a while.'

I had sworn to myself that, no matter what might pass, I would not weep. But at that, I leant against him, feeling his arms around me as the tears came.

'There,' he said, as if all was settled.

I brushed my tears away and regained my dignity. 'You forget, Mr Meredith, that I am already married.'

'To a husband who neither wants, nor deserves you.'

'But in the eyes of the law still owns me.'

'Hmm,' he said. 'I think whatever the scandal and the cost, he may well find he has grounds to seek a divorce.' His fingers traced my cheek. 'Or if not already, the fact of you being here with me might be enough.'

I returned his smile. My heart had begun to race. This was hardly the moment to confess it, but I, who had never felt true desire, found it flooding through my body until I could scarcely breathe.

'Well?' he said softly, as his lips found the corner of my mouth. I turned to meet him, my body softening.

But then I remembered.

He stopped as he felt me stiffen. 'What is it?'

'I cannot,' I said. And I felt as if my heart were breaking. 'I cannot.'

He frowned at me. 'You still have some feeling for him?'

'No!' I exclaimed. 'Never. But I can't build my own happiness on the betrayal of another.'

'Another?' He clearly saw some strapping youth, complete with a posy of violets, waiting at my door.

'How do you think I escaped from Ketterford?' I demanded. 'Not without help. My aunt and uncle would have returned me there in a moment,' I added, hearing the bitterness in my voice.

'Of course,' he said, slowly. 'Miss Treverick. I should have known from her letter of recommendation for you.'

I nodded. 'Judith saved my life. In more ways than one. I can't betray that.' I gazed at him earnestly, willing him to understand. 'She writes to me, sometimes, when she can. She has reassured me that William believes I am still in Ketterford. If he ever finds out I have gone he'll know well enough who helped me. William is Judith's legal guardian, as well as her brother.' I shuddered. 'I know he will punish her. And, knowing his punishments, I could never live with myself if I left Judith open to that.'

He was frowning. 'We could expose his treatment of you. Prove that he is not fit to be a guardian, any more than a husband.'

I shook my head. 'Any legal case would be a costly one. William is too fond of his reputation to give in without a fight, and he has powerful – and wealthy – friends. I can't let you risk this hospital. Or Plas Eden. And besides,' I added, as he began to protest, 'the scandal would taint Judith for the rest of her life. No respectable family would permit their son to marry her. I won't risk her only chance to escape Treverick

Hall, and find happiness.' I met his eyes. 'I let my son die through my own selfishness when I did not even try to prevent my husband from taking him out in the boat, even though I knew Charlie was far too young. Since then Judith has become like a daughter to me. I won't ever, ever allow her to come to any harm.'

'I understand,' he said gently.

Had I been a true heroine, I would have turned and left him there. Left him free to find happiness elsewhere, while I nursed my broken heart to the end of my days.

I was not born a heroine.

'But there maybe another way,' I said, my arms tightening around him once more.

Of course he had thought of it. I saw his eyes gleam. 'If you are certain,' he said.

There was, of course, no other way for it to be done: I returned an answer with my kiss.

ↄ

He found me waiting for him at the hospital the next morning. I saw the joy fade from his eyes as they met mine.

He closed the door to the office behind him. 'What has happened?'

'I have to go back.'

'Back.'

'To Treverick.'

He frowned. 'To him?'

I shook my head. 'No. Never. I would die first.' I held the crushed paper in my hand out towards him. 'Another letter came for me this morning. From Judith. I can't leave her. Whatever happens, I can't leave her now. I have to go back.'

❧

'This is so beautiful,' sighed Karenza, looking around at the restored waterfall of Treverick Gardens. 'I had no idea. It was just a wilderness when I used to play here. It was spooky. Like Beauty and the Beast. This must be how it would have looked then.'

'Then?' asked Carys. 'Oh, you mean in Victorian times. When Ann Treverick was alive.'

'We're not looking for anything, um, buried, are we?' asked David.

Mary, who had been a few steps behind, dead-heading a group of overblown roses, joined them hastily. 'I hope not,' she said. 'We've a lot more digging to do here this coming autumn.'

'Oh, I don't think there's anything hidden here. Mind you, they never did find her engagement ring. At least that's what my grandmother told me. But it might just have made a better story. Along with the curse.'

David and Carys glanced at each other. This was getting more like the brothers Grimm by the minute. Was there a gingerbread house they had missed, or Sleeping Beauty dreaming of her prince?

Mary appeared equally puzzled. 'Engagement ring?'

'Yes,' replied Karenza. 'Judith Treverick. Who made these gardens. She was engaged to some massively rich guy. Of course, I should have known when I found the photograph.' She fished an envelope out of her pocket, extracting a faded sepia print which she held out towards them.

Carys looked down at the portrait. Unlike the others she had seen of the Treverick family, it had not been taken in the

337

studio, but on a steep bank, with the severe outline of Treverick Hall visible in the background. It was of a young girl, probably no more than ten, in ringlets and a frilly dress. She was sitting next to the merest trickle of a stream, her hands tucked under her chin and smiling into the camera as if about to begin a conversation with the viewer, whoever they might be.

Carys smiled. She couldn't help it. The girl had a round, mischievous little face that looked as if it might break into laughter at any moment. Something stirred in the back of her mind.

'There was a pond here, when they made the waterfall,' said Karenza, tracing her footsteps back along the central flowerbed, filled with yellow tea roses. 'It was a family story my grandma used to tell. One of those real ghostly stories that come out at Christmas and Halloween. She always said that her cousin Judith vanished into thin air, just hours before her wedding.'

❧

I found her in the depths of the gardens, gazing into the white rush of the waterfall.

'You came!' she said, turning at the sound of my step.

'Of course,' I replied. 'Do you think I could abandon you?'

Judith smiled though tears and hugged me tight. 'I've missed you so much,' she said. 'The house has seemed so empty since I returned from Italy.'

She had grown. She was almost as tall as I was. No longer a child but a young woman.

'Mr Pawley made the statues, I see,' I said.

'Yes. My brother had them finished for me. They were

placed here last night.' I saw her swallow hard. 'That's how I got them to let me come out here alone for a while. I told them I wanted to see them in the morning light. Now that I will most likely never see them again.' Her chin lifted in that old defiant gesture that had once driven me to distraction, but which now seemed more than a little forlorn. 'William has already ridden into the village to supervise the preparations at the church. He is leaving nothing to chance. Not even for a manufacturer's son from Manchester, who only a few months ago he would not even have acknowledged to exist. These last days, I've allowed him to think I'm resigned to bringing a vast fortune within reach of the family.'

'And are you?'

'No,' she said, vehemently. 'I'd have done anything, if they'd let me. William stopped my allowance the moment I protested. He even took care to remove my jewels for "safekeeping". He knows I have nowhere to go. That there is nothing I can do. And besides…' She stopped.

'He can always remind you that there are places such as Ketterford. And worse.'

She nodded, silently. 'I would not have asked you to risk your own freedom by coming here. I'll do anything. Be anything. But I can't marry that man. And all William will say is that I am too young and foolish to know my own mind, and it's only natural to be nervous, and all will be well and I'll be grateful to him once I have an establishment of my own.' She looked back towards the house. 'They mustn't find you here. They'll be coming to take me back to the house soon.'

And, as if in answer to her fears, there came a crackling of sticks, and footsteps making their way towards us.

❦

🍀 'Vanished?' David was looked uneasily at the roses. Carys took a step away from them.

'Yes. Grandma said she went out in her wedding gown. Although sometimes it was just a cotton dress, but I expect that doesn't make such a good story. Anyhow, just a dress. And shoes, of course. Nothing else. No jewellery, apart from her engagement ring, and no purse. Not even a wrap. They drained the pond. After everywhere else had been searched, that is. But there was no sign of her. They kept on searching, but no one ever saw her again.'

'But I don't see …' began Carys. She came to a halt.

'Don't you?' said Karenza, eagerly. 'Don't you see? Can't you guess?'

'I'm not sure,' replied Carys. Her head was beginning to buzz.

'Of course!' exclaimed Mary. 'I should have realised, the moment you both arrived. I knew there was something.'

Carys stepped back, leaning instinctively on David's reassuring warmth. She felt his arms go around her. 'Well?' he prompted.

Karenza was reaching back into her envelope. 'It was obvious, the moment I found this,' she said. She brought out a second photograph, almost as faded as the first. 'I don't know how she did it. Or why. But she did. I know she did. Take a look.'

Carys hesitated. There were prickles travelling up and down her spine, despite the tightening of David's arms. 'What is it?' she demanded.

'It's the only known photograph of Judith Treverick as a young woman, taken just weeks before she disappeared.'

She knew what it was. Even as she reached out and took the photograph, Carys knew what she would find.

But she still gasped as she turned the sepia portrait towards her, and looked down into her own face.

Chapter Twenty-Three

Two people, a smartly dressed man, and a woman in an old-fashioned cloak, walked slowly through Treverick village towards the Hall that morning. A little later they walked back, arm-in-arm as before.

I watched Judith and Mr Meredith make their way towards the harbour through the crowds gathering for the spectacle of a Treverick wedding. I was certain they would pass unnoticed, just as he and I had passed unnoticed earlier that morning.

I took one last look at the place I had once called mine. I could still feel Judith's grief. For all her desire to escape, it was the only home she had ever known, and we both knew there would be no going back. And for me? I had no regrets at all. I had no wish to lay eyes on Treverick Hall, or its village, ever again.

In the distance, up towards the house, I could hear voices calling. Quickly I pulled the coat I had worn beneath the cloak I had given Judith close about me, and tied the strings of my hat tightly. Then, head down to hide my face, I made my way towards the village. Just another stranger among the wedding crowds. Or so I hoped.

They had both been uneasy at the plan, but I had insisted it was the best way. I was older. Careworn. My hair carefully arranged in the severest, most unflattering manner I knew how. I was the kind of woman who passes unnoticed. Unlike Judith, I was no longer a woman the people of Treverick would

341

immediately recognise. Besides, I knew the back roads and the alleyways so I could take a route that was not direct, so that no one would suspect in which direction I was going.

I paused a few minutes in the square, a little distance from the church. There were flowers everywhere. The heavy scent of roses filled the air. I had lingered too long. I ducked my head down quickly as I heard my husband's voice echoing in the stone porch of the church. I did not dare to take a single step until he had moved away, fussing about the seating arrangements for someone or other. Of the titled variety, naturally.

As William's voice faded into the echoes inside the church, I turned to go on my way. As I did so, my eye was caught by the display set out in front of the village shop, ready for this influx of visitors. It was not for myself, I could have cheerfully lived without any reminder that I had ever heard of a place called Treverick. But Judith, I sensed, would grieve a little for her childhood home all her life.

Hastily, I took the nearest postcard, placing a coin – far more than the thing was worth – on the wooden stand.

I should have known I would not escape unseen.

'Oi!' came the outraged tones of the shopkeeper. 'Oi! Miss!' I tried to gesture towards the coin, to show I was no thief, but it was too late. He had reached me before I could take another step. Heads were turning towards us in the entertainment of the moment. Already he had grasped my arm, preventing my escape.

ꞕ

'My grandmother's first name was Judith,' said Carys, returning her mobile to her pocket. 'Gwenan wasn't sure, but Mam remembered all right.'

'There, you see,' said Karenza, beaming. 'That means we're family.'

'I suppose it does,' said Carys, smiling at her. She looked around at the garden. 'This is such a weird feeling. I think I do remember her, you know. There's a photograph of her, you see, when she was very old, with me and my sisters. I thought it was that. But I *do* remember. There were yellow roses in the vase, and I remember she smelt of lily of the valley. It's still my favourite scent.' She gave a slight shiver. 'Now that is seriously weird.' She turned to David, who was still looking slightly bemused. 'We were supposed to be tracking down something to do with your family, and we found mine, instead.'

'Hey, do you think I mind?' he returned. 'I think it's great.' A slow grin overtook his face. 'I suppose, theoretically, you could have a claim on this place. That would make you a lot posher than us at poor old Eden.'

'Don't be daft,' she replied. 'As if I'd even want to try.' She smiled. 'And, anyhow, my real inheritance is there already. Dad always said that growing things was in the blood. On both sides, so it seems.'

There was a short silence. 'I'm afraid I'll have to get back soon,' said Mary, regretfully, glancing at her watch.

'And me, too,' said Karenza. 'I've a wedding appointment this afternoon. It's already been postponed once, so I can't miss them this time. But we'll keep in touch, Carys.'

'Definitely,' replied Carys. 'I want to find out as much as possible from Mam.'

'And I'll find out everything I can down here,' said Karenza.

'Brilliant,' said Carys. She glanced towards David. 'I think maybe we should come back with you into Treverick and have a look at the church. I'd like to see the plaque to Ann Treverick.

343

It would be like seeing the end of the story. And Mrs Boscawen was right: it did lead us to Judith, after all.'

ᕫᕬ

The church was small and dark, with the faint lingering smell of candle wax and incense in the air.

'It's over here,' said Mary, leading them to one side of the church. 'This wall is where the plaques to the Trevericks were placed. William is over there, nearest the altar. Next to him is Charles William Treverick, the little boy who was drowned in a boating accident. And this one is Ann.'

They paused in front of the figure carved in white marble. It was a plaque on a modestly grand scale in bas relief, with the central figure rising out of the polished stone behind her. A veil covered her features as she leant, head on hand in a gesture of grief. 'Fear no more the heat of the sun' was carved in intricate script beneath the usual inscription to beloved wife and mother.

'1902,' read Carys, bending to see the inscription closer.

'Poor woman,' sighed Karenza. 'I'd forgotten she was so young. She barely reached thirty. I don't suppose we'll ever know how she died.'

'I'd die if I was shut up for life in a place like Ketterford,' said Carys shivering.

David didn't answer. He was staring at the mausoleum, as if he hadn't heard a word.

'What is it?' asked Carys.

'Look,' he replied, slowly. 'Look Cari. Look. Look at her name.'

Ann Hermoine Treverick.

I was too proud to plead. As I met Mr Helyer's eyes, I gave him stare for stare, daring him to call out that the lunatic had escaped. And was on a mission to murder every Treverick in the place, and a few more, no doubt.

'Nonsense!' It was his wife, emerging from the shop door, too deep in gossip with her neighbour to take note of the commotion. 'She can't have gone far. She'll be in the gardens somewhere, mark my words. Where else has she to go, poor thing?'

I thought, for a moment, that she was referring to me. But then I saw across the square that several of the servants from the Hall had appeared. Mr Adamson, the butler, who preserved his dignity at all costs, was clearly out of breath and speaking urgently to his master.

Suddenly, I was afraid. I bit my lip. I could feel my eyes plead with my captor. My mind worked through a thousand plans. Most of which ended up with me throwing myself from the harbour wall to at least give them a chance to get free. Not, of course, that either would have left me. Which made me even more desperate.

'Helyer?' It was his wife, who had turned and seen our little tableau at last. She picked up the coin I had left, and held it in her hand. Out of the corner of my eye, I could see curiosity in every step as she made her way towards us.

Abruptly, his eyes lost their harshness. 'Your change, Miss,' he said, reaching into his pocket. He placed coins into my hand – a random selection including a button carved in bone, as I discovered later – and released his grip.

'Thank you,' I whispered. I felt the tears start to my eyes.

The commotion around us was growing louder by the minute, far more interesting than this disappointing end to our little drama.

'Good luck, Miss,' he said.

I smiled, and turned before Mrs Helyer – still curious – could reach us. Hastily, and most certainly unseen, I made my way through the back streets of Treverick: to where those I loved were waiting for me.

'Are you okay?' said Carys.

'This is what it's all about, isn't it,' said David, gazing around at the yellow roses of Treverick gardens. 'Inheritance.'

'I suppose,' said Carys slowly. She could feel his distress, uncertain of where it had come from.

'It can't be a coincidence,' he continued, as if speaking to himself. 'Hermione might have been a common name in Victorian times, but it's still too much of a coincidence that it was Ann Treverick's middle name. Nainie always said she was called after her mother. Hermione Ann. With all the talk about statues, and those drawings, it can't be a coincidence.'

Carys was still none the wiser. 'Do you think it might have been information about Nainie's mother your parents were trying to find the day they died?' she ventured.

He shoved his hands deep in his pockets. 'Dad would do anything to keep Plas Eden and the village safe. Bloody Edmund.'

'Edmund?' Carys stared at him blankly. 'Oh! You mean your dad's cousin? The one from Patagonia who kept on phoning? I thought you said he was delusional.'

'So I thought. I wish I'd listened more. Bloody Edmund.'

'But surely …' Carys hesitated. 'Surely he must be very old by now.'

'He's dead.'

'Well, then.'

'But his son isn't,' David added, grimly. 'Edmund Jnr is very much alive. He insisted on meeting up with me in London only recently. The day you came with your mam to Plas Eden, in fact.'

'Oh.'

'No wonder he looked so smug. He was quite obviously convinced he'd uncovered some dark secret that could make him a fortune. Someone was asking about Ann Treverick at Ketterford museum not long ago, remember.'

'It doesn't necessarily mean it was him.'

'Who else would it be? Don't you see?' David turned to her with pain in his eyes. 'That must be why Dad didn't want Nainie to know they were coming to Cornwall. Just in case. It's the first thing he would have thought of.'

'The first…' Carys came to a dead halt, light dawning.

'Exactly,' he said. 'Not good for business, I'd have thought, having your lunatics escaping. Maybe after a while, if there were no sign of her, Ketterford Asylum assumed Ann Treverick must be dead. Then the next time a woman without relatives died…'

Carys shuddered. 'Ugh, that's horrible.' They stood for a moment in silence. 'This is my fault,' she exclaimed. 'I wish we'd never come.'

'It wouldn't change anything, even if we hadn't,' he returned gently. 'Besides, I wouldn't have taken Edmund Jnr any more seriously than I took his father. At least this way we're forewarned.' David walked over to the fountain, taking one hand out of his pocket and resting it on the little figure of the winged fairy. 'Funny how something can seem so infinitely precious, when you realise it might not be yours, after all.'

'It was all a long time ago. No one has ever said that Ann Treverick and Hermione Meredith could be the same person,' said Carys, trying to sound cheerful.

347

'Not yet,' returned David gloomily. 'Greed is a pretty powerful thing. Cousin Edmund was always pissed as hell that Plas Eden didn't go down the male line in the first place. I'm sure that's what he's passed down to his son. Edmund Jnr is one sharp piece of work. I bet if he thought he'd get anything out of it, he wouldn't leave a stone unturned. And it looks to me as if he's got the money to do it. Who's to say what he's found out already? Legitimacy and the law. That's what inheritance is about, isn't it?'

'And you can't divorce a dead woman,' murmured Carys.

'Exactly. And if you can't divorce, you can't marry again. Not legally, anyhow. That would have made Nainie illegitimate. Or my great-grandfather knowingly made a bigamous marriage. That would make him a criminal.'

'You don't know that. Even if they didn't marry, you don't know that he didn't legally adopt Nainie.'

'But then why all the secrecy? Why would Dad be so determined Nainie wouldn't find out the reason he was coming down here? Cousin Edmund was always a pain. He never let up. He obviously told Dad he'd found out something. Something that got Dad worried enough to come to Treverick to try and sort it out.'

'But nothing's been said since.'

'Until now. From the way he used to rant on at me and Rhiannon, I'd say cousin Edmund lost it, big time, after Dad died. I can't see Edmund Jnr about to lose anything. It was obvious when I met him that he's convinced he's got one over on us.'

'But it doesn't mean it's true!'

David turned away from her, his face hidden. 'He was so sure of himself. I thought he was just planning a bit of blackmail. It never crossed my mind he believed he can prove that Nainie – and therefore Dad and me and Huw – might have no real right to Plas Eden at all.'

348

Part Four

Chapter Twenty-Four

David and Carys sat at an outside table of the Boadicea café, watching the *Ar Werth, For Sale* sign from Phillips, Edwards and Jones nailed above the village butcher's. Yet another shop had given up the good fight against the odds and was closing. Autumn seemed to have crept into Pont-ar-Eden high street during their short time in Cornwall, bringing with it the edge of a cold wind and the hint of winter around the corner.

'I'm sure everything will be fine,' said Carys, stirring her untouched coffee slowly.

'Mm,' grunted David, without conviction. His coffee stood cooling, equally untouched, on the table in front of him.

'At least Edmund Junior has agreed to meet you. That's a positive sign, isn't it?'

'He thinks I'm about to pay him off, whatever it takes,' said David bitterly. 'You could practically hear the cash tills ringing when he answered the phone.'

'Maybe your solicitor will find something.'

David shook his head. 'There's nothing in the Plas Eden papers. Like he said, there's nothing we can do until we know exactly what Edmund Jnr wants. I wish Dad's old solicitor was still alive. Dad might have spoken to him before they set off for Treverick. But there's nothing we can do about that. No: all I can do is go and listen to Edmund and do my best not to

351

hit him, whatever dirt he thinks he's got on the Merediths.' He sighed. 'Huw's still furious. He's quite convinced we've lost our chance and Beddows won't touch Plas Eden with a barge pole if they get wind of something dodgy hanging over it.'

'I'm sorry,' said Carys. She'd never seen him look so despondent. 'If only I'd never started this.'

'Nonsense.' He took her hand and squeezed it gently. 'You mustn't blame yourself, Cari, you weren't to know.' He smiled. 'We were detectives together in this, remember? Edmund Jnr was always going to come out of the woodwork, sooner or later, whether we had gone to Cornwall or not.'

'I suppose.' Her hand was still being held. Out of nowhere, her heart was beating loud in her ears and she could hardly breathe.

David leaned forward. 'Cari,' he said, his voice low and urgent.

'Morning!' came the cheerful voice of Gwynfor Humphries, hurrying his way towards the Boadicea, Nesta and Haf – eagle-eyed as ever – in tow.

Carys found her hand released instantly.

'Good morning.' David turned his attention to his coffee cup as if there was nothing so important in the world.

'Good morning,' said Nesta, eying the two of them with a distinctly knowing smile.

'Lovely day,' added Haf, beaming at them, misty-eyed, as she passed.

'I'd better get going,' muttered David, as more members of the history group began to appear, watched sourly by Evan Prydderch, who had emerged from the newsagents at the sound of their voices, blinking like a crab lured out of its shell. His eyes sought hers. 'We'll talk more when I get back.'

'Yes of course,' replied Carys, giving the warmest smile she dared while under the scrutiny of Pont-ar-Eden's prime gossips.

He hesitated, as if hoping for the smallest gap in the crowds, but a steady stream was now making its way past them into the café.

'You'll miss your train,' Carys reminded him gently. 'You don't want Edmund to think you're not coming.'

'Hmm,' came the gruff reply. With one last look at the increasing swell of villagers, he swung his laptop bag over one shoulder. 'See you,' he said, sticking his hands in his pockets and making his way to his car for the short drive to Talarn station.

'He'll be back, *cariad*.' Carys found her arm being patted, and looked up to find Sara Jones standing next to her, an understanding smile on her face.

'I wish there was something I could do.' Carys watched the retreating figure. He'd clearly being overdoing things since their return and his limp was as bad as ever. She felt her heart clench. 'I've never heard him sound so low. It's almost as if he's finally given up.'

'David will never give up Plas Eden,' replied Sara, who couldn't know exactly what Carys was referring to, but was watching her with concern. She patted Carys' arm once more as she made her way inside the café. 'Don't you fret, Carys, dear. David hasn't dedicated his life to Plas Eden for nothing. He won't go running out on it now.'

For every second of her life up to that point, Carys would have agreed. But now she was no longer sure. David had been so quiet on the way back from Cornwall, scarcely relinquishing the wheel and apparently lost in thought. It was almost, she felt, as if his whole view of himself, and his life up to then, had been thrown into question.

It wasn't as if he would mind whether Nainie's parents were married or not. Those things didn't matter nowadays, unless you were royalty or serious aristocracy. Carys couldn't remember Nainie talking much about her parents, but everything she had ever said had described how utterly devoted to each other they were, and that Nainie herself had been a much-loved and much-wanted baby. 'They used to call me their miracle baby,' she had said once.

But Carys could see his point. Even she could feel there was suddenly a taint to Eden. A grubbiness that hadn't been there before. Born not of any argument about who should own it and why, but the thought of a stranger viewing it with an eye for the main chance. Someone who didn't care about decades of love for the house and the gardens, keeping the place together against the odds. Someone who didn't give a damn about Plas Eden's long history, or its intertwined relationship with the village on its borders. Someone who could just see themselves walking in to play lord of the manor on the cheap. Or whose only view of the estate was a pot of gold all ready to fund a lifetime of fast yachts, oversized watches and hanging around the tail-ends of C-list celebrities, hoping to make it to page five of the gossip magazines. Not that she knew Edmund Jnr was like this, she reminded herself, but she feared the worst.

Carys watched David's car make its way along the high street and out of Pont-ar-Eden. Maybe, she couldn't help thinking, once out of here he would just want to wash his hands of the place. Lick his wounds and grieve quietly, maybe as much for all those years of wasted effort as for Eden itself.

Sometimes, with something you love so much you cannot bear to lose it, it's easier to stay away, rather than torment yourself with its soon-to-be-lost presence.

In which case, she considered, there would be no more

miracles for Plas Eden. And no reason for the two of them to even see each other again. Even more so if she were associated in David's mind with memories of Eden.

She'd hoped after their time in Cornwall that they might one day put the past behind them and move on. Together. She'd begun to hope David felt the same way. The old ease in each other's company, beneath the initial awkwardness, was still there, and that had to mean they still had a chance.

But it was no good: she had to face it. Without Plas Eden, David's life could be wherever he might choose. This might be the push he needed to let go of responsibility and get on with his life. Perhaps, in the end, he might find himself relieved to leave her behind as well.

Already her heart ached with missing him.

❧

Standing amongst the battered polytunnels of Eden Farm later that day, Carys felt no better. So much for throwing herself into a new venture to keep any negative thoughts at bay.

Everything around her seemed larger and more neglected than on her previous visit. The tangles of autumn weeds and sprays of blackberries across the remains of vegetable beds defied any idea of where to start. At least one polytunnel needed its plastic covering replacing, and in the walled garden the greenhouses were a shambles. As for rest of the kitchen garden – well, she daren't even consider the amount of work that it would take to begin growing. And now, she found, she hadn't the heart to begin.

'I see some of them have made a start,' remarked Rhiannon, emerging from the little sunroom in the cottage and making her way down the path towards her.

'Yes.' Cary turned back to the strips of bare earth, which had begun to appear out of the undergrowth. 'The bit Sara Jones' nephew has taken over is nearly finished. Apparently he's been here after work, as well as weekends.'

'Good for him. I have to confess, I wasn't sure you'd get anyone from Pont-ar-Eden interested in making allotments and growing their own. But Merlin tells me half the spaces have been taken already, and enquiries are flooding in for the rest, and quite a few of those are from young people with families.'

'Yes.' Carys bit her lip. 'It seems such a pity…'

'They all know everything is up in the air with a possible sale in any case, and it might only be for a year,' said Rhiannon gently. 'And at the very least, it's starting something. You never know, this might get some of them to make sure the council creates allotments locally, even if the ones here can't continue. Or Merlin might take them over permanently, depending on what happens with Eden.'

'I suppose so.' Carys pulled herself together. 'So? What do you think?'

Rhiannon smiled. 'The paintings are beautiful. Fancy being there all the time under that whitewash. Someone took real love and care over those.'

'I wonder if they really were done by Nainie's mother.'

'I feel sure they were,' said Rhiannon. 'I know they are very different from those portraits you showed me, but they've got that same sense of life. I suspect they must have been made for your grandmother when she married your grandfather and came to live in the cottage.'

'I like that idea.' Carys could almost see the sprightly figure of Grandmother Judith moving between pots and cuttings in the little sunroom, sheets upon sheets of sketched designs for the garden piled high on a table in a corner. Around it all the curling designs of the leaves and flowers, robins and blue tits hidden in the greenery, along with yellow dots of bees and the smoky wings of cabbage white butterflies, eclipsed entirely by the green iridescent wings of dragonflies. 'I wonder if it could ever be restored.'

'I don't see why not. The paint seems to come off without destroying too much of the pattern, and I'm sure we could work out the rest from the wildlife carved into the statues. There's at least one dragonfly on the statue of Blodeuwedd, and, in any case, I don't think Nainie's mother would mind a little artistic licence to bring it back to life.'

'I suppose it depends on who eventually takes over the cottage.'

'Well, I think it's worth having a go,' replied Rhiannon. 'At least we'll have a record so we could reproduce something like it elsewhere, and it seems to me it's less likely to be painted over if it's fully restored. It will be a nice project. While I have the time, that is.'

'Oh,' said Carys. Absorbed in her own thoughts, she had entirely forgotten. 'You must be so excited.'

'The artist-in-residence, you mean?'

'Of course. And against all that competition, too. It's wonderful.'

The older woman's gaze drifted over to the shadow of Plas Eden on the far side of the lake. 'Yes, it is exciting. And a real confidence boost.'

Carys frowned at her tone. 'You are going to take it? You've got to take it, Rhiannon. After all your hard work, and beating so much competition like that. It's the beginning of a new life.'

'Yes, maybe.' Rhiannon was watching Hodge, who was engaged in snuffling about on the shoreline, following a scent this way and then that, as if in pursuit of the richest of truffles. 'Old habits die hard, I suppose.' She gazed back towards Plas Eden, reflected in the still water. 'I just wish things could be more settled, that's all.'

'You don't have to leave straight away, do you?'

'Oh no. I've got a few months. I'd need to go over to Vermont sometime after Christmas. The end of January, most probably. If I accept, that is.' Carys heard her sigh. 'I can't leave Eden with something like this hanging over it. The things Edmund used to say. Vicious, horrible things.' Rhiannon shuddered. 'Things he was always threatening to take to the newspapers if David didn't "give him his due", as he liked to put it.'

'Maybe David will find his son a bit more reasonable.'

'I hope so: but from the sound of him, I somehow doubt it.'

'Me too,' Carys admitted.

Rhiannon sighed again. 'I would love to walk away from this and concentrate on my career and the residency in America. The trouble is I wouldn't be able to live with myself if I did. Whatever Edmund Meredith is up to, it would feel like betraying Marianne and everything she loved if I were to leave her sons to deal with it alone.'

❧

A delicious smell of cooking filled the air as Carys let herself into Willow Cottage that evening.

'Nice day, dear?' asked Mam brightly, emerging from the kitchen wiping her hands on her apron.

'Lovely,' replied Carys, with the best attempt at cheerfulness she could muster. 'It really is beautiful over there.'

'The best little spot on earth your grandmother Judith used to call it,' replied Mam. Her eyes fell on the laden bags Carys was holding in each hand. 'Oh. Darling, didn't I tell you? I did that "online" thing you showed me with the supermarket. They delivered this morning. There was everything I ordered, and the young man was so helpful. Brought it right in here for me and put the boxes on the worktop. I didn't have to lift a thing.'

'Oh,' said Carys.

'Never mind, *cariad*. The freezer could do with some stocking up, and it's always good to have extra in the cupboard, just in case.' Mam was beaming. 'I thought you might be hungry after all that gardening and then walking back from Eden Farm. There's a shepherd's pie in the oven and the veg is all ready to go on. I thought we'd have blackberry and apple crumble for afterwards, with those blackberries you gathered yesterday.' She clucked impatiently. 'I never thought to order any cream. But it's better with custard anyhow.'

'Much better,' smiled Carys. 'I'll just put these things away.'

Mam shook her head vigorously. 'Now don't you worry about that, Carys, *bach*. You go and sit down, and I'll make us a cup of tea. I'm sure you could do with one.'

'Thank you,' murmured Carys, meekly. 'That sounds lovely.' Protest, she knew well, was useless. And, besides, how could she spoil Mam's obvious delight in her newly returned control of her household?

Of course she was pleased. Wasn't this what she had been waiting for all these months? Shouldn't she be celebrating this sign of being able to return to her own former freedom?

The trouble was, Carys discovered, as she sat down in the little living room, her whole life had been taken over by Mam's needs and Mam's routine and she didn't know what to do with herself without that familiar pattern. Without her old life in Chester with Joe to return to, she didn't even know where to begin.

This must be the feeling you have when you watch your toddler going off to the first day in nursery, she thought. The glee at having time to yourself at last abruptly swept away, as you watch the centre of your existence for the past few years move away into a life beyond you.

For everyone else, life had moved on. Joe was following his ambitions, David was going who-knows-where. Even Rhiannon – whether she took the residency in America or not – was moving into a new career and a new phase in her life. Carys suddenly felt left behind. No one needed her here, while her old life in Chester felt an entire lifetime away. Close as they were, even Poppy was absorbed in babies and keeping a life and business together.

Carys switched on her laptop, fighting down a rising sense of panic. She had the freedom to start something new, and do whatever she wanted with her life. But that freedom seemed more like one scarily large and empty space, with no idea of where to begin.

As she started to look at the accounts she was supposed to be doing, to the sound of Mam humming to herself in the kitchen while the kettle boiled, it felt to Carys that this was the loneliest place she had been in her life.

Chapter Twenty-Five

The following day crawled by. However much she tried to throw herself into her work, Carys couldn't concentrate on anything.

As the afternoon wore on, she finally gave up any attempt on the accounts she was finishing and went through her emails instead. A rapid glance told her that the majority were work-related, plus one from Gwenan with the ominous subject line: 'This year's arrangements for Christmas.' Cary groaned and marked that one to be read later. Possibly with a large glass of wine to hand.

There was nothing from David. There had been no text either, even though he had been due to meet Edmund Jnr in Heathrow this morning at 10 a.m. sharp. Edmund's plane had probably been delayed. They might even have put off their meeting until tomorrow. David could at this very minute be in the process of finding a hotel for the night.

Carys made herself a fresh cup of coffee to sounds of Mam in full spring-cleaning mode, preparing for her bedroom upstairs to receive her bed once more. Forget the family Christmas; Gwenan was going to have enough to say about Mam having press-ganged several of the more spritely members of the Boadicea's history group into hoisting the bed up the stairs after the next meeting. A *bara brith* was already cooling on the kitchen work surface, while a rich smell of chocolate cake oozed in mouth-watering fashion from the oven. Mam had not lost her touch when it came to bribery, Carys noted to herself with a grin, settling down at the keyboard once more.

She'd missed the message from Joe halfway down. Most probably because she hadn't been looking for it. With a sinking feeling she clicked the email open. The message was short and stilted. An offer had at last been made on the flat. Young couple, recently married and moving into the area. No chain. Very keen to move in asap.

'I thought you'd like to know.

Joe'

Carys sat back and sipped her coffee, feeling her heartbeat return to normal and the hurt feelings at the cool sign off subside.

She hadn't been forgiven, then. So much for her idea of returning to some kind of friendship. Even now, he hadn't quite been able to resist including the letters after his name and the impressive signature of his new firm, complete with lengthy confidentiality information and instructions to think of the environment and only print if necessary.

'Arse,' muttered Carys, composing a brief and courteous reply, before consigning his email to the 'deleted items' folder.

About this, at least, she had no regrets. Joe was no longer a part of her life. The breaking of this final connection was a relief. It wouldn't exactly be a fortune to split between them once the mortgage had been paid off, but it was better than nothing. Enough, with the freelance work she was still getting from Tylers, to take the pressure off and give her time to look around.

With nothing to keep her in Pont-ar-Eden, she might have another look south. She and David hadn't had time to see

North Devon, where she'd heard there was still land that might just be affordable. Now was the time to start looking. Carys clicked onto Google Maps. Ilfracombe looked pretty. Right on the North Devon coast, on the edge of Exmoor National Park and not too far from Bristol. She could base herself there for a couple of days and have a good mosey around.

She had just typed 'B&Bs near Ilfracombe, Devon' into Google when her email pinged. It might be David. Or Joe to say the sale was definitely going through.

'Hi Carys! How's the search for the smallholding going? Have you found anywhere suitable yet?' Carys blinked. In her haste, she'd clicked on the email without looking at the sender. This wasn't David, and it definitely wasn't Joe.

Karenza. She'd had a couple of emails from Karenza since they'd got back, but nothing in the last couple of days, and nothing as long as this.

With a sense of a new world opening up in front of her, Carys began to read.

જી

'Sorry I'm late!' Carys hurtled down the last steps into the glade to find David already there. 'I was concentrating on something and totally missed your text.'

'That's okay.' He smiled at her. 'I should have contacted you earlier. I've only just got here myself.'

A breeze stirred the yellowing leaves, sending shadows racing and the branches swaying into life with a soft, dry rattle. Autumn scents filled the air in the slant of bright, delicate sunlight: fungus mixed with the ripeness of fruit.

'Well?' His face was strained and grey. Carys' stomach clenched into one tight, hard knot. 'That bad, eh?'

'Worse. He never turned up.'

'What? You mean he was delayed?'

'No. He just never turned up. No message. Nothing.'

'Maybe his flight was diverted.'

'I checked. He wasn't even booked on the flight. I called and emailed him for several hours. Nothing. There were no diversions and no,' he added at the look on her face, 'no crashes, either. If he'd any intention of trying to contact me, he'd have done it by now. He's a businessman, so he can't possibly be completely isolated from the world for this long.'

'But that could be good, couldn't it? Maybe he's decided to give up.'

'I wouldn't bet on it,' David muttered. 'I've a nasty feeling the next time he gets in touch it will be through a solicitor. He must be very sure of his ground.'

'I'm sorry.'

'Well, it's no more than we expected. There's nothing I can do until he gets back in contact again, so we might as well try and forget it.' He changed the subject. 'How's your mam doing?'

'Oh, fine,' said Carys. 'She's certainly been enjoying finding out about Grandmother Judith's life in Pont-ar-Eden while we were away. It's given her a new lease of life. She's been tracking down clues like nobody's business. I can see she'll be the leading light of the Boadicea's history group in no time. It's built up her confidence, too. She's so much more independent than before we went to Cornwall.'

'That must be a relief for you.'

'Definitely. It means I can finally start moving on with my own life. One thing she found explains why my grandmother wasn't in the line-up of the servants in the photograph we found.'

'Oh?'

Carys nodded. 'My grandmother arrived at Plas Eden as Hermione Meredith's personal maid, but she didn't stay that for long. Mam found the record of her taking over the running of a shop in the village. A little hardware store, in fact. It seems my grandmother Judith was definitely not a conventional woman of her time. From the address, Mam's sure it was on the high street, and probably part of where the 'Boadicea' is now.' She smiled. 'I suppose that's how she got to know my grandfather, if he was popping in for tools and bits and pieces. Although I suppose she probably met him while she was living in Plas Eden. No prizes for guessing it was the love of gardens that drew them together.'

'I'm sure of it, too.'

'Did you know the gardens were completely redesigned just before the First World War? Mam's convinced Grandmother Judith must have had a hand in it somewhere, even if it was behind the scenes. And I suppose she's right: there are so many echoes of the photographs we took of the gardens at Treverick.'

'But much more beautiful.'

'Oh, no comparison,' she agreed wholeheartedly. 'One of my teachers at college always used to say that no one can reach their real creative potential unless they are truly loved, and at the same time feel free. That's how my grandmother could help make such a beautiful garden, and your great-grandmother could create such amazing statues.' She met his gaze. 'And, whatever way you look at it, it was your family, the Merediths, who gave them that love and that freedom. Whatever happens to Plas Eden now, that's something to make us proud.'

'Yes.' He appeared lost in thought. 'Yes it is.' She heard him clear his throat. 'Cari …'

'And Karenza has been in touch,' she rushed on, before he could continue.

'Oh?'

'She says that she's been planning for a while to diversify the cut-flower business into market gardening. She's got the land and local outlets have expressed plenty of interest. She just doesn't have the time or the knowhow. So she's asked if I'd like to go into partnership with her.'

'To grow fruit and veg in Cornwall, you mean?'

'Yes. I know it wouldn't be my own smallholding, but as Karenza says, it doesn't have to be forever. The main thing is to set it up for her, then she can always employ people to keep it going once it's established. That means I'd be free to move on and start up on my own. People are crying out for locally grown food. I could diversify into jams and chutneys. Fruit wines, even. It would be a really good way of making the move to Cornwall and building a reputation down there before I took the plunge. It's strange to think I do have connections down there, after all. I wouldn't be an incomer, but a family member coming home.'

'I see.' His face was unreadable.

'I've said I'll give her an answer by the end of the week. That's only fair. But I'm still not certain.'

David had turned away from her. 'I think you should go for it.'

Carys blinked. Was that it? No regret, not the smallest indication that he might wish her to stay – or stay in touch, even. She'd wanted to be honest. She'd wanted to give him the option of letting her walk away. But that didn't mean she'd wanted him to take it. At least not without the slightest attempt at dissuasion. Hurt flared through her.

'I still need to think about it,' she mumbled. 'It's a big decision.'

'But it's what you want to do. What you've always wanted to do. It would be a fresh start. A completely fresh start.' He gave a little half-smile. 'And you are partly a Treverick.'

'I'll think about it,' said Carys. She needed to get away from there. Now, this minute. Before the disgrace of tears betrayed her.

David cleared his throat again, louder this time. 'I could always come with you.'

'What?' Carys stared at him, not quite able to take the words in.

'If you wanted me too, that is,' he added hastily.

'Come with me? To Cornwall?'

'Yes.'

'But what about Eden?'

'It'll survive. In one form or other, it'll survive. When it comes down to it, what is the Eden estate but bricks and mortar, surrounded by earth? If I phone Huw now, we could get the sale with Beddows moving straight away. We might even get it through before Edmund gets back to us with whatever he's planning next. I'll be able to pay him off if necessary. Huw will be happy and Rhiannon won't feel so guilty about taking up the residency in America.' He grasped her hands, his voice deepening. 'It can be you and me, Cari. Just as it should always have been. Just you and me.'

It was her happy ending staring her in the face. The happy ending she'd always wanted. Always dreamed of, if she was being totally honest.

Damn.

But she was Carys Evans. Straight-talking, loud-mouthed Carys Evans who couldn't love someone as much as she loved David and let them make the biggest mistake of their lives.

She stepped back, pulling her hands free. 'What would you do?' she demanded.

'Do?' He sounded bewildered.

'In Cornwall. What would you do?'

'Oh, that.' He smiled at her. 'Help you. Start a business. Build a home for us.' He frowned, doubts appearing. 'Don't you want me to come with you?'

'Eden is your life, David. It's where you belong. Ever since I've known you, you've been planning and working and dreaming about Plas Eden. It's who you are. It's part of everything you do.' She bit her lip. But it had to be said. If they ever were to have any chance of a future of any kind, it had to be said. 'If I was the cause of you giving all that up, you might end up resenting me. However much you might believe that impossible now.'

He was silent for a few minutes. She saw a struggle pass over his face. He couldn't deny that she was right, however hard she could see him try.

'You seemed happy enough to stay here when you thought Eden was being sold,' he said at last.

'I'd got Mam to consider. And it wasn't intended to be forever.'

'Unless Merlin asked, you mean,' he retorted.

'*What?*' Carys stared at him in disbelief. 'You're not still on about that, are you?'

'That's why he wants to buy the land at Eden Farm, isn't it?'

'Oh, for heaven's sake.' She wasn't quite sure whether she was about to laugh or cry. 'Do you honestly think that I'd have gone to Merlin with a business proposal if I'd thought he had any romantic interest in me? Or if he still wanted to add me to his knicker collection, come to that. At least credit me with enough sense, in that case, not to give him quite such power over me.'

David scowled. 'He doesn't strike me as the kind of guy to benefit all of Pont-ar-Eden for the good of his soul.'

'Of course not. Are you really that blind? Can't you see it's not me Merlin's doing this for. It's not for me that he wants the village to thrive. And if you ever think anything different, I'll never speak to you again.'

'Oh,' said David. He discovered hope had returned and was banging loudly in his chest. Carys sounded very certain on this. Furthermore, she didn't seem in the least upset about it. 'So you still haven't made up your mind about Cornwall?'

'No.' She hesitated. 'Maybe if I hadn't seen the old kitchen garden here…'

He looked at her in despair. 'I hate all this uncertainty hanging over Plas Eden. I hate what it's doing to us all. Huw thinks his chance of a fortune is slipping away. Rhiannon looks unhappy every time I try to talk to her about America. And I can't plan for any kind of future at all. Not until I know. At least if we knew for certain about Nainie's parents, that might be a start. But we've looked everywhere. There's just no trace of Nainie's parents even being married. That's before you start on the whole bigamy thing.'

Carys was gazing at the statues, her eyes travelling from one to the other, as if there might be some answer hidden in their stone eyes. 'There has to be something somewhere. Somewhere we haven't considered yet. Somewhere so obvious no one has thought to look.'

David sighed. 'Trouble is, I can't see Professor Humphries and the history group leaving any stone unturned …' He came to a halt.

'What?'

'Edna.'

'Edna?'

'Yes. What did you tell me Edna said about Hermione Meredith?'

'That she wasn't the lady she made herself out to be.' Carys frowned. 'Which she was, of course.'

'No, not that bit. The other. Didn't Edna say something about Hermione telling everyone that she came from London?'

'Well, yes.'

'That's where they must have met. In London. Which would mean in the Meredith Charity Hospital. Those newspaper articles we found in Cornwall said your grandmother worked with charities while she was living at Treverick Hall, didn't she?'

'Well, yes.'

'So that could be the connection. Judith could have worked with the Merediths, or at least known about them and their charity in London. If you think about it, London would be the best place to vanish amongst so many people. That's where she might have sent my great-grandmother, if she'd helped her to escape Ketterford.'

'It's possible, I suppose.' Carys sounded dubious.

David retrieved his iPhone from his back pocket. 'I know the hospital won't be there any longer, but the building might have survived.' He clicked onto Google, trying first one search, than another. 'Aha!' he exclaimed triumphantly at the third attempt. 'There it is. Meredith House, Lambeth. That's got to be the one. It seems to be the head offices of several charities. Why didn't I think of that before? If there is an answer, I bet that's the one place it can be found.' He met her eyes. 'Well? Are you up for it?'

'Up for what?'

'Going back on the detective trail. Only in London this time.'

Carys nodded. 'Okay, count me in.'

'Great. We'll sort this out between us. I know we will. We make a good team, eh?'

'Mmm,' replied Carys absently. She appeared to have forgotten him already. Her eyes, he found, were searching the stone faces once more.

He took her hand. 'And Cari, whatever you decide, whatever we find in London, whatever happens with Eden…' But Carys, he saw, wasn't listening. She was lost in a world of her own.

'The statues,' she breathed, in a voice that came from a long way away.

'Cari?'

She turned back to him at last. 'The statues, David. The statues: I know who they are. I know who they all are.'

Chapter Twenty-Six

& Meredith House, it turned out, was a tall, unpromising red-brick building, darkened by the fumes of city streets. David and Carys made their way through the imposing gateway into a small paved area used as a car park, following the signs to reception.

The young woman seated behind the clean lines of the reception desk was sleek and efficient, but with a relaxed and friendly air about her.

'Ah, Mr Jackson,' she said, nodding as David explained their appointment with the archivist. 'He's left a message for you. His meeting has overrun, so he'll be another ten minutes, I'm afraid. He suggested you might like to wait in the garden.' She indicated a corridor with a revolving glass door at one end. 'There's a café in there, so perhaps you would like a coffee while you wait. Their cakes are pretty awesome,' she added confidentially, and with some regret.

They made their way along the whitewashed corridor, past a wooden banistered staircase, and out through the revolving doors.

'It's so pretty!' exclaimed Carys in surprise, as she and David emerged into a little courtyard, where the leaves were turning to a soft yellow around them.

'It must be a real oasis in the summer,' he agreed. 'It feels weird that this must have hardly changed since the Meredith Hospital was here.'

It had turned into a blazing autumn in London. Heat still hung between the high walls of offices grouped around the courtyard. It was lunchtime, and on the benches placed between beds of lavender and the last bloom of roses, office workers chatted quietly as they ate their salads, accompanied with the skinny-lattes-to-go from the café.

The café itself took up one corner of the space, its outside tables filled with men and women in dark suits, deep in discussion over their paninis or lasagne, and accompanied by a dance of hopeful sparrows around their feet. Pigeons burbled contentedly in the eaves, landing every now and again in the hope of crusts or abandoned remains of carrot cake. A burst of laughter echoed around the walls, interspersed with the buzzing of text messages, backed by the faint hum of traffic and the howl of sirens.

In the unseasonal heat, a few people were even perched on the rim of the central fountain, bottled water and an apple in hand, faces turned into its cooling spray.

'Look, the hospital hasn't been completely forgotten,' said Carys, motioning towards the statue of a nurse holding a small child in her arms at the centre of the fountain. The statue looked as if it had been made in the 1920s or 30s. The nurse gazed out heroically, in suitably monumental manner, while a group of particularly wretched-looking women and children crouched at her feet.

'In Memory of the Staff and Volunteers of the Meredith Charity Hospital' declared a weatherbeaten legend around the fountain's base.

They looked up as a small, rather bent figure made his way through the revolving door. He stood for a moment, halfway between the offices of 'The Honeybee Trust' and 'Safe Birth for

373

Mothers and Babies in Africa', to peer around, until, spotting the two of them, he began to walk briskly across the courtyard.

David took a deep breath. 'Okay. Here we go.'

Carys felt his hand creep into hers. She gave it a reassuring squeeze. 'You're right,' she said. 'Merediths don't just sweep things under the carpet. Not when it's this important. When it means the future of Plas Eden. Come on. Just you see: the answer will be here.'

ભ

I stood in the little courtyard garden of the Meredith Charity Hospital that day and watched the leaves fall gold and crimson from the trees.

'Mrs Meredith?' I turned as the Matron emerged from the door next to the little office, and approached me hesitantly. She had changed over the long years between, as had I, but she was still the same.

'It's good to see you again, Lily,' I said.

For a moment she continued to scrutinise me, then I saw the smile light up her face. 'It is you,' she said, as she rushed over and embraced me. 'Of course it is. We knew it had to be, when we heard Mr Meredith had married.'

'Was I that transparent?'

She laughed. 'Seeing the two of you together, it was impossible not to know.'

'Oh,' I said, blushing despite myself. I held her hands tight. 'I was so sorry to hear about your Tom.'

Sadness came over her face. 'Thank you. I miss him still. But we had so many happy years together. And two sons. Who are good boys and look after me.' I saw a deeper shadow cross her features. 'Although they say there is a war coming.'

Even in far-flung Pont-ar-Eden, we had heard the rumours that had begun to shadow all our horizons. I could not tell her how much I felt for her. I could not tell her that, but for the storm in Treverick Bay that night, I, too, would now have a son not much older than her boys. One who, with the encouragement of his father and in the impetuosity of youth, might have seen a war as his duty and a schoolboy adventure.

'Well?' she said, pushing her gloom away. 'Mr Meredith said that you had a favour to ask.'

Until that moment, I had not been certain. The Lily I remembered had a good heart and a fair dose of common sense. But this Lily was a woman who had seen grief and loss and returned as a widow to work her way up on merit to be Matron of the hospital. This was a woman I could trust with my life.

'I have.'

She smiled. 'Very well, then. I'll fetch my hat.'

'Don't you wish to know what I am about to ask?'

'No,' she replied. Her smile was suddenly young and mischievous. 'Maybe I can guess?' I looked at her, and she laughed. I could see her old love of romance gleaming in her eyes. 'There had to be good reason why "Mrs Smith" arrived such a lost soul, and left quite so discreetly. Besides, there was a man who came asking questions, not so long ago. He said he came from Cornwall. A private detective, he said he was.'

'A detective?' I exclaimed, unable to hide my alarm.

'Don't worry: he got nothing out of us, for all his questioning. Those of us left who could remember Mrs Hermione Smith loved you too well to say a word that might cause you harm.'

'Thank you,' I murmured, from my heart.

She left, returning in a few minutes in her hat and coat. In her hand, she held a posy of red and white roses. 'I always take flowers to my Tom in the churchyard, of a Friday,' she said, by way of explanation. 'But I feel sure, just this once, he will understand.'

෮෩

David and Carys followed Mr Jackson down to a little room in the basement of the building.

'So you are a Meredith,' the old man remarked, as they made their way between rows of shelves stretching from floor to ceiling, each surface piled high with boxes and files.

'Yes,' replied David. 'I decided it was time to find out more about my ancestors' connection to this place.'

The old man nodded. 'And a good time, too. There has been talk, you know, of setting up a little permanent exhibition in one of the ground floor storerooms. Like the museum to Florence Nightingale in the grounds of St Thomas's Hospital. The British Museum has been making noises about making a temporary exhibition as well, with all this current popularity for the social history of ordinary people. After all, the Merediths, among others, made a significant contribution to the idea of the National Health Service by setting up of a hospital free for all who need it. The mark of any civilisation worth the name,' he added, severely.

'Yes indeed,' murmured David.

'The staff records were what you wanted, yes?'

David exchanged glances with Carys. 'Yes, please.'

'Right at the end here.'

'As we're compiling a social history,' put in Carys, casually, as they followed their guide along the nearest row, 'we thought we'd also like to find the names of the churches the staff and

376

patients would have attended? And maybe see if any are still standing. I know church-going would have been an important part of their lives, and it would add a little local colour.'

'Oh, I can tell you that straight off,' replied Mr Jackson. 'St Catherine's. It's only a few minutes' walk from here. I can show you on the A to Z.' David handed over his copy, and Mr Jackson flicked through without hesitation. 'This is the page. If you walk back from here towards Waterloo Bridge, you'll more-or-less pass it. There it is. It's a bit of a maze, but once you get to Lambeth Palace Gardens you'll soon see the sign.'

'Thank you.' David folded down the page of the guide and placed it back inside his jacket pocket.

'And if it's social history you're interested in…' Mr Jackson paused in his tracks and dodged down a side route through a break in the shelves. He stopped at an old-fashioned iron safe built into the wall. Squatting down in front of the safe, he began to turn the dial rapidly, this way, then that, with an expert flick of the wrist. 'There's a copy in the British Library, of course, but we still have the original.' The last number clicked into place and the door swung open with an impressive creak. Reaching in, their guide lifted out a large box file, placing it almost reverentially on a table to one side. 'This is what we should be displaying. There's been talk of it ever since I started working here, and that's – oh, thirty or so years ago.'

'Oh?' murmured David.

'Indeed. It was quite famous in its day. Quite influential, in fact. It was undertaken in the last years of the nineteenth century by the last Meredith to take charge of the hospital in a personal capacity.' He peered at the top sheet of paper. 'Ah, that's it: David Paul Meredith.'

'My great-grandfather,' said David, exchanging glances with Carys once more. 'I was named after him.'

377

'Were you indeed?' Mr Jackson eyed David with a definite new respect. He opened up the box, laying out a series of smaller files on the table with reverential care. 'It is a detailed study of the living conditions in Lambeth in the last years of Victoria's reign. There were others, of course. But this was one that really seems to have caught the imagination. Your great-grandfather was a shrewd man. He employed an excellent photographer. Some of those images are shocking, even today.'

Carys looked down at the photographs set at regular intervals between close lines of text, punctuated with graphs and lists of statistics. Mr Jackson was right: the gaunt faces of children gazing out from broken-down streets and crowded rooms with plaster peeling from the walls reached out with a desperate pleading across the years.

'And then, of course,' said Mr Jackson, opening the next file with an even deeper reverence, if possible, 'there are these. They're the originals,' he added, as David and Carys bent over the sheaves of drawings, some in pencil, others with a wash of watercolour. 'The faces are quite remarkable.'

'Does anyone know who did them?' asked David, gazing down at the old woman hunched in a corner, the mother with her huge, misshapen hands, pulling washing from a copper, almost extinguished in steam.

Mr Jackson shook his head. 'I'm afraid not. They are only signed with the initials 'HS'. Pity. There have been several attempts to identify the artist, but none have been successful. Whoever 'HS' was, he was a remarkable talent. But then so many promising young artists were killed at the front in the First World War. So many of that generation never reached their potential.'

'Yes, indeed,' said David. And this time he could not keep the excitement from his voice. 'But maybe not this one.'

‹›

'That's the story,' said Carys, eagerly, as they finally said goodbye to an excitable – if slightly bemused – Mr Jackson, promising to return in a few weeks' time, and made their way towards St Catherine's Church. 'That's the story to bring visitors flocking to Plas Eden. That, with the statues, and the drawings from Ketterford. It's more than just Pont-ar-Eden. It's a whole picture of the lives of people – ordinary people – that most of the time are never seen. And seen from a woman's viewpoint, too. It's so rare for anything a woman did in the past to be valued enough to survive. It's totally amazing.'

'I agree,' said David. 'But I can't see that stopping Edmund. If Plas Eden and the statues become famous, he might see that as even more excuse to cause trouble or to try blackmail. We could find ourselves looking over our shoulders for the rest of our lives.'

'Let's see what we find at St Catherine's,' replied Carys, pulling his arm through hers. 'You heard what Mr Jackson said: your great-grandfather was a shrewd man. It'll be there. You see, we'll find it. I just know it will be there.'

Chapter Twenty-Seven

For my first wedding, I had a gown that cost a king's ransom, and a carriage pulled by pure white horses, each sporting enough ostrich feathers to support a stricken Zeppelin in flight. For my first wedding, I arrived at a Treverick Church overflowing with flowers, guests sparkling with gold and jewels. After church came a sumptuous banquet in the great dining room of Treverick Hall, with a great tower of ice at its centre, and bowls overflowing with peaches, grapes and pineapples. Afterwards I accompanied my husband on a half-year tour of Italy, where I was paraded in my finery, for all to see.

For my second wedding there was nothing but a quiet church, and a single bouquet of red and white roses. Afterwards, my husband and I walked along the banks of the Thames, arm in arm, looking exactly what we were: an old married couple, content in each other's company. Unremarkable. Unnoticeable. And yet, perhaps not.

Maybe it was the roses still held in my hand, or simply that pure, heartfelt joy cannot be concealed. Whatever it was, I saw intrigued glances turn, now and again, to follow us. The flower-seller by London Bridge pressed a bunch of lavender into my bouquet, waving away payment with a knowing smile. And as we reached the centre of the bridge, the young man in uniform standing there watched us with a wistful air. His attention was turned from us in a moment, as a young woman

– no more than nineteen at most – ran towards him, holding her hat on her head with one hand. She was, I saw, dressed in the green, white and purple of the suffragette movement, whose banners we had seen draped in corners out of easy reach of the police, demanding equal rights and votes for women.

The world was changing. Even in far away Pont-ar-Eden we had felt it, but here in London it was unmistakeable. The first years of this new century had heralded in a new world. And some of it, I could see in the faces of the men and women passing by, had brought unease. Even dread.

He felt me shiver. 'Shall we go, *cariad*?'

'In a moment,' I replied. In a moment; when I had laid my ghosts to rest.

I looked down into the Thames, flowing beneath. How different I was now from the woman who had stood here, all those years ago, life hanging in the balance between the oblivion of the river, and the Meredith hospital, just a few streets away. Then, I had nothing. Now, my life was rich beyond measure.

I was glad that Judith had not accompanied us this time. Heaven knew where that private detective Lily had warned us of might be lurking, with his questions and his photograph, his holding out of a substantial reward and promise that Miss Treverick would find out something to her advantage, should she appear.

It was old Mrs Meredith who had brought me the copy of The Times containing news of William's death. She was a woman with sharp eyes, for all they were mostly focussed on her books and the current article she was writing. At first, she had been wary of me. Until, at last, we told her the truth.

'Oh, my dear,' she had said, softly, putting her arms around me, with tears in her eyes. That was all she said. That was all that was needed. From that day we were drawn together tightly by our grief for our lost children, and regret for the things that neither of us had said or done to keep them safe.

After that day, she had shared with me the stories that were her study, and her attempts to restore the wilderness of her garden. And maybe also she understood the restlessness that came over me when my work with the children's hospital was done. I had, of course, been proud of the attention given to the Meredith Social Study of Lambeth and the praise heaped on the photographs and the drawings alongside the carefully gathered facts. But it had made me uneasy whenever I held a pencil in my hand, afraid that my drawings might attract a more unwelcome attention, the kind that might destroy my secret – and Judith's – in an instant.

Besides, in this new happiness of mine, all my senses seemed to have been given life, urging me towards more. Towards touch, and feel. It was Mrs Meredith who had given me the courage to approach the younger son of the village blacksmith, who had turned his hand to stone masonry. I think young Mr Humphries thought me slightly touched in the head. But somewhere between his little English, and my little Welsh, we came to an understanding, as he taught me the rudiments of his trade. He scratched his head at my explanation that I wished to make the small creatures that were part of the new garden design. But fortunately being a foreigner, and from the big house, seemed sufficient to explain this eccentricity of mine.

As we worked together on the gardens, Mrs Meredith could not help but notice young Mr Evans and his ideas. Anymore than either of us could miss his head deep in conversation with Judith at every available moment. So when the news came, she gave me that chance to tell Judith, in the quiet of her rooms above her shop on Pont-ar-Eden High Street, before she might come across it by chance.

Poor Judith had wept for her brother and for many days afterwards she was quiet, keeping herself busy in her little shop and avoiding Plas Eden. But a decision could not be put off forever.

'It would give you riches,' I said, the day she returned at last to see the progress of the gardens.

'Yes,' she replied. Her voice was far away.

I was determined to be the voice of reason. 'And independence. It would give you the power to make a garden of your own like this, entirely to your own design.'

'Yes,' she said. 'It was kind of William to think of me.'

'Yes, indeed,' I replied. Now was not the time to comment on the power of a guilty conscience, or the wish to keep one's riches within the family.

I saw the direction in which her gaze travelled.

'You could make him rich beyond his wildest dreams,' I said, quietly.

'He would never accept,' she replied. She met my eyes. 'Lewis Evans is a proud man. I would lose him.'

'You could give him the choice,' I suggested. 'He might surprise you.'

'They would laugh at him. For his manners and the way he speaks.' That old stubborn line had overtaken her lips. 'And they would laugh at me.' Her eyes rested once more on the bowl of the new fountain, where Mr Evans was struggling with the figure of Venus, who appeared to be unwilling to allow water anywhere near her. 'The Trevericks would try to make me the lady I never was. They'd tell me how to look and how to dress. They'd be shocked at my walk. And even more so at my opinions. And the fact that I have opinions at all. Lewis would think me far removed from him, and every man who wished to marry me would be one I would not trust.' She smiled. 'If I were very poor, and had no way of making a living, then being mistress of Treverick Hall would be a freedom. As it is, my freedom, and my happiness, are here.' She took my hand. 'Of course I was tempted, for a little while, at least. But it seems to me that being the heiress of Treverick Hall would bring me nothing but misery.'

Over by the fountain, Venus had given up all resistance. A flute of water shot up, high into the air, sending the workers scrabbling from the bowl, already drenched.

'It worked!' called Judith. She was already running to join them. 'I told you it would work.'

'Typical woman,' I heard Mr Evans say, as he eyed the Venus, his clothes dripping.

'Mind of her own, you mean,' said Judith, tartly. And I saw how the love shone in his eyes, as he smiled in his reply.

❧

On Westminster Bridge, a barge emerged from beneath us, bustling on its way with a loud warning hoot towards smaller vessels straying towards its path, and bringing me back to the warmth at my side and the roses in my hand.

'Happy?' asked my new – in law if nothing else – husband.

'Completely,' I replied. 'I wish things could stay as they are now, forever.'

'Mmm,' he grunted. He was watching the throng of people passing us, as if lost in thought. 'Maybe we should ask Evans to arrange for the bottom field next to the kitchen garden to be ploughed up, when we get back to Plas Eden. If there is to be a war, I suspect food could soon be in short supply, and if we wait until the event, there will be few young men left in the village to undertake the task. We could then at least supply some fresh fruit and vegetables to the village and to the hospital here.'

I put my arm through his, and held him tight. Once, I had thought it was the rich and the titled, the beautiful and the extravagant who would inherit the earth. How differently I felt now. And that idea I had been talking over with David's mother and with Judith, as the gardens at Plas Eden were brought back to life, came back into my mind. This time with utter certainty.

The little people, my Uncle Jolyon used to call them. As would William, too, had he spared the energy to think of all those who worked, day and night, putting the food on his table and keeping his house clean and warm. The brick-makers who made each brick to build Treverick Hall. The cotton spinner in the factories and the weaver who made the cloth. The seamstress who sewed the garments that covered us. All the men and women who would keep the world turning, whatever the outside world might decree, and whatever sorrow might be inflicted upon them. The children, who would take our world, and make it grow into the future.

All of us, I thought, as I looked down into the waters of the Thames, where my life might have ended so long ago, have our stories to tell. Lives to be celebrated. The self-styled great and the good make a hideous amount of noise concerning their existence. But we who have survived whatever life has thrown at us, who have learnt the hard lesson of what it is to be human, are the ones whose stories should be told in stone. Ours are the stories that should be remembered forever.

A fire began inside me that day. A flame that would carry me in ambition beyond a small dragon or even the most graceful of garden nymphs. That would also carry me through whatever might lie ahead for us. One I knew would never die.

'Ready?' I said, lifting my eyes from the river to those of the man I loved, and would love, until the end of time.

He smiled, his eyes warm on mine. 'Yes,' he said. 'Time, I think, for us to go home.'

❧ St Catherine's was a simple, whitewashed church, flooded with light from Victorian stained-glass windows featuring scenes of Mary Magdalene, small children and the poor.

'Mr Jackson phoned to say you were coming,' said the vicar, making her way down the aisle to greet them as they entered. Maggie Day was a tall young woman with sleek cropped hair and the confident stride of a marathon runner. 'The Merediths built this church, you know.'

'Really?' said David.

'Oh, yes. They were always very particular that everyone was welcome, including the 'fallen' women they worked with.' She smiled. 'And that compassion was preached, rather than hell-fire. We're proud to keep up that tradition today. Mr Jackson said you were interested in the social history of the hospital?'

'Yes,' David replied.

The vicar gave him a sharp glance. 'Anything special you might like to find out about?'

'Well,' he began, before stumbling to a halt.

'We'd like to know more about the people who used the church in Victorian and Edwardian times,' put in Carys.

'And I believe my great-grandfather might have been married here,' said David.

'Really?' Maggie Day's eyebrows rose. 'How very strange.'

David exchanged glances with Carys. 'There hasn't been someone looking already, has there?'

'Oh, no. Not in the time I've been here, anyhow.' She smiled at them. 'We've just been clearing out at the back of the church, that's all. It was Sam Jackson and his plans to open a museum in the old Meredith Charity Hospital that started it. We've just had a grant to turn the offices at the back into a community café and workshop space, so they needed to be cleared anyhow, before the building work takes place next year.' She led them through a small doorway into a dusty room with books and files piled high all over the floor. Picking her way between the mounds, Maggie began unlocking a metal filing cabinet beneath the single window. 'That's when we came across this.' She pulled out a battered and stained book. 'It's one of the old registries. We found it wedged down behind one of the bookshelves that used to be in here. It could have fallen by accident, of course.'

'Or placed there for safe keeping?' suggested David.

'Possibly. I doubt that the church has entirely escaped unscathed from trouble over the past hundred years. Plus it was used for all kinds of different purposes during the two world wars. The dates all seem to be 1911. There's water damage to some of the pages and the handwriting isn't always the easiest to decipher, but I'm certain I saw a Meredith there. I assumed it must be another family with the same name.' She steadied the book on a pile of papers and flicked through until she came to the right page. 'Ah, yes. There we are. Could that be him?'

David bent over the faded scrawl. 'David Paul Meredith, bachelor. Yes, that's him.'

Carys peered over his shoulder. 'That's definitely an Ann.'

'The handwriting is pretty appalling, I'm afraid,' said Maggie.

'That's got to be 'Hermione',' said Carys. She met David's eyes. 'And that scrawl looks like 'Treverick', to me.'

'Widow,' read David.

'What's the date?' Carys was peering at her little notebook, to make sure there was no mistake. 'According to the plaque in Treverick church, William died in August 1911.'

David peered closer. 'It's 1911, but the month is under a water stain. It's completely blurred. And the ones above.'

'I take it the date of the marriage is important?' said Maggie.

'Just a bit,' muttered David.

'Very,' said Carys.

Maggie turned the book towards her. 'I'm assuming you don't necessarily need the exact day, just that it's – ah – in the last six months of the year?'

'Yes,' said David. Carys nodded.

Maggie inspected the page. 'For what it's worth, I'm pretty sure one at the top of the page says September.' She turned to the previous page. 'There's still damage here, but I'd say those are September, as well.' She flicked back still further. 'It must be. Near the end of September, I'd say. That's the first one that looks as if it could say August.'

'September.' David's face relaxed.

'Almost exactly a hundred years ago,' said Carys. 'Long story,' she added to Maggie, who was clearly intrigued. 'Thank you for all your help.'

Maggie smiled. 'My pleasure. I'm glad you found what you were looking for.'

'They must have been very discreet about it,' said Carys, as she and David made their way out of St Catherine's, with a promise to return for a longer visit the next time they came to meet with Mr Jackson at Meredith House. 'They must have been well loved and respected here by people who made sure their secret remained safe.'

David shivered slightly. 'Thinking about it, I'm sure it

wasn't so much about not wanting people to know how long they had lived together without being married, but making sure that no one ever found out about Ketterford. Hard to explain, especially given the attitudes to women in those days, that Ann wasn't really mad.'

'You're right,' replied Carys. 'And rumours of insanity would be passed on to her descendents, too. It was Nainie and your dad, and you and Huw too, they were trying to protect. No wonder we kept on coming up against a brick wall. Thank goodness we found them.'

David came to a halt. 'You don't think it was the madness thing that Edmund was on about, do you? I don't fancy having to fight off suggestions that the Merediths are lunatics. My grandfather took Nainie's name when they got married, so that there would always be Merediths in Eden. It would be a bit ironic if the Meredith name helped Edmund start mudslinging and suggesting we're all raving lunatics who shouldn't be allowed out after dark.'

Carys thought for a minute. 'Even if he does, it's hardly going to matter now, is it? Not with those incredible drawings. They are so clear-eyed and compassionate. Like Mr Jackson said, the drawings have already established a reputation of being the work of a hugely talented artist. Just because the artist turns out to be a woman rather than a man, doesn't change that. Her drawings will form Hermione Meredith's reputation. Nothing else.'

'Yes, you're right.' David tucked her arm through his. 'And at least Edmund can't say Nainie was the result of a bigamous marriage and therefore the daughter of criminals.' He gave a wry chuckle. 'I suppose a scandal like that from the past might have brought the tourists into Plas Eden, but I think we can manage without the ghoulish obsessives, whatever happens.'

'Definitely.'

He tightened his arm around hers. 'Cousin Edmund must have known Dad would have done anything to protect Nainie from any hurt and public humiliation, whatever his son thinks now. Dad always said Edmund was a liability. He was so right. I hope we never hear from Edmund Jnr again.'

'Me too.'

Carys, he discovered, was busily counting on her fingers. 'What?'

'Nainie always said she was a miracle baby. She was right: at their age, they must have given up the idea of having children at all. Nainie was born just six months after they were able to marry. I wonder if they knew, that day they came to St Catherine's?'

'I hope they did. Or guessed soon after,' replied David, with a smile. 'I think Nainie would have liked that.'

They walked for a little way in contented silence, until they reached the busy thoroughfare of Westminster Bridge. Open-topped buses lumbered by, as David and Carys dodged tourists taking photographs of each other with Big Ben and the Houses of Parliament. At the centre of the bridge, they paused side by side to look down the river towards St Paul's, with the London Eye slowly turning, its little capsules full of passengers admiring the view.

'So what happens now?' said David.

'I don't know,' replied Carys.

'With you and me, I mean,' said David earnestly. He clasped her hands. 'Cari, what I've been trying to say all this time is that I love you. That I want to be with you. I don't care how, I don't care where. I just know that you are the most precious thing in my life, and I couldn't bear to lose you. Not again.'

'I love you, and I don't want to lose you, either,' said Carys.

Crowds or no crowds, his arms came around her, as she was swept into his kiss. Carys held on tight, feeling the warmth of him being absorbed into her, until she could no longer tell which was which. His kisses were becoming more insistent. She could just relax, let go, and let happiness overwhelm her.

'We could still sell Plas Eden, you know,' David murmured against her mouth.

'Oh?'

'Mmm. Huw could buy a holiday home in Barbados and set up any business he wanted.' He kissed her again. 'We could make Rhiannon put herself first for once. And you and I –' His kiss was longer, this time. 'We'd never have to worry about money for rest of our lives. We could do whatever we wanted.'

Carys gently disengaged herself. 'And you'd be happy?'

'Yes. If I was with you.'

'Rubbish,' she said softly. 'I love you more than ever for saying so, but life isn't like that. I think, in our hearts, we both know it. We're neither of us into buying things just for the sake of it.' She put her arms around him again, holding him tight. 'An eternal holiday sounds fine in theory. But everyone needs a purpose in life. You included. You're a Meredith, through and through. Plas Eden is *your* purpose. Always has been, always will be. How could I be happy unless I knew you were happy, too? I'm not sure love would survive, unless both of us can follow our dreams.'

'But what about Cornwall? I don't want you to throw that away.'

She kissed him. 'Of course I was tempted by Karenza's suggestion. Who wouldn't be? A few months ago I would have jumped at the chance. But not now. Oh, I want to visit there, just like we'll be coming back to London, and I want to get to know Karenza better. I'll always love Cornwall and be glad it's a part of me. But I'm a Pont-ar-Eden girl at heart. Then there's Mam. I'm not sure I'd want to live so far away as Mam gets older. Not now. I've learnt so much during the time I've been looking after Mam. Most of all, I've learnt that Pont-ar-Eden is where I belong, too.'

His gaze was earnest. 'Are you sure? Are you absolutely sure? I lost you once before because of Plas Eden. I couldn't bear losing you again.'

'You won't,' replied Carys, smiling. 'In those days, I was a child. I didn't know who I was, or what I wanted. I saw Eden as a trap I could never escape, and that would suffocate me.'

'It might well do yet,' returned David.

'I don't think so. In fact, I'm certain it won't. It was your great-grandmother who taught me that.'

'Really?' said David, in surprise.

'Yes. I've been wondering, ever since we got back from Cornwall, how I'd feel if my husband had shoved me into a lunatic asylum just to get rid of me. I'm not sure I'd ever be able to love or trust in anyone ever again. But Ann did. She made her life in Plas Eden without even the protection of being married. In those days, that meant she could have been thrown out on the streets at any moment, with no means of supporting herself.'

'I suppose so,' said David, with a shudder.

'I couldn't imagine what gave her such mind-blowing courage. But then, when we were waiting in that courtyard for Mr Jackson just now, it suddenly struck me. It was love that gave her the courage to go with your great-grandfather to Plas Eden. She wasn't afraid of taking on the responsibility either. I'm certain she helped him with his work, as well as setting up the Children's Hospital. I realised it was love that gave her true freedom, too.'

'How do you mean?'

'The statues,' said Carys. 'Ann's drawings are amazing, but Eden's ghosts are something else. They are so ambitious, so alive, and so beautiful. So few women in the past ever had the time or the confidence to achieve anything like that. They are the work of someone who has been able to reach their full potential. I think that's something money could never buy, and the greatest freedom and happiness anyone could find. That's what I want to find, too.'

David kissed her. 'I know exactly what you mean.' He grinned. 'Now all we've got to do is persuade Huw and Rhiannon and work out exactly what we are going to do with Plas Eden.'

Carys smiled. 'Oh, I think between us we'll be able to come up with something. We make a pretty invincible team, remember?'

David laughed as he pulled her towards him. 'You can say that again.'

They stood together in silence for a while, looking down into the ever-flowing waters of the Thames. Then, arm in arm, holding each other close, they made their way through the cheerful jostle of the crowds. Past Big Ben and St James' Park: making their way towards Buckingham Palace and the green heart of the city.

Chapter Twenty-Eight

♣ 'It looks just like it used to when you were children and your dad was alive,' sighed Mair Evans on the morning of Christmas Eve, gazing round at Willow Cottage with the happy gleam of nostalgia in her eyes. 'You've worked miracles, Carys.'

'Oh, I don't know about miracles,' replied Carys, mentally checking off her list of preparations for Gwenan and Nia and their families to descend complete with carols at midnight in Pont-ar-Eden square. 'As long as it looks festive. And I think we've certainly managed that between us.'

Mam smiled. She was looking tired after the exertions of shopping for presents and sorting through the old decorations during the past few weeks, but there was colour in her cheeks and a gleam in her eye. She hadn't had all her children home together for Christmas in years, and who know when it might happen again. She was going to make the most of it.

Willow Cottage shone clean and sparkling in the cold, clear sunlight. In order to keep Mam from taking over the broom and the mop and wearing herself out completely, Carys had kept her firmly supplied with holly and mistletoe, brought over in large armfuls from the Eden estate, defying each knowing glance as she made her way down Pont-ar-Eden high street.

Mair Evans had once been famous in Pont-ar-Eden for her winter wreaths. It was a pleasure to see her getting back into the swing of things, binding sprigs of red berries and milky mistletoe into glossy circles that adorned the front door and the kitchen. Longer swags of greenery dotted with tiny white rice-lights wound around the banisters in the hallway and over the paintings in the sitting room.

For the past few years, Mam had brought out the old faithful artificial Christmas tree, but a few days ago Carys had given in to the temptation of the largest fir leaning outside the grocery shop, and returned with Sara Jones' husband Alun clutching the other end, clearly delighted that someone other than Rhiannon at Plas Eden was going overboard this Christmas.

The tree now took up one corner of the sitting room from floor to ceiling, sending the cut-pine scent oozing through the house, between the richness of freshly cooked mince pies and the burnt-wax smell of the fat red advent candles nestled happily amongst Mam's tour de force of berries and prickly leaves.

Carys made room for the last of the Christmas cards on the crowded mantelpiece and stood back to admire her handiwork. 'Tea?'

'That sounds good,' said Mam, who had the look of one who needed a good sit down and a nap before her family could arrive.

'Then I suppose we'd better get changed.' Carys peered out into the slant of morning sun that was sending the mountains into sharp relief against a pale blue sky. 'I know they were talking about a white Christmas this year, but it doesn't look like it at the moment.'

Mam joined her. 'It'll snow,' she said. 'Look, there are clouds gathering over Moel Eden already. Those look like snow clouds to me.'

'Maybe,' said Carys, not entirely convinced.

'They are. You mark my words. Besides, you can smell it on the air.'

'I didn't know you could smell snow.'

'Of course you can,' replied Mam, smiling. She tucked her arm through Carys'. 'It's been good having you here,' she said. 'You've been wonderful, *cariad*.'

'I've enjoyed it.' Carys watched her anxiously. 'And I'm not going anywhere, Mam. Even when I move into Eden Farm, I'll still be popping in to see you, and I won't be far away. You know you can call on me, whenever you need me.'

'Now stop fussing. I'll be fine. You know you're going to have your work cut out getting a business started in Pont-ar-Eden.' Mam sighed. 'That's my only regret, you know. That your dad didn't live to see you bringing that old walled garden back to life.'

'If I can,' muttered Carys. Thank heaven for the mild autumn, but even with the help of the growing number of allotment holders, clearing the walled garden of weeds ready for the spring planting was proving a mammoth task. But she was determined to do it without recourse to too much machinery, rediscovering in each corner the evidence of fruit and vegetable beds left by her ancestors. After all, they were the ones who knew how best to use every patch of ground to its most productive potential.

And then there was the small matter of Plas Eden…

'You'll make it, *cariad*,' Mam was saying. 'If anyone can, you can. I never worried about you, you know.'

'You don't need to worry about me, Mam,' smiled Carys.

'No.' Mam was thoughtful. 'You know, nothing ever quite prepares you for being a mother. You try to be fair, and do your best. But sometimes the whole experience is so overwhelming, it's just survival that takes over.'

396

'You were a brilliant mother,' said Carys stoutly.

'Thank you, darling. It's very sweet of you to say so. But I'm afraid I was not always fair.'

'Mam…'

'No, listen *cariad*. Nia was always so clinging, and Gwenan … well Gwenan was always a bit of a handful, if I'm honest. Always so set on getting her own way. I never knew quite how to deal with her. I was such a dreamer when I was a girl; I never thought what it would be like to be grown up. And, well it wasn't anything you really talked about, in those days. Then it happened so fast, once I met your dad. I think maybe I was still in shock for half of my life. And you were always the one that was so quiet. So sensible.' With her free hand, she was adjusting the set of a bunch of holly on the windowsill. 'I should have known. When I used to help with the children's reading at Pont-ar-Eden Primary, it was always the quiet ones that were overlooked. You noticed the very good and the very naughty. But sometimes, it seems to me, it's the ones in the middle, who simply get on with things and don't demand your attention, who are the ones who may need the most, after all.'

'You're my mam, and I wouldn't have you any other way,' said Carys, kissing her mother.

Mair smiled. 'Dear me,' she said, feeling in her pocket for a tissue, 'we haven't half finished, and those girls will be here any moment.'

'They're going to meet at the hotel first,' replied Carys. 'Gwenan's arranged for them all to have lunch there, and then come on here for the evening.'

'What were they thinking of?' said Mair, who had entirely forgotten this arrangement in the flurry of preparations. 'There's no need for that. We've plenty of food here.'

'Gwenan thought it might be easier if they all got themselves settled first,' said Carys. 'And, anyhow,' she added with an affectionate smile, 'we all want to make the most of you for the next few days, and we don't want to tire you out straight away. Where would the fun be in that?'

'Nonsense. I'm not in the least tired,' stated Mam, who was by now heading for the nearest chair, hardly able to keep her eyes open.

'I'll make that tea.' Carys slipped out into the hallway so that Mam didn't have to fight the doze that was rapidly overcoming her.

As she reached the kitchen, the telephone rang. Carys grabbed it hastily, cutting off the summoning peal before it could disturb Mam.

'Nia hasn't got here yet,' came Gwenan's voice, tired and decidedly in full night-before-Christmas stress. A cacophony of squabbling teenagers erupted in the background. 'Her mobile's switched off. We've got lunch booked in half an hour.'

Carys took a deep breath. 'They'll be there,' she said, soothingly. 'I expect the traffic from Birmingham is really busy. You know what the reception is like once you get near the mountains. They're probably just going through a bad spot…' She jumped as the mobile in her pocket bleeped and vibrated. 'Just a minute, Gwenan. I think this could be Nia now.'

'I keep on getting 'missed call' from Gwenan on my mobile,' wailed Nia's voice, though a crackle of breaking signal and a background of Sam and the children halfway through 'Silent Night'. 'Tell her we'll be there as soon as we can. Sam forgot his toothbrush, so we called in Talarn first.'

'I'm sure they'd have had toothbrushes in Pont-ar-Eden,' came Sam's voice, over a mildly hysterical 'our Sav-ior is bo-orn' from William and Alexandra in the back seat.

'Not electric ones, and you know they are much better for your gums,' said Nia.

'Chri-ist our Sav-iour is born,' roared out Sam, in reply.

Carys stifled a giggle. 'Look, don't worry about it, Nia. I'll let Gwenan know. She can always put back the lunch booking if need be.' Nia mollified, Carys turned her attention back to the landline. 'They're nearly there, Gwenan. They're just on their way back from Talarn. Something about last minute Christmas presents,' she lied blithely.

'Nia is always so disorganised,' sighed Gwenan.

At a padding of footsteps behind her, Carys turned to find Mam back on full alert, watching her with an anxious expression, and clearly with motorway pile-ups and suddenly collapsing bridges looming large in her mind.

'It's fine,' she mouthed silently, before turning her attention back to her elder sister. 'Look, Gwenan, why don't you see if you can arrange for lunch to be put back a bit. I'm sure they won't mind if you let them know now. After all, they know you're both coming quite a distance, and traffic is always bad on Christmas Eve, so it can't be entirely unexpected. That way, you can all get unpacked and have a relaxing drink before you eat. We're not going to have a meal until late here, anyway.'

'Okay.' The stress eased a little in Gwenan's voice. 'If that's okay with Mam, of course.'

'Mam's saying yes,' replied Carys, smiling at her mother, who was shaking her head in mild exasperation.

'Okay. I'll talk to them.' Gwenan's voice sharpened. 'And what are all those cameras doing at Plas Eden?'

'Cameras?'

'A full film crew,' said Gwenan. 'They were heading into the woods where the statues are. The van said 'BBC Wales' on the side.'

'Oh, right,' said Carys. 'Long story. They must be wanting to get some pictures of Plas Eden before the work starts. They're going to be following David over the next year. It's turned out to be quite an exciting project, especially the statues. We'll tell you all about it over supper.'

Gwenan suitably intrigued, Carys placed the phone back in its receiver. Her eyes met those of Mam's. 'It seems they've started filming already.'

'Well, then let's hope it snows for them,' said Mam. 'Plas Eden always did look like a picture postcard in the snow.'

'Mmm,' replied Carys. A sudden feeling of sadness had overcome her. 'I can't imagine Plas Eden without Rhiannon next year. It won't be quite the same, will it?'

'But at least Plas Eden will be there,' said Mam. 'Even if she doesn't live there any more, Rhiannon will be back to visit. I know she's looking forward to it, and this thing in America is a marvellous opportunity for her, but I've got a feeling there's part of Rhiannon that will stay in Plas Eden forever. And that, in the end, is what counts.'

'Like Nainie's mother, and Grandmother Judith, and all those people from Pont-ar-Eden.'

'Exactly,' said Mam. 'I think it's wonderful. And so clever of you to spot it.'

'I didn't really,' smiled Carys. 'It was you and everyone at the Boadicea going through all those old photographs and finding out about all the people in them. Without that, I'd never have made the connection. And anyhow, it was you and Dad who took me to that exhibition of Julia Margaret Cameron's photographs when I was a kid. That's what was niggling at me, the moment I saw the old photographs of Plas Eden. I should have known.'

'You mean because Julia Margaret Cameron used her domestic servants as models for her photographs?'

'Yes. I wonder if that's what gave Nainie's mother the idea to use the people of Pont-ar-Eden as models for her statues?' She frowned, searching her mind. 'And I suppose Granddad's photographs of the ordinary people around him, as well. Except I have a feeling it was more than that. When I look at the statues now, it feels as if she just simply loved human beings, in all their strengths and their weaknesses. And I suppose the story of a life you can see in a face.'

'My argument for not having Botox, any day,' said Mam, brightly.

Carys laughed. 'Me too.'

'And maybe it was Pont-ar-Eden,' said Mam.

'Pont-ar-Eden?'

'Yes. You know, I'm sure both those women were happy here. Nainie's mother creating the statues, your grandmother creating the garden for them. Both of them doing what they loved, and with husbands and children, and a community that accepted them for what they were, not for some idea of what they ought to be. I think Nainie's mother created those statues out of love, not just for her husband and her children, but the people in the village, too. It's like I've always said, *cariad*: Pont-ar-Eden isn't such a bad place to live, after all.'

'Yes, Mam.'

Behind them the kettle boiled.

'Perhaps we should make that a sherry,' said Mam. 'It is Christmas, after all. Although I'm sure you'd prefer a glass of red wine.'

Carys smiled. 'Well, maybe. But I know you like sherry.' She peered out of the window. 'I think you're right, Mam. Those clouds are thickening over the mountains. Looks like it might snow, after all.'

By the time the short day turned towards dusk, a light sprinkling of snow covered the landscape around Plas Eden. From Nainie's bench on the ridge behind the house, the Eden estate lay spread out, a network of houses, trees and roads marked in black like a sketch in charcoal amidst the soft gleam of white.

'Beautiful, isn't it?' said Carys, a little shyly, as she approached the slight figure sitting alone on the bench.

'Stunning,' replied Rhiannon. 'I think I shall never tire of looking at Plas Eden, whatever the season and whatever the light.' She stuffed a camera deep inside the pocket of her padded walking coat and pulled on her gloves. 'Are you going to join me?'

'I don't want to disturb you.'

'Not at all.' A faint smile appeared on Rhiannon's face. 'Do I detect a fellow escapee from last-minute Christmas preparations?'

Carys laughed. 'I suppose so. Plus David said I might find you up here.'

'Oh?' enquired Rhiannon as Carys sat down beside her. 'Nothing wrong, is there?'

'Oh, no. I just wanted to make sure you were okay. About Eden Cottage, I mean.'

'Of course,' replied Rhiannon. 'It makes perfect sense for you and David to settle in the cottage. I don't know why anyone didn't think of that solution before.'

'But we don't need to stay there, not once the work on Plas Eden has been done. There will still be room in the east wing, even though most of it is being turned into function rooms and being set up for courses. David and I could still live there. We don't have to live in the cottage forever.'

'If I wanted to use Eden Cottage as my home when I'm in the UK, you mean?'

'Yes. David says you're fine about it, but I don't want to feel that I'm throwing you out of your own home. Not after everything.'

Rhiannon let her gaze travel over the winter landscape below them. 'I will always love Eden,' she said quietly. 'It will always be my home. And yes, there's something very sad about packing away the remains of my life here. But I'm also looking forward. When I leave for America, it will be to a completely new life.' She smiled. 'Funny, isn't it? I feel like a teenager, just about to leave home for college. I'm a bit scared, but I know I have to go.'

'But you'll be coming back?'

'Keep me away! I'll be back for visits and to see the new Eden. I'll want to keep up with how the courses and the B&B is coming along. I'm happy to run painting courses, if you and David are still interested.'

'Yes, of course. That's what gave us the idea for concentrating on functions and courses in that wing of the house in the first place.'

Rhiannon smiled. 'I wouldn't want to see you and David crammed into the new flat in the east wing. At least in the cottage you'll have space to call your own and a chance at a normal life. It makes much more sense for me to use the flat, or the barn conversion David is talking about as a studio and place to run my painting courses, if they take off.'

Carys hesitated. She didn't want to start her own new life with a shadow hanging in the background. 'You know, don't you, Rhiannon, that I love David with all my heart, and that's why I want to be with him?'

'Of course.'

'And you don't still think I've agreed to marry him just because of Plas Eden?'

Rhiannon, she found, was scrutinising her face. 'Was that what you thought? When David wanted to marry you, all those years ago, was that what you thought?'

'I don't mind. And I understand. In your place I'd probably have thought the same. And anyhow, who is to say it wasn't true? I just don't want you to think it's true now.'

'Oh, Carys.' Rhiannon reached out with her gloved hand to touch Carys' face. 'I didn't know you thought that way. I believed you and David marrying so young was a mistake, yes. But I never meant you to take it like that. It wasn't David I was worried about, it was you.'

'Me?'

'Yes. Do you remember what I once told you about me coming to Eden saved me from the worst mistake of my life?'

'From going with the famous artist to America, you mean?'

'Exactly. I only understood later that I would never have found my way as a painter and always lived in Jason's shadow. That's what I was afraid of for you. You were so young and so bright, and so full of energy and ideas. I saw a girl who could be anything. I was afraid that Eden would suck that life and that energy out of you. That you would live your life in David's shadow. Or, even worse, in the shadow of Plas Eden. And that one day, when you were much older, perhaps with children, and with so few options open to you, you would see that. Don't you see, Cari? I saw myself in you. That's why I was afraid.'

'Oh.' Carys attempted to get her head round this. 'And now?'

Rhiannon chuckled. '*Cariad*, I have no worries in the least for you now. Especially not as mistress of Eden Farm. I feel certain you will follow in your grandmother's footsteps quite magnificently. David is going to have to watch his step from now on.'

'You make me sound quite terrifying.'

'Only to those who don't know you,' replied Rhiannon, gently. 'You're good for David, you know. You always were.'

'We make a good team,' said Carys with a smile.

'I can see that. Believe me, that's what you're going to need to make Eden work for you. And you will. I've no doubts of that at all. I'm looking forward to watching your progress.'

The last of the light glinted on the distant sea, throwing the shadow of Talarn castle into sharp relief.

Carys glanced at her watch. 'I'd better get back.'

'I'll come with you,' said Rhiannon, rising and taking out her torch. 'It'll be dark soon, and I've still one or two things I need to finish before the carol singing.'

'Me too.'

As they began to make their way down, swirls of white began to fall. Scarcely perceptible at first, but growing into a sweeping dance around them.

Rhiannon removed her glove and held out her hand to catch the icy softness. 'It's going to be a proper white Christmas,' she said.

❦

Snow fell quietly and steadily all evening. As midnight approached, it seemed as if the whole of Pont-ar-Eden had gathered in the village square.

Gwenan and Nia settled Mam in the folding chair brought for the purpose, complete with blankets and an Arctic-conditions sleeping bag, while Carys filled up three hot water bottles from the 'hot water bottles only' urn simmering gently just inside the Boadicea's door in the cause of helping the more senior members of Pont-ar-Eden to keep hypothermia at bay.

'In the bleak midwinter, frosty wind made moan, Earth stood hard as iron, water like a stone …' began the crooning voices of Pont-ar-Eden, hushed almost to a whisper, as Carys returned to join the carol singers around the tree. She paused for a moment just outside the cafe, feeling almost like a child again as the scent of hot mince pies and mulled wine spilled out with her into the white, gently swirling world, pristine in the glow of streetlamps.

In front of her, Pont-ar-Eden glistened in the heavy weight of snow, beginning to freeze as the temperature dropped, covering the fluffy surface with a crust of shimmering ice crystals. Under the eaves of shops and houses, white icicle-lights chased each other, as if trying to outdo curtains of brilliant blue hung across the Boadicea's windows, and the multicoloured baubles wound around the central Christmas tree.

'It's times like this, it feels as if nothing ever changes,' she remarked to Merlin, who was stamping his feet as quietly as he could manage.

He smiled. 'Funny, I was thinking just that.'

'In the Bleak Midwinter' faded away into silence. There was a moment's coughing and shuffling, following by a rousing rendition of 'Ding, Dong, Merrily on High', accompanied by an almost-in-tune school band and buckets being shaken for donations towards the local children's hospice.

'Coming to join us?'

He shook his head. 'It kinda feels weird,' he said, pulling the folds of his cashmere overcoat closer around him. 'I sort of became a Buddhist when I gave up the booze,' he added apologetically.

Carys grinned. 'I don't think that matters. Not everyone goes into the church for the service afterwards.' She nodded towards the young couple in hand-knitted gloves and bobble-hats emerging from the new health-food store where the old butchers had once stood. 'And Pete and Saffron are definitely New Age and unashamedly pagan. I'm not sure Pont-ar-Eden will ever recover from that one.'

'Mmm.' He was still hesitating. Carys glanced back to where she could just make out Buddug putting the finishing touches to the Boadicea's tables, ready for the frozen hoards to descend the moment the carols ended.

'You could always join her,' she remarked.

Merlin grunted. 'She's had enough trouble, if you ask me. Last thing she needs is another alcoholic in her life knocking her around every Friday night.'

Carys watched him thoughtfully. 'When did you last have a drink?'

'April fifth, two-thousand-five,' he replied automatically.

'And when did you last hit a woman?'

'I have never in my life…' he began, indignantly. 'Ah,' he said, meeting her eyes. 'I see what you mean.' He swallowed. A look of blind terror overtook his face. 'I've never done this without half a bottle of Jack Daniels inside me,' he muttered.

Carys kissed him firmly on the cheek. 'Take it slowly. Play it by ear. You'll be fine.'

Merlin smiled. 'David Meredith's a lucky man.'

'And I'm a lucky woman,' she returned.

'*Tawel nos, dros y byd…*' began the gentle lilt of 'Silent Night' in Welsh, humming in the snow around them.

'Well, go on, then,' said Carys, steering him around so that he was facing the Boadicea's door, and giving him a gently encouraging push on his way.

She waited just long enough to see him make his way inside, then hurried to take the hot water bottles to Gwenan, who was hovering on the edges of the carol singers, wondering what had kept her.

'*Stille Nacht, heilige Nacht, Alles schlaft, einsam wacht...*' came the murmur as 'Silent Night' transformed itself into the original German.

As Gwenan shot back towards Mam, the crowd closed behind her, forming a tight, perfect circle around the Christmas tree. Carys hesitated, not wanting to disturb the unity, as 'Silent Night' was sung in English, before returning back for a final time in Welsh.

But then she spotted it. The place that had been left for her. The place that would always be hers.

Quietly, Carys made her way to join David, as the midnight bells rang out across the roofs of Pont-ar-Eden.

Epilogue

In the trees of Plas Eden a wind stirred, sending the shadows rustling amongst the leaves and over the still features of Eden's ghosts.

David Meredith pulled the last of the brambles from the shield of King Arthur and sat back on his heels to view his handiwork. He glanced over to where Carys was kneeling, planting yellow primroses where the figure of Blodeuwedd rose out of her carved sheaf of willow and meadow flowers.

'There, that's looking better,' he said.

Carys looked up and smiled. 'Much better. Much more like a garden again.'

Over the past year, the overgrown branches of the trees had been thinned and neatened, leaving a larger circle of sky above them. Encouraged by the increased light, daffodils were already springing up amongst a swathe of snowdrops, with the first stirrings of bluebells amongst the longer grass. The creamy flowers of hawthorn were coming into bloom next to Ceridwen's cauldron, while a bank of bright yellow celandines and pink-tinged wood anemones nestled at the feet of the small child beneath.

Spring flowers completed, Carys settled down to trays of lavenders and purple sage she had brought from her greenhouses at Eden Farm. Pots of honeysuckle and clematis lay waiting to be trained up and around the benches that had been placed strategically at the edges of the little glade, interspersed with clumps of oriental poppies promising an exotic touch of large scarlet blooms in a few months' time.

All of her plants, Carys was proud to see, looked green and healthy and all ready to burst into new growth. Over the past year, while Rhiannon had been in America and the scaffolding had enclosed Plas Eden within a ring of steel, the gardens at Eden Farm had come on in leaps and bounds.

Although, she had to admit it, if she'd known just how hard the work would be, Carys would have thought anyone mad to start it. But last summer the polytunnels had been full to bursting with tomatoes and chillies, and the ramblings of squashes of all shapes and sizes. The beds had yielded potatoes and broccoli and enough peas and green beans to feed her and David, and keep the Boadicea Café and the thriving little health shop on Pont-ar-Eden high street supplied. This year, by the time the cookery courses got underway in early summer, there would be enough veg and salad leaves for the students to pick their own each morning. It still gave her a buzz each time she thought about it.

Last year, Carys had only made brief experiments with plums and raspberries, while most of the bilberries and blackberries she had harvested had simply gone straight into the freezer. They had enjoyed the delicious bursts of fresh fruit in pies and crumbles all winter and supplied the first home baking course with a tasty selection of fillings that had sent their first clients home in a state of ecstasy. Word had clearly got about, as even before their marketing plan went into full swing the second baking course was almost fully booked. This year, alongside growing for the courses and their own use, she was determined to begin making jams and preserves in earnest.

The breeze stirred once more. Between the slowly unfurling leaves, Plas Eden gleamed pristine white, every window shining, the roof mended and cleaned of moss.

'I suppose we'd better go,' said David, a little regretfully. He had finished tidying the empty pots into the wheelbarrow, and was engaged in watering each newly placed plant, filling the watering can from the stream running alongside the statues. He eyed the little glade with a smile. 'It's perfect.'

'Not exactly perfect.' Carys eyed her planting critically. 'It

412

all seems horribly last minute. I should have done these weeks ago.'

'They look fine,' he replied. 'Last minute, isn't that what weddings are about?'

'So I've heard,' she returned with a smile. 'I suppose we should have known when we said we wanted something small and quiet that it would just grow and grow.'

'Doomed from the start,' he agreed, laughing. 'I'm still not sure we'll all fit in here tomorrow morning.'

'I expect we'll manage,' she returned, with a grin.

With Buddug currently in full charge of Plas Eden's shining new kitchen, Karenza having driven up that morning from Cornwall with a carful of flowers, and Poppy due to arrive at any minute, this had been their last chance to get everything ready. And only just in time, it seemed. Footsteps were making their way down the steps towards them, accompanied by the murmur of voices.

The next moment Gwynfor and Rhiannon appeared, with Hodge trotting in full adoring attentiveness at Rhiannon's side.

'I'm afraid we've been sent as a delegation from Huw,' said Rhiannon.

'He's worried you've forgotten that David is staying with Rhiannon in Plas Eden tonight,' added Gwynfor.

'He isn't still trying to get me out to the Taliesin, is he?' demanded David, in alarm.

Gwynfor chuckled. 'I did suggest the full Pont-ar-Eden stag night might get out of hand and end up in the local paper, however hard you tried. That seemed to do the trick. And I did point out you'd probably prefer a cup of tea and Rhiannon all to yourself for the evening, in any case.'

David let out a sigh of relief. 'Thanks.'

'So Angela's arranging tea and cake for us all before Carys

413

goes back to the cottage,' said Rhiannon, with a smile. Her eyes travelled around the little glade. 'That is so beautiful. You've transformed this place; this must have been how it was when they were first made. You can really see the statues clearly now.'

'Stunning,' agreed Gwynfor, wholeheartedly. He patted the newly cleaned staff of Merlin the magician that appeared to positively gleam with contained magic. 'No one who could make these could possibly have been in the slightest bit insane.'

David looked up at his tone. Gwynfor was gazing at the face of the statue, deep in contemplation.

'It was you,' said David. '*You* phoned Ketterford Museum, asking questions about statues.'

'Ah,' replied Gwynfor, turning back to face them. He cleared his throat. 'I wondered if they might have mentioned it.'

David frowned at him. 'So you knew all along. About Ketterford Asylum?'

'Oh, good heavens, no. Well, not exactly. There were always rumours in the village about Nainie's mother, when I was young. She was such an extraordinary person, and didn't seem to come from anywhere or be of any family.'

'So the private detective Sara Jones and the others were talking about had found out about Ketterford?' said Carys.

Gwynfor shook his head. 'No, no. Not at all. That private detective was paid to uncover the trail of a missing heiress, not a woman who had been declared dead many years before.'

'Oh,' said Carys. 'Grandmother Judith, you mean.'

'Exactly.'

'So who…' began David. He met Gwynfor's eyes. 'Don't tell me: Edmund Jnr.'

Gwynfor coughed. 'He did contact you, then. He swore to

me he hadn't, but then his father always had a cavalier attitude to the truth. I should have known the son would be the same. I take it you haven't heard from him recently?'

'Not since he failed to turn up for a meeting we'd arranged last year.'

'Good.' Gwynfor looked smug.

'So how…?'

'Well, there were, shall we say, a few little things Edmund failed to mention to his offspring.'

'Such as?'

'Fraud. Embezzlement. Attempted blackmail. The family gave Edmund the option of emigrating permanently to South America or facing the police here.'

'But I didn't find anything about that when I looked.'

Gwynfor's eyebrows bristled. 'Oh, don't worry, the papers are safe.' He smiled. 'I might have mentioned to Edmund Jnr that his father got himself entangled with some pretty unpleasant low-lifes. The kind that have long memories and might not be too fussy about how they got their money back and when. Besides, with all the detective work you two did and the drawings and the statues creating such a stir already, everyone knows there is nothing to be ashamed of, and nothing whatsoever to hide. I very much doubt you'll have any trouble again.'

There was a moment's silence.

'Come on,' said Rhiannon at last. 'We've given our message, and I think we can trust these two to follow us in their own time.'

'Ready?' said David, as Rhiannon and Gwynfor disappeared once more, Hodge trotting cheerfully behind, fulfilling the promise of his collie ancestor as he made sure no one went missing along the way.

'Just these two,' replied Carys, heeling in the final clematis and turning her attention to the last of the lavender. 'They won't take a minute.'

'Okay,' said David, sitting down to clean his spade. Carys bent again, trowelling amongst the slate-filled earth to settle the little plants in position at the base of Ceridwen's cauldron. High above, a line of swans flapped noisily, landing a few minutes later on the lake with much honking and rushing of water. Then it was silent again.

She would never be afraid here, Carys thought, pressing the last plant into position and wiping her trowel on the grass. A plaintive meow came out of the dark of the undergrowth, followed by the silky blackness of Tash stalking out to join them. Absently, Carys pulled off her gardening gloves and stroked the warm fur, which promptly wound itself around her, purr rumbling gently against her legs.

And suddenly it was very still. She could feel the statues near her, almost as if they were bending towards her, listening to the very beat of her heart.

She lifted her head towards them: The people who had lived and died within the lands of Eden. The people who had worked the earth and raised their children, and whose hopes and dreams, joys and sorrows of lives richly led, lay silently in the earth around them. Lives captured for a moment by the photographs of her grandfather and celebrated in stone for all to see by Hermione Meredith.

Carys looked at the faces above her. She gazed at Ceridwen, in reality a widow who had raised a family of nine on her own, taking in washing and scrubbing the floors of Plas Eden to ensure they survived and made better lives for themselves. And whose granddaughter had brought life back to Pont-ar-Eden within the bustling walls of the Boadicea Cafe.

416

She smiled at Merlin, the old gardener who had raised melons and pineapples and any fruit you cared to mention, for the delight and envy of visitors to Eden. She smiled at the forlorn lovers, released from their ivy, who had not parted forever like Tristan and Isolde, but had lived together in their snug little cottage below Eden's walls for the best part of sixty years, with only the occasional pot or pan seen flying through the window of a Friday night.

She let her hand rest on the head of the giant Bendigeidfran, the stable lad who had died with his horses amongst the mud of Flanders, and let her eyes travel past the seamstress, who never went further than Talarn in her entire life, riding away on her uncatchable horse, trailing moons and stars in her skirts.

Finally, her eyes rested on the figure of Blodeuwedd, the young woman poised beneath the arch of honeysuckle, eager for life to begin. In amongst the leaves, the figure of a bronze owl gleamed; every feather of its flower-like face picked out in exquisite detail. For, as Rhiannon said, if you looked, really looked, an owl had an untamed beauty all of its own. And an owl was a symbol of wisdom – or at least of wisdom gained – after all.

In the shift of shadows across the stone faces, Carys could have sworn the blank eyes were watching her, bending close in a protective circle around her and David. As if they were trying to tell her something.

Her head was spinning. She closed her eyes to force back the giddiness. She could smell the green newness of the leaves, and the distant exotic richness of the yellow azalea by the lake, and the world pulsating to the slow beat of new life.

She opened her eyes again, and found herself gazing into the face of Little Gwion Bach. The child with the face of the little boy of the photograph with Nainie's mother. It was only recently, looking through Mam's photographs again, that it had dawned on her that the familiarity in the mischievous little face was her own. It was Dad's face as a child, just as much as it was Grandmother Judith's. And it was her own.

Carys smiled at the child with the face full of such eagerness and promise. A child who held the future, and could become anything they chose.

The rustle amongst the leaves was a warmth on her cheek, almost like the soft breath of a kiss. In her ears was the sound of laughter. Small figures seemed to flit in and out between the statues, turning now and again towards her with eager children's faces. One moment they were the mischievous features of Grandmother Judith, the next the loving seriousness of Hermione Meredith, until they blended together so completely she could no longer tell which was which.

And the suspicion that had been growing in the back of her mind over the past couple of months was back again: this time a complete and utter certainty.

'David,' she whispered.

He put his arms around her, as he bent to touch the softness at the base of her neck with his lips. 'Yes?'

She turned to meet his kiss. 'We'd better get going. I can hear more cars arriving, and we don't want them sending another search party out.'

Beside the Venus fountain, now cleaned and with water dancing high into the air, Tash was already making her way home, tail held high, glancing back every now and again to make certain they were following.

Carys took one last look around at the statues. In the whispering of the breeze and the flick of shadows over their faces, she could have sworn they were smiling.

'I've something to tell you as we go,' she said, as she slipped her arm through David's, holding him tight.

And they set off together, walking upwards in the soft brightness of the day, towards Eden.

Acknowledgements

I would like to give a big thank you to everyone at Honno Press. With special thanks to my editor, Janet Thomas, without whose guidance this story would never have come to life and from whom I have learnt more than I can ever express.

Thank you to my family and friends for their help, patience and understanding. With special thanks to Fran Cox and Salena Walker, and also to Dan and Linette for the beautiful photographs taken at Brondanw Gardens.

Thank you, as ever, to Dave and Nerys, Catrin and Delyth Haynes for being the best of neighbours and for help with the assorted menagerie. And a big thank you to my colleagues at Tape Community Music and Film for all the support and allowing me so much flexibility of working. I couldn't have done it without you!

Many thanks to my friends and fellow writers in the North Wales' Novelistas, the 'She Writes' Forum, and the RNA. And especially to the wonderful RNA's New Writers' Scheme, without which I would never have become a published author. And to my bookclub for cheering me on and tactfully not noticing when I haven't quite managed to read the book. Again.

MORE FROM HONNO

Short stories; Classics; Autobiography; Fiction

Founded in 1986 to publish the best of women's writing,
Honno publishes a wide range of titles from Welsh women.

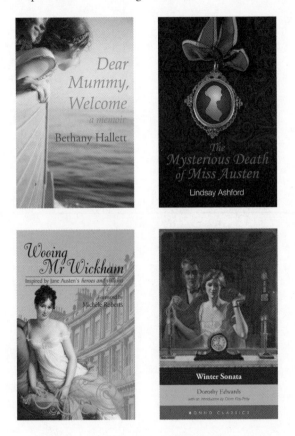

All Honno titles can be ordered online at
www.honno.co.uk

ABOUT HONNO

Honno Welsh Women's Press was set up in 1986 by a group of women who felt strongly that women in Wales needed wider opportunities to see their writing in print and to become involved in the publishing process. Our aim is to develop the writing talents of women in Wales, give them new and exciting opportunities to see their work published and often to give them their first 'break' as a writer.

Honno is registered as a community co-operative. Any profit that Honno makes is invested in the publishing programme. Women from Wales and around the world have expressed their support for Honno. Each supporter has a vote at the Annual General Meeting.

To receive further information about forthcoming publications, or become a supporter, please write to Honno at the address below, or visit our website:

www.honno.co.uk

Honno
Unit 14, Creative Units
Aberystwyth Arts Centre
Penglais Campus
Aberystwyth
Ceredigion
SY23 3GL

All Honno titles can be ordered online at
www.honno.co.uk
or by sending a cheque to Honno.